daddy

JANET INGLIS

daddy

POCKET BOOKS

New York   London   Toronto   Sydney   Tokyo   Singapore

This book is a work of fiction. Names, characters, places, and incidents are products of the author's imagination or are used fictitiously. Any resemblance to actual events or locales or persons, living or dead, is entirely coincidental.

POCKET BOOKS, a division of Simon & Schuster Inc.
1230 Avenue of the Americas, New York, NY 10020

Inglis, Janet.
    Daddy / Janet Inglis.
        p.   cm.
    ISBN: 0-671-88747-5
    1. Fathers and daughters—England—Fiction.   I. Title.
PR6059.N522D33   1994
823'.914—dc20   94-2971
                                                                              CIP

First Pocket Books hardcover printing September 1994

10 9 8 7 6 5 4 3 2 1

For Jimmy
sine qua non

Oh pity my condition
Just as you would your own,
For fourteen long years
I've been living all alone.

—*Old song (1)*

What did you fall out about,
Oh dear love, tell me?
About a little bit of bush
That might have made a tree.

—*Old song (2)*

Hold your tongue of your weeping, said he,
Of your weeping now let me be,
I'll show you how the lilies grow
On the banks of Italy.

—*Old song (3)*

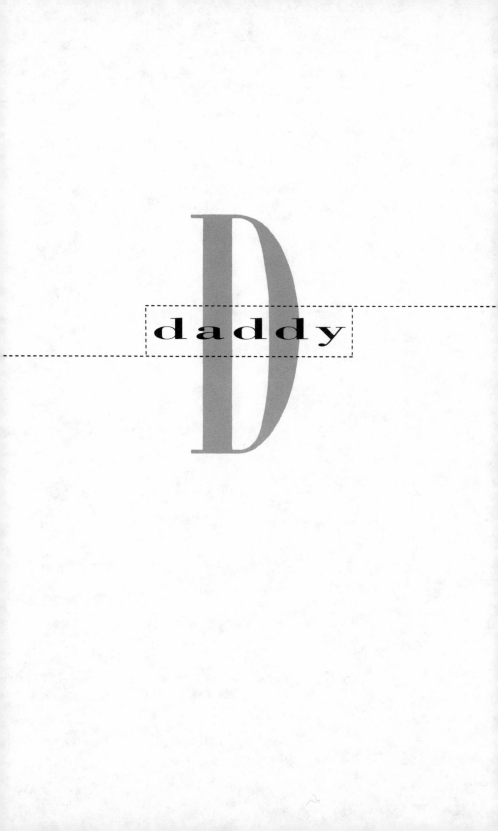

daddy

1

The sound came from outside the room. Below the window, she thought.

She was in her own home, in her own room like an eyrie at the top of the house, in her own bed in the safety of that room, but there was no safety now. She knew with a dreamer's knowledge that whatever was scaling the back of the house to reach her dormer window was no ordinary intruder but a nightmare thing.

Shards of glass flew across the floor. The casement banged open. A head and shoulders loomed against the night. It looked like a man, but by the way the pale eyes regarded her she knew it was not.

She had only the brief instant that the thing would need to climb over the sill. She jumped out of bed and fled downstairs, slamming her bedroom door in pointless defiance of the monster.

Every child knows, even she at fourteen knew, the only real place of safety against dream-world terrors is your parents' bed. She ran down the steep, narrow flight of stairs, running in her dream to her parents' bedroom on the floor below and slamming the door again behind her as she ran inside.

They were there, sleeping, and they woke when she called out to them. She could hear the creature coming down the stairs, but her parents would keep her safe. She begged them to help her, to save her from the terror on the stairs.

They looked at her and she saw their eyes. Strangers' eyes. The nightmare opened the door.

Olivia woke up. She always woke up at that point. The rest would be anticlimactic. Being torn to bits or whatever the monster had in mind was a less terrible prospect than the idea that her parents were not her parents anymore.

Since her father left two and a half years ago, she had suffered through that nightmare many times. The terror and shock did not grow less with repetition. But she hadn't dreamt it for quite a while now. She had hoped it had gone away. Maybe it was the divorce being made final that had brought it back.

She made her eyes open wide. The nightmare was still hanging around her in the darkness, waiting for her to fall asleep so it could begin again. She turned on the bedside lamp to see what the time was but her eyes refused to focus. Funny how you could be panic-stricken and dead sleepy at the same time.

The skeleton on the wall, a gift from Megan, glared down at her. He was only half a skeleton, left side blood and bones, right side soft tissue, muscle, and other organs. He had one flayed eyeball with which to glare. Her mother would say it was him that had brought on the nightmare—"How can you sleep with that horrible thing in the room?"—but Olivia thought of the cardboard corpse as a guard dog to keep evil spirits away.

She wondered if her mother had come home yet. She was far too old to creep into her mother's bed for comfort, but the thought of having the nightmare in an empty house was a particularly dreadful idea. Though not dreadful enough to keep her awake.

She woke again with a start, as if she had dreamt of falling out of bed. Or had she heard something? She strained to listen, confounded by the thumping of her own heart. Was she really awake, or back in the nightmare, only dreaming of being awake? Was it her mother coming in? Or was it another noise, and her mother not yet home . . .

She decided to make herself get up and go to the loo. She could check on the way to see where her mother was. She hated going to bed before her mother had come home, but there was school in the morning and anyway, she was old enough to be left in charge of other people's children, so it seemed babyish to complain. Especially to complain of nightmares.

She didn't dare switch on the hall light, for fear of disturbing she didn't know what. She went carefully down the stairs from her attic room, holding the handrail and reaching out with a tentative toe for the next step. Even now her eyes were barely open.

Her mother's bedroom was the first door on the left. Olivia felt in the dark for the gap that would mean she was still alone in the house. Her hand touched the door, firmly shut.

Her mother was home, then. Olivia let out her breath. But before she could take another step toward the bathroom, she heard a sound—the sound, maybe, that had wakened her.

Coming from behind her mother's bedroom door.

Her hand seemed to be stuck to the door panel. The sound waves went through the wood and entered her body through the palm of her hand, passing up her arm and making her shiver inside. It was something between a groan and a whimper, repeated and repeated in a terrifying rhythm, as if someone were being incessantly beaten.

As she stood frozen, she heard the voice. The words were indistinguishable. Maybe there were no words, just a muttered counterpoint to the moaning. What it was saying did not matter. What mattered was that it was a man's voice.

Her hand came free of the door. She fled down the hall to the bathroom and locked herself in, in the darkness.

She was going to be sick. She was afraid to be sick; they would hear her. She was afraid to move. She crouched by the toilet, hugging her knees to her chin.

Her mother had a man in her bedroom.

Once she would have assumed—would have hoped, would have prayed—that it was her father. But not now. Her parents were officially divorced, and her father was marrying Althea in three weeks and two days. That thought made her feel sick all over again. She pressed her mouth against her knee to make the feeling go away.

There was a stranger in her mother's room.

He would be a stranger even if she had met him before. Her mother's man friends (she couldn't call them boyfriends; a boyfriend was what girls her own age had) were not people she wanted to know. They were smarmy and creepy, or fat and sweaty, or old and bony. She had only met them in passing, when they came round to take her mother out some-where. She hated them because they were not her father, be-cause they kept her mother out while she was left home alone, because they were not good enough for her mother anyway. Now one of these awful strangers was here in her house, doing *that* to her mother.

She really was going to be sick. She vomited into the toilet as quietly as she could. Maybe they wouldn't hear her, they were making such a racket themselves, moaning and mut-tering in the way she had overheard.

When she stopped heaving she stayed on her knees, sweat-ing and shaking, listening to see if her mother had heard, if her mother was coming out.

There was no sound now but her own breath and blood.

She was relieved, and desolated. If she had been younger she might have made a fuss, made her mother come out and be a mother to her. But she was too old to do that now; she was supposed to know about these adult affairs and under-stand that your parents actually did the things they told you about in biology class. But understanding all that did not make it any less disgusting or diminish the sense of betrayal.

She rinsed her mouth out with a glass of water, unlocked the door, groped her way along the hall and back upstairs to her room. She shut the door tightly. She wished it had a lock. She wanted to lock out the man, the sound, the thought of what they were doing. She got into bed and turned out the bedside lamp, pulled the duvet over her head, and curled up on her side, hugging herself for comfort and defense.

What if her mother had been doing this all along, ever since her father left? What if strangers had been coming into the house at night without her knowing? In a way that made it better, since it would mean that this man would be gone by morning. She would never need to look at him and be reminded of the sounds he had made, the sounds he had made her mother make behind the closed door; never have to look at him and think about what the sounds must have meant.

She couldn't even bear to think about it now. Deliberately she shut her mind to it. She had learned to do that long ago, to shut out painful knowledge. Especially after her father left.

The thought of the empty half of the bed in her mother's room had been as dreadful then as the thought of it no longer empty was now.

She shut off her mind and pictured the stars. They were soothing, stars: mysterious, ancient, beautiful, unfathomably far away. She supposed they must have a life and awareness of their own, an astral existence that had nothing to do with biology or physics.

She imagined herself flying through black space, cold nothingness, diamond points of light wheeling all around her. She flew closer to one of the lights. It was a red star, Betelgeuse, a vast glowing body in the shoulder of Orion. White stars and blue stars were hottest; this great star was only as warm as bathwater when she entered the red haze. Cozy as firelight, comforting as candles, its substance was all about her, enfolding her, making her safe from strangers and nightmares. Making her invulnerable.

She fell asleep.

2

Her mother was opening the curtains and calling her. A fine May morning was shining through the casement window at the eastern end of her room, the one through which the dream man had burst last night.

"Lia, get up, you're late. I've got to run."

Olivia pushed back the duvet and heaved herself up against the headboard. She stared at her mother, who looked the same as she had yesterday: tall, nervously slim, elegantly dressed, flawlessly made up, still the same dark blue eyes and the pale blond hair Olivia had unaccountably failed to inherit. She was wearing a cream and red outfit, jacket, blouse, and trousers, which suited her perfectly with her fair coloring and slim figure.

It was unnerving to think that her mother could have done what she did last night and show no sign of it this morning. It suggested that all sorts of other unpleasant things could be happening without her knowledge.

"Are you all right, Lia? You're looking sort of pale and peaky."

"I'm okay. I was sick last night, but it's okay now." Olivia swung her legs over the side of the bed and said to her mother's back, "What time did you get home last night?"

"Later than I expected, I'm afraid."

Olivia stood up and stretched and combed out her hair with her fingers, anything to avoid looking at her mother. She was terrified now that her mother would say something like As a matter of fact, or Now that you mention it, and go on to tell her about the man. She didn't want to hear about the man. She was just glad he was gone. "Are you going out tonight?"

"No, I should be home by six-thirty. Don't forget it's Friday, I've got to pay the weekly visit to Sainsburys."

"Can I come with you?"

"I thought you hated grocery shopping."

Olivia shrugged. She couldn't very well say she didn't want to be alone in the house. "It's half term next week. I want to get something for my lunches."

Her mother lingered, to no apparent purpose. Olivia thought she was trying to work herself up to saying something. She knew her mother could chatter for hours to her friends on themes of no interest or importance whatsoever, and that on the other hand she would go to any lengths to avoid coming to grips with vital matters. On the subject of menstruation, for instance, she had ducked out of her maternal duties by providing Olivia with a booklet. As to sex, even the provision of booklets was too near the knuckle.

It was probably the midnight man her mother was so anxiously not wanting to talk about. Olivia rescued them both by saying, "I'll see you tonight, Mummy," and disappearing down the stairs to the bathroom.

She had a shower and washed and dried her hair. It always

took ages to dry because it was so long, and every time she dried it she thought about cutting it off. That was what her mother was always telling her to do. Her mother had a very short hairstyle that followed the shape of her fine-boned skull. That was okay if you were ash blond. Olivia's hair was rather mousy, dark blond or light brown, whatever you wanted to call it, not really curly and not exactly straight. Until two years ago her mother had managed to persuade her to cut it every time it started to grow. Now it reached halfway down her back.

At first it had been a sort of vow, like people in the Bible: she wouldn't cut her hair until her father came home. But he would never come home now; he was marrying Althea. Althea was going to be his home.

She brushed and combed her hair in front of the full-length mirror. It was long enough to cover her breasts. And a good thing too.

Her legs were okay, there was nothing wrong with long legs. Models and dancers and athletes had them. The boys in Kilburn High Road were not going to shout obscenities at her on account of her legs.

Nor was there anything seriously wrong with her hips and waist and bottom. She would have preferred one of those straight-hipped boyish bodies that all models seemed to have, but not being built like that wasn't going to ruin her life.

The only thing that did matter, that she couldn't disguise or get rid of, was the size of her bust.

She had always assumed that she would grow up to look like her mother, without the blond hair, of course. Her mother was five foot eight and yet people described her as delicate, fragile, petite. As a child Olivia had applied, or had heard others apply, quite different words to describe herself: gawky, clumsy, awkward. She had consoled herself with the ugly duckling story. When she grew up, she would be a swan like her mother.

It wasn't happening like that. She was already ten pounds heavier than her mother. But the worst thing was the bust.

Back in January she had told her mother she needed a new blazer for her school uniform. Why, said her mother, you can't have grown that much since last summer, have you?

Olivia demonstrated: she couldn't do the buttons up anymore.

Her mother had looked at her then in a funny way, with surprise and displeasure, as if she had turned out to be not an ugly duckling but a cuckoo in the nest. A stranger's child. How could her own daughter not be made in her image?

"Well," her mother had said in a cool, brittle voice, "you are going to be a big girl, aren't you?"

Olivia had heard that euphemistic expression before. It meant you had large breasts. Big tits. Boobs, knockers, jugs, bazooms—lewd, crude things stuck on the front of your body as if someone had grafted them on while you were asleep and you woke up and there you were, stuck with the horrible things forever.

Worse than that, she had been dispossessed. Now she would never be her mother's daughter.

Her best friend, Megan, said that the size of your breasts didn't matter. If anything, men preferred big ones. Thinking of the boys from Kilburn, Olivia replied that that was just the trouble. Anyway, it was all very well for Megan to talk; she hadn't got great boobs like these ones bouncing around all over the place. On account of them, if for no other reason, Olivia was glad she attended a single-sex school.

She pushed her hair aside. She set the palms of her hands under her breasts and pushed them up. She tried to imagine a man's hands doing that. The thought gave her a funny feeling, like a shudder somewhere deep inside her, the idea of a stranger's hands on her breasts. Of course he wouldn't be a stranger, whoever he might be, if he was doing that to her. But she couldn't imagine wanting anyone she could think of to touch her breasts, so the hypothetical man had to be a faceless stranger.

Like the creature in her dream.

That thought put her off the whole idea. She picked up her pajamas but didn't bother to put them back on when she left the bathroom. She was only going upstairs to get dressed, and there was no one else in the house.

Her mother's bedroom door was closed. It was never closed, except when her mother was inside. She always left it open, for the air, she said. But now it was closed.

Olivia flew up the stairs to her own room. She shut the door and dressed herself as fast as she could. She had a horrible thought, a monstrous suspicion that she knew what was behind that closed door, and she did not want her suspicions confirmed. She did not want to meet the stranger who was her mother's man.

Supposing he had opened the door while she was strolling upstairs stark naked? It was like the nightmare; she wasn't safe in her own house.

When she was ready she ran down the two flights of stairs, almost holding her breath for terror of that door opening, and paused only to snatch up her bag and books before she left altogether, leaving the faceless stranger in possession of the house.

— — — — — — — — — — — — — — — — — — **3**

Over the weekend, when her mother made no mention of any particular man, past or present, Olivia began to think that she had dreamt the whole thing. There was no evidence, aside from the sounds she had heard, that anyone else had been in the house that night or the morning after. Maybe it had just been a continuation of the nightmare. Maybe in a new version of the dream the alien creature went downstairs and did unspeakable things to her mother—who, in the dream, she recalled, had been turned into an alien herself.

All things considered, Olivia thought she would prefer the incident to have been real rather than dreamt. Real men were easier to deal with than a nightmare man from Mars.

The next week was half-term holidays. Next year these would be ruined by the approach of GCSE examinations, but this year nothing serious was happening, only the school's own year-end exams, which could be swotted up the night before.

Monday was the Whitsun bank holiday and she went to the seaside with Megan's family. On Tuesday she had the house all to herself and deliberately did nothing that could have been described as work. She sat out in the sunny garden and read all day.

The roses were just coming into bloom, the wisteria just fading. The garden was not large, but it enjoyed the southern sun and backed onto a park. The great oaks and sycamores, rooted in the park, spread their limbs across the footpath that ran behind the terraced row of Edwardian houses to reach over the high garden wall. It was a pleasure to be home by herself on such a fine bright day, not at all like being left alone at night. Bad dreams were unimaginable right now.

Her mother would be coming home soon; the art gallery where she worked closed at six. Olivia bestirred herself enough to go into the kitchen and refill her glass with lemonade. She had just opened the refrigerator door when she heard the sound of a key turning in the front door.

Her mother must be home early. She went into the hall.

A stranger was standing in the front doorway.

Olivia stared at him, speechless. A girl at school had told her how her father had gone into their dining room one evening and discovered somebody stuffing the silverware into a plastic bag. But this was broad daylight. The front door. Locked. She always kept it locked.

He was staring too, but not like a burglar surprised. More like he had walked into his own house and found her, a stranger, making herself at home. She was struggling to find her voice, to say something suitable—*Who are you?* and *Go away!* were the only phrases that came to her stunned mind—when he spoke.

"You're Lia."

He sounded surprised and amused. Not at all embarrassed, not remotely like someone who has just walked into the wrong house. And he knew her name.

She hadn't dreamt it. This was the man in her mother's room.

"You've got a key," she said stupidly.

He shut the front door behind him. "Em gave it to me." He put the key into his pocket. He was smiling. He seemed to be amused by some private joke. "She told me she had a little girl."

Olivia flushed. "I'm not a little girl."

"So I see."

He was looking at her in a way that made her feel even more alarmed. She was wearing cut-off jeans and a sleeveless cotton top, suitable clothing for the privacy of her own garden, but not the outfit she would have chosen to confront a stranger in the front hall. He was staring at her as if she had nothing on at all, as if she was just a pair of naked tits. She wanted to run up to her room and pull on three more layers of clothing, to put on her anorak and zip it to her chin, anything to make him stop looking at her.

She edged over to the stairs. "Who are you? What are you doing here? Why did Mummy give you a key?" She spoke sharply, accusingly, because she knew who he was. She knew the answers to all her questions. "Why didn't you ring the doorbell?"

"I did."

"I didn't hear. I was out in the garden."

"Sorry if I startled you." He glanced at his watch. "Em said she'd be here by now. When no one answered the bell I thought she must have been held up. I didn't know you were home, and I thought I'd rather wait for her inside than hang about the doorstep." He smiled again. "Do you mind?"

She minded horribly. She minded him setting foot in the house, with or without her mother. She minded him looking at her, laughing at her. She minded his masculine confidence and conceit that let him walk into her house as if he owned it. She minded him sleeping in her father's half of her mother's bed. She minded the noises she had heard in the night.

Thinking of that, looking at him, she thought she was going to throw up again.

"You wait for her if you like. I'm going out."

He stood between her and the front door, so she ran out of the back door and through the garden gate. She didn't care just then that he had won, that she had left him in possession

11

of the house. She didn't care about anything but getting away from him.

She held back the tears until she had reached the right place. There was a duck pond in the park and a particular oak tree that she and Megan had discovered, oh, a lifetime ago, with a huge limb that overarched the pond so you could sit nestled in the boughs of the oak and watch the ripples on the water below and pretend, if you were very young and the world still seemed wide and mysterious, that you were in a magic wood.

Olivia had grown out of the magic, but it was still a private place. She didn't even climb the tree, she just sat among the roots and wept.

They are all disgusting, she thought. My parents are disgusting, both of them, and their paramours or whatever they are. Daddy is marrying one of his former students, a horrible person young enough to be his daughter. Mummy picks up men and brings them home. Even gives them a key to the front door.

That was unfair, of course. She had no idea how her mother had met this man or how long she had known him. Maybe he ran the sandwich bar where she bought her lunch.

That was unfair too. He might just as well be a property tycoon or own a chain of betting shops. The one thing she knew was that he was not an academic like her father. In fact, he was what her grandmother Hardy would have called common. She wondered how her mother could have imagined him as a replacement for her father, enough to take him to bed and give him a key to her house.

What did the key mean? Was he going to come and go, walking in unannounced as he had done today? Was he moving in? Was she going to be expected to live with him as if he were her father?

In her heart she knew the answer. He was going to be an uncleman.

Megan's mother, who was head teacher of a primary school in Kilburn, used that word to describe the men who came and went in the homes of so many of her little pupils. Daddy, if he had ever existed, was long gone for these children. Instead they had Uncle Fred, Uncle Pat, Uncle Kevin, for a month, a year, a decade. The unclemen.

It was shocking that people's mothers should behave like that. Especially her own mother. Olivia had seen Mel Gibson playing Hamlet, gorgeous as always. She remembered the scene with his mother. "At your age the heyday in the blood is tame. . . ."

Her tears had subsided by now. The sun was low. Her mother must have come home. She climbed up into the oak tree and stretched herself out along the limb over the water. Since she was thinking of Hamlet, this reminded her of Ophelia's fate, falling from a tree into a stream and drowning. She considered drowning herself. But you would have to try very hard to drown in a duck pond. Like drowning yourself in the bathtub, really: absurd and undignified.

And not really worth it. She had thought from time to time that one or other of her parents did not love her, her father because he had left her and was marrying Althea, her mother because she was never home, spent all her time working or doing what she called building up a clientele or going out with creepy men, and left her daughter alone. Perhaps they would be relieved to have her out of the way.

But she was not going to oblige them. It wasn't her idea to be born. They had had her, and they were stuck with her. So there.

4

After sunset, when they locked the park gates, she went down the path that ran along the narrow back gardens of the terraced houses, the same path that led up to the back gate of the park. She came in through the back door, reckoning that wherever he was, it would not be in the kitchen.

She was wrong. He was sitting by the table, reading a tabloid paper while her mother did the washing up. He had a glass of whiskey on the table beside him, and he was smoking a cigarette.

Olivia was astonished. Her parents had always had fanatical views on smoking—drummed it into her, bribed her even, not to smoke. Since the idea had never seriously tempted her, she was happy to take the money her father offered. But now here was her own kitchen stinking of tobacco like a pub, and her mother taking no notice. Conniving, even; she had given the stranger an ashtray, which she normally kept hidden to discourage visitors from smoking unless they insisted.

And she was not, apparently, angry or worried by her daughter's long disappearance. She glanced up when Olivia came in. "Hello, darling. I've kept your dinner for you. I'm sorry, we got tired of waiting."

"I'm not hungry."

She was trying not to look at the man by the table. Her mother's glance went where she was ostentatiously not looking. "Nick says you've already met."

"Sort of," mumbled Olivia.

The intruder looked up from his paper. It must have been the *Sun;* she could see the outsize headlines and large print. Not to mention the outsize breasts on the page-three bimbo.

This was even more astonishing than cigarettes. She wondered if he bet on the football pools. She didn't know what football pools were, precisely, but she knew that *Sun* readers were big on them. She also knew that the sports pages had nothing about cricket, which was the only sport that interested her father; instead they were almost entirely devoted to listing the results of various horse- and dog-racing events.

"Yeah, we met." He was looking at her and smiling, and again it was a private joke that she did not understand. "I gave you a bit of a scare, didn't I, Lia? I didn't know you were here and you didn't know who I was."

But I know you now, thought Olivia, I think. The cigarette and the *Sun* had unsettled her. People who belonged in her parents' lives didn't do those things.

Nor did they stare at her breasts, as he was doing right now.

"I'm going upstairs," she told her mother.

"Don't you want your supper?"

"I told you, I'm not hungry."

On the first-floor landing she stopped to look into her mother's room. It was the same as it had been ever since her father left: neat, practical, but unmistakably feminine, with no sign, except for the large double bed, that a man had ever crossed the threshold.

Then, since the coast was clear, she peeked into the spare room. There was a suitcase on the bed, a leather jacket slung over the back of the chair. Her heart sank. She closed the door and went up the narrower second flight of stairs to her own room.

She couldn't stop shivering. She felt chilled to the core. She had stayed too long out of doors in the cool May evening with bare arms and legs and only a thin, sleeveless cotton top. She got into her pajamas and dressing gown and pulled the duvet up to her chin, like an Eskimo battening down the hatches for an arctic blizzard.

Her mother came in. "What are you doing? Are you feeling ill again?"

"I'm cold. I think I got a bit too much sun."

"Shall I make you some cocoa?"

"Yes, please. Can you bring up my book? I left it out in the garden."

She waited, shivering, for her mother to come back. The cocoa would help, and the fact that her mother was mothering her.

The cocoa came, and the book. Her mother looked at the cover with distaste before handing it over to her. "Why do you read this science fiction rubbish?"

"I like reading about other worlds. It's exciting, anything can happen. Nothing ever happens here, nothing exciting. Anyway," she added maliciously, "it's better than the *Sun*, isn't it?"

To her surprise her mother smiled. "The *Sun* is strictly for adults. And you can't change people when they're grown up, you just have to take them as they come."

"What's he doing here?" Olivia demanded. "Why did you give him a key?"

"I'm sorry, Lia. I meant to tell you, I meant to be here first, but I was held up with a client." Her mother sat down on the corner of the bed and folded her hands in her lap, in the prim formal way she had when she was Talking to Her Daughter. "He's going to be using the spare room. He'll only be here on weeknights; he just needs a pied-à-terre in London." She added defensively, "I thought we could do each other a favor. God knows I can use the money."

"So he's a lodger."

"I suppose you could call him that." Her mother gave a little laugh. "That's an old-fashioned sort of word, isn't it?"

It was. Lodgers were strange old-fashioned people in old books like Sherlock Holmes and Agatha Christie, people with odd haircuts and old-fashioned clothes who turned out to have killed somebody. And the lodger's landlady was always an elderly widow with a suspicious cast of mind and an obsession with respectability.

But this was the 1990s, not the 1930s, and the man downstairs was not her mother's lodger but her lover. Perhaps her mother too was obsessed with respectability.

"Who is he?"

"He's a photographer. His name is Nick Winter. I needed a photographer to do a brochure and someone recommended him. He's very good; you'll be impressed when you see the brochure."

"Where has he been living till now? Where does he live on weekends? Why doesn't he just buy a flat if he needs to be in London?"

Her mother got up and paced around the room, touching, straightening, adjusting everything in sight. Since the room was in a mess as usual, there didn't seem much point. Applying a feather duster would have made as much difference to the chaos. But that was not the point. The point was distraction.

"He did have a flat, and a cottage in Norfolk. But his marriage broke up, and his wife got the flat. He's stuck with a cottage in the middle of nowhere. In fact, she's claiming half the cottage as well, which I think is a prize bit of brass. Anyway, he's put it up for sale, but the housing market is absolutely dead. So he's had to drive all the way down from Norwich every day."

He was married. That surprised Olivia. "Does he have any children?"

"What?" Now her mother was surprised. "No, no children."

"You told him I was a little girl."

Her mother looked at her and laughed. "Did I? I'm sorry, darling. But fourteen is still a long way from being grown up, you know."

"I'll be fifteen next month."

"But you're still such a child, Lia." Her mother came over and brushed Olivia's hair away from her face. "I wish you'd get a proper haircut; you look like the missing link with your hair all over the place. All right, I'm sorry, I shouldn't have called you a little girl, but it doesn't matter now. He's met you now, he knows how old you are, he can draw his own conclusions."

- - - - - - - - - - - - - - - - - - 5

She slept very late the next day. When she got up she crept down the stairs to make sure she was alone in the house. The door to her mother's room was open, the room obviously empty. But he had been in there, she could tell; her mother would never have left the bed in that state.

She went into the bathroom and was confronted with more evidence of his habitation: a razor on the shelf above the sink. It had been nearly three years since her father's razor had disappeared from that shelf, along with shaving foam and aftershave lotion and other such mysterious masculine paraphernalia.

Now they were back again, courtesy of the lodger. Nick Winter.

She resented them there. Even with the door locked, she

felt as if she were being spied and intruded upon, as if she were somehow sharing the bathroom with him while she did those things that you only do when alone.

She spent the afternoon with Megan, poking around Oxford Street and Regent Street. The excuse for their expedition was that she had to find a dress to wear to her father's wedding.

"He's given me the money, so I have to have something to show for it. Not that he'd notice if I turned up in some rag he'd seen a dozen times before."

"How much did he give you?"

"A hundred pounds. He said he'd give me more if I needed it."

"That's very generous of him."

"Well, he wouldn't want Althea's family to think he was too cheap to buy proper clothes for his daughter, would he?"

She tried on at least a dozen dresses. Megan tried some on too, just to keep her company. The one they both liked best was a soft silky fabric of deep ruby red, with a short, full skirt that swung out when she swirled and full sleeves that came to just below the elbow. The neckline had a drawstring that tied at the front. You could draw it as tight or loose as you pleased, raising or lowering the neckline.

"What do you think?" she asked Megan. "Will Mummy like it?" She had never bought anything more ambitious than a pair of jeans without her mother's approval.

"Why not? The color makes your skin look tanned. Anyway, if she doesn't like it you can always bring it back."

She bought the dress. It was quite a lot more than the £100 her father had given her. She hoped he wouldn't mind too much.

When they were on the bus headed northwest toward Kilburn/Cricklewood/West Hampstead, Olivia said, "Meg, can you ask your mother if I can sleep over at your place tonight?"

"Yeah, sure. Is your mother going to be away?"

"Worse than that. She's got a man."

"Are you keeping out of the way because you don't like him, or because you do like him and you're hoping to help the romance along by leaving them alone together?"

"Officially, there isn't any romance. The story Mummy's handed me is that he's a sort of weekday lodger, renting the spare room."

"And what's the real story?"

"He doesn't sleep in the spare room. He sleeps with her."

It was humiliating even to say it. Much worse to have to picture that cocksure man with the insolent eyes climbing into her mother's bed. Naked, no doubt. The thought was even more disgusting than humiliating.

"That's good, isn't it? She must have been feeling quite depressed about your father getting married. Now she can feel that her own life is going forward again."

Megan was always so horribly reasonable, even about her own emotional crises and desperate passions. Sometimes this rational approach was exactly what Olivia needed. Other times she could have shaken her truest, dearest, oldest friend until her teeth rattled. "What about my life?" protested Olivia. "Why should I have to put up with a stranger in my own house? And she didn't even tell me first, or introduce him to me. He just appeared in the front hall last night. I got the fright of my life, I thought he was a burglar."

"Maybe she just forgot to tell you."

"She didn't forget, she just chickened out."

"If she was that nervous, she must really like him."

"Thanks for cheering me up."

"Maybe you'll like him too, when you get to know him," Megan offered optimistically. "You always dislike the men your mother goes out with. They can't all be total wallies. I mean, the law of averages—"

"This one is worse than a wally. He's a low-class creep."

They reached their stop and got off the bus. Megan inquired clinically, "Is he actually creepy, or are you just being jealous and resentful?"

Megan always analyzed everything: feelings, jokes, novels, social situations. Sometimes it was like being best friends with Dr. Freud. She wanted to be a doctor, but her grades were probably not going to be good enough, so she was already resigning herself to being a nurse instead.

"He is definitely horrible," Olivia said emphatically. "He

smokes and reads the *Sun*, and he looks at me in a funny way."

"What does that mean, in a funny way?"

"Well, you know what I mean." Olivia wished she hadn't mentioned that bit. "He looks at my breasts."

"Sexist, you mean. He doesn't really sound like your mother's type," Megan allowed.

"My father is my mother's type." As they walked down the street, Olivia brooded, getting more outraged at her domestic situation. "I have a good mind to go and live with Daddy."

"I thought you couldn't stand Althea."

"Well, I can't. She talks to me as if I were a retarded two-year-old, and she does it on purpose. It's so embarrassing, the idea of having a stepmother who's more like my sister. She looks more like Mummy than I do. Even my gran remarked on it."

"Does this lodger look like your father?"

"No, not at all."

"What does he look like?"

Olivia conjured up a mental image of Nick Winter in the front hall. She found she could visualize him with surprising clarity. "Tallish, blond, light blue eyes. Early thirties, I guess. Definitely not fat, but not thin either. Sort of athletic and muscular. I'll bet he works out in a gym." She added, with reluctant honesty, "If he weren't such a creep he'd be quite good-looking."

"It sounds like your mother's done all right for herself, in spite of the *Sun* and the smoking."

Olivia glared at her. "Meg, you're disgusting."

Megan was not offended. She laughed. "That reminds me, I've got something really disgusting to show you tonight."

"What is it?"

"You wait and see."

Olivia had to wait until it was time to go to bed. Megan's mother had said it was okay if she stayed over, so she rang up her own mother and told her what Megan's mother had said. "Is that okay?"

"That's fine, darling. You'd better pop home to get your pajamas and toothbrush."

"Megan says she'll lend me some pajamas. And it won't be the end of the world if I don't brush my teeth tonight."

Ordinarily her mother, who agreed with the received wisdom concerning cleanliness and godliness, would have argued that it might indeed be the end of the world, but tonight she didn't seem to care. "Well, I suppose it'll be all right. Have a good time, and I'll see you tomorrow."

Olivia rang off, obscurely displeased. It was bad enough being at home when her mother and that appalling man were practicing methods of human reproduction on the floor below, but now she discovered that it was even worse for them to be doing it when she wasn't there. Worse, because of the thought that her mother was happy to have her out of the way.

Feeling like an orphaned refugee, she put on her borrowed pajamas. They were not Megan's, because Megan was five inches shorter than her; they belonged to Megan's brother, Teddy, or Ted as he had preferred to be called since he started shaving. They fit reasonably well, except that being boy's pajamas the bottoms had an opening at the front. This reminder that the previous wearer had had a distinctly different anatomy made Olivia vaguely uncomfortable.

It reminded Megan of something else. She reached under the bed and produced a handful of magazines. "Here, have a look at these."

Olivia glanced at the covers. They were all the sort of publication that news agents put on the top shelf, and they showed signs of having been read many times. "Where did you find these?"

"In Teddy's room."

Olivia was scandalized. Teddy had always seemed an inoffensive, rather remote, faintly pimply sort of boy. Not one she would have dreamt of putting into a sexual context. "Won't he notice they're not there?"

"I only took a few. He's got a huge stack of them stashed away in his wardrobe. Pretty gross, aren't they?"

Some of them were grosser than others. One featured women with breasts like balloons; the effect, with the absurd tongue-in-cheek text, was far more comical than sexy. Others, where the models were attractive young women in less grotesque poses, Olivia found faintly shocking. She stared at a picture of a girl holding the crotch of her knickers aside to show her vulva. The girl stared back at her, bold and languorous. The genitals were revealed as clearly as in the diagram in her biology textbook. A case might be made, she thought, for the female breast as an object of beauty, but the vulva was just plain ugly.

"How can men possibly find this sexy?"

"No imagination, I suppose. There are some better ones—I mean worse ones—in here."

Megan paged through another magazine to find some even more explicit photos, this time taken from the rear. Olivia browsed through her own publication. "Where do they find these strange clothes? Nobody wears underwear like this, do they? They must make them expressly for pornographic purposes."

"I think that's the sort of thing you can buy in sex shops. This looks really uncomfortable, doesn't it?"

They studied a photograph of a woman contorted into what looked like a yoga posture that hadn't quite worked out. "Don't the women feel, you know, ridiculous?"

"Not half as ridiculous as Teddy would feel if he knew we know about these."

"He deserves to feel ridiculous. Fancy spending money on sexist rubbish like this."

"Maybe it's just sex that's sexist. I mean, you can choose how you behave, but you can't really choose how you feel. Apparently everybody's ideas about what constitutes hot stuff are fixed when we're still very young."

Olivia giggled. "You mean Teddy is a helpless prisoner of his infancy."

Megan laughed too. "Listen, this stuff is normal." She tapped the magazine. "Some people can only get it off in really weird ways. They're attracted to old ladies, or shoes, or train wrecks."

Olivia couldn't stop laughing. "Train wrecks! What do you mean, train wrecks?"

"Honestly. I read about a man who deliberately caused train wrecks because it was the only thing that excited him."

"It would be a man, wouldn't it? All perverts are men. Why is that, Dr. Davies?"

"Well, Dr. Beckett, if you look at the situation from a biological point of view—"

"Surely, Dr. Davies, it must be biologically counterproductive to make love to old ladies or shoes or smashed-up trains."

"Yes, yes, but there's a more basic principle at stake, it seems to me, Dr. Beckett. The embarrassment factor, I call it."

"What's that?"

"Well, as far as nature is concerned, the most important thing is that everybody should get out there and reproduce. This would be a nonstarter if it depended on the likes of me and you. I mean, can you imagine going up to a strange man at a party or in the pub, and chatting him up or propositioning him? Or supposing he agreed to go home with you, how would you get around to making a pass at him? Or even inviting him out to McDonald's for a hamburger? Just the thought of it makes me cringe."

"Me too. So what?"

"Well, somebody's got to get things started. So what's happened is that men have been made a lot more desperate than women. So that they don't mind being rejected nine times out of ten, as long as they make it the tenth time. And if all that desperation sometimes ends up as a flasher or a rapist, maybe from nature's point of view that's the price of progress."

Olivia thought about that. "You make men sound like Martians."

"Maybe they are."

Olivia looked down at Teddy's pajama bottoms, with the strategic gap in the front. "I'm not sure I want to be wearing these."

"It's okay," said Megan, "they've been through the laundry."

6

Since she couldn't stay at Megan's house forever, Olivia did the next best thing and brought Megan home with her the next evening.

"What am I, your bodyguard?" Megan wanted to know. "Do you think this guy is going to creep upstairs in the middle of the night and cut your throat?"

"*Creep* is the operative word. But no, I'm not worried about that, he's too busy in the middle of the night screwing my mother."

She said it with casual scorn, but it was a deeply disturbing thought. She remembered the noises in the night. Megan's joke about him coming upstairs, like the creature in the nightmare, was hardly less disturbing.

Megan was not disturbed at all. "I can hardly wait to meet him."

Olivia went into the kitchen to put the kettle on. The sound of a piano came from the sitting room. Megan must have turned on the radio. She returned to the sitting room just as someone—a large black woman, by the sound of her—began to sing.

I dreamed last night that I was dead.

Olivia stopped short in the doorway, shivers running up and down her spine. The singer was describing a trip to hell. The piano sounded so eerie, the woman so woebegone, Olivia was entranced. She had never heard anything like it.

"This is awesome," Megan exclaimed. "What is it?"

"I don't know. I've never heard it before."

"But it's one of your CDs. It was in the machine when I turned it on."

"I never heard it before." Olivia went over to the player and picked up the empty plastic case. A large black woman, just as she had guessed. "It's Bessie Smith."

"Who's she?"

"Who knows? Maybe it's one of creepy Nick's."

By this time the singer had moved to a different sort of hell and was begging someone to give her some. The tune had an engaging, danceable rhythm, and she sang with gusto and unerring musical mastery. Megan remarked, "He can't be that creepy if he likes this music."

When Olivia went out again to make the tea, Megan followed her and pounced on a copy of the *Sun* that Nick had left behind.

"Oh Meg, leave that alone," Olivia said crossly, as if Megan were a dog and the paper a particularly vile and smelly bone. It irritated her intensely that Nick should leave his rubbish around in her house. He hadn't emptied the ashtray either; it sat on the table, reeking. He was like a gorilla, fouling his own nest. She picked up the ashtray and threw it, butts and all, into the trash bin.

Megan read aloud, "Crazed woman plots to murder her children."

"What's that about?"

"It's how they describe the play I saw last week."

"How would you describe it?"

"Well, the way they produced it did sort of reduce it to crazed woman plots murder. But they did it all wrong. It should be very topical, all about divorce and remarriage and what happens to the children. It could be quite electrifying if it were done right."

Olivia tsked. "Armchair critics."

"Well, why don't we do it?"

"Do what?"

"Put it on properly. We could rewrite it and make it totally relevant."

"Are you serious?"

"Sure, why not?"

"You can't go rewriting someone else's play. There are laws against that sort of thing."

"But this one was written by some old Greek, he's been

dead for thousands of years. The copyright must have expired by now. Come on, Lia, do let's do it. You can ask your father to find a few different translations and we can write our own version."

"Oh, all right," Olivia agreed, knowing that the probability was against anything actually happening. "Why are you so keen on this play?"

"I like it because the heroine beats the men at their own game."

"What game is that?"

"Mass murder."

Olivia's mother came home in good humor and looking remarkably pleased with herself. "Hello, Lia. How are you, Meg? I've got something to show you in a minute."

New clothes, Olivia mouthed to Megan as her mother disappeared upstairs. Her mother had a wardrobe large enough to outfit an entire tribe of impoverished Africans. She always said that buying something nice to wear cheered her up when she felt depressed. Today it must have really done the trick.

But it wasn't clothes. At least it wasn't clothes that her mother had in mind. She came back down with a brochure in her hand.

Olivia took it. "Is this the one Nick did for you? It looks very posh," she added in surprise. Posh was not a concept she would have associated with anything Nick had a hand in.

"Yes, doesn't it? I'm absolutely thrilled."

Her mother had worked for years in an art gallery in the West End, but after Olivia's father left she had decided to turn herself into a proper career woman. Now she rented space above the gallery to use as a workshop where she spent her mornings designing and making jewelry, which the gallery obligingly displayed and sold. This brochure was supposed to advertise the jewelry.

It succeeded admirably in that aim, but it was also an ephemeral work of art in itself. The jewelry was displayed on the body of a woman—arms, hands, neck, ears, and associated parts—but the woman remained anonymous: turned aside, out of focus, not in the frame. The back page had the most striking image: a pair of hands with a pair of rings on every finger, covering a pair of bare breasts.

Olivia went back through the other pictures. There was no sign of clothing in any of them, though the photography was done so skillfully that it was only on the last page that the model's toplessness became apparent.

Something else became apparent this time. "Mummy, is this you?"

Her mother actually blushed. As well she might, thought Olivia. "I didn't think anyone would notice."

"Maybe no one will. I didn't at first."

"I certainly didn't," Megan said, examining the pictures more closely. "You look terrific. You should have been a model."

"It's a bit late for that, I'm afraid," Olivia's mother observed, not displeased by the remark. "Maybe if I'd met Nick fifteen years ago . . ."

If her mother had met Nick fifteen years ago, Olivia reckoned, he might have been her father. A totally disgusting idea. She was outraged that her mother could say such a thing, outraged that her mother should have let Nick take pictures of her naked breasts. That seemed somehow much worse than merely going to bed with him. Though there was nothing remotely scandalous about the pictures; if an unknown woman had done the modeling, Olivia would have thought absolutely nothing of it, and any newspaper would have printed them without demur. "Whose idea was it to show the jewelry like this?"

"Nick's, of course. I don't know anything about photography."

"And was it his idea for you to be the model?"

"Well, yes. It did save money," her mother added defensively.

"These are excellent." Megan was still poring over the brochure. "Lia, you've got to take this to school next week. Everyone will be madly jealous of you for having such a gorgeous mother."

"More to the point," said Olivia's mother, "they might like the jewelry."

Megan said obligingly, "That's excellent too."

Olivia caught sight of Nick coming through the front door. She looked away quickly to avoid catching his eye. She saw her mother's face light up when he appeared in the doorway, saw her mother take a step toward him and then check herself.

"We were just admiring your brochure. It's come back from the printers."

"Let's have a look."

Megan brought it over to him. He took it and smiled at her. "Thanks. I don't know you, do I?"

"I'm Meg."

"I thought you might be." He flipped through the brochure, apparently just to check that everything was there and in the right place, then handed it to Olivia's mother. "That looks all right to me. You're the customer, what do you think?"

"I think it's brilliant."

"You're the kind of customer I like."

They smiled at each other in a way that made Olivia's toes curl, made her want to hide behind the sofa. She was sure that if it hadn't been for her and Megan, they would have kissed or touched somehow. If she had seen her father and mother look at each other like that she would have fallen on her knees to thank God. As it was . . . she didn't want to see, didn't want to know.

And as it was, nothing happened.

Her mother said to Nick, "I'll get you a drink while Lia and Meg entertain you."

When she went into the kitchen, Nick collapsed into the nearest armchair. He ran a hand through his short fair hair like a man at the end of a hard day, and smiled at Olivia and Megan on the sofa opposite. "All right, ladies, entertain me. Did you enjoy yourselves last night?"

"Yeah, we did," Megan said cheerfully. "We—"

Olivia interrupted her. She had a sudden dreadful notion that Megan was going to tell him what they had really done, about the girlie magazines and all. So she said quickly, "It was okay, except for Meg's cat coming in through the window in the middle of the night with a live mouse."

Megan turned to her in surprise. "I don't remember that."

"I know. You slept right through it. Tig came in with a mouse and took it under the bed and tortured and ate it."

"I didn't hear anything. Are you sure you didn't dream it?"

"I was wide awake. It took me ages to get back to sleep. Tig was making ferocious noises and the mouse was squeaking and shrieking and then I had to listen to the mouse being torn limb from limb and crunched up, right underneath me. It was like having a baby ogre under the bed."

"How do you know it was Tig? Maybe it was Mog."

"It was horrible, whichever one it was. But it was definitely Tig, he stood on my chest afterward wanting a cuddle."

Megan explained to Nick, as if he might be remotely interested, that Mog was the mother cat and Tig was her kitten. To apologize for their barbaric behavior, she added, "I'm mad about cats but I do wish they weren't so cruel to the mice. And they're even worse with birds."

Nick didn't feel this called for apology. "They're not cruel, it's just the way they are. If you treated mice like that, Lia here would ring up the RSPCA. But cats are cats, aren't they? You can't make them behave any differently."

Olivia's mother returned with a small glass of white wine and a large glass of beer, and no prizes for guessing which was whose. "What are we talking about?"

"Meg's getting a biology lesson," Olivia told her.

"Not in my sitting room she's not." She handed Nick the beer and perched herself on the arm of his chair. She took a sip from her glass of wine. "Lia, I don't know when I'm going to find time to take you shopping for a frock to wear to the wedding. I've got so many things to do, I'm going mad. Maybe we can squeeze in an hour tomorrow morning."

"That's okay, I bought one yesterday when I was out with Meg."

Her mother stared at her. "You bought a frock to wear to Ross's wedding?"

"Yeah, I did. I told you he gave me the money, and I've spent it. More than he gave me, in fact. He owes you fifty pounds."

Her mother didn't look totally pleased at this evidence of independence. "You'd better show me what you bought. You can't wear just anything to a wedding, you know."

"It's really super," Megan assured her. "Come on, Lia, try it on for your mother."

When they got up to her room at the top of the house, Olivia said, "You are absolutely horrible, Meg. I shall never speak to you again."

Megan was unmoved by these threats. Nothing ever appeared to distress her; she was solidly constructed, physically and emotionally. A typical Taurus, as she herself always pointed out. "Why?"

"Crawling to that awful man like that."

"I wasn't crawling, and he's not awful. I like him, he's kind of hunky."

"That's disgusting. He's old enough to be your father."

"So is Mel Gibson, and you don't mind drooling over him."

"Well, it's bad enough to have my mother drooling over creepy Nick. Don't you start."

"You can't hate him all that much just because he smokes and sleeps with your mother."

"I hate him because he's hateful. If he were a cat I'll bet he'd invent new ways to torture mice. And he wouldn't let you pick him up and cuddle him like Tig."

Olivia pulled her new dress over her head, smoothed down the skirt, and looked at herself in the mirror. Her breasts seemed much more obvious than they had in the fitting room at the shop. She wasn't going to go downstairs and parade around in front of Nick with her bosom hanging out for him to stare at. She pulled the drawstring around the neckline tighter, retying it only an inch or so below her collarbone. "Do you really think my mother will approve of this?"

"How could she not? You look beautiful." Megan looked at her and at her image in the mirror. "Everyone thinks you're beautiful, Lia. I don't know why you don't like the way you look."

It wasn't something that could be explained. Certainly not to Megan, whose breasts, though substantial, were just the right size to match her substantial torso. Olivia turned away from the stranger in the mirror. "Come on, let's go down and see what she says."

When they came into the sitting room, Nick was still in the armchair, but her mother was standing up, sipping self-consciously at her wine, and looking faintly flustered, as if she had been doing something quite different a few seconds before.

She removed her composure enough to examine Olivia with a critical eye. "That's very pretty." She sounded surprised. "The color's good, it suits your complexion. But you've pulled the neckline too tight. The bodice isn't draping right." She adjusted the drawstring to her own satisfaction and Olivia's embarrassment. "That's better. What do you think, Nick?"

Olivia could have kicked her mother for inviting that man to look at her. He was just in the process of lighting a cigarette. He glanced up over the flame of the lighter, then snapped the lid down and leaned back to consider her through a haze of smoke.

She didn't want him inspecting her, staring at the draping of the bodice and her breasts beneath. She folded her arms across her chest and stared back at him.

"That looks great."

He wasn't smiling; maybe he actually meant it. Not that she cared what he thought. She ignored him and spoke to her mother. "Is the dress okay, then?"

"I should think it will do," her mother agreed. "At least you won't embarrass me by wearing it."

"Lia always looks good," Megan remarked. "I keep telling her she could be a model. What do you think, Nick?"

Olivia flushed. "Shut up, Meg. I don't want to be a model."

Nick was looking at her again with the cool, assessing X-ray gaze that she found so unsettling. He couldn't see through her crossed arms, surely? And how could he look at her like that in front of her mother, like the wolf sizing up the meat on Red Riding Hood's bones?

No, he was sizing up her bones as well. As she retreated up the stairs to change out of the dangerous dress, she heard him tell Megan, "The bone structure, that's what they look for. Lia has good bones."

So he did have X-ray vision.

7

The pub was noisy and crowded. The publican might have put its popularity down to the trendy decor and live music (on Saturday night). But for Olivia and her friends the attraction was quite different.

"They were definitely coming here," Clare repeated, with a touch of anxiety or impatience. "I heard Danny on the phone after dinner, arranging to meet Will."

Olivia repeated her objection to this whole scheme. "Won't they think it's kind of suspicious, just happening to turn up at the same pub?"

"Maybe we came to hear the band. Don't be such a baby, Lia. Don't you know how it works?"

"I just thought maybe Danny won't like us hanging round him and his friends."

"Bugger Danny," Clare said coarsely, to emphasize her disregard for social convention and her brother's feelings. "It's Allie I want to see."

"Well, maybe Allie—"

"Do shut up, Lia. Here they are. Look the other way."

Olivia and Megan dutifully stared at the pinball machine instead of the door. Clare was the sophisticate in these matters. She had already had a boyfriend, though not one she was very keen on, who used to take her to films and rock concerts. Now she had developed an interest in her brother's friend Alistair, and taken steps to pursue the matter.

Olivia was impressed by Clare's nerve. Perhaps it came of having very curly, bright red hair. That must have made it hard to play shrinking violet. Olivia's own romantic experience had been limited to playing postman's knock at parties and falling in love with André Agassi.

She was even more impressed when Clare managed to lure her brother and his friends over to their table.

There were four of them: Clare's brother, Danny, her *inamorato*, Allie, and Will and Charlie. They were all in the upper-sixth form at Danny's school, a boys-only establishment. Clare flirted shamelessly with Allie, who didn't seem to mind. Megan was too straightforward to stoop to flirting, but she was obviously enjoying the masculine company. Olivia just felt shy and rather stupid. Maybe it was because Clare and Megan were nearly a year older than her. They would both turn sixteen in September, whereas she was still ten days short of fifteen.

Eventually she escaped to the loo, which was crammed with girls chattering and smoking and combing their hair and fixing their makeup. It was even more crowded, smokier, and noisier than the bar itself.

When she escaped from the loo she bumped—literally—into Danny's friend Charlie.

"There's luck," he said, smiling down at her through the tobacco haze. "Will's at the bar ordering another round. What'll you have?"

"Just a Coke, please."

"I'll pay, but you'll have to come and carry it."

He waded through the crowd toward the bar. She followed in his wake and found herself pushed up against him by the mob jostling for position and a drink. She didn't mind being nudged by strangers, but it was embarrassing to be pressed against someone she actually knew. She tried to move back, but there wasn't any room.

"Sorry." She giggled to hide her embarrassment. "It's too crowded in here."

"Come and stand here." He maneuvered her up against the bar and stood behind her, leaning his hands on the counter on either side of her so that his arms and body protected her from the crush. "That's better," he said in her ear.

Olivia wasn't sure about that. Their bodies were still touching, but at least it wasn't her fault anymore. She squeezed herself right up against the counter and stared into the mirror opposite. She could see Will on the other side of the man next to her. Behind her she could see Charlie's face, smiling at her in the mirror.

He was tall and dark and handsome in a lean, loose-limbed way. He had been sitting on the other side of the table, so she hadn't even spoken to him till now. She watched him dip his head to talk to her. "Clare introduced us, but I didn't catch your name."

"Olivia," said Olivia.

"I thought she called you something else."

"She called me Lia. That's supposed to be short for Olivia."

"But much more exotic."

He wasn't looking at her in the mirror now; he was looking at her in the flesh. Specifically, he was looking down the front of her shirt. She wished she had left it buttoned up. Clare had persuaded her to undo the top buttons to make sure they wouldn't have any hassle about their age. Clare was drinking spritzers.

To distract his gaze she wiped her hand across her face. "It's horribly hot in here, isn't it?"

"Do you want to go outside?"

"Well—"

"There's a garden out the back. Not many people know that," he added dryly, glancing round the room, which, except for the animated chatter and laughter, might have been a scene from hell. "Here come the drinks. You head for the back door and I'll meet you there after I've given Will a hand with these. Here's your Coke."

There were half a dozen boys, about the same age as Danny and his friends, standing outside the back door, smoking and joking among themselves. They looked Olivia over as she came out. One of them made a remark that made the other boys laugh and Olivia go pink. She hated boys. Especially in bunches.

The witty one addressed her as darling and asked her if she was looking for someone. She ignored him, but she had lost her nerve. She started to go back inside and met Charlie coming out.

"Come on, let's get away from this rabble."

He led her across the lawn, away from the colored lights and the noisy boys. The air was cooler and fresher at the back of the garden. The sunset had not yet vanished from the high clouds overhead.

He leaned back against the garden wall and took a drink of beer. She rested one shoulder against the wall and sipped at her Coke. She wasn't hot anymore, she was chilly. She couldn't think of anything to say. She wished she hadn't come out.

"I like your earrings." He wasn't looking at her ears, he was looking at her bosom, even though he couldn't see it with her hands and the Coke glass in the way.

"Thanks." Olivia liked her earrings too. They had been made from one of her mother's designs, plain gold and shaped something like the Greek letter delta. She knew all the letters of the Greek alphabet because the stars had Greek letters in their official names, just as plants and animals all had formal Latin names. "My mother made them."

"Does she do that a lot?"

"That's what she does. She's a jewelry designer."

"I'm impressed."

Not knowing how to respond to that, she changed the subject. "Are you at school with Clare's brother?"

"Just for one more month, then I'm free." He grinned at her. "I don't care if I've failed all my A levels, I'll still be free."

"Aren't you going on to university?"

"Not a chance. They don't want me and I don't want them."

"Have you got a job lined up?"

"I'm going to work for my father."

"What does he do?"

"He has his own company. Cahill Construction, you ever heard of them?"

She had. It was posted at construction sites all over London. "Do you have to start as a brickie and work your way up, or do you wear a tie and get called a management trainee?"

"My dad says I have to do it the hard way. The hard-hat way, that is. Boring, eh? But I don't know how long he'll stick to that. My brothers have already been through this routine, and the stretch in purgatory gets shorter each time."

He grinned again. "At least it's money in my pocket, and I can get on with my life."

"What do you want to do, besides becoming a property magnate?"

"I don't know, travel a bit, maybe. I haven't thought." His eyes did some traveling of their own, from her face to her breasts and back again. "You've still got a few more years of school, do you?"

"Yeah. Boring, eh?"

They both laughed.

"You finished your Coke?" He held out his hand for the empty glass and set it on the nearest table. Then he looked at her again. Her chest. She was hugging herself. The silk shirt was thin, the wind suddenly cool. "Are you cold, Lia?"

"A bit." She shivered. "Maybe we should go back in."

"Let's try this first."

He took the single step between them and put his arms around her. Her arms were still crossed between her body and his. She stared at him, watching his face come closer. He kissed her on the mouth.

He did it quite gently. She trusted him enough to unfold her arms and bring her hands up to his shoulders.

"That's better." He kissed her again, sliding his tongue along her lower lip like people did in films. He took her shiver for pleasure and pushed his tongue inside her mouth.

She had never been kissed like that before. She quite liked it. She touched the tip of her tongue to his, timidly, for fear he should think her a brazen hussy. She put her arms around his neck. He moved one hand up to cradle her head, the other around to cradle her breast.

The sensation was not at all unpleasant. But her head was suddenly filled with the image of Nick Winter. In her front doorway, staring at her breasts under her tank top. In her sitting room, staring at the bodice of her new dress while her mother watched benignly. Staring at her with cool insolence, stripping her naked with his stare, as if he had every right to look at her naked body.

Suddenly what this boy was doing to her seemed horribly shameful and sordid. The idea of any man touching or even looking at her breasts seemed degrading. Her breasts themselves were degrading, grotesquely heavy, obvious, inescapable, like an obscene cartoon.

She pushed away Charlie's hand and clutched at the front of her shirt.

"Lia?"

"Sorry." She turned away from him, toward the wall, one hand protecting her breasts, the other pressed to her mouth. "I felt sick all of a sudden." She took three deep breaths, aware of the rough brick against her body. She felt better now, stupid rather than sick, embarrassed instead of ashamed. "Sorry," she repeated. "Maybe I'd better go home."

"I'll drive you home."

"I can't, I came with Megan. I have to go home with her."

"I'll take you both home," he offered with reckless gallantry.

That sounded better. Safer. "Okay."

She took his arm by way of apology as they recrossed the lawn. She liked him. She was sorry she had inadvertently humiliated him. "Charlie, I'm sorry. It wasn't anything to do with you."

"I hope not." He sounded faintly offended, but also amused. "When someone says you make me sick, it's only supposed to be a way of speaking."

She collected Megan and said her good-byes to Clare, when she could pry her away from Allie. Clare was very interested when she learned how they were getting home. "Oh, Charlie, he's quite gorgeous and very sweet, and his father's filthy rich, but Danny says that's just as well since he hasn't any brains."

Olivia was indignant on Charlie's behalf. "I think he's nice."

"He is. I said so, didn't I? He's just a bit dim."

The two girls sat in the back of the car. Safety in numbers, no conquest by division. Olivia let Megan carry the conversation, which her friend was entirely capable of doing. Charlie stopped at Megan's house first. When he came to the terrace where Olivia lived he got out and opened the car door for her, and walked with her to the front door. Her mother had left the outside light on.

"Are you still feeling sick?"

"A little. Not so much. I'll be okay in the morning."

"Good." He was looking at her face. He had nowhere else to look, since she had done up her jacket. "Maybe we could try again tomorrow."

"I have to visit my father tomorrow."

"Where is he, in the hospital?"

"No, he—he just doesn't live here." She looked away. "Don't ask! I live in a zoo."

The dream came back again that night.

This time, when the creature climbed through the window, she found herself unable to run. She knew she should have run, somehow she knew she could have run, but she stayed frozen in her bed. He—it—that—came over to the bed and stared at her with pale, alien eyes. He/it jerked away the duvet. She discovered to her horror that she was naked. Her shame grew greater than her terror, shame above all that she hadn't made herself run away.

The man-thing reached down and touched her naked breast.

8

Her father lived in Highgate village, in a small but perfectly formed eighteenth-century terrace house, the middle one in the row. Every second Sunday was Olivia's day to visit him. They had established this rigid routine soon after his desertion, as soon as she discovered that if it wasn't set in stone it didn't happen. There was nothing new about that, of course. Even when he had been at home he had never been at home.

The pattern of the visit was a routine too. She always cycled over the heath when the weather was good; it was a horrible long hill going up but a wonderful long hill going home. When she arrived and rang the bell, Althea always answered the door. It was a message, which Olivia received loud and clear: This is my house, not yours. He belongs to me, not to you.

As always, Althea invited her in, in a gracious, formal way, as if there were not nine but nineteen years between them. "Ross is upstairs in the study." She never said your father, only Ross. Then she would call up the stairs, "Lia's here, Ross," as though he wouldn't have known who it was at the door if she hadn't told him. No one cometh unto the father but by me.

Her father had his own routines. He always kissed her on the cheek. She hated that; it made them seem like strangers. If he had picked her up and swung her round, if he had hugged her and kissed her three times like Russians meeting, that would have been best. But next best was no kiss at all.

The next bit of the routine was sherry in the sitting room. Olivia liked this room, in spite of Althea's presence made obvious in the elegant floral arrangements and the sophisticated color scheme. It was full of books, her father's books, all the books that used to be in her own house, that he had taken away when he left. She had always associated him with books, and it was the absence of the books more than his own absence—since he was hardly ever there anyway—that had made her understand he would never come back.

She always had a glass of amontillado, which didn't taste as good as Bristol Cream but was more romantic on account of Poe's story. Her father drank whiskey, and Althea had vodka with tonic. It was all very cool and adult, which was one way, Olivia supposed, of pretending that the person sitting opposite was not your only child whom you had abandoned. Maybe he was hoping to make the visits so boring that she would give up coming.

While they had their drinks Althea would do her routine of playing aunt. She asked about school. She asked about violin lessons. She asked about extracurricular activities. She asked about Olivia's mother—in the hope, Olivia supposed, that her mother might have dropped dead sometime in the previous fortnight without its having come to Althea's attention.

Althea really did look like Olivia's mother. She was a couple of inches shorter, her glossy, smartly cut hair was black instead of yellow, and her eyes were brown instead of blue, but otherwise she might have been trying to make herself a copy: slim, neat, beautifully dressed, even the sense of style that was Olivia's despair because she lacked it herself. The same nervous energy and rigid self-control. The same small, elegant breasts, Olivia thought bitterly. But Althea was eleven years younger than her mother.

The routine after lunch was that Olivia went for a walk with her father on the Heath. By tradition Althea stayed behind, on the pretext of doing the washing up, even though they had a dishwasher. But Olivia had her father to herself. Sometimes if the weather was bad they went down to the Tate or the National Gallery after lunch, which should have been more interesting but was actually worse because Althea came along.

Olivia asked her father about his book. He was writing a book about the Wars of the Roses. He talked to her as if she were one of his university students. She was flattered and grateful. She pleased him by listening and asking careful questions. This was important. It was the only way she had of getting him to love her.

The first time she saw him after he left she had asked him—shamelessly, as it seemed to her now—if he didn't love her anymore. He had said of course he did; he was still her father, he said. He had seemed embarrassed and angry. So she must suppose that even if he loved her, it annoyed him to have her ask, to have to say it. You weren't supposed to talk about love.

It had always been best between them, as long as she could remember, when he was absorbed in telling her about something that interested him. She recalled years ago when they had gone up to High Barnet and he took her down a lane to see the battle site, and Dead Men's Ditch beyond, where the losing Lancastrians had tried to flee and mostly failed. He had walked around the field, describing the movement of troops on that fatally foggy Easter Sunday. She had had a funny feeling then, a pang in her ten-year-old heart, an idea that those dead Lancastrian soldiers were more real for him than she was, his own daughter, his living flesh and blood.

She wished at least, every second Sunday, that he would put his arm around her as they walked together. When she was little she used to hold his hand; he had held her hand at Barnet, on the battlefield. But she had grown too big for that now. She had grown too big almost overnight, it seemed, when he left and she got tall and her horrible tits appeared.

She put her arm through his the way her mother used to do, the way Althea did now. He didn't seem to mind. So that was all right.

"We've got a lodger," she told him.

"A what?"

"A lodger. He's renting the spare room."

Her father stopped and stared at her. "When did this happen?"

"Last week. He's only there on weekdays. Mummy says it's his pied-à-terre."

"Anyone I know?"

She knew then that he understood. A lodger wasn't anyone he would be likely to know, but a lover, a lover might be. "His name is Nick Winter. He's a photographer."

"Where did he come from?"

"He did a brochure for Mummy. To advertise her jewelry."

"Was it any good?"

Olivia had to admit that it was. "He used Mummy as his model. She looked quite terrific and so did the jewelry. Only she didn't have anything on up top."

Her father made a sound between a choke and a cough. She didn't look up at him. "It's a bit late in the day for her to start practicing public nudity."

Olivia felt obliged to defend her mother from this masculine sneer. "She really did look okay. Not old at all."

"I expect he used filters or something," her father said vaguely. "What are her clients going to think about this burst of exhibitionism?"

"I don't think they'll even notice that it's her. It was done quite cleverly. And don't blame Mummy, it was Nick's idea."

"I believe you."

They fell silent, both perhaps contemplating the same mental image, of Nick removing her mother's clothing. Olivia almost blushed, not so much at the image itself, though that was embarrassing enough, but at the idea of her father sharing the thought. Though of course he didn't even know what Nick looked like.

"What's he like?"

"Meg thinks he's hunky."

"What do you think?"

"I don't like him. He's a yob. And he smokes. But he's not around much."

Her father seemed relieved. It was as if he was more jealous for her than for her mother. Her heart lifted at the thought.

She changed the subject. "I bought a frock for the wedding, by the way. Meg and I picked it out ourselves. But it cost more than you gave me."

"How much do I owe you?"

"You owe Mummy fifty pounds."

"Fifty pounds?" He pulled his arm free of her grasp. "You spent a hundred and fifty pounds on a dress?"

"What's wrong with that? Althea does it all the time, doesn't she? And you said to get whatever I wanted. And it's really super, Daddy."

"I should bloody well hope so, at that price. But Lia, you'll have grown out of it in six months."

"Daddy, I haven't grown for over a year. Not upward, anyway. This is the size I'm going to be."

Her father looked at her as if he hadn't seen her at all in the two and a half years since he left home. His eyes kept coming back to her breasts, as if they were the least credible part of the changes in her. It made her feel very strange to have her father stare at her bosom like that. She folded her arms across her chest to hide it.

He said, "Well, I don't suppose you'd want to get much bigger, would you?"

"I should be smaller," she said bitterly. "I weigh too much."

"Is that why you never eat your lunch?"

She didn't eat her lunch because it made her sick to eat food that Althea had prepared. But she couldn't tell him that. "Well, I am on a sort of diet."

"You're like Emma; she was always on a diet."

"She still is. But it keeps her beautiful, doesn't it?"

"For what that's worth," her father said dryly.

He could afford to talk like that. Men could stay beautiful in spite of wrinkles and a thickening waist and gray hair. It was so unfair, her mother always said.

Pondering the unfairness of matters between men and women reminded her of Megan's daft idea about the play, and what she had promised to do. "Daddy, can you find me some translations of a Greek play? Meg has this big idea that she wants to produce it and I've got to help her rewrite it."

"What's the play?"

She knew the title was a woman's name, but the only name that came into her head was Emma, her mother's name. Also one of Jane Austen's novels. "I forget what it's called. It's about a woman whose husband leaves her and she kills his new wife."

"*Medea.*"

"Yeah, that's it. I knew you'd know it. I need you to dig out some translations from the university library. We want to compare them because we can't read Greek."

"Nobody can anymore. It's a lost art, classical Greek."

"So what? It's a dead language, isn't it? Even the Greeks don't understand it."

"Their loss, surely," her father said acidly. "You'll have to wait till I get back from holiday. I've a formidable pile of exam papers to plow through before we go away."

They had come full circle back to the house. "Can you give me the money for my frock? I have to pay Mummy back."

"I'll write out a check." He gave her another faintly incredulous look, as if he still couldn't believe this tall, buxom wench was his young daughter. "Did Emma approve of this solid-gold garment?"

Olivia was pleased that her father still recognized the authority of her mother's taste in these matters. "Yes, she did." To her own surprise she added, "So did Nick."

"Oh well, then," said her father. "He should know. In his line of work he must spend all day looking at women wearing fancy frocks. Or taking them off, as the case might be."

9

Olivia had to put up with only two evenings of Nick that week: on Wednesday he didn't arrive till after dinner, and on Thursday she herself was late getting home on account of her music lesson.

She discovered that the daily routine of a photographer, whatever it might be, and assuming that photographers had daily routines the way schoolgirls and jewelry designers did, seemed to keep him in bed until after she had left for school. That way at least she didn't have to see him in the morning. Though she would rather have had him get up and go out early, along with her mother. She didn't like going past her mother's bedroom door when she knew he was in there. It was like tiptoeing past a dragon's lair, hoping he wouldn't wake up.

When Megan told her she was being irrational she couldn't really defend herself. It was true what Megan said; he was always perfectly pleasant and polite to her, but of course he would be, wouldn't he, while her mother was around.

She had called him a creep, but he wasn't really, not like some of her mother's previous man friends who had been rather rodential types. The comparisons Nick brought to mind were not of small, sly creatures but of large, dangerous, even carnivorous beasts. You might be alarmed and unhappy about your mother keeping a bear in the bedroom, but you couldn't really say that it was boring.

The bear wasn't there the following week. Her mother said he had gone to Spain on a job, or a shoot as she called it. He'd be gone all week, she said.

But she was wrong.

On Thursday evening Olivia came home late, as usual on Thursdays, because she had her violin lesson after school. Her mother was also going to be late that night; they had a private view on at the gallery.

She was just coming up the hill to the house—third from the bottom of the row it was, the one with the stone lion over the front door and the attic window of her bedroom like a pineal eye in the slope of the roof—her violin case in one hand, her bag of schoolbooks and music books in the other, when somebody called her name.

She had never seen Nick with his car before. She hadn't happened to see him coming or going, and he had to park wherever he could in the street, so it was only now she discovered that the gunmetal blue XJS convertible she and Megan had admired last week belonged to him.

She was impressed in spite of herself, and in spite of the fact that the car was rather old and had been knocked about quite a bit. Not unlike its owner, come to think of it. But after all, as Megan had observed, a Jag is a Jag, and he did look good in it, though she wasn't going to let him know any of that. She had to admit that Megan was right: he was kind of hunky. His hair was unevenly blond, very fair on top, slightly darker beneath. Maybe a few days of Spanish sun had done that for him.

She set down her book bag and violin and leaned over the door to examine the interior. "I thought you were in Spain."

"So I'm back."

"Mummy's out tonight. She won't be home till about ten."

"Does that mean you're the cook?"

The idea of acting like some sort of scullery slave for him filled her with indignation. "What do you think?"

"Just joking. Tell you what, I'll take you out to the local Taj Mahal."

"I'm all right," she said stiffly. "You go by yourself."

"You'll have to come. I don't know where it is."

"I'll draw you a map."

"Come on, kid." He reached up and caught her wrist, tugging playfully. "You know we'll have to make friends sometime. Let's make tonight the night."

Olivia tried to pull her hand away. "Who said I wanted to be friends with you? Let go of me."

He didn't let go. It was not a painful grip, only a very strong one. "Don't you want a ride in my car?"

She said scornfully, "Is that your standard pickup line?"

"No, I save that one for kids."

She looked down at him and he smiled, and she started to laugh. He was so outrageous he was funny. "Okay, let me put my gear in the house and get changed. And I have to be back by eight o'clock because there's a program I want to watch."

"Whatever you say, sweetheart."

She was so flustered as she collected her things that she wasn't sure if she had heard him right. It didn't mean anything, of course; he was the sort of person who would call everybody something like sweetheart. But it flustered her, and she resented that.

She resented him even more when they got to the Curry Palace and he managed to bully her into eating more than she had meant to. She ordered a small salad and he said in a rather belligerent tone Is that all you're going to have? She said yes, so what? and he said she was going to faint from hunger before she'd even left the restaurant, for Christ's sake, and he made such a fuss in front of the amused and incredulous waiter that she ended by ordering chicken tikka and pilau rice as well just to shut him up, telling herself she wasn't actually going to eat any of it.

"I can't believe you," she muttered when the waiter had gone away smirking. "Do you do that to Mummy when you take her out to dinner?"

"Em's old enough to starve herself if she wants to. You're just a silly kid."

"There's nothing silly about it. I'm the same height as her and twenty years younger but I weigh ten pounds more."

"Maybe she's too thin, did you ever think of that?"

Olivia wanted to say If you think she's too thin why are you screwing her? "Are you going to try to fatten her up?"

He smiled. "Maybe I will. But you don't need slimming down or fattening up, Lia. You look good just the way you are."

She crossed her hands over her breasts, an almost automatic defensive gesture she had developed whenever any male appeared to be showing interest in them, as he was definitely doing now. "Don't call me Lia."

"Why not?"

"It's a stupid baby name. When I started to talk that was all I could make of Olivia. My parents thought it was cute, so they started using it too." She glared at him, irritated that this stranger should have managed to insinuate himself into any sort of intimate family arrangements. Though she admitted to herself that was rather a grand way to describe a childish nickname. "But you're not my father," she added, "so you ought to be calling me by my proper name."

"Who else calls you Lia?"

"Just my family and friends."

"That puts me in my place, doesn't it? All right, I'll call you Olivia if you call me Nicholas."

Olivia looked at him and covered her mouth with her hand to hide an urge to giggle. Nicholas was as likely on him as Frederick or Bartholomew.

"If you laugh, you have to call me Mr. Winter."

"Okay," she conceded, "you might as well call me Lia."

It was his turn to be amused. "Well, why not? It saves time."

Two girls from her school came in to collect a take-away. They were a year ahead of her and she knew them only by sight, not well enough to speak to. She was amused and perversely pleased to observe that they were clearly impressed by Nick, and by the fact that he was with her. If only they knew . . .

Nick had noticed them too. "Friends of yours?"

"They're in the fifth form of my school."

He watched them go out. She hated the way he was looking at them, with clinical interest, rating their female attributes like a judge at a gymnastics competition. She had never really watched a man do that before. Boys did it, loudly amongst themselves, like the ones outside the fish and chip shop on Kilburn High Road, or the boys hanging around the back door of the pub last Saturday, but they were only doing it to impress each other. Nick was doing it just because he did it all the time.

She wondered if her mother had noticed, and if it bothered her.

He finished his beer and lit a cigarette. "I like your friend Meg."

"I like her too." To get even with Megan for her betrayal the other night, Olivia added, "And she likes you. She thinks you're a real hunk."

He smiled. "You don't agree?"

She flushed and looked down at her hands. "It's nearly eight o'clock."

"All right, let's go home."

The XJS really was terrific. She even had the luck to go past the two fifth-form girls and the pleasure of seeing them recognize her.

After making such a fuss about wanting to see the TV program, which was about Darwin's voyage on the *Beagle*, Olivia found it hard to concentrate. After ten minutes she went into the kitchen to make herself a pot of tea. She stuck her head around the sitting room door to ask Nick if he wanted a cup.

"Two sugars."

Well, he would, wouldn't he? He was so predictable— exactly the same tastes and habits as her mother's cleaning lady. Unlike the cleaning lady, he didn't actually drop his h's or put them where they didn't belong, but he did pronounce the first letter of her mother's surname, Hardy, as haitch rather than aitch.

And he called her mother Em. Inexplicably, her mother didn't seem to mind.

She poured the tea and stirred in the sugar and brought it through to him. Evidently Darwin's adventures were of no interest to him; he was browsing through one of her mother's glossy fashion magazines.

Professional interest, she supposed. "Is that the kind of thing you do?"

"Now and then. The real money is in advertising."

Olivia sat down at the opposite end of the sofa, nursing her own tea and thinking about what Megan had said the other day, about her being a model. Megan was a loyal friend, but she was also the last person to practice flattery. Nick would know if Megan was right, or if Megan was crazy. He dealt with models every day. He looked at women all day, and sized them up. It wasn't that she wanted to be a model, mind. Just perhaps that she might not be so far from her mother's ideal, her father's Althea, as she had supposed.

"Nick, do you think I could be a model?"

"I thought you said you didn't want to be a model."

"I just want to know if I could be one. Don't they have to be, you know, a certain height and weight and so forth?"

Now he looked up. "Your height's all right. Let's have a look at the and so forth." He dragged on his cigarette, watching her. "Stand up and take off that tent you're wearing."

"My jumper?" Olivia was startled. "What for?"

He said patiently, "How can I tell if you look like a model when I can't see what you look like? You've got something on under that sweater, don't you?"

"Yes," she admitted. "But . . ."

"The answer's no."

He returned his attention to the magazine. She stared at the top of his head, obscurely outraged. "What do you mean, no?"

"You can't be a model if you don't want anyone to look at you. That's what modeling is all about."

She really truly hated him. Right now she particularly hated the fact that he had so readily guessed what was in her head. She wanted to escape upstairs, but that would be letting him win. And she wanted to know.

She pulled off the sweater and stood in the doorway in an equally oversized T-shirt.

"Well?"

"You want me to be honest?"

"That's why I asked you."

"I'm flattered." He smoked and studied her and she wanted to die. "Let's see." He stubbed out the cigarette and stood up with the magazine in his hand. "Go over there, face the mirror in the hall. That's what you think you want to look like, right?" He handed her the magazine, open at a full-page photograph of an impossibly slim, impossibly tall, long-boned, small-breasted, glossily over-made-up young woman wearing what appeared to be artistically shredded rags.

"I suppose so," she said faintly.

"All right. Now you look at that, and then you look in the mirror."

She looked at the mirror. He was standing right behind her, three or four inches taller than her. He gathered her hair into his hands and piled it up on top of her head. "What do you think?"

She could feel the warmth of his body behind hers, the warmth of his hands in her hair. He had astonished her, coming so close, touching her, rearranging her hair. She didn't look at the image in the magazine; she looked at the image of herself, and closed her eyes in despair at the sight.

"I'm too fat. I'll never be that slim."

"You couldn't be fat if you tried, kid. That stupid slag lives on cucumber and cottage cheese and without her makeup she looks like death warmed over."

He took away his hands. Her hair came tumbling down. He slid his arms around her waist.

She froze.

"Sweetheart, you're the best shape there is. They'd love you on page three."

He terrified her. Holding her like that, talking to her like that. Yet it was ages, years, since anyone whomsoever had held her in any way at all. Except for the boy at the pub.

He drew her back against him. She dropped the magazine and put her hands on his arms, which were linked like iron around her midriff. He was talking to her, breathing his words in her ear the way a lion might purr over his dinner. "You've been neglected, kitten. Someone should have told you how beautiful you are."

His hands were like his voice, warm and coaxing, warm and persuasive. She watched the mirror in amazement as those hands slid up to cup and stroke her breasts. She could feel the heat of them through the thin T-shirt and her bra beneath. She could feel the pressure of his caresses, especially on her nipples.

The pleasure of his caresses. She had never felt anything

like this: the way he held her, stroked her, talked to her. Comforting and terrifying, shaming and exciting her.

"Let me go," she whispered.

He let her go.

She turned to confront him. He was looking at her, neither smiling nor angry nor apologetic. Just looking at her, in a way that made her feel funny inside.

"You're not supposed to do that."

She shouldn't have said it like that. It sounded stupidly childish: you're not supposed to eat sweets before dinner, you're not supposed to jump on the sofa. He was an adult. The rules were different in his country.

She could only invoke adult authority. "I'll tell my mother."

"She'd like that, wouldn't she?"

"What do you mean?"

"You're a smart kid, you think about it."

Despite the sarcasm, he was serious. She decided to think about it upstairs.

She went upstairs and shut her bedroom door. I need a lock on the door, she thought. She went to the front window, the pineal eye of the house, and looked out at the street below, at the terraced line of roof gables marching down the hill, at distant windows in Kilburn reflecting the low-lying sun. The most familiar sight in the world to her, that cityscape.

She didn't know how her mother felt about Nick. Her mother was the last person in the world to come home and say something like, I've met this gorgeous man and I'm mad about him. On the other hand, she was also the last person to invite a man into her home and life simply because she fancied him. And this man was so totally unlike all the men with whom her mother had ever had to do. The fact that he went against her grain and yet was here, living here, could only mean that she really had met a gorgeous man and was mad about him.

So he was right. The last thing her mother wanted now was to have her, Olivia, her daughter, come to her and say, By the way, your boyfriend has been feeling me up and what are you going to do about it?

Besides, what had he really done? Only what Charlie Cahill

had attempted on Saturday night. And he could always say, she asked me about modeling. Or, I was only hugging her.

Or else he could say, she liked it.

She could hear Megan's persistent questions in her head, mildly curious, horribly frank. Megan was fearless even with herself, a sort of psychological crown prosecutor. Megan would say, well, did you like it?

And Olivia on oath would have to answer, well, yes.

10

On the day of his wedding her father came round to collect her, to take her down to Marlow. Althea's parents lived near there. They had a large Victorian house and a long lawn sloping down to the Thames, an admirable setting for a wedding, and they were determined to have a wedding there. Althea was their only daughter, their only chance.

Althea was already there. Propping up her mother while she had the vapors, Olivia's father said. He was on his best behavior, quite noticing. "You look very pretty, Lia. Is that the new dress?"

Irony was not Olivia's style, but he tempted her. She thought of saying, No, I just threw on any old thing. But she loved her father and knew his shortcomings, so she agreed that it was the new dress.

"And you've put your hair up."

"Mummy did it. Don't you like it?"

"Yes, of course. It makes you look very grown up. Much older than fourteen."

"I'm fifteen now, Daddy. My birthday was on Tuesday."

"So it was." He sounded alarmed, vaguely displeased. He had obviously forgotten about it. Again. "I was so involved with exam papers and this wedding business ... We'll have to celebrate that when I see you again."

She felt as if she were seeing him off on a long sea voyage in the old days, when people as often as not never came back. She remembered something she had read about Sir John Franklin's ill-fated expedition to the Arctic. A ship had come afterward looking for them, bearing letters from England. Letters, among others, from a mother to her sons, both of them long since dead when she thought they were still alive on the other side of the world.

She felt as if her father were setting sail for the Arctic. Or maybe she was.

It wasn't a proper wedding because it couldn't be held in a church. Church marriages could only be held between bachelors and spinsters, or widows and widowers. Althea qualified, but Olivia's father did not. So they had actually got married the day before in a registry office. The wedding to which Althea and her parents had invited an enormous number of people was really only the wedding feast, after the deed had been done.

There were lots of people at the house near Marlow, hardly any of them people that Olivia knew. None of her mother's friends and relatives were there, of course. Her father's parents lived in Yorkshire and had declined the invitation on the grounds of distance. But her father had said they didn't approve of the divorce. At any rate, her grandparents were not present, and neither was her father's brother, her uncle John.

Out of shyness among so many strangers, she stuck close to her father and ended up being introduced to everyone. Among the wedding guests were Althea's brother and sister-in-law, two grandmothers, a grandfather, and even a very frail great-grandmother. The grandparents all seemed confused about where Olivia fitted into the family scheme. The idea that Althea was marrying a man who had a teenage daughter seemed scandalous, improbable, or intriguingly risqué.

Another guest was the local vicar. He was not the vicar of Marlow but of some village closer by, the one who would have had the privilege of marrying Althea to Olivia's father if such an event had been permissible in church. He apologized to them for having been unable to do the honors.

"You know how it is," he said to Olivia's father. "Totally irrational, these matters. The Queen's own family can marry as often as they please, it seems, but you and I, we're not allowed to know. Perhaps before the twenty-first century dawns, we might be prepared to meet it."

He turned to Olivia with an inquiring glance at her father. Her father cleared his throat in a vaguely embarrassed way. "This is my daughter, Olivia."

The vicar was not at all abashed to be confronted by a product of the marriage that he was so eager to declare irrelevant history. He took Olivia's hand in both of his. "How do you do, my dear? So nice to meet you. You must be pleased to be with your father on this happy day."

Olivia smiled politely. She thought for a moment about what he had said. Was it a happy day for her father because after living with Althea for two and a half years it was no longer adultery? But according to the vicar himself nothing had changed as far as his church was concerned. And if her father was going to have sexual intercourse with Althea tonight, it would presumably be no different from the intercourse they had enjoyed for nearly three years past. So the only thing the vicar could have meant was that her father was happy to be finally rid of her mother and her. And why should she be glad of that?

She smiled again, more stiffly. "I'm pleased if Daddy's happy."

The vicar looked at her more carefully. He looked at her bosom, to be precise. He was still holding her hand. He said to her father, "It must be a great source of pride and pleasure for you, to have such a beautiful daughter."

Beautiful was a code word, she understood. It meant the same thing as grown-up. It meant she had big tits. The idea of a vicar, of all people, commenting to her father, of all people, on the size of her breasts was enough to make her want to jump in the river, no matter what Nick had said about the fans of page three. She disengaged her hand and excused herself.

Althea's father gave her a glass of champagne. Olivia

sipped it cautiously. It tasted a bit like very dry ginger ale. A little while later he came back and filled her glass up again. She refused a third glass when he offered it. Instead she went off to look for her father, who had disappeared.

She found him talking to some people she didn't know. She hung around politely at his elbow, not really listening, just watching her father. He had told her in the car that she looked nice, and she had returned the compliment. But it wasn't a fair exchange; he didn't look nice, he looked wonderful. He had always looked like a film star, dark hair, blue eyes, tall and slim, fit enough to fight the villains and win. But he wasn't a film star, he was a professor. Not only beautiful but brainy.

No wonder her mother had loved him. No wonder Althea wanted him. Olivia loved him too, but no one had asked her. She was the child of the marriage that was no more, and that left her out of all consideration.

He finally noticed her, and disengaged himself from his conversation to turn to her. He was all in black and white, formal and prim. Except that it was his wedding day, and he had been drinking champagne.

"What's the trouble, Lia?"

"Nothing's the matter. Mummy said she'd pick me up at five and it's five o'clock now."

"Are you all right? Are you enjoying yourself?"

"Not quite," she said frankly. "Daddy, I want to talk to you before I go home."

He made an uncharacteristically expansive gesture. The day, or the drink, no doubt. "Let's have it."

"No, I want to talk to you alone. Let's walk down toward the river."

She was speaking quietly, so he took her seriously. She tucked her arm under his and walked close to him. His long-legged stride meant she had to skip to keep up.

"Daddy, I ..." She took a deep breath. "When you get back from your holiday, can I come and live with you?"

"Why? What's wrong with things at your mother's?"

"It's that man I told you about."

"What's wrong with him?"

"Well, he's ..." She wondered if her father would understand what an uncleman was. Yes, probably all too clearly. "He's not just—you know—just a lodger. Where Mummy's concerned, I mean. But as far as I'm concerned he's a total stranger. How would you like having to live with a stranger?"

Her father didn't say anything for a minute. "Have you discussed this with Emma?"

"No."

He had come to a halt. She lowered her gaze to his chest. She thought that she would have liked to reach out and touch him, the way you would touch a person you loved, but he was forbidden to her. She could have touched him, true, but she would have discomfited him. Only Althea could touch him now.

"No," she repeated. "I don't think she's even twigged that I know—you know—what goes on between them."

He moved away, moodily. He doesn't want me, she thought. She had guessed it before but never dared put it to the test. She was doing it now only because of Nick. She wondered what her father would have said if she had told him, Mummy's boyfriend was groping my tits.

"Not now," her father was saying. "Maybe next year."

"Why not now?"

He was looking away, looking across the river as if the farther bank were a paradise where such awkward situations never arose. "Althea's pregnant."

"She's going to have a baby?" It had never crossed her mind that her father and Althea were capable of making a baby. He was too old, he was over forty. The very idea was disgusting. He was looking at her now, waiting for some reaction. She supposed she was supposed to be pleased but she was just shocked. All she could think of to say was, "When?"

"Christmastime." After a pause he added, "By this time next year we'll be over most of the sleepless nights and colic. Maybe you can come then."

To mind the baby, thought Olivia in a dreadful, cynical, hard-hearted heave of understanding. Althea was going to have a baby. Her father would have a new daughter or, better still, a son. He would have a new family altogether, but she could creep in as a skivvy. Cinderella.

"Lia, it's just the timing. Do you understand?"

She didn't answer him. "Did I have colic?"

"You were terrible," he told her, smiling. "You kept us awake every night for six weeks running."

"Are all babies like that?"

"I hope not. Lia, I've got to go back up to the house. Are you coming?"

"Not yet. I'm going to admire the river for a while."

"Well . . ." He didn't have time to worry about her just then. "I'll see you later."

By the waters of the Thames Olivia sat down, but she wasn't going to weep with all these strangers about. The champagne had made her a little giddy; it was easy to close off the part of her brain that wanted to brood on what her father had said. She just sat and watched the water flow by, feeling as if it were running through her head, washing her thoughts downriver to drown them in the salt sea.

Althea came down to call her. "Lia, someone's come for you."

Olivia was too distracted with looking at Althea's long white silk frock and trying to imagine a baby inside to take any notice of what she had actually said. It was an awful shock to come into the house expecting to see her mother and find Nick Winter.

Instead of his usual faded jeans he was looking amazingly respectable in a very sharp suit. He was talking to Althea's father, or rather Althea's father was talking to him. "Have some champagne," Althea's father was saying, having had quite a lot of it himself.

"No thanks, I'm driving Lia home."

"Plenty of time," Althea's father persisted. "Come in, sit down, we'll get you something to eat."

Nick glanced at Olivia, who was keeping her distance, staring at him. "I think Lia wants to go home now."

Olivia's father came up. She had another shock, seeing him next to Althea's father and realizing that the age difference between them was less than that between her and Althea. Didn't Althea's father think it was funny to have a son-in-law his own age? It seemed medieval, even barbaric: a custom from other cultures, other times.

No introductions had been made and none seemed to be needed. Althea's father neither knew nor cared who Nick might be, while Olivia's father had clearly deduced exactly who he was and disliked him for it.

Olivia's father came and stood beside her and put his hand on her shoulder, but he was looking at Nick, speaking to Nick. "Emma sent you to chauffeur Lia, did she?"

He meant to sound insulting, and Olivia thought he had succeeded pretty well. But she saw that Nick had been sent not as her chauffeur but as her mother's champion. On her father's wedding day, her mother would not humiliate herself by turning up here. She meant to represent herself not as the cast-off wife but as a woman with another, younger, lover to replace the former husband. And her father, quite unfairly, resented that.

"I'm taking her home," Nick answered coolly. "Are you ready, Lia?"

Little Red Riding Hood wasn't quite ready to get into the wolf's car. "Wait a minute, I have to say my good-byes."

She pulled away from her father's proprietorial hand. She said good-bye to Althea's parents and brother and sister-in-law, grandparents and great-grandmother, and to awful Althea herself. Then she came back to her father and hugged him and kissed him and fought back tears. She felt as if she were saying good-bye to him forever. Maybe it was the wedding, maybe the baby.

"Daddy," she whispered desperately, "can't you take me home?"

"You know I can't, Lia. These people are my guests. Anyway, we'll have to leave for Heathrow soon."

"I know that. But I don't want Nick to drive me home."

"Why not?"

She knew she had to be careful here. She couldn't say, I don't want to be alone with him. She didn't know what to say when the truth would clearly not do. She invented a probable lie. "He drives too fast. He's got an XJS."

"The speed limit is the same for an ape in a Jaguar as for us lesser mortals."

Her father came out into the front drive with her. They all came out, Althea and Althea's parents and Nick. They all looked at Nick's XJS. Everybody but Olivia and her father admired it without reservation. Althea even tried out the driver's seat.

Olivia had a crazy notion that if Nick had tried his hand he could have abducted Althea on her wedding day. It was a crazy notion because she knew that Althea was the last person to be seduced by romantically impractical things like an elderly sports car and a fashion photographer who called everybody sweetheart. Althea was made of sterner stuff.

Anyway, Nick didn't have a chance to come on to Althea because Olivia's father was reading him the riot act. He had taken Nick to one side so that no one else could overhear, which Olivia realized was a mercy when she eavesdropped on the conversation.

Her father said Look here, Lia's just told me she's nervous about riding in this car. Take it easy, will you? She's apt to get carsick.

Olivia was ready to sink into the earth. She heard Nick say No problem, as long as she pukes over the side it'll all come off in the car wash.

Her father said How wonderfully convenient these tinpot convertibles are, but the point is she doesn't want to get sick in the first place, Emma doesn't want her to get sick, the M40 isn't Silverstone, do you catch my drift?

Olivia thought she should be a mile below ground level by now, but strangely, she could still hear Nick's reply. "I hear you all right, but I'm not sure you heard Lia." He turned away from her father to her. "All right, Lia? Let's go."

Her father let her go.

Nick put her into his car. Her father and Althea and Althea's parents stood and waved. Which was backward, it was supposed to be the guests seeing off the bride and groom, not the other way round.

When they were out of sight, Olivia settled back into her seat with a sense of desolation and relief.

"Have a good time?"

She had almost forgotten Nick. She sighed in spite of herself. "It was okay."

He gave her a funny look but did not comment on her lack of enthusiasm. "How do we get back to the motorway?"

"Go straight through the town to the second roundabout, then turn left."

"You come here often, do you?"

"I've only been here once before." She studied her fingernails and selected one to chew on. "I suppose they're my stepgrandparents now, aren't they?" She preferred that awkward phrase to the alternative, my stepmother's parents. Althea was not going to be any sort of mother to her. "What are you doing here?"

"What do you think? I came to get you."

"I mean—it's Saturday, you're supposed to be in Norfolk, aren't you?"

"Is that a rule?"

Olivia didn't answer. She was feeling rather dizzy. The aftereffects of champagne, she supposed.

Nick turned left at the roundabout as instructed and drove north toward the motorway. The wide, straight road and the open car should have made her feel better, but it didn't. By the time they reached the motorway she was queasy as well as dizzy. She tried closing her eyes, but that only made her head spin. If she looked at the verge or the cars passing in the opposite direction, she felt disoriented. She sat hunched in her seat, gnawing her knuckle and staring straight ahead, hoping the feeling would go away, praying she was not going to be sick.

"Lia, are you all right?"

"Of course I'm all right."

"You look like a ghost. Are you going to puke?"

"No," she lied, near tears. She could have killed her father for what he had said to Nick. It was true that she used to get carsick when she was younger. What she had hated most about it was not having to throw up but that it was a childish affliction. Adults didn't need to stop the car and get out and heave. So she was not going to do it in front of this man, especially after the conversation she had overheard. "I'll be all right."

"You sure? There's a lay-by coming up."

Without waiting for her answer he moved out of the fast lane, right over into the nearside lane. By the time he pulled into the lay-by she had both hands to her mouth. If there was anything more humiliating than vomiting in front of him, that would be doing it in his car.

As soon as he had stopped, Olivia opened the door and scrambled out. "It's the champagne," she mumbled.

The ground was uneven and she was in haste. She stumbled and fell to her knees.

She retched without result, swaying on hands and knees to keep from soiling her new dress. Riding in the convertible had whipped some of her hair free of the knot her mother had tied it in, and now the wind blew the long, loose hair in her face. She pushed at it helplessly, blinded by the hair and her tears of embarrassment. Her stomach ached, her throat hurt. She seemed to have a great hole in the middle of her.

She crouched beside the car, breathless and sobbing. She was so empty she had nothing to throw up. Her father had thought she was a pathetic little girl. Now Nick would know she was a pathetic little girl. She wished she was dead.

"Come 'ere, kitten."

Nick went down on his knees in front of her. She saw him dimly through her veil of hair and tears. He pulled her onto his lap and held her against him, cradling her head against his shoulder. He stroked her hair, smoothing it away from her face.

"You're all right, sweetheart," he said.

She was not all right. She wept, burying her face against his designer shirt. She had a great ache, in her belly, in her heart. She had lost her father.

When she could speak she said, "Althea's going to have a baby."

"Surprise me."

She lifted her head enough to look at him. "You knew?"

"Well, I guessed. Why d' you think he married her? And in such a fucking hurry."

"In a hurry?"

"He didn't have time to argue, he needed a divorce. He signed over the house to Em."

"Why did he do that?"

"Maybe Althea's old man didn't want any of his guests talking about shotgun weddings. Or else she didn't fancy getting married in a maternity outfit. It was supposed to be a trade-off—your old man gets off the hook for your maintenance—but that doesn't add up." He ruffled her hair, a casual gesture, something her father would never have done. "It's a hard world, kid. A house in London is worth a hell of a lot more than you."

She didn't understand the financial or legal implications of what he was saying. She just grasped that her father had been particularly eager to wash his hands of her so that he could marry Althea before she had his baby. Maybe that was why he hadn't wanted Olivia to come and live with him; he had already paid her off.

"You mean he bribed Mummy to let him go."

"You could say that. Or you could say he was just passing on a bribe. Em told me that Althea's old man offered to make it up to him."

"You mean, to make sure Althea was married to Daddy before the baby was born?"

He shrugged. "Money comes down to blood in the end."

Or blood comes down to money. That would explain why she was being left out of her father's new life. It was all biological, even the money.

She laid her head down on his shoulder, her eyes wide, focused on nothing. Her father didn't want her. Nick thought she was a stupid little girl who puked in the car. The traffic was only a few yards away, on the other side of the car, making a steady, swift, alarming rhythm, *shoom, SHOOM, shoom, SHOOM,* dominating her efforts to think. She found herself trembling like a frightened kitten.

Nick stroked her hair and the back of her neck. With his thumb he brushed away the tear stains at the outer corners of her eyes. He tipped her face upward. She closed her eyes rather than look him in the face.

He touched the tip of her nose with the tip of his tongue. She had never thought of kissing somebody with your tongue like that. Didn't Eskimos kiss with their noses? She giggled and opened her eyes.

He was looking at her as if he might have been smiling, but he wasn't smiling now. "Feeling better?"

"Mm." But she didn't move away. She snuggled closer to him, happy for the moment to be cradled and caressed.

He lifted her chin again. This time he touched his tongue to the corners of her mouth. She opened her mouth to say something, even just to say Oh in surprise or pleasure, and he put his tongue into her mouth.

She said Oh again, in her throat this time because she couldn't speak while he was kissing her. He was much better at it than the boy at the pub. It made her ache inside again, but differently, in a rather exciting way.

She was still perched sideways across his thighs. He pulled off her sandal and caressed her foot. He moved his hand up slowly, all the way up her ankle, her calf, her knee, her thigh, pushing up her skirt to stroke her bare skin. His hand went up to the top of her thigh and slid inside her knickers, stroking the smooth skin of her bottom as if it were silk. His fingertips came to rest in the cleft between the cheeks of her bottom. The palm of his hand cupped her left buttock. When he stroked her with his thumb she shivered and wriggled against his hand.

Nick said *Christ!* and took his hand away.

He stood up, pushing her off his lap. "We've got to get going. I told Em I'd pick her up from the gallery at six. She's got some fucking dinner party lined up."

The harsh tone of his voice alarmed Olivia. She scrambled awkwardly to her feet.

He was dusting off the knees of his trousers. He had mucked up his very expensive, very fashionable suit by going down in the dirt to comfort her. That should have made her feel good, but instead it alarmed her. She guessed he would blame her for it.

He leaned against the car, lighting a cigarette. He exhaled and watched her struggle to put her sandal back on. It made her feel sick, the look in his narrowed eyes as if he hated her.

"You're not going to puke again, are you?"

It was less a question than a threat. She shook her head.

"Good. Get in."

She got in and he shut the door on her. As soon as he started the motor he turned on the radio. Someone began to beg them to tell Laura he loved her. Lucky Laura, thought Olivia. She wished somebody loved her. She wished she were

Althea, to be loved by her father. Or even her mother, to be loved by Nick.

Why would she want to be loved by Nick? The mere idea gave her a hole in her middle, a horrible, bottomless ache like the times when she dreamt that she was falling out of the sky and the pressure of the fall built up inside her until she felt that she was going to fly to pieces.

Just now when he had held her and kissed her, she had felt good in a way that she couldn't remember feeling for years, the way she felt in her dreams when the warmth of a star surrounded her: safe and secure, knowing that everything was going to be all right.

But it wasn't all right. When he looked at her afterward with his cold blue eyes it drove away all the warmth inside her. He didn't love her; he hated her. He was disgusted with her. She had seen it in his face.

She folded her arms across her stomach. She felt sick. But she wasn't allowed to be sick.

11

The man came again. If it was a man.

This time it came up the stairs. She heard it coming and she couldn't run. Maybe she could have escaped through the window; sometimes in dreams you could do things like that. But she stayed frozen and trapped in her bed. While the door burst open and the stranger stalked into her room.

Again he came over to the bed and dragged the duvet off her. Again she was naked and afraid, naked and ashamed. The shame was stronger this time because she was waiting for him to touch her. Wanting him, even, to touch her. In the dream she writhed in shame upon the sheets, not even daring to cover herself with her hands, knowing that he knew what she wanted. He looked down at her with his stranger's eyes full of loathing and contempt for her nakedness and her desire to be touched by him.

She saw that it was a man after all. A man she knew.

It was her father.

Olivia was almost too mortified to get up and face the world on Sunday morning. Even her nightmares were an embarrassment now. And it was true, her father would certainly regard her with loathing and contempt if he knew what had happened on the way home from his wedding. Even Nick had been disgusted by her. It should have been Nick in the dream.

Did that mean she really did want him to touch her?

She couldn't begin to contemplate that thought. How low would she have to sink to earn the contempt of a man she thought beneath contempt? Low enough to want her mother's lover to put his hand up her skirt?

Her mother came into her room and opened the curtains at both ends. "Are you planning to get up at all today, Lia? I thought since it's such a fine day we'd go up to St. Albans for lunch."

Olivia knew St. Albans well. Two battles had happened there; her father had described them both to her, on the spot, as it were. "Is Nick going to come with us?"

"Of course. I can't leave him here to eat bread and cheese."

"I thought he was a lodger. You're not obliged to take your lodger out to Sunday lunch."

"He's taking us out to lunch, actually."

"How kind." Olivia didn't want to be in the same room as Nick, let alone eat lunch at the same table. Not after what he had done yesterday. And then he had sworn at her and pushed her away and glared at her with icy blue revulsion as if she had leprosy. After that she didn't want to know him—even if some decadent part of her did want him to touch her again. "Why is he here on a Sunday? I thought this was supposed to be strictly a weekday arrangement."

"He was away in Spain last week," her mother said vaguely, as if two wrongs made a right. "Anyway, we had that dinner party at Kay and Simon's last night."

"How did that go? Did Nick enjoy it?"

Olivia asked with real interest. Kay wrote cookbooks and Simon was somebody at the BBC and they lived on the other side of Finchley Road, the posh side. Her mother must be truly besotted if she was actually introducing Nick to her friends. If he had been ten years younger she could have passed him off as a toyboy, but at thirty-something he was supposed to be a serious person. Perhaps her mother's friends would be too well-bred to say anything.

"Yes, of course," her mother answered. "Everybody enjoys Kay's dinner parties, she's such an amazing cook. Now do get up, Lia, we'll be leaving soon."

"I don't want to go to St. Albans. I promised to do something with Meg this afternoon."

"All right, we'll leave you to your own devices. But get up anyway."

So it was okay to leave your daughter to eat bread and cheese. Olivia agreed to get up. She went down to the bathroom and had a long, leisurely bath and washed her hair and shaved her legs. By the time she came out her mother and Nick had gone.

When Megan came over she wanted to hear about the wedding.

"It was boring, actually. It wasn't a real wedding anyway because they'd got married the day before. It's a funny thing—my father's wedding and I hardly knew anyone. It was more like a party that Althea's father was throwing for his friends and relations and business colleagues."

"Weddings are always like that. The bride and groom are just an excuse."

"But I'll bet if we looked at my parents' wedding pictures there'd be lots of people there that I know. And that all happened before I was born."

She knew exactly where the wedding photos were because her mother had had all the old albums out last week, on Olivia's birthday. Her mother did that every year, hauling out Olivia's baby pictures and getting sentimental—for the good old days, maybe, when Olivia herself had been manageably small and her father had still been around. Only sentimentality could explain how her mother could look at a photo of newborn Olivia, red and wrinkled and blinking like an elderly bat, and announce in defiance of her own eyes, "You were such a beautiful baby." Then she had sighed and said, "I can't believe you're fifteen years old today."

Her mother said this every year—not fifteen, but whatever age was appropriate. But this year her mother had looked at Olivia when she said it, and her expression changed. As if she had just said, I can't believe you're only fifteen years old.

Olivia turned the pages of her mother's wedding album with Megan, pointing out the faces she could identify. Some of the faces belonged to dead people, her grandfather, for instance. She recognized the church; it was the one in the village in Devon where her grandmother lived. Everyone looked pleased, the dead and the living alike.

Her mother in these pictures was a slighter, finer-featured version of the Princess of Wales. Her father looked very handsome and very young, more like a student than a don, though he had already earned his Ph.D. They were smiling, arm in arm, ready to live happily ever after.

"How did they meet?"

"Mummy was one of Daddy's students."

"Like Althea."

"Yeah. Maybe his students are the only women he ever meets."

"At least the only ones he notices. Hey, your parents were married in December."

"December twenty-first. The first day of winter."

"And you were born six months later."

Olivia looked at Megan and then at the photograph of her parents. How could she have failed to work it out for herself? Her mother must have been three months pregnant when that picture was taken. And that meant ...

She knew that her mother had never completed her university degree because she had left when Olivia was born, at the end of her second year. Olivia had supposed, because adults always seemed to have the privilege of doing what they wanted to do, that her mother had married her father and had a baby because she preferred that to slogging on with her studies. After all, people didn't have babies if they didn't want them, did they? Not with the pill and abortions.

But if it was true what Nick had said, that her father was only marrying Althea because she was pregnant ...

Supposing Althea had wanted to get married and her father had not. Supposing Althea had got pregnant so that he would have to marry her. Something like that was surely what Nick had been implying. So Althea wanted the baby and her father didn't. Or maybe, given Althea's defective maternal instincts, she didn't really want the baby either, except as a way of getting Olivia's father to marry her.

If things like that could happen now, today, what had happened fifteen years ago?

Maybe her father had never really wanted her either.

She wanted to ring up her father for the comfort of hearing him deny it. But he was a thousand miles away in Amalfi. And even if he said no, it wasn't like that, at least not with her—how could she tell if that was the truth? All she knew was that he had left her and made excuses about why she couldn't come to live with him.

"Lia, don't look like that." Megan touched her arm. "What difference does it make? Even in those days people weren't likely to be virgins when they got married. And there's no such thing as a bastard anymore."

"It's not that. I meant to tell you, Althea's pregnant. Daddy told me yesterday."

"At the wedding? That was good timing." Megan paused to consider the news. "So he's going to have another six-month baby. What's that line from Oscar Wilde, one is misfortune but two looks like carelessness."

"Nick says that's why he married Althea."

Olivia waited for Megan to make the connection, but it didn't happen. "Nick says? How come you're discussing these intimate family secrets with Nick?"

"He drove out to Marlow to bring me home."

"I thought he wasn't around on weekends."

"He's here this weekend. Something to do with Spain and a dinner party, according to Mummy."

"Maybe they're really falling in love."

Megan found this notion romantic. Olivia did not. "That's an appalling idea, Meg. But I can't imagine Nick in love with anyone except himself." She closed the album. "Let's do something. Let's go to a film."

The film they decided to see was classified 18-only. Fortunately, since Olivia's mother wasn't home, they could put on loads of makeup to make themselves look about eighteen without her wanting to know what on earth they were up to. Olivia borrowed a pair of her mother's sandals with four-inch heels and one of her sweaters because her own were all too baggy to make it glaringly obvious to the ticket seller that she had a real grown-up bosom. The theory was that anyone standing six feet high with breasts like Elizabeth Taylor's simply had to be eighteen years old.

Then they put each other's hair up. While Megan was doing Olivia's hair, Olivia was reminded of Thursday night when Nick had piled her hair up with his hands. And told her she had page-three tits, and stroked them with his hands.

Even the recollection was excruciatingly humiliating. It made her think of how he had looked at her yesterday, cold and despising. It made her tremble uncontrollably.

Megan looked at her in the mirror. "What's the matter, Lia?"

"Nothing, why?"

"You looked just now as if you were going to cry."

"Did I? Well, I'm not."

After all their efforts they admired themselves in the full-length mirror in the hall downstairs and were enormously pleased with the results. They went out, feeling like *Elle* on wheels.

They managed to get into the film without any trouble. It was about a man who went around murdering women. The murders were done in Technicolor gore, which was bad enough, but the really unnerving thing was that the murderer had a girlfriend who didn't know about his lethal hobby. As the film went on and the girlfriend began to get suspicious, the tension grew as to whether she would (a) confront him, (b) turn him in, and/or (c) get murdered by him.

On the way out Olivia said, "Maybe we shouldn't have gone to see that. I can tell I'm going to have nightmares tonight."

"I don't mind the gory bits," Megan said cheerfully. "After all, I'm going to have to deal with accident victims and people who get cut up in fights."

Olivia put her hand over her mouth and mimed a heave. "Better you than me. Anyway, I meant nightmares about being murdered."

Megan didn't mind murder either. "Most people get murdered by a member of their family. The chances of your being attacked by a stray lunatic are about zero, Lia."

No man, in or out of his right mind, would try to murder Megan. She had straight, fair hair and large, wide-set blue eyes and a sturdy, athletic body, and she was the bravest, most resourceful person Olivia had ever known. At the age of twelve she had saved a small child from drowning. Last winter when a drunken man had come up and made obscene and menacing remarks to the two of them as they were walking through the park behind Olivia's house, Olivia had been terrified, but Megan gave him a lecture on the impropriety of his behavior and he went away abashed.

Olivia left Megan on her own doorstep and came home through the park. She discovered that she didn't need to unlock the back door because her mother was already home. Once upon a time this would have comforted her, but now it meant Nick. Her stomach started to churn at the thought.

She opened the door and came into the kitchen. He was there, all right, sitting at the table with the inevitable cigarette, a glass of beer, and a newspaper. The *Sunday Sport*, I bet, she thought bleakly, or else the News of the Screws. He said hi and she ignored him.

Her mother was doing something domestic at the sink. "Hello, darling. I was beginning to wonder where you were." She glanced up and took in Olivia's appearance for the first time. "Where on earth have you been, all made-up like that?"

"We went to a film." Olivia added defiantly, "Don't you like the way I look?"

"You look very nice," her mother said doubtfully. "But I think I recognize my jumper and shoes."

"So what? It's not a crime to borrow them, is it?"

"I didn't say it was a crime, but you should ask me first."

"You weren't here."

"If I'm not here to ask, you shouldn't use my things."

"But you're never here."

That was a low blow, designed to hobble her mother's argument with guilt. It worked, as it did every time. "Never mind," her mother said stiffly. "Just go and get changed, please. I want you to help me with the dinner."

"I'm not hungry."

"You have to eat something, Lia, you can't live on air. Anyway, you're not the only person living in this house. Nick's hungry, I'm sure. He's entitled to his dinner."

Olivia looked at Nick. He had given up on the newspaper—too many long words, maybe, she thought spitefully. He was leaning back in his chair, his arm hooked over the back of the neighboring chair, watching her with a cool blue stare.

She felt horribly naked in that stare. It made her insides clench to see him looking at her like that. How could her mother not notice?

She thought maybe he was staring at her breasts, which were so obvious in her mother's borrowed jumper, maybe remembering how he had held and stroked them. Maybe he was looking at her bottom and recalling how he had put his hand inside her knickers. Or maybe he was only thinking that she had let him do those things.

That she had liked it.

She glared at him. "He can get his own dinner," she said to her mother. "He's not even supposed to be here tonight. Why should I be his skivvy?"

"Lia, don't be rude." Her mother glanced anxiously at Nick to see if he had taken offense. "Nick pays for his bed and board, he's entitled to it."

Nick hadn't been offended, apparently; he gave her mother a brief, easy smile. Her mother smiled back at him, responding with uncharacteristically ingenuous pleasure to his casual approval. Like a dog after a pat, Olivia thought. How can she crawl to him like that?

And then she thought, It's not fair; he smiles at her but he looks at me as if I were the dirt beneath his feet. She felt a wrench of some profound emotion.

It made her say something truly unforgivable. She could hardly believe it was her own voice speaking. "Oh, he pays you for it, does he?"

Her mother stared. Her mouth opened speechlessly. Her normally pale skin had gone dead white except for two red points at the outside corners of her cheekbones. She looked as if she was about to faint.

But even now she didn't lose her temper the way other people did. She was profoundly insulted, humiliated in front of Nick, furious with Olivia, but all of that only put ice into her voice. "Go up to your room, Olivia, and don't come down again until you're ready to apologize to both of us."

Which will be never, thought Olivia as she stormed up two flights of stairs. Her mother could have an apology, maybe even deserved an apology. But that man, never. She would die before she humiliated herself by apologizing to him for anything, ever.

When she got up to her room she discovered she had lied to her mother; she was hungry after all. Starving, in fact. She ate a chocolate bar that she found in her bedside drawer.

Then she lay down on the bed and listened to something called *Glassworks* on her personal stereo. It had been a Christmas present from her father. Usually this music soothed her like Orpheus playing to the savage beast. It moved continuously but went nowhere, like huge swells in midocean. It had no end and no beginning. It seemed to come from far away, maybe from some other world, and it stirred immortal longings in her. But tonight she was beyond even *Glassworks*.

More than ever now she wanted to go and live with her father. But more than ever it seemed her father didn't want her. She was stuck with her mother. And Nick.

Did Nick know she had been, as Megan put it, a six-month baby? He knew other things that she hadn't known herself, about her parents' divorce, about money. Her mother had told him those things. Told the lodger, ha. Olivia felt exposed and betrayed.

She knew that her father paid for her school fees and music lessons. The divorce settlement that he had made with her mother, the one that Nick had told her about, did that mean her father wasn't going to pay for that anymore? Her mother couldn't afford it, she knew that much. Maybe she would have to change schools. She couldn't really ask because she didn't think she was supposed to know what Nick had told her.

Just like she couldn't tell what he had done to her.

Well, what had he done? Maybe he had only meant to cuddle and console her. Maybe it was an accident that his hand went so far up under her skirt. Maybe that was why he had been so put off when she wriggled against him.

But then he had been kissing her, not soothing baby kisses but real, deep, penetrating, sexy kisses like people in films who were about to make love. And she had been kissing him back. If you put your hand inside somebody's knickers while you were kissing like that, it was no accident.

Thinking about it made her feel that strange excitement again, and also the humiliation of his abrupt rejection.

It was nearly midnight and she was wide awake. She had to get up for school in the morning. She had to get to sleep sometime.

She composed herself and thought of the stars, her favorite fantasy. This time as she drifted through space she was drawn into the atmosphere of Rigel, a great, hot star burning blue-white in the thigh of Orion, the Hunter.

If Betelgeuse had been bathwater, Rigel was a very hot tub, verging on discomfort. She breathed in the substance of the star. It burned in her windpipe and lungs like smoke from a cigarette, scalded her esophagus and stomach like neat whiskey. Molten star-stuff coursed through her veins.

She spread out her hands and saw them dissolve into brightness. Then her arms and legs were absorbed into the being of the star, a voluptuous, euphoric dissipation. Soon she would cease to exist as herself; soon she would be a starsomething.

12

She woke in a sweat when her mother came to get her up. Her mother was still angry; she called her Olivia instead of Lia.

Olivia put her arms over her face when her mother opened the curtains. She wasn't ready for morning light; she wasn't ready to face her mother. She had been dreaming. Not the sort of dream she wanted her mother to know about.

When her mother had gone downstairs again, she lay in bed remembering the dream. It had been about the film she had seen with Megan. But in her dream the murderer had become Nick and the murderer's girlfriend was her mother.

She had tried to warn her mother, but her mother didn't seem to hear her; it was as if she were speaking a foreign language. In the end, dreamlike, she found herself struck dumb. The Nick-murderer grabbed her from behind, like his victims in the film, and she couldn't even scream. But it wasn't murder he had in mind.

She couldn't remember now what had happened after that. It must have been terrible, and exciting; she was still in turmoil.

Her mother called her again from the first-floor landing. "Olivia, get up, for heaven's sake. I've got to go now."

Olivia made some suitably promising response and snuggled down under the duvet. It was uncomfortably hot—rather like the star Rigel—but she had several reasons for not wanting to get up. One, she hadn't had much sleep last night and she had a headache. Two, her friends at school would be asking about her father's wedding and she didn't want to think about her father. She didn't want to think about anything at all.

The next thing she knew, it was ten o'clock.

In a panic she stumbled down the stairs to the bathroom and washed her face with cold water. The headache had lifted. Too bad, that deprived her of an excuse for missing school. On the other hand, turning up at school in midmorning didn't seem like such a great idea either. She wandered out of the bathroom, undecided what to do.

The door of the back bedroom opened. Nick came out.

It was a terrible shock, seeing him there. He was dressed and shaved; he must have been about to go out. But he should have been long gone. He usually got up just about the time she left; she often heard him running the shower as she went out of the front door.

"I thought you were gone," she said sharply. "What are you doing here?"

If she had surprised him, it didn't show in his sardonic stare. "I could ask you the same question, kid."

"I overslept. I had a headache."

"Your head's all right now, is it?"

"I really did have one. Not that it's any of your business."

He was standing in the doorway of his room. She still

thought of it as the spare room, because although he kept his clothes and things in there she knew very well that he slept in her mother's bed. She had to go past that doorway to reach the second flight of stairs that led to her room. She had to get up to her room to get dressed, because she was still in her pajamas.

It reminded her of a game that she and Megan used to play when they were younger, a game they had called the Witch's House. You had to try to sneak past the witch's house without the witch coming out and grabbing you. If you were caught you got eaten. Then you had to take a turn at being the witch.

She came closer, edging along with her back to the banister, challenging him. "You can't tell me what to do. You're not my father."

"If I were, I'd have laid a belt to your backside long before now." He took a step forward, freezing her against the banister. "I didn't say anything last night because I wasn't going to give you the chance to stir it up. But I'm bloody well telling you now, if I hear you talking to Em like that again I'll see you're sorry for it."

The threat was obscure but powerful. She stared at him. She knew how strong he was. She remembered his hand on her wrist beside his car, inviting her to come out to dinner.

She discovered that the thought of physical chastisement at his hands was at least as exciting as alarming. Neither of her parents had ever offered her so much as a smack on the bottom, as far as she could recall. Her mother practiced sweet reason or cold withdrawal; her father employed bribery and threats. So the notion of being slapped or spanked by Nick was purely a theoretical experience, without any previous pain and rage to give it terror. Whereas the thought of his hands on her . . .

"You wouldn't dare touch me," she said with appropriate scorn.

He didn't look impressed. "Yeah? Why not?"

She couldn't tell her mother; he had already shut that door on her. She remembered her father and Nick at the wedding, growling at each other like two great hostile dogs. "I'd tell my father." She added in the smaller voice of childish candor, "When he gets back."

As she spoke of her father she suffered a wave of homesickness, hollow in her middle, as if she had found herself marooned on Mars. And yet she was home. This was home.

She put out her hand toward Nick to push him back. "Go away," she whispered. "You keep your hands off me."

With her fingertips she could feel the rough denim of his shirt, the broad, hard bone and muscle of his chest beneath the shirt. She stared at the coarse, fair, curling hairs below his throat, above the first shirt button. Her father had dark hair on his chest. The sight of the blond body hair mesmerized her.

Her hand crept up to touch it.

He made a sound in his throat, an animal growl. He pushed himself right up against her, pinning her against the banister. It took her breath away, the warmth and the hard, unyielding angularity of his body that she felt through her cotton pajamas. She looked up into his face.

He was staring at her, his eyes opaquely intent, as if he couldn't see anything but her, yet he couldn't really see her at all. The way the witch might have looked at its victims before it ate them up. Just for that instant Olivia was terrified.

Until he kissed her.

She should have been even more alarmed. They were cannibal kisses; he took her lower lip between his teeth, thrust his tongue into her mouth, nipped at her neck below her ear, tipped her head back to reach the tender point between her throat and chin. But kisses meant love, as far as she knew.

His hands were doing the sartorial equivalent of unseaming her from nave to chaps. He jerked her pajama top open, sending the buttons flying. He held her against him with one arm and ran his other hand down over her naked breast, over her ribs and waist and hip and buttock, sliding her pajama bottoms down as he went.

Olivia hardly knew what she thought about this, even if he had given her time to think. She was being flooded with feeling, physical sensations and emotional reactions. The main physical feeling was that her skin had turned into something between silk and ice cream, smooth and delicious. Inside she felt exhilaration and terror, triumph and shame. She was caught up in some powerful event over which she had not the slightest control, like falling overboard in a gale.

It seemed that no more than thirty seconds and no less than three hours had passed since he had begun to eat her up. He picked her up and carried her into his room to lay her on the neatly made, never-slept-in bed. He took her pajama bottoms right off. She felt another twinge of shame and excitement. Bare breasts were one thing, a bare bottom quite another. She felt horribly vulnerable. She curled up her legs and clenched them together, out of shyness and fear of what was to come.

He pulled her legs apart without effort, as if she had not been resisting. When he lowered his head between her thighs she pushed at him ineffectually.

"Please, no, don't, please . . ."

She knew he hadn't even heard her. She had only whispered anyway. Her voice wouldn't work properly. Like the dream.

He caught the sensitive skin of her inner thigh between his teeth, in the hollow where her leg met her torso. That didn't hurt, but it made her squirm and intensified the strange restlessness inside her.

Then he did other things to her with his mouth.

Her body wanted desperately to move; her mind was frozen with shame. There was a picture in one of her father's books that had fascinated her ever since she had first come across it. As a child, maybe, it was the brightness of gold in the painting that had caught her eye. It showed a naked girl lying back with her legs curled up, her eyes closed, her mouth a little ajar with some inexpressible emotion, and a shower of gold coins pouring down between her raised thighs. The painting was called *Danaë*.

She had never asked her father about it; she had a vague idea, growing more certain as she grew older, that it was one of those things he wouldn't really want to explain. And the older she got, the less she wanted him to find out that she liked to look at it. It had always given her a strange sensation when she studied it, a mixture of longing and shame, as if the nameless longing was a shameful thing. She had tried to imagine how the gold coins would feel, running like water over her belly and bottom and inner thighs. How the girl would feel, or how she would feel if she were the girl, lying naked and open to the whim of heaven.

Then only a few months ago she had come across a line of Tennyson, "Now lies the earth all Danaë to the stars," and her English teacher had explained about Zeus and Danaë and the shower of gold. So she knew then what the picture was about.

And now she knew how the girl must have felt.

She buried her fingers in Nick's hair—thick, fair hair between her thighs like the gleaming gold in the picture. "Nick," she whispered, wanting him to stop because she couldn't bear the intensity of her shame and longing, or the ache that he roused in her belly. "Don't do that to me."

He stopped. But not because she wanted him to.

He stood up, stripped off his shirt, and unbuckled the belt of his jeans. She curled up again, shivering under his stare. When he was naked she nerved herself to look at him in return.

The blond hair went all the way down his torso. It tapered to a narrow trail below his chest, ran down through his navel and abdomen and expanded luxuriantly at his crotch. But unlike the female arrangements she was familiar with, his pubic hair provided no modesty. Everything he had was arrestingly visible.

She had seen pictures of penises. Someone at school had got hold of a magazine with some photographs of naked men, their dangling vulnerable genitals more comical than arousing. And her biology textbook had a drawing of an erect penis. But his was much larger, much more intimidating, than anything she had expected.

She had only a few seconds to look before he lay down between her legs. He was so big she had to draw her legs up toward her hips to make room for him.

He kissed her mouth and her breasts and called her a beautiful kitten in a husky, rusty voice that made her quiver inside. He said it would be all right if she relaxed. He wouldn't hurt her, he said.

But he did.

Megan had told her, in one of their discussions about such matters, that physical incompatibility between a man and a woman was impossible because the vagina was so elastic. If it could accommodate a baby being born, Megan had pointed out, it could certainly cope with anything a man could come up with. But coping was one thing, Olivia discovered, discomfort another. And pleasure, which was supposed to be the point of it all, didn't even enter the picture.

It wasn't the size of any particular bit of him that was the problem, it was just that he was so much bigger and stronger and heavier and more forceful and violent than she would have imagined, and terrifyingly single-minded. If earlier the vehemence of his attention had made her feel adrift in storm waves, right now she was struggling to survive in a violent and lethally indifferent ocean. She was not now Danaë caught in the shower of gold but Europa mounted by the bull.

He shook and groaned in a terrifying way, more like extremes of pain than heights of pleasure. She clung to him to comfort him, to comfort herself.

"Jesus, I must be out of my mind." His voice was rough and breathless. "I could get sent down for this, you little witch."

"What do you mean?"

"It's a crime to fuck a fourteen-year-old. Even if she's asking for it."

The crude language disconcerted her as much as the meaning of what he had said. "I'm fifteen now," she said, unable to think of any more relevant response.

"That's off-limits too. The blokes who make the laws don't approve of randy little girls."

"I'm not," she whispered. Not a little girl, not randy. He made it sound shamefully unnatural for her to want him to touch her. She couldn't have wanted any more than that, she hadn't known any more, in spite of what they had taught her in biology class. She was afraid of seeing loathing and disgust in his eyes, as she had in the lay-by. If touching her bottom had made him despise her, how much more would he despise her now? She despised herself.

She closed her eyes, shutting out his face above her. Her eyelids squeezed out tears.

"Don't do that, baby." His voice went soft and smoky. "It wasn't as bad as all that."

She felt his mouth nuzzling her face, his tongue licking away teardrops, like a large, unpredictable dog alternately amiable and threatening, dangerous even in its friendly overtures. She opened her eyes. He was almost smiling. Maybe he didn't despise her after all.

When he rolled off her she turned over onto her stomach for the sake of modesty. She still had her pajama top on, though the buttons were gone. She watched him dig out a cigarette from the heap of clothing on the floor, watched him light it and lie back to smoke it, one arm tucked behind his head. She wanted to touch him but she didn't dare.

She looked at his face. It was an oddly familiar type of face, a Saxon type, nothing patrician about it. The bones beneath the skin were strong, not coarse or raw, just English oak. The tip of the nose was slightly sharp rather than fleshy. When smiling or at ease, as now, it was a pleasant, even amiable face, but at all times opaque to emotion. There were creases at the corners of his eyes, deep lines between his brows and at the sides of his mouth, like her father's face.

She thought he must be at least as beautiful as Zeus in any of his divine disguises.

Nick reached over to touch her face with the hand that held the cigarette. "I'd like to do a shot of you."

"A photograph, you mean?"

"Just the way you are right now." He propped himself up on his elbow to survey her. His hand traveled down her back to her bottom, where the pajama top ended. "That's a great pose. I couldn't have set it up better myself."

She thought of the brochure, the photograph of her mother's bare breasts. Her mother had said that was how she met him, hiring him to do the brochure. Olivia wondered if that was when he had seduced her mother, persuading her to take off her clothes for him, saying he wanted to take a shot of her. Presumably he had had to go to the trouble of seduction with her mother, rather than merely ripping off her clothes and throwing her on the bed as he had done with Olivia herself on the grounds that she was a randy little girl who was asking for it.

He pushed away the pajama top to stroke her bare bottom, still with the cigarette burning between his fingers. He leaned down and kissed her bottom. An hour ago she wouldn't have believed anybody could want to kiss someone else's bum. It would have seemed even less probable than the idea of him sticking his tongue up her vagina, which he had already done, to her shame and amazement. He was like some blind beast that got knowledge of her by touching and tasting, licking and biting. The idea repelled and excited her.

He kissed her on the other buttock, touching her soft skin with his tongue, nipping it with his teeth. She scrambled to her knees to ward him off. "Stop it, Nick, don't do that."

She pulled the lapels of her pajama top together like the shreds of her lost virginity, crossing her arms to cover her breasts, staring at him, breathless and terrified. He was going to do it all again, do something worse this time. She didn't know what worse things he could do to her, but she was sure that he knew.

Nick sat up too, smoking the last of his cigarette and watching her through the smoke. Her terror seemed to amuse him. But he didn't try to touch her.

"Take it easy, kitten, you're all right." He swung his legs over the side of the bed and stubbed out the cigarette. "I've got to go. Get dressed and I'll drive you to school."

The thought of school appalled her. How could she walk into class as if nothing had happened? "I can't go now, it's too late."

"Sure you can. Come on, let's get on with it."

He had already pulled on his underpants and jeans. He leaned over, took hold of her by the upper arms, hauled her off the bed and onto her feet. He did it as easily as if she really were a little girl, not woman-sized.

As if to remind her—as if she needed reminding!—how vulnerable she was to him, he cupped the bare cheeks of her bottom in his hands and pulled her tight against him, tucking her thighs between his. He had buttoned up his jeans but not yet fastened the belt. The dangling buckle prodded her stomach, cold and sharp.

Olivia clutched the front of her pajamas and stared up into

his face, his pale eyes. She thought of Tig and the mouse. He was going to torment and devour her all over again.

"Maybe we'll do it again sometime. If you want." He kissed her quite gently on the mouth. "D'you want to do it again?" He was teasing her; he knew very well it didn't matter what she wanted. Or maybe he knew what she wanted. He slapped her on the bottom, again quite gently. "But not now; now I'm taking you to school. You go and get dressed, and be bloody quick about it."

When he let her go she fled up the stairs to her room and dressed as quickly as she could. But first, when she took off her pajamas, she looked at herself in the mirror. She hadn't turned green or anything. There were no teeth marks on her throat or breast or bottom. She was sore but not, to her surprise, bleeding. He had left no external sign of his possession.

But she felt possessed. She felt shamed and debased. Not because he had done all those things to her but because he hadn't bothered to ask her. He had just done whatever he wanted, as if her consent didn't count because she was too young to give it.

How did he know she wasn't going to bleed all over the bed? Virgins did that sometimes. How would he have explained that to her mother, bloodstains on the duvet of the bed he never slept in? Maybe he had thought she wasn't a virgin. But she knew that he had known, she knew somehow that it had been part of the pleasure for him. I won't hurt you, he had said, knowing that he would.

She heard him yelling up the stairs at her. She put on her uniform in about thirty seconds, for fear that he would come up after her. When she came down he had restored the bed to its original tidy state and collected the buttons from her pajama top.

She was in a daze. She had no idea, and cared even less, what excuse she was going to give for her late arrival. When he stopped the car outside the school gate she fumbled with the door, unable first to find the handle and then to get it to work.

He reached across to open it for her. She slid out and looked back at him, afraid of finding that terrible cold look in his eyes. But he was smiling. Sort of.

"See you later, kitten. If you tell anyone I'll kill you."

13

He didn't need to warn me not to tell, Olivia thought with vague indignation. Normally the first thing she would have done after an adventure or in possession of a secret was run to tell Megan, but this time she was not even tempted. This was an adult secret, the kind that could have catastrophic consequences if it got about. She understood that perfectly well.

The only trouble was that since she couldn't tell Megan about it she had to tell herself, over and over again. For days she could think of nothing else. She spent all her waking hours, at school and home and in between, reliving that incredible quarter of an hour.

She tended to skip over the bit on the bed where he had actually made love to her. She didn't know what to think about that yet. They told you in biology class about the mechanics of the sex act (being biology, of course, they called it insemination), erection and penetration and ejaculation and so forth, but they might as well have been talking about life on Mars for all the relevance that bore to her experience with Nick. Painful, confusing, scary, those were the sort of adjectives she might have chosen to describe it. But maybe that was only because it was the first time.

The part beforehand—she supposed that was what was called foreplay—was the most exciting. And the absolutely most exciting thing to think about was what he had done to her that reminded her of the painting of Danaë. If somebody had told her beforehand that men actually did that sort of thing to women she would have thought it a revolting idea. And it wasn't romantic; even now, it was too gut-wrenching for romance. It was sexy.

At this point in her reveries she most regretted not being able to tell Megan. She wanted to be able to describe to Megan what sex was really like. Megan was full of all sorts of useful and interesting information, especially about sex. She had pinched a condom from Teddy's dresser drawer and shown it to Olivia. (They had filled it up with water and burst it and got soaking wet and sick with laughter, but that bit had nothing to do with sex.) She had been the first to find out what gay men do to each other (and pretty disgusting it was too, thought Olivia, though Megan was more tolerant). Now finally Olivia had some practical experience of the matter that she could have dazzled Megan with, but she couldn't tell.

Having survived a day at school, she didn't want to go home. She didn't know how she was going to look at Nick again, let alone her mother. But Nick wasn't there. He was off on a shoot again, her mother said, the Orkneys this time.

It was almost like nothing had happened, almost like Nick had never been. Olivia made peace with her mother in a roundabout way by volunteering to help with the dinner preparations and the washing up. Her mother took this in the right spirit and was quite cheerful and chatty all evening.

"Meg has a bee in her bonnet about putting on a play," Olivia told her mother, by way of contribution to the conversation, "and she's roped me into it. She wants me to help her rewrite it."

"What is it, a modern English version of *Hamlet?*"

"No, this is some old Greek play. She's got Ms. Pankhurst to sponsor it so we can put it on at school next year." Ms. Pankhurst was her father's joke. He had taken to calling her English teacher that, after the famous family of suffragettes, when he met her at a parents' night at school. He always went to the parents' nights instead of her mother. Olivia supposed it was because he paid the fees and wanted to make sure he was getting his money's worth. The English teacher's real name was Kate Reid and she was generally regarded as a fanatical feminist. The girls in her class quite admired her for the strength of her seditious views, and when Olivia reported what her father had said they all began to call her Ms. Pankhurst, or Ms. P. for short.

"What's the play about?"

"It's about a woman whose husband leaves her for some-body else."

"That sort of thing happened in ancient Greece too, did it?"

"Yes, but she doesn't take it lying down, according to Meg. She murders her husband's new wife and then she kills her own children so he can't get custody."

Her mother dropped the tea cup she was washing. Luckily it fell into the dishwater. "Ms. Pankhurst has approved this play?"

"She said we had to put it all in context. She said Greek men were allowed to kill their children when they were born, if they didn't want them. She said they mostly killed the girls. They put them out on the mountainside to die of starvation or be eaten by wolves."

"Charming! I thought ancient Greek society was supposed to be the foundation of Western civilization."

"That's what Ms. P. said too. I think she was being ironic."

"About the ancient Greeks or about Western civilization?"

"Both, probably." Olivia turned away to stack the plates she had dried back in the cupboard. With her back to her mother she said, "Is Daddy going to pay my school fees again next year?"

Her mother answered casually, "I presume so. I certainly can't afford to pay them. And this whole private school busi-ness was his idea in the first place. I thought it was kind of old-fashioned, but he claimed that girls do better in a single-sex environment."

Olivia remembered that discussion. When she was eight her father had had a row with her teacher about what she was or was not learning in school. The upshot was that he had taken her out of the local primary school and got her a place at a private girls' school, the under-school to the one she was in now. Her mother had said sarcastically that she thought socialists were supposed to be dedicated to nonelitist comprehensive coeducation. Her father had said socialism didn't oblige you to allow your child to be taught by a men-tally defective madwoman, and anyway it wouldn't be right to sacrifice Olivia's education on the altar of abstract princi-ples. Her mother had said then why had he accused her of being a snob on numerous occasions, just because through no fault of her own her parents had sent her to a private school instead of a state school like him. Her father had said that went to prove that an expensive education didn't prevent some people from turning out pig-ignorant, and if he had been her father he would have demanded his money back.

"So if Daddy doesn't want to pay the fees I'll have to change schools."

"What makes you think Ross might not want to pay? Did he say something?"

"No, it's just that babies are expensive, and he's always complaining about how badly lecturers get paid, and Althea won't like him spending all that money on me when they have their own child." She set the last dish in the cupboard before turning again to face her mother. "Besides, didn't he give up this house so he wouldn't have to pay maintenance for me anymore?"

She didn't say that Nick had told her that. She didn't dare mention Nick. Her mother just assumed that her father must have told her, and was irritated. "A lot of good that's going to do me, until I come to sell the house. In the meantime I've got to pay the mortgage myself. If it weren't for Nick I don't know what I'd do."

Olivia didn't want to hear her mother talking about Nick. It reminded her that he slept in her mother's bed. She wondered if he did the same things to her mother that he had done to her, if he did them every night when he slept with her mother, sliding his middle finger down the cleft of her bottom, stroking her anus, licking all the folds and crevices between her thighs . . .

Her stomach turned over at the thought. With disgust at the idea of her mother in such a vividly sexual context. With jealousy, that what he had done was not special to her.

With yearning, wanting him to hold her again.

She must be mad. He was horrible; she hated him. He was a child abuser, he had admitted it himself. She told herself, not very convincingly, that she hoped he would stay in Scotland forever.

"The school fees," she persisted, "are they tied up in the house too?"

"Not as far as I'm concerned. That's between you and Ross, Lia. He knows I don't have the money, he can't be expecting me to pay. Though it wouldn't be the first time he's tried to get out of his obligations toward you."

"Well, at least you won't have to kill me."

Her mother gave her a blank look. "What are you talking about?"

"That play. If Daddy doesn't want me, you're not about to lose custody of me."

She tried to split her mind into two halves. The thought of Nick and what he had done and, worst of all, how she felt about what he had done—all that was intolerable in the light of her ordinary life. If her mother or father, or her friends and teachers and neighbors, or any passing stranger in the street, ever came to hear of it, she would die of mortification. She tried to put it right out of her head while she went about her daily business. It was easier to do that when Nick wasn't around.

But in bed at night, sinful subterranean thoughts came into her head, bubbling up like poisonous gases from a hidden volcano seething somewhere belowground. Even Ms. Pankhurst, who talked so forthrightly about female sexuality, would not have approved of these images.

The first time she had set eyes on Nick, for instance. What if he hadn't just stared at her breasts; what if he had actually done what he did three weeks later? Maybe he had wanted to do it even then, the first time he saw her. She imagined him stripping and penetrating her without a word spoken between them, in her own front hall.

In reality that would have been rape. In fantasy . . . well, she wouldn't want Ms. Pankhurst—or anyone else for that matter, not even Megan—to know about that fantasy.

She was disgusted with herself for not being sufficiently disgusted. For having lain there like a wimpish hamster while he treated her like a doughnut. A freshly baked and iced doughnut, mind, but still basically a doughnut.

No, no, she was even worse than that. At least hamsters and doughnuts didn't get turned on by recalling what some pervert had done to them. She shivered uncontrollably when she remembered the way he had looked at her. As if she were the only person alive on earth.

Would he do it again? He had said they would do it again. If she wanted, ha, ha. But maybe that was just the sort of thing men said afterward, the way her mother would say to acquaintances she met in the street, We must have a drink sometime. Maybe we'll do it again sometime. If you want . . .

She lay in bed and embraced herself. She stroked her breasts and arms, her throat and hair, wishing her hands were someone else's hands. Wanting someone to love her. Nick wasn't going to love her, whatever. She had given him an itch and he had used her to scratch it.

It was shameful, shocking, *sick* that she might want him to do it again. She couldn't, he couldn't, she couldn't live with herself if he did. The first time he had taken her by surprise. The next time she would have to know, would have to connive and collude . . .

Like in the dream.

14

On Thursday after her music lesson Olivia went over to Megan's house. They had a French exam the next day and wanted to swot up on vocabulary by testing each other. Megan's parents had gone to the theater and her brother, Teddy, the closet pervert, spent the whole evening shut up in the study, cramming for his A levels and consulting with his friends on the phone, emerging only to find something more to eat.

The two girls dutifully conjugated verbs for a while but ended up watching a film on television. At eleven o'clock Teddy came out of the study.

"Lia, your mother just rang. She says she's coming over to collect you."

"What time is it? Oh, God, I was supposed to be home by ten at the latest. Maybe if I dash home through the park . . ."

"She said for you to wait here. She didn't want you coming home in the dark. I said Meg and I would walk you home, or else my parents would give you a lift when they get back, but she said not to bother."

"You should have said I'd already left. She'll have the hump."

"Sorry." Teddy shrugged off this ingratitude. "But she's right, you shouldn't be out alone at night."

"Why not? It's only a ten-minute walk, and this isn't Kilburn. Anyway, Ms. Pankhurst says that male violence is meant to intimidate women into restricting their own freedom and activities. It's our duty to refuse to submit to intimidation, don't you think, Meg?"

Speaking as a woman, Megan had to agree. In fact, she thought some intimidation of men might be a good idea. Teddy deplored this.

"It's already happening," Olivia pointed out, gathering up her French notes and stuffing them into her school bag. "They do it to each other. I'd better wait out front for Mummy so she doesn't have to get out of the car."

Megan came out with her. She turned on the porch light and closed the front door and they sat on the front step, discussing various recent atrocities against women, waiting for Olivia's mother's battered Volvo to turn up.

What turned up was Nick. On foot.

Olivia recognized him as he came up to the house. She recognized his gait—he always moved with cock o' the walk confidence, as if he owned the earth he trod on—even before she could see his face. She was appalled, too appalled to say hello.

Megan said it for her. "Hi, Nick. Where's your super car?"

"I walked over."

"That's a shame. My parents will be home in a few minutes and my father could have driven Lia home. It's also a shame because I wanted to have a good look at your car. Lia and I were in love with it even before we knew it was yours. Why didn't you bring it?"

Olivia stared at her sandaled feet, mortified. Nick said, "I could say it's a nice night, and that would be true, but I'd be lying. The fact is, I walked because I've got three pints with whiskey chasers inside me."

"My father won't be stone cold sober either," Megan replied with equally casual frankness. "But he wouldn't mind chancing it because it's such a short distance."

"I can't afford to take a chance. I was nailed last year and got off easy. But next time . . ." Olivia looked up to see him draw a graphic finger across his throat.

She was amazed and appalled by this exchange. Amazed because the tone of the conversation was as if Megan were twenty-five instead of fifteen. Appalled, because her father had never been brought into court for so much as a parking ticket, never mind drunk driving. And here was Nick admitting to it quite cheerfully. She began to think that he and Megan were not unlike in their conversational candor and blunt style of speaking. Megan had never to her knowledge uttered the word *fuck,* but when she did Olivia wouldn't be surprised.

Megan wished them good night. Olivia turned to go home. Megan called after them, "Hey, Nick. Sometime when you're sober will you take me for a ride in your car?"

Olivia could see Nick's grin in the darkness as he looked back at Megan. "Anytime, sweetheart."

Megan blew him a kiss.

Olivia hated them both.

Nick took her school bag out of her hand and carried it for her. She crossed her arms over her chest and walked in quick silence, ignoring him. The street was totally deserted. Her sandals made a great racket, slapping against the pavement with every step.

"I thought you were in Scotland," she said at last.

"I'm back." He added dryly, "We had this conversation last week, didn't we?"

"Why didn't Mummy come for me? Is she drunk too?"

"She had a few glasses of wine. Enough to put her over the limit."

"What have you two been doing all night, sitting around getting pissed?"

"We went to the fucking pub. Does that offend your delicate sense of propriety?"

Olivia would have blushed if she hadn't been so enraged. He was the one to speak scornfully of propriety, of course, after having treated her like a Kings Cross streetwalker on Monday morning. "So she only noticed I wasn't back yet when you both staggered home a few minutes ago."

He said flatly, "D'you want a smack?"

She had a sudden head-spinning image of him throwing her across his thigh, skirt up and knickers down, and spanking her bare bottom with the flat of his powerful hand, right there in the public but deserted street. The image made her muscles clench. The sphincter muscles they must be, the ones doing the clenching; the one that would feel the strength of his hand was the gluteus maximus.

She was almost tempted to say yes, to see what he would do. But she wasn't quite certain that he wouldn't actually do it. "Don't talk like that."

"Like what?"

"Like a—like a barbarian. My father would never talk to anyone like that."

"Yeah, I know, I've had the pleasure of meeting your old man, remember? He's a fucking saint, I could see it at once. Watch out for Lia or she'll puke in your car, he told me. He's a real gentleman."

She did blush this time; she could feel herself go hot with humiliation. He had managed to hit her in so many places at once that she didn't know how to hit him back. She would far rather have been spanked. "Well, you're not. You're horrible," she spat, skipping away from him. "You can go home without me, and explain that to Mummy."

She ran across the street and round the corner. It was only a short distance to the main gate of the park. He wouldn't even know where that was. Their house backed onto the other side of the park, and if he had ever entered the park at all he would have used the little gate that opened onto the footpath behind their back garden.

Both gates would be locked, of course, they were always locked at sundown, but that had never stopped her and Megan from taking their customary shortcut even after dark. The locked gates meant only that no one else would be in the park.

If she could climb over the gates as usual and disappear into the darkness before Nick reached the corner, he would have no idea where she had gone. With any luck she could even be safe in her own bed before he got home.

Her sandals flapped as she ran, so noisy that she couldn't hear if he was coming after her. She didn't dare to look back in case he really was. She reached the wrought-iron gates and began to climb. From habit she knew the best places to put her feet. She hiked up her skirt so it wouldn't catch on the palings at the top, and swung her legs over. As she turned to climb down she looked back up the street and saw him, alarmingly close.

In panic she jumped straight down to the safety of darkness instead of climbing down, and grazed her knee on the gravel path. She pulled off her sandals and scampered away barefoot across the grass. When she looked back over her shoulder Nick was standing on the other side of the gate. As she watched he dropped the book bag over the gate and began to climb.

She debated whether to hide or to run home. She could hide here till morning if she wanted. What would her mother do if she didn't come home? Would she come out to search? Would she notice, or care?

It was a fine, warm night; the stars hung huge and close. That was the best thing about the park at night; the lamps were turned off and you could see the stars. In winter when the dark fell early Olivia sometimes came in here on a clear evening with a torch and a star map so that she could learn their names and places. Their places were unimaginably far away, their names were magical incantations: A for Antares, Arcturus, Aldebaran . . .

She stopped on the wide lawn to look up at heaven. Her grandfather in Huddersfield had taught her the names of the summer stars. All the bright, familiar constellations were spread out there, the Swan, the Eagle, the Northern Crown. She looked down and saw the starlight gleaming on her bare arms and legs.

"Lia!"

She could see Nick in the starlight, at the edge of the lawn. He was coming toward her. She couldn't hide now. The thought of crouching among the bushes, holding her breath and hoping he wouldn't blunder across her, was worse than the idea of running home to the safety of her mother. Relative safety, anyhow. She turned and ran toward the back gate.

The area nearest the gate was the playground. Little feet had left little grass, and the exposed earth around the path was still slippery from a recent rain, as she found when her bare foot slid and she landed on her knees. She scrambled up again, wincing. The grazed knee didn't like being bruised. She limped across the last stretch to the gate.

Nick was right behind her. She could hear him calling to her, keeping his voice low. He was laughing. "Hey, Lia! I'll throw your books in the duck pond if you don't stop. You'll have to go swimming to get them back."

He grabbed her arm as she started to scale the gate. She kicked out at him, with a poor aim and bare feet. "Let me go, you bastard. Stop bullying me. And don't you dare throw my books in the water."

"Come down, you little bitch."

He started to shake the gate. That was easy to do; it was locked only with a chain and padlock. She didn't dare climb over for fear of impaling herself on the points at the top. She hit at him with the sandals she was carrying.

"You do want your arse smacked, don't you?"

Then he did something she couldn't believe. He let go of the gate and put his hand up under her skirt and pulled her knickers right down to her ankles.

Olivia didn't know what to do. She couldn't climb with her knickers round her ankles. She couldn't pull them up without coming down. And she was mortified.

She didn't get to decide, as it happened. He had only been playing Tig with her. He reached up and pulled her down, like peeling ivy off a wall.

She tried to kick him as she fell—a heel in the crotch was supposed to discourage attackers—but the displaced knickers made the maneuver impossible. All she managed to do was lose her knickers altogether.

He dragged her down to the grass, gripping her wrists so she couldn't scratch him. He lay across her, one leg between hers. Her skirt had got rucked up in the tussle and his jeans chafed the tender flesh between her thighs.

His face was so close that she could taste the sour, yeasty smell of beer on his breath. It made her think of unwelcome encounters with drunks on the Tube. The sense of strangeness disturbed her more than anything. She wasn't used to men with beer on their breath. Her father drank whiskey and wine and she had never seen him even halfway drunk. Or in a crazy mood like Nick was in now. He scared her.

"Get off me! You're too heavy, I can't breathe."

He didn't answer and he didn't budge. What he did do was rub against her, nudging his denim thigh into her naked crotch, pressing his denim-clad erection against her belly. Her panic grew. This wasn't romantic at all; it was terrifying, here in the dark on the ground and he maybe too tipsy to keep in mind or even care exactly who she was. It was like being dragged into the bushes by a drunken stranger.

She heaved upward against him, uselessly. He moved his other leg over so that he lay between her legs, forcing her thighs apart. He let go of her left wrist and fumbled to unfasten his jeans. With her freed hand she tugged at his hair, trying to hurt or at least distract him, but afraid of provoking his anger.

"Cut that out," he growled. "I'll throw you in the pond along with your books." He captured both her hands in one of his and pinned them down above her head. His other hand covered her mouth. "Someone's coming."

She could hear the footsteps, coming along the footpath on the other side of the high hedge, between the back gardens and the park fence. It was probably one of her neighbors. If she could have called out the person would hear her.

Nick took his hand off her mouth.

She stared into his shadowed face, inches from hers. His eyes were too dark to decipher. He was looking down at her as a stranger might look at a stranger. Worse, maybe: she remembered the cold ferocity of contempt in his eyes, the day of her father's wedding. All the ugly words, the curses that men use to describe what she knew he meant to do to her, came flooding into her mind, freezing her beneath him.

The footsteps came abreast of them.

She could feel the heat of his unsheathed erection. He said in her ear, "Don't you like it rough?"

The tip of his penis nuzzled her vulva, rubbing against the most sensitive spot. In spite of her terror the pressure produced an agreeable if uneasy sensation, like squirming astride a bicycle seat or a tree limb, but better than that.

The footsteps faded, the passerby passing away. Nick invaded her.

"No," she whispered, too late.

Maybe he had taken it for consent when she didn't call out. More likely he didn't care if she consented or not. The sense of powerlessness roused humiliation and excitement in her.

To her surprise and relief it didn't hurt this time, even when he thrust into her quite violently. He put his arms around her, taking her weight off the hard earth and lifting up her bottom to meet the rhythm of his strokes. The sensation his movements were producing in her genitals grew stronger. In a way it was a pleasurable sort of prickle. In another way it was a deep and terrible craving, like being sick for something, homesick, lovesick.

She drew his head down till his face pressed against the side of her neck. She could feel the heat of his breath on her skin as he uttered muffled rhythmic grunts—like a rutting animal, she thought, which was not at all romantic but horribly sexy. Even the smell of beer and the smoky tobacco scent of him was sexy. She was dying for him to kiss her.

He jerked like a man in a fit, and nearly cracked her ribs. The full weight of him pressed down on her once he had stopped moving.

"Nick." She whispered, trying to shake him, to rouse him.

He raised his head, bleary-eyed like a man recovering from a fit. "Sorry, kitten."

She could breathe again. He had called her kitten.

He got to his feet and fastened up his jeans. Olivia sat up and looked around for her knickers. Luckily they were white and easy to see in spite of the darkness. She retrieved them, replaced them, and stood up, smoothing her skirt down.

She wasn't rid of him yet; she was wet between her thighs, enough to get her knickers wet too. That was annoying and embarrassing, but it stirred a pulse in her belly. She looked at him, not knowing what to do. She wanted him to hold her and kiss her, to do all the things he should have done before-hand instead of just pulling off her knickers and . . .

A number of degrading words presented themselves to describe what he had just done to her. She didn't think men did it like that to women they loved. But of course he didn't love her. He was her mother's lover.

She ached, low down in her body. She wanted to curl up and hug herself.

He put his arms around her. "Sorry, baby," he said again. "Next time I'll do you justice."

She didn't know what he meant, but she did know what *next time* meant. She put her arms round his neck, laying her head on his shoulder, pressing her face against his neck. She felt his arms tighten around her. She thought she was going to cry. Instead she kissed his neck, down by the ridge of his collarbone. She was afraid to say any of the things that she would have liked to say, for fear he would take his arms away from her.

"I can't go home with mud all over my legs."

"We'll fix that when we get out of here."

She found her sandals and he retrieved the book bag (un-ducked) and they climbed out over the little gate. This time instead of shaking it he held it steady for her.

Under a street lamp Nick used a tissue to clean the mud from her knees. He spat on it first, the way her mother used to do when they were out somewhere and the infant Olivia got a smudge of ice cream or chocolate on her face.

She set her hand on his shoulder to keep her balance. She looked down at his bent head, the nape of his neck, his broad shoulders and upper back. She had never looked down on him from above before. He looked powerful, in a very basic physical sense. She thought that when he stood up he would lift her with him, like Leviathan rising from the deeps. Maybe he had no more regard for her than the sea monster would of the sunken ships in its wake.

"You're bleeding."

"I cut myself on the gravel. It's your fault, you scared me and I jumped down."

"Sure, it's all my fault, isn't it?"

She saw his face tilted up at her, half smiling. Then he touched his tongue to the graze, the way an animal might lick another's wound. She nearly fell over in spite of holding on to him.

"Why the hell did you go into the park?"

"That was your fault too. You were being horrible to me. Anyway, I always go through the park. After dark I like to look at the stars."

He let go of her leg and straightened up. Now she had to look up at him again. "Fuck the stars. You stay out of there when the gates are closed, you hear me? Anything could have happened to you."

15

C oming home was terrible.

Olivia thought her mother would be able to look at her face and guess what had happened. She wanted to sneak upstairs and go to bed, but her mother wanted to express her disapproval of a young girl getting in at eleven-thirty on a school night, especially a girl who had been told to be home by ten o'clock. Olivia was too shattered to defend herself, for instance by pointing out that to get home by ten o'clock she would have had to disobey another commandment about walking home alone in the dark, since nobody had been around to come and get her.

She finally escaped up to her room. As she climbed the stairs her mother was apologizing to Nick for Olivia's thoughtlessness in not being ready to leave when he got to Megan's house. Olivia was mortally relieved, as well as amused, to hear that. It meant her mother had made up her own explanation for the extra ten minutes they had taken getting back.

Nick said it was all right, it didn't matter.

Olivia wondered how he could manage to talk to her mother as if nothing had happened. Maybe as far as he was concerned nothing much had happened. Maybe it didn't count for him because she was only a kid. Maybe he made love to other women all the time. Sometimes it seemed from what she read that men were more interested in having sex than in who they did it with. And maybe that was true; how else could anyone explain prostitution?

After she had closed her door she heard her mother coming up the stairs. At first she was afraid her mother was coming right up to the top of the house to her own room, but then she heard her go into the bathroom.

She heard Nick come upstairs and go into the bedroom below hers, her mother's bedroom. She wondered if he was going to make love to her mother tonight. The thought filled her with nausea.

She got undressed. She took off her knickers last of all. They were still wet with semen. She wanted to go down and show them to Nick, to put him off sleeping with her mother.

But maybe it would only turn him on. First the mother, then the daughter; now the daughter, now the mother. His own domestic harem.

Ms. Pankhurst would disown her if she knew. Especially for not screaming when the footsteps went by. Most especially for the terrible ache she was suffering right now when she thought about what Nick had done, wanting him to come upstairs and do it again. It was like wanting to be screwed by a bear.

She wondered if he really did make love to other women. She wondered about his wife. It shocked her to recall that her mother's lover was a married man. Separated, not divorced.

First her father had gone to live with Althea while he was still married to her mother. Now her mother was divorced but living with a man who was still married to someone else. Everything seemed fluid and changeable. Anything could happen, anything was okay.

The only thing not okay, that definitely mustn't happen,

was a fifteen-year-old girl getting laid by her mother's lover. Nick in her knickers was the one big no-no.

Putting the knickers into the laundry hamper, she thought for the first time of the biological point of what had happened. What if she got pregnant?

The possibility didn't alarm her much because she didn't take it very seriously. Nor did there seem to be much she could have done to prevent it. In the first place, she hadn't intended to have sexual intercourse, either time, and in the second place, there hadn't really been anything she could have done to stop it from happening. It was just like an act of God. Or more like an act of one of the old Greek gods who took a sudden fancy to a woman: Nick had got the idea he wanted to screw her, and he did it.

He had said something about next time, but she didn't know when that would be, if ever. She couldn't carry a condom around with her on the unlikely chance of persuading him to use it, if or when next time ever arrived.

She examined her wounded knee. It had stopped bleeding. His tongue must have done the trick. She wasn't going to wash it ever again.

She pulled on her nightgown, and got into bed, turned out the light, and closed her eyes. The comfort of stars eluded her tonight. All she could think of was Nick saying Fuck the stars. She imagined him standing naked in space, like Orion the Hunter with a huge erection, impaling the Pleiades, the circle of Seven Sisters, upon the white-hot tip of it.

She shivered and straightened her legs and tried to relax. It was very late, very quiet now.

Beneath her the springs of her mother's bed began to groan, protesting the weight of two bodies combined.

The next day was Friday. Sainsburys, no Nick. No Nick all weekend, hallelujah. He had gone to Norfolk, where he was supposed to be every weekend. Maybe he had a mistress up in Norwich.

Olivia spent most of the weekend in her room, playing the violin obsessively like Sherlock Holmes in a fit of detecting. She was dying to go and see her father on Sunday but he wouldn't be back from Amalfi till Tuesday, and she wasn't due to visit him until the following Sunday.

She imagined him asking her over the amontillado what she had been up to during the previous fortnight. She imagined herself telling him. Daddy, I've been deflowered, despoiled, debauched. Mummy's old black ram has been tupping your white ewe-lamb. In her imagining she was suddenly stark naked in her father's sitting room, semen dripping down her inner thighs. Her father stared at her crotch with cosmic rage and revulsion in his eyes.

He would never pay her school fees after that.

On Monday she discovered that she had failed Friday's French exam. It was, as her teacher pointed out bitterly, the first time she had ever failed in any subject. Her father would be even more furious than in her daydream.

She didn't mention the disastrous French exam to her mother. In fact, she didn't see much of her mother because she spent most of Monday evening skulking in her room, avoiding Nick. She couldn't bear to be around him, especially not around him and her mother together. And the way he looked at her, cool and casual as if he hardly knew her from Adam, when in fact he knew her as well and in the very same way as Adam had known Eve . . . well, she couldn't stand it.

On Tuesday her father would be coming home. If she could only reach Tuesday without anything happening . . .

On Tuesday morning while she was ironing her blouse in the kitchen the phone rang. The phone never rang before she went to school. She had a wild thought that it might be her mother with news of some disaster. But it was a female voice asking for Nick.

Olivia resented this. As far as she knew, Nick was upstairs in bed. He didn't usually get up until after she had left the house. There was a telephone extension in her mother's bedroom, about three feet away from where he must be lying asleep. If she had known it was for him she would have let it ring until he answered it himself.

"He's not up yet," she told the woman. "You'll have to ring back later."

"Could you please call him for me? It's very important."

Olivia went to the foot of the stairs and called Nick.

No response. She went upstairs and banged on her mother's bedroom door.

Still no response. Perhaps he had already gone out. She opened the door and peeped in. The curtains were half drawn, the duvet so rumpled that it was impossible to tell from the doorway if anyone was under it or not. Her mother always opened the curtains wide and straightened the duvet religiously, but Nick had no such Calvinist compunction.

"Nick?" She came closer to the bed, tiptoeing timidly into the ogre's lair. She could see him now, sleeping on his ventral side, as her biology textbook would have put it, sprawled facedown across the far side of the bed. Her father's side.

"Nick?"

He was dead to the world. She set one knee on her mother's side of the bed and reached across to touch his bare shoulder. "Nick, there's a phone call for you."

He might have slept like a deaf man, but his sleeping was not senseless. At her touch he woke and rolled over in her direction. "Lia," he muttered, "what the hell?"

"Someone's on the phone asking for you. She says it's important."

"All right. Thanks." He picked up the receiver with his right hand and transferred it to his left, propping himself up with his left elbow. "Yeah?"

Olivia took her knee off the bed and turned to leave. He reached out to grab her wrist with his right hand and pulled her back toward him. He covered the mouthpiece with the fingers of his left hand. "Hang on."

"I've got to go. I'll be late for school."

She tugged to free her wrist, but his grip was like iron. He wasn't even paying attention to her anymore, he was talking to the woman on the telephone, with pauses between each remark.

"Yeah? What's that mean? Don't give me that shit."

Olivia stopped trying to escape and started listening to the conversation. Who could this woman be, that he felt at liberty to speak to her in this manner? By the time he had called her a fucking cow and told her to turn up or else, Olivia was absolutely electrified.

"Who was that?" she demanded when he hung up, too curious to pretend she hadn't been eavesdropping.

"One of my regular models. Irregular, I should say. A totally unreliable tart."

It made her feel very strange to hear him talk like that. It made him seem alien and threatening. No one among her family or friends used words like s*** or f***, at least not when she was around. Anyone who did was not part of her world—boys on the street corner, strangers on the Tube, people in films or plays on TV. It excited her to think that in him her safe sunlit world touched another, more dangerous, underworld.

He still had hold of her wrist. He pulled her toward him. She resisted. "I've got to go downstairs and hang up the phone."

"Bugger the phone. Come on, kitten, don't you want a cuddle?"

She did want a cuddle, but that wasn't what he meant. Anyway, she couldn't get into her mother's bed with him.

He was very strong, she discovered. She had discovered that before, come to think of it. He hauled her down onto the bed and rolled her over beside him.

She discovered something else: he didn't wear pajamas. There was something about lying right up against a naked, hairy, muscular male body that scared her silly. Perhaps it was the fact that he had a very palpable erection.

And there was something about this that was worse even than that. It felt almost sacrilegious to be lying in her mother's place in her mother's bed. When she was very small her parents used to let her climb into bed with them on Sunday morning. She still remembered the sense of absolute security, of being safe at the center of the universe, that she had felt when she snuggled under the duvet between her mother and her father.

But now she was in her parents' bed and neither of her parents was there. Only Nick on her father's side and she in her mother's place. She thought if he touched her now God would surely strike him dead.

Or maybe her.

"You've been avoiding me," he said in a sleepy, husky voice. A sexy voice, she thought unwillingly. "What's the matter, don't you like me anymore?"

"I never said I liked you in the first place."

"Just an impression I had."

She was wearing a cotton nightgown because she hadn't finished ironing her blouse and because she hadn't yet got round to sewing the buttons back onto her pajama top. She had her legs firmly pressed together. He put his hand on her knee and moved it gradually up her thigh, displacing the nightgown as he went.

She grabbed his wrist to stop him. "You're disgusting," she hissed, trembling with unattributable terror and rage. "I know you do that to my mother, right here. You did it to her last night."

He said in that husky, sexy voice, "Doesn't that make it more exciting?"

She stared at him. She remembered what he had said in the park as they lay half naked, half conjoined in the darkness while one of her neighbors went by. Don't you like it rough, he had said. Maybe he was a pervert.

Maybe she was a pervert.

She tried once more to shove him away. "It makes it more disgusting."

God was getting very late with that thunderbolt. Nick had pried his thumb between her close-held thighs and continued to slide his hand slowly up toward her crotch.

As he caressed her she discovered the difference in sensitivity between the outer and inner thigh, the lower and upper thigh. It was as if her body was built to give him green lights the closer he came to his goal. When he pushed she yielded, whether she had thought she wanted to or not, and it was not just a question of his greater strength.

She knew—he made sure she knew—that he could have simply taken what he wanted, as he had done before. But he was not now a sexual pirate on a raid. He was demanding some response from her. He wanted her to desire him, to desire whatever he wanted of her. And she did not yet know the meaning of that desire, except as an ache in her belly and an itch in her crotch.

He came to her mount of Venus and ran his middle finger down the cleft in it, stroking up and down. The effect on Olivia was as if he had pressed some open sesame. Her guarded thighs fell apart, her pelvis came up to meet his hand. She didn't mean to do any of that. It just happened.

She was a thief in her mother's bed. Nick was the king of thieves; he had taken her father's place and her mother's love, and now, rather than merely taking her, he was insisting that she give herself to him.

She knew what he was doing, but it didn't make any difference. Or maybe, as he had suggested, it made everything more exciting. She found herself making small moans. She felt his finger go right up inside her, and she writhed. The thought of him within her made her melt with shame and desire. She wanted him in her as much as she should have wanted to keep him out. Even the shame, the sense of surrender, added as much to the wish as to the revulsion. He was teaching her the meaning of desire.

He made her feel sick, sick with desire for him; she had a bellyache that wanted him to come into her and cure it. Her shame was indescribable, her craving insatiable. She whimpered to the movement of his hand, like a child being beaten.

He made a sound, a soft growl in his throat. She heard it because his head was down close to hers. He bit her neck, the way tomcats do with queens. She moved against him more and more urgently, moving from passive response to overt demand. She had no more shame, only desire: in a larger sense, desire for him, in a narrower but increasingly more compelling sense, the desire for him to do very particular things to her. That desperate, insistent, impossible craving stuck in her belly till she thought she would die ... till the world seemed to sneeze and she had blissful relief.

Before she had time to recover herself, let alone have any thoughts on what had just happened, he got between her legs and pushed himself into her. She was too dazed to protest. And those same sensations that had just come to a climax were already building within her again as he moved in and out of her.

It was better this time. Whatever he made her feel, she was

making him feel it too. She could tell by the catch in his breath, the tension in his arms around her, the rhythm in the movement of his body. She felt as if they were each two people at once, themselves and the other. She was moving to please him, he to give her pleasure, alongside the demands of their own bodies.

At some point, briefly, awareness of him disappeared from her consciousness, and then awareness of herself.

When she had her mind back again she found she was still embracing him, he was still holding her. She wanted to say something appropriate to the occasion. Something like I love you. But she knew that nothing could have been less appropriate or more unwelcome. He didn't want her to love him, he just wanted her to open her legs for him.

"Jackpot," he said in her ear. "If only it could be like that every time."

Every time implied some future, some repetition. She stirred herself, stroked him with her legs and arms, turned her face toward his. He kissed her but not deeply. It was more of a nuzzle, his tongue flickering into the concavities of her face the way a cat might do. She didn't mind. She had the code now: invasive kisses meant fucking, a nuzzle and a cuddle meant love. Maybe.

There was something worse after all, something more shameful and degrading and soul-shattering than the abandonment of her sense of self into which he had seduced her. That worse thing was a hopeless yearning for him to love her, to give her some expression of love. She felt as if she was scavenging for scraps beneath a table where a feast was taking place. Where she would be kicked outside if anyone noticed what she was doing there. Begging would have been dreadful, but she didn't even dare to beg. She was an emotional jackal, Nick the lion she was obliged to dog.

He talked to her while he kissed her. The warmth of his breath made her skin tingle.

"You're magic, kitten."

That sounded like a line. "Am I?"

"Mm." He bit her earlobe, not hard, just tasting her. "You have a fantastic body."

"Big tits, you mean."

105

"You have first-class knockers, but that isn't what I meant."

"What did you mean?"

He ran his hand down her hip. She shivered at his stroke. It wasn't just the sexual frisson, though that was there. It was just as much the sense of possession implied by the gesture, like patting a horse's flank while riding it. She knew that he felt her shiver, that he knew why she shivered, and that he liked it. He knew more about her than she did herself. It was as if in making love to her he had made her altogether, as if she had become his creature in the biblical sense. A thaumaturge was a wonder-worker, a demiurge was a divine creator, and he was both.

But he didn't talk like a divinity. "Christ, you're good."

"What does that mean, good?"

He wasn't giving anything away. "It means you're a great lay."

She felt as if he had slapped her. "That's not funny." She pushed at him. "Get off me, I'm going to be gruesomely late for school by now. In fact—oh God, we've got a physics exam this morning, it's probably started already. You're going to ruin my education as well as my morals."

He moved off her, amused. "Don't panic. I'll give you a lift."

She sat up and swung her legs over the edge of the bed, pulling her nightgown down. Before she could get to her feet he was kneeling behind her, tucking her bottom snugly between his thighs, his arms around her waist. Because he was still naked she could feel his erection pressing against her back and bottom. He's going to do it again, she thought in despair and elation.

She leaned back against him. His hands cupped her breasts. She wished he loved her, but if he didn't she would take what she could get.

"Jesus, I could screw you all day." His voice, coarse and ragged, and his hands stroking her breasts, made her want him to do just that. Fuck the physics exam, fuck Nick instead. But he saved her from herself by saying, "That'll have to be another day. I've got to get going."

To deal with the fucking cow, she supposed, the unreliable tart.

He let her go. Pushed her gently away, as if it were she who had been delaying him. Indignant and embarrassed, she ran downstairs. She had belatedly remembered the iron and the telephone receiver.

Ten minutes later she came into the front hall and found him waiting, car keys in hand.

"Ready?"

"Okay."

He opened the front door and held it for her. He was looking at her in a funny way. "That's your uniform?"

"Yeah." You've seen it before, she wanted to say. But she didn't want to remind him of that occasion, after the first time he had taken her to bed.

"Pretty old-fashioned, isn't it?"

"I think that's the idea. It's supposed to keep our minds on higher things."

He laughed and opened the car door for her. "Does it work?"

She stared at the front of his trousers, just about at her eye level as he slammed the door. I wish it did, she thought with self-loathing, I wish it worked like magic. I wish I didn't want you to screw me all day long.

16

Ms. Pankhurst accused Olivia of being lost in space.

The idea appealed to Olivia. There was nowhere left on earth for someone to be a hermit. If you went to live on a desert island, people in round-the-world yacht races or anthropologists in dugout canoes or ecologists charting the decline of the dolphin population would be banging on the door of your palm-frond hut every day. Antarctica was a popular tourist resort. People climbed Mount Everest hundreds at a time. Anyone seeking solitude would be driven to living on the moon.

The really good thing about life on the moon was that she would never have to see Nick again.

She was sure she would give herself away by blushing when she saw him. She could hardly keep from blushing at the thoughts in her own head. She was horribly conscious of all the sexy bits of her body, erogenous zones they were called, except that she seemed to have developed these sensitive places in every part of her. Maybe she really was a pervert. She imagined that everyone would know just by looking at her what had happened to her that morning, and be appropriately appalled and disgusted. Especially Ms. Pankhurst.

In one way it had been magic. She had never experienced anything like that before. She felt a strange shudder inside her every time she thought of it, and a longing for him to do it to her again.

The horrible, shameful part of it was that he had somehow got inside her head and taken control of her thoughts. And he was such an appalling person. It was like something out of the rags he read: I WAS THE SEX SLAVE OF A MALE CHAUVINIST PIG.

It was bad enough having her mother's lover doing the same things to her that he was doing to her mother. Actually, that wasn't just bad, it was intolerable, it felt like someone squeezing her heart and wringing her guts when she thought of it like that. But she could have told herself, not having Megan's ruthless style of introspection, that it wasn't really her fault; he was so much stronger than her that she had no choice.

Call it rape.

Except that the time in the park he had deliberately taken his hand off her mouth; he had given her the chance to scream. Knowing very well that she wouldn't.

But the thing that really made her want to kill herself was the knowledge that she liked what he did to her. More than like it. He had made her come, for the first time in her life. He had *made* her come.

Anyone who knew what she had done would despise her.

She was despicable.

Her mother would never forgive her. Her father would be revolted. The thought of anyone else finding out, her friends or teachers, for instance, was enough to make her want to throw herself under a bus.

A less drastic course of action would be to convince her father to let her come to live with him and Althea. Having Althea around would be dire, but not half as bad as the consequences of continuing to live with Nick. Besides, if she could persuade her father to let her move in, it would be some sort of proof that he really did love her, that she hadn't been born unwanted after all.

Only now she would be getting his love under false pretenses. Now, if only he knew it, there would be every good reason not to love her, to despise her.

He was supposed to be returning from his honeymoon today. After school she rang his house and got only the answering machine. She left a message.

He rang her back that evening. She knew she should ask him if he'd had a good time or good weather or something, but she couldn't bring herself to do that because of its being his honeymoon with Althea.

"Daddy, can I come and see you tomorrow after school?"

"Can't it wait till we see you next Sunday?"

We, what did he mean we? Althea wouldn't care if she never set eyes on Olivia again, and vice versa. Olivia went to Highgate to see her father, full stop.

"Not really. It's sort of urgent. When can I come?"

"I'll be home just after six."

"It has to be before that. Can I come and see you at the college?"

"I have an important meeting at five. I'll be in my office before that."

She would have to skip games, which she wasn't strictly allowed to do. Well, too bad. "Okay, I'll be there about four-thirty."

"Do you want to tell me what this is all about?"

"It's a project. I'll explain when I see you."

She consulted with Megan about the best tactics to use. She didn't tell Megan the whole truth, of course. She just said she wanted to go and live with her father for a while because she didn't like Nick being around the house.

"What is it you don't like about Nick?" Megan wanted to know.

"I just don't like him. Why should I have to live with someone I don't like?"

"But you don't like Althea either."

"I know, but my father doesn't know that. Besides, he doesn't like Nick. When Nick came to get me at the wedding they hated each other instantly, I could tell."

"Well, they would, wouldn't they? Your mother's not crazy about Althea, is she? You'll have to have some really good reasons why you don't want to live with your mother and Nick."

Olivia thought carefully. The irony was that she had a real, unanswerable reason that she couldn't tell. Telling would ruin her mother's life and land Nick in prison, if her father didn't kill him first. And besides, then she would never again be able to feel the way she did when he held her and hugged her and let her put her arms around him. Safe and warm, that was how she had felt. Safe in a puny little boat on a stormy, shark-torn, ice-tormented sea.

"He smokes like a chimney," she announced at last. "My father is a fanatical antismokist."

"That might help, but you'll need something better than that."

"I could say he beats me."

Megan looked interested. "Does he?"

"No," Olivia admitted. "Not yet. But he looks the type. And he did threaten to kill me."

"My parents threaten to kill me at least once a week," Megan said dryly. "Lia, why do you really not want to live at home?"

"I feel like a fifth wheel." That was as close to the truth as Olivia dared to come. "My mother's all giggly and girlish and she fawns over him. She thinks the sun rises and sets on him. We used to do things together, but now he's always there and she does things with him instead."

"They won't carry on like that forever. Why don't you just wait awhile and put up with it till they get over this passionate bit?"

"I will wait awhile, but I want to do my waiting somewhere else."

"If you go and stay with your father, you'll be complaining that he fawns over Althea."

"My father doesn't fawn over anyone," Olivia said indignantly. "It's Althea who does the crawling. Whose side are you on anyway, Meg?"

"I'm on your side, idiot. That's why I'm pointing these things out to you. Lia, if you tell your father all that, he'll just say you're being childish and jealous and your mother has a right to her own life and you should grow up."

"He wouldn't say that, Meg. He might think it, but you're the only person who would actually say it." And Nick, she added to herself.

"In that case your best bet is to pitch him your pathetic yarn and basically use emotional blackmail to get him to let you move in. Either that, or behave so badly at home that your mother tells your father he's got to have you for a while because she can't cope."

"I already tried a bit of that." Olivia giggled. "That's when Nick said he'd kill me." She added more seriously, "The real trouble with that idea is that I'm not sure my mother would even notice anymore if I didn't come home."

"She'd notice if you came home at three in the morning, pissed as a newt."

"Sure she would, but I don't want to get drunk. I'd have a hangover afterward."

"You're hopeless, Lia."

"And it's no use my starting to smoke and swear. He does all that and she thinks it's great."

They both began to laugh.

Finding her father's office was a matter of working her way through a maze: first left, second right, through the double doors and up the stairs, and so on. She always reached it with a sense of relief and accomplishment.

Someone was in the office with him when she arrived. A student, she supposed, because it was a boy rather than a man. She hovered timidly at the door.

Her father finally noticed her and beckoned to her. "Come in, Lia. This is my daughter," he said to the student.

These are my daughter's tits, thought Olivia, as the boy gave her a cursory smile and focused his attention on her breasts. She was wearing her school uniform, but without the blazer because it was so warm. For the first time she hated summer. Nothing on earth was going to get her into a bathing suit.

She turned away from them. "I'll wait outside until you've finished."

"It's all right," the boy said to her back, "I won't be a minute, don't go on my account."

She ignored him and stood in the hall until he came out, almost immediately and still apologetic. At least he was apologizing to her face. She went into her father's office, shutting the door on the boy's apologies.

Her father gave her a look that meant he thought she had been rude, but he didn't say so. What he said was, "That was a very suave performance."

Olivia wondered what he would say if she said, I didn't like the way he was staring at my tits. It was a purely theoretical speculation. She would no more have made reference to her breasts in her father's presence than he would have used a word like *tits* in her presence. Anyway, she didn't want to get on the wrong side of her father right now.

But she wasn't going to apologize for refusing to be made a spectacle of. "What did he want?"

"He wasn't happy about the mark I gave him."

"Well then. I got rid of him for you, didn't I?"

Her father laughed. "You're going to be a tough lady when you grow up, Lia."

"I hope I don't grow up much more. I'm already five foot eight."

He looked at her in vague surprise, as if he could have forgotten or failed to notice how tall she was. "I should have said, when you're a grown-up." She had flustered him; he didn't like to be caught out, especially in a silly play on words. She was doing everything wrong today. "I was just about to have a cup of coffee. Would you like one?"

"Please, Daddy." She would rather have had tea, or better

still a cold drink, but she didn't want to cause him any more trouble.

He went off down the corridor. She wandered about the small office, poking at the books on his shelves and the papers on his desk. One of the drawers in the desk was partly open. Automatically she tried to shut it and found it had got wedged. She pulled it out to give it a clear run. Under some miscellaneous rubbish, dead pens, broken pencils, and so forth lay a photograph. Out of idle curiosity she took it out and looked at it.

A photo of a woman. Althea in a very un-Althea-ish pose. She was wearing nothing but a shirt, and the shirt was unbuttoned and hanging open. She was straddling the arm of the sofa in the sitting room of the house in Highgate. One leg was tucked up on the sofa, the other knee was flexed so that her toes rested on the floor. Her hands gripped the front of the sofa arm, her dark pubic hair was only just visible. She was leaning slightly forward toward the camera. Her small, shapely breasts swayed forward too, clearly visible through the open shirt front.

The most uncharacteristic thing about her was the expression on her face. Her mouth was half open, her eyes half closed, her head raised, her attention focused on the camera— on Olivia's father, that is, since he was the only one who could have taken the photograph.

Olivia stared at the photo. It was interesting to see what Althea looked like naked, even though she resented her stepmother's elegantly understated bosom. But it wasn't the sight or the size of Althea's breasts that held her riveted. It was the expression on Althea's face.

She remembered the way Nick had looked at her when he was just about to come into her: terrifyingly intent on her, but only half aware of her. The other half of his awareness was submerged in some primeval sea of sexual desire which every man carried within him. The thought of it made her tremble.

Now here was Althea, looking at her father with the same expression. When the picture was taken they must have just been or were just about to be making love. She tried to imagine her father lying on top of the Althea in this photo, looking down at this Althea the same way Nick had looked at her, doing to Althea what Nick had done to her. Was it even possible that her father spoke to Althea then with the same four-letter language that Nick used to her?

She felt sick.

It was only instinct that made her put the photo away and shut the drawer just before her father returned with the coffee. She couldn't have heard anything, with her heart hammering in her ears and a cramp in her belly.

She sat down heavily in the chair the student had vacated. Her father set a cup of coffee on the desk beside her and sat down in his own chair. She looked at him and tried again to imagine . . .

It shouldn't have been difficult. Her father was forty-one; the age difference between him and Nick must be about the same as between her and Althea. She knew he was definitely handsome because her friends were always comparing him to one or another film star. And he too must have roots in that spring, that deep well, that underground river of male sexuality. That was how she had come to be born.

But it wasn't for that she hated and envied Althea just now. It was the thought of her father holding Althea the way Nick had held her afterward in the park, tight enough to make her feel wanted, gently enough to make her feel he might really love her. She wished her father would hold her like that.

It was pushing imagination too far to conceive of her father ever under any circumstances calling Althea something equivalent to kitten or baby or even sweetheart. In her whole life she had never heard him address anyone by anything except their own name. So she didn't have to be jealous about that, because it just wouldn't have happened.

"Well, then," her father said briskly, "what's this project you're doing?"

Olivia had to wrench her thoughts into more acceptable channels. "Oh, yeah. It's not a project really, not official I mean, but we are going to do it at school. Remember, I told you that Meg and I need some translations of that play, the one where the heroine kills her husband's second wife and also her children when he's going to take them away."

"I remember." Her father looked at her oddly. "Does Ms. Pankhurst by any chance have something to do with this?"

"Well, we've discussed it with her and she's agreed to sponsor it." She blinked at her father. She couldn't seem to see him clearly. "She didn't write the play, you know. It was written thousands of years ago."

"I know. Euripides was too advanced in his views. He's had to wait twenty-five hundred years for the likes of Ms. Pankhurst to come along and appreciate his message."

He was being sarcastic, she could tell. She had an idea that Megan would have been better able to cope with this. Megan disregarded space and time in her cosmic view of things. "But isn't she right? She says that men are always murdering their wives and children to prevent somebody else having them. I don't mean having them," she added hastily, "of course you can't really possess another person, but Ms. Pankhurst says men think that—"

"That they own their wives and children. Be serious, Lia. Can you honestly believe, for instance, that I think like that?"

Olivia shook her head, staring down at her coffee cup. Her hands had started to shake. Her voice went thin and lame. "I'm just telling you what Ms. Pankhurst says. She said they think they can own them, and then they think they can disown them."

There was quite a long silence, during which she kept her eyes firmly fixed on the shivering surface of the coffee. At last her father cleared his throat. "What's the urgency about this? You didn't say it was urgent before."

"It's not. I just said that."

She dared to look up at him. He was staring at her. "Why?"

"Because you asked. I had to tell you something."

He was still staring, but she was too miserable to be nervous. "Presumably you had some reason for wanting to talk to me today, rather than waiting till Sunday."

She couldn't face him while she spoke. She kept seeing that photograph. She jumped up and stood in front of the window, looking out at Bloomsbury. "Do I need a reason? I'm not one of your students, I'm your daughter. Can't I just come to see you because I want to see you? I haven't seen you for nearly a month, if you don't count the wedding."

When he didn't answer right away she said, "Don't you

want to see me? Don't you like to talk to me? Don't you miss me at all?"

She turned to look at him. She had taken him by surprise; he was too confused to organize an emotional withdrawal quite yet. "I always like to see you."

"Then why do I have to set up appointments? Every second Sunday at one. Today between four and five. Daddy, when you lived at home you used to see me every day. Don't you miss me?"

"It's not as if you were a little girl anymore," he said stiffly. "In a few years you'll be leading your own life and you'll have to make time to see me."

She sat down in the chair again and took a sip of her coffee. She hadn't made a conscious effort, it had just burst out of her, but it left her feeling drained. She wanted to ask him the big question about her own conception, but she didn't think she was up to it just now. She chose the less personal (to her) topic of Althea's pregnancy. She couldn't bring herself to think of it as her father's baby. She was her father's baby.

"Did you and Althea mean to have this baby?"

He was staring at her again. This time his mouth had actually fallen open, as if he were witnessing some prodigy against nature. "I—we meant to do it sometime, I suppose. Maybe not quite yet. But it won't really make any difference."

Score one for Nick, she thought. "Would you have married Althea if she hadn't been pregnant?"

"Well, I—I—"

She interrupted his uncharacteristic stammer. "I mean, did you just decide to get married when she told you she was pregnant? She must have already been pregnant when you told me you were going to marry her."

He closed his mouth firmly on his own astonishment. He was looking quite grim. "Did Emma bring these considerations to your attention?"

Score two for Nick. "I haven't discussed it with Mummy," she said angrily. "I never talk to her about you and Althea, it just upsets her. Anyway, do you think I can't work it out for myself?"

"I'm sorry, Lia." He rubbed his face and ran his hand through his hair, looking handsome and harassed. "All right, the truth is that Althea and I got married when we did because of the baby. What might have happened otherwise we'll never know. Are you satisfied?"

"No, I'm not. Is it true you signed over our house to Mummy so that you could marry Althea in a hurry? And did Althea's father say he'd make it up to you? And did you say you wouldn't give Mummy any more money for me?"

"Oh, for God's sake, Lia, you can't tell me you didn't get all that from Emma."

"No, no, I . . ." She couldn't say Nick had told her. "I overheard her talking to Nick."

"Ah, yes, the boyfriend." Her father seemed perversely satisfied. "Emma is the only person in the world who would be conventional enough to call him a lodger and foolish enough to expect anyone to believe it. But I still can't believe her taste. A peroxided superannuated sub-Chippendale with his inarticulate cockney knuckles dragging on the ground."

Olivia felt simultaneously pleased and pierced to the heart. On the one hand her father had confirmed her original—and not wholly revised—views of Nick. On the other hand she was by now obsessed and possessed, penetrated and corrupted, by that same superannuated, et cetera. She also knew now that the peroxide jibe was unfair, as Nick was not; she knew that he was honestly blond, right down to his root.

Where had her father been when she needed him? Off on his adulterous honeymoon. It was too late now. If he learned the truth he would throw her forever on the same scrap heap as her mother. He would never let her live with him if he knew the truth.

But all this ad hominem attack on Nick was just an attempt by her father to distract her. She said sternly, "But Daddy, is it true?"

At least her father was not a liar. "Yes, it is."

"Does that mean you're not going to pay for my school fees and music lessons anymore?"

"No, it doesn't. I'm not giving Emma any more money. I owe her nothing now, I've wiped that slate clean, thank Christ. But I will pay directly for the things I want you to have. That means school and violin lessons." He paused. "Any other questions, Ms. Torquemada?"

That was a joke, but she didn't understand it and disregarded it. "Do you want it?"

"Do I want what?"

"The baby."

He said wearily, "It doesn't matter what I want. Althea wants it and it's on the way. I expect we'll make friends when I get to know it better."

Win, place, and show for Nick. There was no doubt in her mind that her father could have said the same thing of her, fifteen years ago. And it wasn't clear, even after fifteen years, that she had ever succeeded in making friends with him.

She had never heard her father speak so frankly, and she didn't want to hear any more. This was grown-up talk with a vengeance. Megan might have taken it in her stride, but Olivia was floundering now.

Apparently he had reached his tolerance level as well. "Is that all, Lia? I have to go to my meeting in about two minutes."

She couldn't bring herself to ask the last question, the only one she had come to ask. She got up and went over to the door. He pushed back his chair and stood up, about to follow her out. She stopped with her hand on the doorknob and looked back at him.

"Daddy, please can I come and live with you? Just for a while? Please, Daddy, I'm . . ."

She couldn't say what she was. Defiled, depraved, despairing, a juvenile slag, a child concubine. She burst into tears.

Her father stood and watched her while she wept. He didn't touch her at all, not even to stroke her hair. He should have held her and hugged her, like Nick in the lay-by. Unlike Nick, he wouldn't have had to ruin an expensive suit to do it.

She supposed she must be too big to cry, too big to be cuddled. In the grown-up world apparently your only comfort came from getting fucked, and that caused as much unhappiness as it cured.

Her father handed her a tissue. She dried her eyes and blew her nose.

He said, "I'll have to talk to Althea. It's her house too."

17

On Thursday evening, instead of avoiding Nick, Olivia found herself taking the Tube down to Wapping to meet him.

It was all her mother's fault.

The evening before had been largely Nick-free because he had flown to Paris for the day, in pursuit of some lucrative advertising commission, her mother said. Olivia, having grappled with her father before dinner, decided to have a go after dinner at tackling her mother about her birth date.

She hauled out the album and found the photo of her infant self as a fried tomato. "Did Daddy take this picture?"

"Yes, he did," her mother agreed readily. "He wasn't present at the birth, of course. I expect it was just as well, he'd probably have fainted. And I have to say I wasn't in any mood to appreciate you myself when the picture was taken. I was too worn out from the labor, I just wanted them to take you away and let me sleep."

"Weren't you excited at all?"

"I was too exhausted to be excited." Her mother recalled her birth all too clearly, it seemed, down to the goriest gynecological detail. "It was dreadful. I was in labor for over twenty-four hours. I was absolutely dead. Finally they used forceps to haul you out. You were enormous. Nine pounds, it nearly killed me. I was so shattered I couldn't even look at you, I just wanted to go to sleep. And then when we brought you home you cried every night for weeks, and nothing I could do would comfort you. I was about ready to send you back."

Her mother laughed at the recollection. Olivia said, not

sure how sarcastically she meant it, "I'm sorry I was such a nuisance."

"After you stopped crying all the time, you were beautiful. But never a cuddly baby, always independent."

"That's better than crying, isn't it?" Olivia took a deep breath. Maybe this was the moment to broach the big question. She said with deliberate ingenuousness, "Megan just pointed out the other day that you must have been carrying me when you got married."

"You were premature," her mother said quickly, her fair skin going faintly pink.

"Not three months early, not when I weighed nine pounds."

"It was just a coincidence. I mean, the timing was wrong. We would have got married anyway, but not till I'd graduated. But you can't guess about things that didn't happen. And in the end it didn't matter. Reading history wouldn't have helped me to design jewelry, would it?"

"What did Daddy think about it? About me, I mean."

Her mother shrugged. "He married me, didn't he? So he must have wanted you. At any rate, I wouldn't dream of sending you back now."

"Thanks for that." Olivia was definitely sarcastic now. At least she had been born, not aborted, if that was something to be glad of. As her mother had just said, you could never know about the things that didn't happen, including your own nonexistence. So she had resulted from a muddle, been born in a muddle, and stayed in a muddle ever since.

It seemed a monstrous injustice, almost an argument against God, that people could be born by accident. Unless Megan was right in her belief that everybody arranges their own birth. Which didn't prevent them from making a mess of things afterward.

That was when Nick had come in, looking pleased with himself because he had bagged the Paris commission, as it turned out, and proposing to take Olivia's mother out to dinner the next night, to celebrate.

"I don't expect to be back from Bristol in time for any serious celebrations," her mother said regretfully. To Olivia's amazement she added, "Why don't you take Lia out to dinner instead? Otherwise you'll both be eating cheese sandwiches."

Nick looked at Olivia without expression. When he looked at her like that, as if nothing at all had ever happened between them, almost as if he hardly knew her, it was easy to return the look. Instead of being embarrassed, she felt forsaken.

He said to her mother, "Sure, why not?" And then he smiled at Olivia. "If you feel like dressing up, we can go someplace upmarket of that curry palace."

Olivia perked up at the suggestion and the smile. Dinner sounded safe. And she was secretly thrilled at the idea of being taken out to dinner like a grown-up. By Nick.

Her mother sounded no less grateful. "That's so sweet of you, darling." Darling Nick, that was, not darling Olivia. "But don't forget, Lia, you have your music lesson after school tomorrow."

"Can't I just skip it?"

"No, of course not. You know very well Ross would make an absurd fuss if he found out you'd missed a lesson for no reason. And Mrs. Stone would charge him for it anyway at this short notice, so you'd better go. But that means you'd have to come all the way back from Golders Green and get changed and start out again, and it takes forever to get down to Wapping. Why don't you take your dinner dress with you to school and Mrs. Stone's house, and get on the Tube from there? You can get changed at the studio."

So now Olivia was traveling southward on the Northern line, still in her school uniform, clutching a small overnight bag and her violin in its case. Not a propitious start to a supposedly adult evening.

The music lesson had not been promising either. Mrs. Stone had spoken sternly about Olivia's want of attention. Mrs. Stone had always been a bit of a dragon—maybe she had learned that breathing fire down the neck was the best way to make her pupils perform—but today she had gone beyond that. She had accused Olivia of wasting God's gift.

Olivia had been horribly embarrassed, first by having God dragged into it, then by the information that she had a musical talent. She didn't want to be told things like that. Talents meant expectations and disappointments and obligations and confirmation of the dismaying suspicion that perhaps you were not basically just like everyone else. If she wanted anything more than any other thing, it was to be understood, to know that she was not a changeling from another planet, which often seemed to be the only explanation for the way she felt about her life. Mrs. Stone was no help on that front. Though she had the idea from time to time that Mrs. Stone understood her better than she would have liked.

As an end-of-term present she had been given a Bach partita to learn to play over the summer. In her heart Mrs. Stone must have felt that the sun of the musical world had risen not with Apollo but in 1685, and set not with Schönberg but in 1750. Olivia hated Bach. He was like geometry; she could see very well how he worked, and in a dryly intellectual way it was mildly interesting, but it had nothing to do with the real stuff of life. It reminded her of someone her father had described, a conceptual artist who didn't actually produce any works of art, just the ideas for them. It was surprising that no one had named a computer after Bach.

Her mother had described in detail how to get from Wapping station to the studio. Unfortunately, as usual with her mother and navigation, the details were confused or simply wrong. She remembered going on holiday with her parents and the appalling rows they used to have when her mother said left instead of right and couldn't tell north from south, even though Olivia had pointed out to her that in the northern hemisphere the sun was always in the south, never in the north. Olivia had never been to Wapping before and by the time she had found her way to her goal she thought she would be quite happy never to go there again.

She tried to take a shortcut through a council estate and got lost. She felt such a fool, wandering about with her violin like a demented busker in search of an unlikely pitch. Some boys began to follow her, calling out obscene comments. It was hours till sunset and there were plenty of people about, so she had no real reason to be afraid, but she had to force herself not to run. By the time she found the renovated warehouse in which Nick had his studio, she was so glad to be there that she hammered on the door like a benighted traveler in a Grimm tale.

She was looking over her shoulder, hoping the boys were not going to reappear before Nick came down, when she realized that the door was open and he was standing there.

"There's a bell," he pointed out dryly. "All mod cons, despite appearances."

"Oh," she said stupidly. "I didn't see it."

There were four bells, in fact. She followed him up the stairs and discovered that the doors belonging to the other bells were on the ground floor and the first floor and the second floor, since his door was on the third floor. So when she banged on the street door she was knocking on four doors at once, or none, depending on who happened to be listening.

"You're late." It was an observation, not an accusation.

"I got a bit lost. Mummy's directions weren't the best." She added in a rush, "Some yobs started following me. It was awful."

"I should have come to meet you at the station."

"I did manage to get here in the end," she said sharply, taking his comment as a reflection of her presumed childish incompetence. But when he opened his door at the top of the stairs and stood aside to let her go in, and put a hand on her shoulder while he closed the door behind her, she understood in a bewildering way that he had made the remark not as an adult to a child in his care but as a man offering a courtesy to a woman.

Embarrassed by her misunderstanding, she pulled free of his hand. She turned away from him and saw the studio.

The ceiling was more than ten feet high. A wall of windows faced south across the river, making the space a broad, bright, high, airy eyrie. The large room was broken up by movable screens. The floor was checkered with rugs of various sizes and patterns, some rich and bright, some anonymously muted. The furniture was eccentric and sparse, some items purely decorative, some brutally functional.

Olivia had never tried to imagine what Nick's studio might be like. It had never been real to her the way her mother's workshop above the art gallery was real, the way her father's small office within a maze of corridors was real. But if she had tried, she would never have imagined this.

She looked back at Nick, as if to ask his permission to wander around. He took the bag and the violin case out of her hand, which was an answer of sorts.

She walked up to the windows and looked out. The Thames was wide here, the tide high. The waters in the evening sun seemed to be struggling at cross-purposes, the tide taking the role of Canute in trying to defy gravity by making the river run upstream, at least on the surface, while underneath, the undeflectable current pursued its destiny downriver, toward the open sea.

She came back and stood in the middle of the wide space and turned slowly in a full circle.

"It's like a Roman church," she said, recalling memories of an Italian holiday the summer before her father left home. "Drab on the outside and beautiful inside."

Then she could have blushed at her presumption. As if he cared what a fourteen-year-old—fifteen-year-old, she corrected herself—thought about the space he had created to work in. She knew nothing at all about such things.

He didn't reply to her brash approval, at least not directly. He went over to the window and glanced out and down, over the river. "Sorry about the trouble you had. I'm so used to this place, I don't think about the neighbors."

She stared at his broad back and licked her dry lips. "How long have you been working here?"

"Five years." He glanced out again, his hand flat against the glass as if he would have grasped the sky beyond. "I was born over there."

"Over there?" Again it was something she had never tried to imagine. He had sprung into creation fully formed and fully grown the day he had walked through her front door.

"Across the river. Bermondsey." His mouth twisted in what might have been a smile. "Hell of a place to come from, even before they let the niggers in."

Olivia was profoundly scandalized. All his effing and blinding was tea-party talk compared to the taboo he had just broken. "Don't talk like that, it's racist."

He turned his head to look at her, the smile definitely sardonic now. "You mean I'm not supposed to call a spade a spade?"

She refused to be amused. "You know what I mean."

"And you know what I mean." He came away from the window, toward her. "I've got a surprise for you. Two surprises. Come here."

She followed him behind the line of screens. In one corner was a sort of kitchenette: a sink, a small fridge, an electric kettle, and a microwave oven. In the sink was a bucket of ice and in that, a bottle of champagne.

"Oh," she said, taken by surprise for the umpteenth time in the last five minutes. "You weren't joking about celebrating."

"I brought it back from Paris. Along with a present for you."

"For me?"

"I missed your birthday, didn't I? Em didn't tell me about it or I would have brought you something from Spain. So it's all a little bit late, but what's a fortnight between friends?"

He took the bottle out of the bucket, uncorked it, and spilled champagne into a couple of glasses. He handed her one and then touched it with his. "Here's to fifteen."

She sipped and giggled. "The bubbles are flying up my nose."

"You're supposed to drink it, not snort it like coke."

She took a substantial gulp this time. He was watching her.

"Don't pour it down your throat either. It's not meant to be mainlined."

"Mainlined?"

"Brought up in a convent, were you?" He took her hand and turned it over, palm up. "There's the mainline." He ran a fingertip up from her wrist to the visible blue vein just below the inner bend of her elbow. "The needle goes in best right about there."

"Ugh." Olivia pulled her hand away, disturbed by his touch and his words. "The idea of sticking a needle into yourself gives me the creeps."

He shrugged. "Some people like the needle better than the dope."

She didn't want to know about that. An idea came into her

head and she couldn't keep from glancing at his arms. He had his shirtsleeves rolled up to the elbow, and there were no obvious scars or marks. Not that she had the faintest idea what to look for.

He caught her look and laughed. "Would you like to check out my feet as well?"

"Your feet?" She felt herself going red.

"Isn't that the only thing the Devil can't hide?"

She turned away from him and walked round the corner of the screens into the open area. It was undisguised retreat, but there was nothing she could do about that. She swallowed more champagne and looked around.

Some of the screens were covered with photographs. She came up close to examine them. They were all of women: modeling clothes or presenting themselves to the world as they wished the world to see them. There must have been a hundred images of women pinned up for display, every one of them passably beautiful, and every one, as far as Olivia could judge, a 34B or less.

She felt depressed in spite of the champagne. She moved over to a bank of photographs, all but hidden in a corner, that were not of women displaying themselves.

These pictures might have been taken by another person. The others were a standard type, publicity photographs or the sort of portfolio a model might have. These ones in the corner were ... nonhuman, she called them, because there were no people in them, and they could have been taken on Mars for all the sense she could make of them. The longer she stared at them the more she came to see how they were composed of ordinary things but strangely abstracted, uprooted, isolated, as if only the pure form was of interest to the photographer, and the context, the meaning, the emotional human baggage, had been thrown away.

Rather like Bach, she thought. Or like the Tuilleries. She remembered her surprise at finding that famous garden not really a garden at all, more like an idea for a garden. Very French, her father had observed.

She was so absorbed in these peculiar photographs that it startled her when Nick came up behind her.

"I thought you'd be looking at the others. I thought you wanted to be a model."

She glanced at the rows of perfect women. "They're just—pictures of pictures."

He was standing beside her now. "What about these?"

She stared again at the strange photographs. She could smell him. He was the first person she had ever associated with a distinctive smell. It was mostly the smell of burning tobacco, actually, but in the olfactory nerve center of her brain it became the smoky scent of him. It went with his voice. Even his eyes were smoky, the pale blue-gray tinge of smoke in sunlight. She tried to ignore his presence and concentrate, to connect these harsh, dry, emotionally bleached images with a man who read the *Sun* and called women fucking cows.

"These are pictures of you," she said suddenly.

When she realized what she had said she was so embarrassed that she swallowed the rest of her champagne at one go.

Nick looked at the photographs and then at her, with an expression she had never seen on his face before. It reminded her of Mrs. Stone. Which was inexplicable, because she could not imagine two people less alike in character and appearance than Nick and Mrs. Stone.

But all he said was, "More champagne?"

She gave him her glass. On the way back to the bottle he stopped to put a tape in the player. By the time he reappeared with two full glasses someone was playing the cello. That surprised her.

"What's that?"

"Lloyd Webber. Julian, that is. Not really my taste. What d'you think?"

She listened. The tone was rich, the melody seductive. The whole effect was beautiful and appealing, but uncomfortably like eating two Mars bars at one go.

"I love the sound of the cello," she remarked tangentially. "I would have liked to learn to play it, but it's kind of awkward to lug around, and even more awkward to play."

"You don't fancy fiddling between your legs for an audience?"

This time Olivia knew she had definitely gone bright red.

She turned away, furious with him for his deliberate coarseness and with herself for having responded exactly as he must have wanted her to.

"I wish you wouldn't talk like that." She added, in a tone somewhere between malice and pathos, "You wouldn't talk to Mummy like that."

"But she's not here, is she?"

He came up behind her and put his arms around her, lacing his fingers together across her stomach. He pressed his hands against her, pulling her back in to his body. She put her hand over his. His hands were strong and warm and powerfully disturbing. Like the rest of him. She let her head fall back against his shoulder and closed her eyes.

"D'you want to open your present now?"

Her eyes flew wide. "Is that the other surprise?"

"You can have it on one condition."

She twisted her head on his shoulder to look at his face. He was smiling. "What's that?"

"You have to put it on and wear it tonight."

She was too intrigued not to agree.

He took his hands off her. "Go and look round the back, by the mirror."

Olivia went behind the row of screens again. There was a big table back there, and a door to a room, which she supposed must be a darkroom, and a lot of clutter and incomprehensible photographic gadgetry. There was also a sofabed. She wondered if this was where he had shot the pictures for her mother's brochure. She wondered if he had made love to her mother on that sofa. Maybe that was how it all started.

She didn't want to think about that. It tied a knot in her stomach. She looked around for her present.

One of the folding screens had a mirror on all three panels, like the mirrors in a dress shop. There was a designer carrybag hooked over a wooden chair in front of it.

That looked promising. Carefully she set her glass of champagne down on the floor beside the chair. Inside the bag were several small, professionally wrapped parcels.

She opened the flattest one first. It was a pair of very sheer black silk stockings with a seam up the back.

After that she was almost afraid to open the others. But

128

there they were, the stuff of subterranean fantasies: garter belt, knickers, and bra, all in black.

And she had promised to put them all on.

"Nick, don't you dare come back here."

"I wouldn't dream of it."

She turned away from the mirror to get undressed. It was like taking off one self and putting on another. Taking off her flat shoes, her blazer, her navy skirt and white cotton blouse, her flesh-colored tights and plain white bra and knickers. Putting on . . .

The garter belt had to go on first, then the stockings. The knickers were silk and lace, much more lace than silk, and not a lot of either. The bra was very low-cut and had strictly liberal ideas about how her breasts should arrange themselves. She looked at herself in the mirror at last and saw a very sexy stranger.

It made her feel scared, as if she had got on a train familiarly labeled Edgware and discovered too late that it was heading for Hainault instead. She didn't know where Hainault was, but she knew she didn't live there.

At that point she realized that she had left the bag with her dress and shoes in it around the other side of the screens, by the door.

"Nick, can you hand my bag over to me?"

"No."

"What do you mean, no?"

"You just wear what you've got. You can put your dress on later."

Olivia was taken aback, then angry. If he thought she was going to parade around got up like this for him, he had another think coming. The mere idea was too embarrassing for words. She pulled her blouse back on, and her skirt and blazer and flat scuffed shoes. The only bit of his present now visible was the stockings below the knee. Not much titillation there.

She took another swig of champagne and came out from behind the screens. She was expecting, hoping, to disappoint him, but instead he was amused.

"Did you like your present?"

"It's quite . . . breathtaking. Thank you."

"My pleasure." He was looking her up and down with lively interest, just as if she had been wearing nothing but the underwear he had given her. "I said two surprises, but there's another one. I want to take your picture."

"Not in this grotty uniform! Let me get changed."

"No, I want you just the way you are. I'll take another when you're done up the way you think you ought to be. Like these." He indicated the rows of smiling beauties behind her.

She didn't want to be one of those. But neither did she want to be the human equivalent of the photographic Sahara on the other side of the room.

Her hesitation amused him. "Trust me, kid. I make a living out of this."

"Oh—I suppose so."

"Good girl." He turned the screen with the mirrors around and folded it so that each mirror reflected the same thing from a different angle. Then he set a high stool in front of the mirrors and patted the top of the stool. "All right, kitten, get your arse up here and face the mirror."

Olivia climbed up onto the stool and faced the mirror. Nick topped up her glass of champagne and handed it to her. "Work on that while I do something with your hair."

"What's wrong with my hair?"

"Nothing. It's terrific. But it can look terrific in a lot of different ways."

Sipping at the champagne, she watched him in the mirror while he drew her hair back to the nape of her neck. She was feeling relaxed, enjoying the sensation of his hands in her hair. "I wish I was blond. Mummy's blond. I was cheated."

"Everybody's blond. You're different."

"Mousy."

"It looks more like honey to me."

Honey-colored hair. She liked that idea. She wished he would put his arms around her again. "What are you doing, plaiting it?"

"That's the idea. Hold still, I'm nearly finished."

He draped the braid over her shoulder. She was surprised to see how far down it came. "I look like a little girl," she protested.

"You look like a schoolgirl," he corrected. He took the glass out of her hand. "Take a deep breath and put your hands in the pockets of your blazer. That's good. Stay like that and look at yourself in the mirror. You can breathe again, by the way."

He took several shots from different angles, some of her and some of her image in the mirror, before setting the camera down.

"Can I move now?"

"You hold still, we're just getting started. Have a drink." He held up the glass of champagne for her to take a sip, then had a drink himself from the same glass. How could that possibly, she wondered, be a sexy thing to do, for him to drink from her glass? But mysteriously it was.

He stood behind her and made adjustments to her pose. They were all the same sort of adjustment. He hiked up her skirt and made her rearrange her legs so that the tops of the stockings showed, with the briefest flash of bare thigh above. He unfastened the top two buttons of her blouse. The result, because of the uplifting function of the bra beneath, was to reveal a cleavage of Hollywood proportions.

Olivia felt obliged to protest. "Nick, what are you doing?"

"Reading the daily papers." He touched the hollow at the base of her throat and trailed one fingertip downward. "We've done the *Telegraph,* now we have the *Express* and the *Mail.* If it's in one, it'll be in the other."

His finger slid down her cleavage to the first buttoned-up button. She watched it move down in the mirror. Then she saw that he was watching too. Their reflected eyes met.

His gaze moved from her image to herself. He brought his hand up to take her by the throat, tipped her head back against his shoulder, and kissed her mouth.

She clenched and unclenched her hands in the pockets of her blazer. She couldn't embrace him; he was standing more or less behind her. Except for the arm against which she was leaning, he didn't touch her below the neck. He pinched her earlobe and stroked her jaw and ran the ball of his thumb across her lower lip, all of which was astonishingly sexy. And he kissed her.

When he finished kissing her he sat her up straight on the

stool. He made her readjust the length of her skirt and the angle of her legs, which had got out of kilter on account of the kissing. Then he put her hands back in her pockets and took some more shots.

She began to find this amusing and exciting. "What next?"

He looked at the mirror and considered. "Take off the skirt and blouse, I think, but put the blazer back on."

She slid off the stool, removed her skirt and blouse, and pulled her blazer on over the bra. He shared another glass of champagne with her, interspersed with serious kisses, before setting her back where he wanted her.

Olivia was feeling distinctly high by now, but she wasn't sure if it was Nick or the champagne that was making her lightheaded. The cello was still playing, a sound like black velvet on bare skin. She hummed along with Julian while Nick rearranged her to his satisfaction.

This time she had to sit with her legs slightly apart, her outspread hands on her thighs, and slide her thumbs under the stocking tops. He undid the plait and tied the hair at the nape of her neck, bringing it over her shoulder to curl around her left breast. He did all this in a businesslike fashion, even when he touched her bare thigh or breast.

"Which newspaper is this going to be in?"

"We're still in the *Mail* and *Express*. Lingerie fashions or something to do with a diet plan." He added dryly, "The *Times* would publish anything if they could call it a promotional shot for some opera."

They hadn't come to the *Sun* or the *Star* or the *Mirror* yet, still less the *Daily Sport*. Olivia had seen large photographs of virtually naked women in these papers. That meant she would be virtually naked when he photographed her.

And that was one of the most exciting ideas that had ever entered her head. Not the idea of being photographed naked, but the idea of being photographed naked by Nick.

When he finished shooting this pose he refilled the glass, upending the bottle. "This is the last of the champagne, kitten. And about time for you, I reckon."

She took off the blazer and tossed it aside. "What do you want this time?"

"You're getting the hang of it, I see." He came over to her

where she sat on the stool, came to stand behind her and lay his hands on her shoulders. "Having a good time, are you?"

She nodded, then ducked her head in sudden embarrassment. She shouldn't be enjoying displaying her body like this. Especially not letting him take pictures.

He gave her a sip of the champagne. Then he unhooked the black bra and took it off. He untied her hair and draped it artistically around her bare breasts, not to conceal but to emphasize them. While he arranged it he looked in the mirror, as hairdressers do, and she looked too, as hairdressers' customers do. She watched him stroke her breasts and seemed to feel it twice, once as herself and once as somebody else, somebody outside herself. She looked like somebody else. She looked glamorous and grown-up and sexy.

He rubbed her nipples between his finger and thumb. She watched them stiffen and swell in the mirror. She had learned about erectile tissue in biology class. But nobody had told her that when he did that to her breasts, she would feel it between her thighs. She bit her lip to keep from squirming.

His hands moved down to her hips. He pushed the black silk knickers down over her hips and bottom. She raised herself to let him take them off. He slid them all the way down her legs and over her feet with sensual attention to what he was doing. She could tell that her whole body from head to foot was sexier now, to him and to her, now that no flimsy impediment of silk and lace prevented a sudden possession. Yet she was still wearing the garter belt and stockings. Naked in every way that mattered, but wearing quite a lot of clothing.

This was a game too, she understood. First of all there was the newspaper game, but they were down to the *Sun* now, almost the bottom of the ladder. Then there was the game of clothes, how fully dressed she could be and still be vulnerable to him. Last of all and most riveting was the game he was playing with himself of how long he could hold off before taking her.

He turned her a little to one side, so that her breasts showed in profile. Her naked flank made it clear to the viewer that she wore no knickers, only the garter belt. He had her slide the fingers of her right hand down inside the top of the stocking. He made her put her left hand at the top of her left thigh, her right leg lowered to leave the hand visible. She could see in the mirror what it must imply. She had never understood before the visually erotic implications of the female body. As Sam Gardener had said of some quite different thing, it might have been put there a-purpose.

Nick leaned over her, making adjustments. "You're on page three now, baby," he muttered, making her laugh. He looked ready to laugh himself, watching her watch him in the mirror. "Don't laugh. Look sexy."

"I don't know how."

"Sure you do."

He showed her. He slid his hand between her thighs, just to remind her that he could touch her anywhere, that she had no private parts now. The effect on her was astonishing, especially when amplified by the fact that she watched him do it in the mirror. She could see her pose and expression change, grow languorous and yearning. Her breasts enlarged themselves as if to make bigger targets for his caresses; evolutionarily speaking, he might have been the last man alive, blind and cack-handed, needing all the help he could get. In photographic terms, maybe, that covered nearly all the male readers of the *Sun*.

He took pictures of her like that.

She took a deep breath. "Now what?"

"Now we take the belt off." He unfastened each of the garters, unhooked the belt, and tossed it aside. The stockings stayed on. But she was naked from the top of her thighs to the top of her head.

"Okay, maestro, what now?"

He told her what now, in great detail. She was to cross her left leg over her right. She was to put her right hand on her bottom. Her left hand had to spread and slide between her thighs. She was to let her head fall back slightly and then turn to look at the mirror.

She did all that and saw what she looked like. Rather good, actually, but hopelessly vulgar. "What's this for? We've done the *Sun*."

"Call it the *Sport*."

He touched her breasts. The pose made them jut out, and

his touch stiffened the tips. That too was immortalized on film, from all angles. She could hardly wait to see what came next.

Even with only a pair of black stockings to work with, he had plenty of ideas. He got her down off the stool and onto the rug, still in front of the three-way mirror. He made her sit on her left foot in a very particular way, so that the heel and ankle fitted snugly into her crotch. Her right leg was extended gracefully and she removed the stocking slowly, with a photographic record of her progress.

After that he laid her on her back, with her right leg bent in a sketchy salute to modesty, while she raised her left leg and removed the last stocking.

"This is pretty low," she observed with a champagne giggle. "Where are we now?"

"Channel Four."

She giggled again. She was totally naked now. She thought he must have to come into her at last. She had paid her dues, she deserved his loving. She wriggled against the warmth of the carpet. He was standing over her with the camera. She wished he would come down to her.

"One more," he said.

She pouted deliberately. She would never have done that normally, but she was tipsy and she wanted to play up to him. "What more?"

"Put your left hand behind your head. That's a good kid. Now bend your right knee just a little. Bring your left foot up closer to your arse, that's it, and put your right hand down here. Perfect."

He stepped back to look at her through the camera. She heard him say *jesus* under his breath. She became aware, now that the cello music had finished, aware of the way he was breathing, rough and audible. His heart must be pounding like mine, she thought. If he touched her anywhere she would fly to bits.

"You're a good kid," he repeated. His voice was like a rusty hinge, thick with the thought of her. He set the camera down and took his clothes off, quickly, urgently. He wasn't stripping for her the way she had for him. He was stripping for action.

She stared at him standing naked over her. He might have

been a Martian for all the understanding she had of what it must be like to have a body like that. There was nothing soft or superfluous about it, nothing there for the comfort of others in the way that a woman's body was made for bearing and suckling and comforting babies. His body was an instrument for imposing his will on the world.

He lay down on top of her, between her legs. He was poised to enter her, but he didn't yet. He looked down at her. No one else had ever looked at her like that. She did not know how to describe it, except to say that it might have been the Devil looking out of his eyes, and that if it were she would happily let him take her straight to hell. She could see in his eyes how much he wanted her; and she wanted so much to be wanted. She put her arms around his neck.

He grazed her mouth with his. "This is for your birthday, baby. What d' you want?"

She wanted him to love her. But it was forbidden to say so, even now. "You know."

"Tell me."

He moved against her, caressing her body with his like a stallion nudging a timid mare through the gate of a corral. She could not help responding. "Make love to me," she whispered.

"I've been doing that for an hour already. Didn't you notice?"

He nuzzled her, kissing in passing the angles of her face, the corners of her throat, touching her with his tongue in randomly unerring design. She squirmed beneath him. She didn't want to play games anymore, she wanted him to do what he had meant to do all along. "You know," she said again.

"Say it."

"I can't."

"Sure you can. It's only four letters."

She didn't want to play semantic games, she wanted him to love her. Love was four letters too. But she knew what he wanted. "Fuck me, Nick."

Somewhere in the back of her mind she was horrified to hear herself say such a shameful and humiliating thing. But the language of love seemed to have quite different parameters from the speech of everyday encounters. It used words that Beowulf would have blushed at.

Love was not one of them.

Even so it was a magical language. What you asked for, you got. He thrust himself into her. She was so grateful she wanted to say it right then, the one forbidden word: I love you, I love you, I love you.

It wasn't so much the sexual sensations, as wonderful as they were, but the sense of closeness, the loss of loneliness. Maybe being a woman meant you were always empty, always wanting a man to fill you. Maybe only the right man would fit. Did men never have that inner emptiness? Were men and women like nuts and bolts, totally opposite, completely complementary?

She clung to him with her arms and legs, letting him go only to draw him back again. Maybe it was just the champagne, but she felt as if they had both become transparent, so that she knew how he fitted her, how he liked her to move. He growled in her ear, words of ancient but obscene provenance. That made her more desperate for him. She let him take her as roughly as he pleased. The rougher he was, the more he wanted her, or so she reckoned with her calculus of need. But for herself the only four-letter word she uttered in extremis was his name.

He came with her, in half a dozen violent, shuddering thrusts.

"Jesus." He opened his eyes to look at her, and shut them again. He could hardly speak. She thought it was from lack of breath.

She loved him so much at that moment she couldn't have spoken herself. She stroked his hair. It was the least of the things she longed to do. Every inch of him was beautiful, every ounce of him desirable.

He gathered his strength. "You're the best fuck I've ever had."

Something inside her pounded on her ribs, bruising her. She wanted to say Do you love me, do you love me? but that was a different language. His native tongue was Anglo-Saxon and there was no use asking him questions in Greek. She would have to be content with fucking for loving.

He pushed himself up and looked away from her. "Christ, I'm starving. Let's go and eat."

18

He took her to a restaurant in Hampstead, a nice cozy one, not intimidating.

"Why Hampstead?" she wanted to know.

"It's close to home and parking's easier. And I like this place."

Olivia liked it too, but not as much as she had a moment ago. "Have you been here with Mummy?"

"I might have, I can't remember. What d'you want to eat?"

She wanted to say I'm not hungry. The temperature had dropped twenty degrees when she mentioned her mother. Another forbidden word. But she couldn't really blame him for that. She didn't want to talk about her mother either. She didn't even want to think about her mother when Nick was around.

Anyway, upon consideration she was hungry after all. "I don't mind. Tell me what's good."

"At these prices everything had better be good." He leaned across the table to run his finger down her menu. The menu was inevitably in French, and upside down from his point of view. "If you like chicken, that's all right."

She looked at the item he was indicating. It did appear to be chicken. He could read French, and upside down too, apparently. But she didn't really care what it was he had recommended. Octopus, haggis, hominy grits, whatever, she would have eaten it, seeing that everything had warmed up again between them. "All right, I'll have that."

The waiter came and went away with their requests. Olivia sipped at the drink that Nick had ordered for her. It had an interesting taste but no alcohol. I've got to get you sobered up before we go home, he had said. What he meant was, before your mother sees you.

Going home was a sobering thought in itself. He had done something magic in the studio, turned her into someone else, someone glamorous and sexy, for whom it was okay to do forbidden things. The mere thought of her ordinary self doing those things was enough to make her cringe and feel sick with embarrassment and shame. Right now she was, as he had said, close to home, and she didn't know how to think about it. So she thought about something else instead. He had mentioned it himself, it wasn't forbidden.

"Did you grow up in Bermondsey?"

"I got bigger. I don't know about growing up."

"What was it like?"

"The pits." He drew on his cigarette. He seemed to be focusing on something beyond her left shoulder. "But my old man would have made anywhere hell."

"Why?"

"He'd thump you as soon as look at you."

He spoke flatly, indifferently. But when his eyes returned to her face she felt a flicker of unease. Maybe it was his tone of voice, the way one might speak of growing up in some hellish corner of the earth where people routinely suffered floods and plagues and died of famine. She couldn't imagine a famine, any more than she could imagine her father so much as smacking her.

"Does he still live there?"

He shrugged and stubbed out his cigarette. "No idea. I haven't seen the bastard for almost twenty years. He could be dead. I hope he is."

"How can you say that about your own father?"

"It's easy. I hated him." This time there was no facade of indifference but real venom in his voice.

"Because he beat you?"

"Among other things."

There was no point asking about the "other things," she could tell Nick was not going to elaborate. "What about your mother?"

He shook his head. "The last time I saw either of them was

eighteen years ago." He smiled suddenly, a faintly ferocious expression. "I was your age."

"You left home at fifteen?"

"Fourteen."

The idea made her feel quite dizzy, as if she had suddenly aged five years in five seconds. "What about school?"

"That was the best part, getting shot of school."

The waiter came back with food. When he had gone again Nick said, "The night I cleared out, he came home pissed and picked a fight with my mother. That stupid cunt never did learn to keep her mouth shut. I told them both to put a sock in it, so he started on me."

"He beat you up?"

"Not that time he didn't. The good guy won for a change. I beat the shit out of him."

Olivia stared at him, open-mouthed. He might have been describing everyday life on Mars. Totally alien to her; to him, by the tone of his voice, unremarkable. "You beat up your father?"

"Fucking right I did. One for the hundreds he'd given me. Not really evening the score, but better than nothing." He glanced down at what the waiter had brought. "Let's eat."

She had to wait to hear more. Fortunately she was hungry, and too tipsy to remember the diet she was supposed to be on. She ate her chicken, whatever it called itself on the menu, and watched him eat. She had thought more than once before, having supper at home, that there was something odd about the way he ate. Nothing basic like using the cutlery wrong or anything obvious like that. She couldn't put her finger on it. But now she understood. He ate like a man who had come late to the concept of the dinner party. The idea of eating as entertainment, eating as a social experience, was not one that came naturally from his background. He ate methodically, efficiently, the way he would have filled up his car—a routine chore that had to be done, without intrinsic enjoyment.

But he didn't make love like that.

When he had cleared his plate he lit a cigarette and finished his glass of wine. He had had only one glass because of having to drive home; apparently the champagne didn't count.

He watched while she picked at the bones of her dinner. "Was it good?"

"Yes." She thought maybe he meant more than the chicken, and for that reason she didn't say thank you. For everything beforehand, they owed each other.

"What about afters?"

"Are you having something?"

"Why not?" When she hesitated, Nick added with amusement, "Go on, it's for your birthday. You're not setting any dangerous precedents."

She pondered the alternatives on the menu. "What's a syllabub?"

"It's good. D' you want to split one?"

"Okay." She closed the menu and took up the real conversation where he had left off. "I suppose after you'd . . . done that to your father, you had to leave home."

"It wasn't quite like that."

"How was it?"

He smiled, without warmth. "More like, if I was big enough to teach my old man a lesson, I was big enough to do whatever the hell I wanted. And what I wanted was to get the fuck out of there."

"But you were only fourteen. Didn't anyone try to find you? I thought the police—"

"They'd have been bloody glad to see the back of me. We're not talking about Hampstead, baby. Where I came from, if some troublemaker dropped out of sight everybody just said thank Christ. Especially the coppers."

Olivia didn't want to speculate about how the police had even known of his existence. "Where did you go? What did you do?"

"I just wanted to see things. I'd never been out of London before. I took the rent money to keep me going for a while and hitched my way around the country. After a while I took a ferry to Holland and moved across Europe."

That explained the French, if not the reading upside down. But she had other concerns just then. "You stole your parents' rent money?"

"They owed me, don't you think? I would have done somebody else but I didn't have any time to waste." He smiled suddenly, a real one this time. "Jesus, Lia, you should see your face. I think you did grow up in a convent."

She floundered between embarrassment and indignation. "I'm not surprised you did it, just surprised you'd admit to doing it."

"It's a secret between you and me, kitten. Are you going to turn me in?"

"You mean you've never told anyone about all this?"

"I've never told anyone anything." He inhaled on the cigarette and slowly exhaled, looking away again at nobody. "As far as I'm concerned my life began when I left all that shit behind me. I invented some cock-and-bull story to entertain the lorry drivers who gave me lifts, and that's the story I've stuck to ever since."

She stared at him. She wanted to touch him. Everything he had told her made him more alien, more desirable. Nothing in her biology classes had enabled her to conceive of a craving to engage in sexual intercourse with a Martian.

"Why are you telling me?"

"You're still in it, aren't you?"

It. Childhood, that time of life when adult others ruled. Her parents, her teachers, Mrs. Stone. Nick.

The waiter had returned. Nick ordered the syllabub. His glance came back to her. "Coffee?"

She was an adult tonight. She had coffee.

It was past ten o'clock when they left the restaurant. The meal had done Olivia's head some good, but she was still coming down from the champagne high. And depressed by the prospect of reentering everyday life, where Nick was her mother's man. Where she could neither look at him nor touch him, for fear of giving terrible secrets away.

She put her arm through his, as she had seen her mother do, while they walked uphill to the car. She did it to be close to him, but what with the champagne and her high heels on the uneven pavement she was glad of some support.

The street lamps were coming on, sunset still glowed in the sky, a fine calm evening. In the twilight she saw another couple coming down the hill toward them. At first she only noticed them because they were just coming abreast of Nick's

XJS. Then she looked again, and recognized her father and Althea.

"It's Daddy," she whispered to Nick, taking her hand from his arm. Suddenly the thought of what she had done, what Nick had done to her in the studio, made her feel quite vile. She became horribly conscious of the black underwear, even though none of it was visible under her dress, the red dress her father had bought her for his wedding. If he had known . . .

She stopped and waited for her father to come down. Nick stopped too, standing near but not too near. On the one hand she was glad of his presence, on the other hand in her father's presence the thought of him made her feel sick. Anyway, she had no choice.

Her father came down and stopped. He stood a little closer to her than to Nick, not quite standing between her and Nick, not quite turned away from Nick. A very literal and unmistakable cold shoulder. Althea had her hand on his arm and she didn't let go.

"Hello, Lia, what are you doing here?"

"Hi, Daddy. Mummy had to go to Bristol, so she asked Nick to take me out and we've just had dinner. We're going home now," she added to reassure him when he frowned.

After her speech she felt distinctly lightheaded, or maybe it was the high heels. She felt herself swaying toward her father. She put her hand on his shoulder to steady herself. "Sorry."

"Did you eat dinner or drink it?"

The dry, sardonic tone was sharper than usual, which meant he was very angry. She took her hand away. "Sorry, Daddy," she said again. "I've only had two glasses of champagne. That's as much as I had at your wedding."

Her terror in the face of her father's anger made her feel even more lightheaded. She moved away from him and missed her footing. This time it was Nick who caught her and held her upright.

"All right, Lia?"

He had spoken quietly, but of course her father heard. "She's not all right. She's drunk."

"Daddy, I'm not," Olivia protested. She tried to pull away from Nick but he held her firmly by the elbows. Maybe that was just as well; she was tempted to faint from embarrassment when she saw her father and Nick glaring at each other.

Her father said icily, "Is this your idea of an evening's entertainment, getting a fourteen-year-old plastered?"

"I'm fifteen, Daddy, I've had my birthday and you forgot it."

He ignored her reproach and continued to address Nick. "Are you fit to drive? I doubt it. You're certainly not fit to be in charge of a young girl, if this is the result. I've a good mind to take her home to Emma myself."

"Daddy, please—"

Olivia could feel the tension in Nick's grip on her arms. She was terrified he might do something horribly physical. Her father was taller, but Nick had broader shoulders and more experience—as she had just learned—of assault and battery. He also had a pretty good line in arctic sarcasm. "Yeah, well, if you think you've done enough to embarrass Lia, we'll be on our way."

Althea was hanging on to Olivia's father's arm as if she thought he might take a swing at Nick. "Ross, Lia's all right. She's just had a good time. Kids like to have a good time. Let her go home to bed, she's got school tomorrow."

For the first time in history Olivia was grateful to Althea. "I'm all right, Daddy, really. And I do have to get to bed."

Nick was practically dragging her away. Althea was doing her best to move Olivia's father along in the opposite direction. Finally her father said grudgingly, "All right, Lia, you get home. I'll talk to you tomorrow."

Nick bundled her into the Jaguar and drove off with rather a lot of sudden acceleration and gear changes.

Olivia found herself shaking. She put up her hand to her mouth, thinking she was going to cry or throw up. She knew what her father would do. He was going to phone her mother. And Nick was so angry she could feel it inside her, making her pulse leap every time he moved his hand to the gearshift or looked in her direction. She leaned her head against the windowpane and closed her eyes and wanted to die.

"Nick."

He didn't answer.

She opened her eyes and took her hand away from her mouth in case he couldn't hear her. "I'm sorry, Nick."

"About what?"

"About my father."

They were coming down toward Finchley Road. He braked abruptly and pulled over to the curb.

He unlocked his seat belt and released hers as well, then leaned over and put his arms around her. He hadn't done that all evening, except when they were actually making love. She embraced him. She couldn't stop trembling. Anybody would have thought she was freezing to death on a warm summer night.

"You're shaking, kitten. What's the matter?"

"Nothing." She buried her face against his neck. "I'm scared."

"Of what?"

"I don't know." She couldn't say, Scared of what we're doing. "Daddy was furious. So are you."

"Not with you, baby. With him."

"You don't like him."

"He doesn't like me. What did you expect?"

She sighed. "I hate Althea."

"Yeah, I know."

He was still caressing her, comforting her, stroking her with his hands and with light, undemanding kisses in relatively unerogenous places like her temples and the top of her head. Gradually she stopped shaking and began to relax. She turned up her face to him. He kissed her mouth, first a little kiss like the others, then a deeper one.

She started to tremble again.

"We've got to get home, kitten."

"I don't want to go home."

"Neither do I. I want to take you back to Wapping and screw you all night. But we can't do that."

He let her go. She watched him light a cigarette, roll down the window, do up his seat belt. But he didn't start the motor right away. He sat smoking and looking out of the window. If he would say that he loved her, she thought she could have borne anything. But he didn't say that.

He ran his hand through his hair, the hand that held the cigarette. "Christ, what a mess," he muttered. Then he turned the key in the ignition, put the car into gear, and drove home.

19

Megan and Clare and Sissy went over to Olivia's house on Friday night. Olivia's mother obligingly disappeared for a while, leaving the girls to play music and dance and talk and giggle uninhibitedly in the sitting room.

Olivia might once have supposed that the contrast between the way in which she had celebrated (if that was the right word) the night before and this innocent little hen party tonight would make her feel daring and grown-up and superior to her inexperienced friends. But it wasn't like that. She felt horribly corrupted and estranged. Her family and friends thought she was a normal, ordinarily innocent girl of fifteen. Instead she was what her grandfather would have called a whited sepulcher.

Nick had isolated her from the rest of the world. He had contaminated her with a sort of moral leprosy to which he himself, being Martian, was immune.

"Where's this lodger you told us about?" Clare wanted to know.

"He's not here tonight. I told him you were coming, so he stayed away."

Clare stuck out her tongue. "Horrible child. Meg says he's gorgeous."

"Don't you believe Meg?"

"I do believe Meg. All the more reason to see for myself."

"Well, you can't. He's up in Norfolk, that's where he spends his weekends." Olivia deliberately changed the subject. "How is your romance with Allie coming along?"

"I haven't seen him for ages. Danny says everyone's gone into purdah till A-level exams are over. Allie's got to get at

146

least one A or his career as an engineer will be finished before it starts. You'll be the first to know when there's any progress to report."

The subject of Megan's play came up. Sissy hadn't heard about it yet, and Megan had to give her a brief résumé of the plot.

"Bags I the villain's part," Clare said quickly.

"Who's the villain?" Olivia wondered.

"Well, whatsisname, the errant husband, of course."

"What about Medea? She's the one who murders everybody."

"Well, she can't be the hero *and* the villain."

"Why not? What about Macbeth?"

"If she were meant to be the villain, she wouldn't be allowed to escape at the end," Megan ruled firmly. "She's definitely more sinned against than sinning."

"But you could say that about most of the people in prison," objected Olivia. "Even the ones who've committed horrible crimes, it turns out their mother rejected them and their father beat them and their girlfriend cheated on them and their teachers flunked them and their wife ran off with another man."

The others hooted her down. "Oh Lia, what are you, some kind of Nazi? Next thing you'll be wanting to bring back the rope. Anyway, the men can look after themselves. They usually do."

Olivia persisted in her heresy. "I just meant, I don't think Medea is supposed to be a passive victim of circumstance. She's supposed to be a strong, independent woman, isn't she? You can't have it both ways. Either we're responsible for the consequences of our actions or we're not. And if we're not, who is?"

"The system. Society."

"Mrs. Thatcher said there's no such thing as society."

"Yeah, well, my father says she knows better now, since society threw her out of her job." Clare was browsing through a stack of CDs. "Lia, what are you doing with all this antique music? It wasn't here the last time I was over."

"That's Nick's nigger music," Olivia said maliciously.

They all looked at her. "Wash your mouth out with soap!"

"I was only quoting him."

"He sounds very nice, not. Who's this Mississippi John Hurt?"

Olivia didn't know but it didn't matter. The pictures on these recordings were all the same. The men—there was an occasional woman with a pleasant round face and motherly figure and no glamour at all—the men might be young or old, thin or fat, but they were all weather-beaten black men in funny hats and ill-fitting 1930s suits. "He's just some old blues singer."

"I like that name. Let's have him."

They had him. He was singing "Candy Man," a slyly obscene song about all the women being stuck on the candy man's nine-inch candy stick. They giggled and joked and swapped folklorish tales about men and their sexual apparatus, like Desdemona repeating to Emilia what Othello had told her concerning the Anthropophagi.

Olivia listened to the music and didn't say anything at all.

After Clare's mother had come for her and Sissy, Olivia walked Megan partway home through the park. It was well past sunset. The groundskeeper came by and said they would have to leave, and they said they were leaving anyway. Olivia wondered what Megan would say if she knew what had happened to her, Olivia, on her way home through the park last week. Guess what, I was raped, she could say. He raped me and I'm in love with him.

"Do you remember what you were saying about my coming home drunk as part of a campaign to go and live with my father? I did it last night. By accident."

"You got drunk by accident?"

"Well, I certainly wouldn't do it on purpose. I felt terrible this morning."

"What happened? Was your mother appalled and distressed?"

"She didn't even notice. I told you she wouldn't. But Daddy was furious."

"How did your father find out?"

Olivia gave her an edited version of her adventures, leaving out the events in Nick's studio. "He must have phoned her at work, because she came home tonight looking glum and asked me exactly what had happened."

"Did you tell her?"

"Why not? Althea's father was trying to pour champagne down my throat at the wedding, and Daddy didn't say anything about that."

"Well, he wouldn't, would he? Was your mother mad?"

"She was mad at my father. She said he was hypocritical and vindictive, which for her is practically raving."

They had reached the farther gate by now. The little man showed them out and slammed the iron gates behind them. They lingered there to finish their conversation, leaning on the bars and looking back wistfully like exiles from Paradise.

Megan undertook to analyze the situation, as usual. "If your father wasn't all that keen on your coming to live with him, why is he making such a fuss?"

"Because he's hypocritical and vindictive, I suppose."

"You mean he's trying to get at your mother?"

"That's what Mummy thinks. Why else would he ring her up and yell at her?" She used the word metaphorically; neither of her parents ever yelled at anyone. Her father just got venomous and sarcastic, which was far worse than being yelled at. Her mother got offended and sulked. Screaming and shouting didn't come into it. But she added, "Actually, I think she's wrong. I think it's Nick he's getting at, trying to put Mummy off him."

"That sounds pretty vindictive and hypocritical to me. He left your mother for Althea, why shouldn't your mother get herself another man?"

Olivia recollected the scene, Nick and her father ready to come to blows almost on sight. "Maybe it's me," she said slowly, disbelievingly. "Maybe he's jealous about me."

If he's jealous he must love me, she thought. She didn't say it aloud, because she hadn't dared to confess that terrible insecurity even to Megan. Your father should love you automatically, shouldn't he, whether or not he wanted you to begin with? Once she had simply assumed that magic parental love. But first her father left her, then she found he hadn't meant her to be born, and now ... She remembered what Nick had said about his father. A brutal man, nothing like

her own father. But it meant that nothing was magic or automatic about a father loving his children. He might hate or
despise them.

Yet her father had been jealous. He had been ready to fight
on her behalf. Unheard of, unimagined!

"Well then," said Megan practically, as if she had been
following Olivia's thoughts, "he'll probably want you to come
and live with him."

On this optimistic note they parted. Megan went to the
curb to cross the street; Olivia started the long way round
the park. Megan looked back to wave and saw what she
was doing.

"Oi! He's gone now." She pointed to the gate, meaning the
little man.

Olivia looked up at the advancing night. "I can't. Nick told
me not to, after dark."

"Is he giving the orders now?"

Olivia knew that Megan wasn't daring her, because Megan's own parents would have said the same thing if they
knew of their daughter's habit. She was just asking out of
interest. If Nick was playing daddy now, Olivia's father might
well be jealous.

Olivia's own thoughts were slightly different. Who was
Nick to give orders, after all? Her mother's lover, not even
her stepfather. As her own lover he had no authority at all,
his status was entirely illegitimate. Criminal, in fact. He had
said so himself. He had no right to lay down laws for her.

She ran back and scaled the gate, waving to Megan before
heading off into the deepening dark.

She went round to the front street anyway, so that her
mother wouldn't know she had come through the park. When
she let herself in the front door she heard voices, her mother's
and Nick's, clearly having an argument. She shut the door
very quietly so as not to interrupt them.

She knew what they must be quarreling about. She leaned
against the wall beside the sitting room door. The hallway
was dark. The mirror opposite faced into the sitting room,
but only the fireplace was visible.

"I'm not blaming you, darling," her mother was saying in

a sweet, understanding voice. "No one could reasonably object to a fifteen-year-old having a glass of wine with dinner. Ross gives her a drink himself when she goes over there on Sundays. She's big enough, God knows, you wouldn't think it could make her tipsy. It's just unfortunate . . ."

"It's unfortunate," Nick broke in coldly, "that you're taking any notice of anything that shit says. Why didn't you just tell him to fuck off? For Christ's sake, Em, he's out of your life. You've divorced him, he's married to someone else. The only thing you have in common now is Lia, and she's old enough to deal with him herself."

"She's done just that, it seems." Her mother's voice had gone cold now too, angry not with Nick but with Olivia. "Did you know she went and begged him to let her come to live with him? She said she didn't want to live in this house with you here."

"When did she do that?"

"This week. Wednesday, I think he said. I'm sure it's true. He may be everything you say, but he's not a liar."

Nick said slowly, "What did he say to that?"

"He told me he might take her for the holidays. He said he told her he'd have to speak to Althea about it. I don't imagine she'll be keen on the idea." Her mother added, warmer and quicker and softer, "I'm sorry about this, Nick. I know Lia resents you just because you're not Ross. She's at an awkward age right now, nobody understands her and so forth—"

He cut her off impatiently. "Yeah, all right, I don't need a map. And I'm not insulted, so don't apologize. What the fuck does it matter why she wants to go? If it's all right with him, let her go."

"But I feel I must have failed her somehow." Her mother appeared in the mirror, facing the front window, striking an unconsciously dramatic pose with her long, slim hands interlinked against her breast. "If she wants to leave so badly that she's willing to put up with that dreadful girl . . ."

"That's Lia's problem. She's a big girl now, as you just observed. Let her sort it out herself." Nick came into view behind her mother. He put his hands on her shoulders.

"Wouldn't it be kind of nice to have the place to ourselves for a while? We could take a holiday."

He was caressing her mother's upper arms and shoulders, massaging the back of her neck with his thumbs. Her mother resisted this seduction long enough to ask, "Can we afford a holiday?"

"Holidays are necessities. When was the last time you had one?"

"I can't remember. Not since Ross left."

"High time, then. Let me take you away from all this. We'll go somewhere nice and sunny and study the *Kama Sutra*. A thousand ways to add spirituality to your sex life. D'you fancy that?"

Her mother leaned back into him and laughed. "You could write a new *Kama Sutra* yourself: a thousand ways to turn a woman on."

"Let's try number thirty-four, how to talk dirty to a colonel's daughter." He said something in her mother's ear that Olivia couldn't hear and didn't want to hear.

He unzipped the front of her mother's trousers and put his hand down inside. Down inside her mother's knickers. Her mother wriggled against his hand. Olivia nearly threw up.

Her mother put her hands behind her and stroked the front of his jeans. Stroked his erection. "Stop that, you horrible, vulgar man. Lia will be home any minute."

Olivia didn't want to watch Nick masturbating her mother and vice versa. She didn't want to hear that smoky, sleepy note in his voice. Or remember when and where he had spoken to her like that.

Right here in front of the mirror, the first time.

Nick took his hand out of her mother's knickers and said in a different voice, "Speaking of Lia, where the fuck is she? It's already dark."

"Maybe she stopped over at Megan's house for a while."

That was Olivia's cue to go to the front door and open and shut it as if she had just come home. She managed to open it quietly enough.

"If she's gone through the park I'll kill her."

"She can't go through the park. They lock the gates at twilight."

"She climbs over the gate. Didn't you know? I caught her at it last week and told her I'd give her hell if she did it again."

Her mother laughed. "Maybe that's why she wants to go and live with Ross."

Olivia closed the door. She was on the outside. She ran to the top of the street and round the corner before they could come out and find her.

She was never going back, never. Neither of them wanted her; they couldn't wait to get her out of the house. Her mother's only concern was not looking like a bad mother. Nick's only concern was fucking her mother.

For him to talk so casually about the time he had found her in the park . . . as if he had forgotten all about what he did between catching her and warning her. The memory of that should have tripped up his tongue in front of her mother. But he didn't care. She could go and good riddance.

She had nowhere to go but Highgate. Her father was going to get her whether Althea liked it or not.

The air had cooled off since the sun went down. She wished she could have gone back to get a sweater and some money for taxi fare, but there was no chance of that now. She couldn't even get her bike because it was locked up in the garden shed. She would have to walk all the way to Highgate.

At least she couldn't get lost. It was straight down to Finchley Road and up across the Heath. Maybe if she walked fast it would keep her warm.

When she was crossing Finchley Road a man in a car asked her if she wanted a lift. She ignored him, and he went away.

By Jack Straw's Castle her sandal strap broke. She couldn't walk with one shoe off and one shoe on, so she carried them both and walked in her bare feet.

The pavement near the pub was littered with broken glass, which she failed to see in the darkness. She had to stop to pick bits of glass out of her feet. But even under a street lamp some pieces simply couldn't be found, so she had to limp along and suffer. Her feet felt as if she had been walking on upended razor blades. The soles were bleeding, and her right foot had a sliver of glass embedded in it that sent excruciating pain through her body if she put her weight on it in the wrong way.

If she could have found somebody to ask, she would have begged for ten pence to phone her father. If she could have found a telephone booth. But she was crossing the Heath now, a benighted traveler such as her father had told her about from the good old days. No one lived right near here. No one needed to make urgent telephone calls. It was a jolly place, when the sun was shining.

She sat down at the side of the road, near tears. She simply couldn't walk any farther. She might have to sit there till morning, dead tired and chilled to the bone.

She wondered if her mother was seriously wondering where she was. It was Nick, not her mother, who had remarked on her absence. She really couldn't go back now; Nick had said he would kill her. She wondered what that meant. Maybe he meant he would beat her the way his father had beaten him. In the old days people used to beat their children all the time and no one thought anything of it, not even the children, though presumably they didn't exactly enjoy it. Would he hit her with his fists, or slap her face, or spank her bottom, or even whip her with his belt? It was all unknown territory to her. She recalled watching him unbuckle his belt, though not for purposes of physical chastisement. The memory made her shiver.

Right now she thought she wouldn't mind him beating her in any or all of those ways, if only he loved her. But he didn't.

After she had sat there for about a century, a police car went by. It came back again and pulled over to the curb. One of the policemen rolled down his window and asked her if she was in trouble.

She limped up to the patrol car and showed him her sandal strap and explained, in a rush of words, how she had no money to phone her father and was trying to get home to Highgate. By the time she had finished her explanation she was wiping away tears with the heel of her hand and feeling totally humiliated for crying like a lost toddler.

The policeman said they would take her home. She gave them her father's address and got into the car. When they drew up outside her father's home the policeman on the passenger side got out and opened the car door for her. She climbed out and started to limp toward her father's front door, wincing and biting back an exclamation when she forgot and stepped on the sliver.

The policeman came over and took her arm. "Have you hurt your foot, miss?"

"I stepped on some glass."

"Maybe you should have that looked to. We'll see you to your front door."

"No, please!" Olivia pulled away from him. "I'm all right, I'm home now. Please go away."

"Take it easy, love." He took her arm again. She protested too much, she realized. It had made him suspicious. "What's your name?"

"Olivia."

"How old are you, Olivia?"

"Fifteen," she said, too exhausted to remember to lie.

"Well, Olivia, we can't just drop you and drive away. Your parents must have been expecting you home a fair while ago."

"Yes," said Olivia. "No." She could imagine what her father would say about her landing on his doorstep in the middle of the night, escorted by the police. "Please let me go. Please go away."

She started to cry again. She was shaking with terror and cold. She knew her behavior was only making things worse, but she couldn't seem to regain her self-possession. Maybe she should have taken a leaf from Nick's book and hitched a ride up the Great North Road to see the world.

"What's the matter, love? What are you afraid of?"

How could she even begin to explain the problem? She got no farther than "My father—" before her voice stopped working.

"I'm going to talk to your father," the policeman said firmly. "Lean on me, I'll get you to the door."

He hooked her arm around his neck, his arm around her waist, and helped her hobble across the pavement. She was resigned to her fate by now. After all, she would have to ring the bell and make some explanation to her father anyway, so maybe it was better if this determinedly helpful policeman ran interference for her.

He rang the bell. After a long time a light came on and her father appeared in his dressing gown.

At first he was too surprised and confused, and sleepy too, perhaps, to be angry. The policeman brought a tearful Olivia into the sitting room and settled her on the sofa and picked up her feet, one at a time, to look at the soles, while her father hovered, awaiting an explanation. Olivia looked down and saw she had left bloody footprints on Althea's pastel Chinese rug.

"Daddy, I'm sorry. About the rug, I mean," she added between a hiccup and a sob. "I've ruined it."

Maybe Nick would have said Fuck the rug, but her father didn't give ground so grandly. "What happened to your feet?"

"My sandal broke. My feet are full of glass, they're killing me."

"We found her on the Heath, sir, near the Spaniards," the policeman put in firmly. "You shouldn't let a young girl like that be out so late without some way to get home."

Althea appeared at this point. She came in and stood beside Olivia's father. She looked at Olivia and at the blood on the Chinese rug and back at Olivia again, not very kindly.

Olivia's father was saying, "I didn't know she was out. She lives with my ex-wife over in West Hampstead."

The policeman looked at Olivia. To her surprise he seemed more amused than annoyed. "Yes and no, eh? I get it now." He said to her father, "I'll leave you to sort that out for yourself then, sir. Maybe her mother would like to know where she's got to."

"Very likely," her father said grimly.

He went to the door with the policeman. She could hear the policeman saying something about getting a doctor to look at her feet and her father being politely impatient and trying to shoo the policeman out. Her father was the sort of person who expected to encounter the police only when he wanted to complain about his neighbor's dog barking. He would not anticipate or welcome any contact or advice of a social-work sort; that would put him in the same class as an unwed mother on a council estate.

Althea took advantage of his move to the doorstep to hiss at Olivia, "What have you done to my rug?"

"My feet." Olivia held one up for her inspection. "Blood."

Her father came back, having disposed of the persistent policeman at last. "Lia, are you drunk?"

"Of course not." She added indignantly, "I wasn't drunk last night either, not really."

"So when you say you're not drunk now, does that mean you're not drunk or you're not really drunk?"

"Daddy, don't talk like that." She was angry, and afraid of his anger, and embarrassed because of last night. "You're the only one who gives me anything to drink, when I come over here on Sundays."

"Somebody else gave you something to drink last night."

"I explained about that. Please, please, don't go on about it." She added sarcastically, "While we're on the subject, maybe I should tell you that I also don't smoke pot, sniff glue, snort coke, or do Ecstasy. Okay?"

Her father sat down in the chair across from her. Althea perched herself on the arm beside him. Olivia suddenly remembered the photo of naked Althea sitting on the arm of the very sofa that she herself was lying on. As soon as she thought of that, she couldn't bear to look at either of them.

"If you're not doing any of those things, would you mind telling me what you were doing wandering across Hampstead Heath at half past one in the morning?"

Althea's presence made everything a hundred times worse. "I was coming here," Olivia muttered. "I didn't have any money for cab fare so I had to walk."

"You were coming here?" he repeated sarcastically. "You thought you'd drop by for a visit in the middle of the night?"

"I've come to stay with you," she burst out. "I can't stand it anymore."

She thought for a moment he was going to ask her what exactly it was she couldn't stand, but perhaps the lateness of the hour got the better of him. He rubbed his hand across his cheek. It was the middle of the night; he had a bad case of five o'clock shadow. "Does Emma know where you are?"

She shook her head.

"I'd better ring her." He stood up and said to Althea, "I'm sorry about this. If you could make up the spare bed . . . Then you can go back to sleep. I'll get Lia sorted out."

Althea shrugged sulkily and went upstairs.

Olivia's father went into the kitchen to phone her mother. Olivia didn't want to know about that conversation.

She had made a complete botch of everything. Instead of sympathizing with her, her father was practically chewing the carpet. He seemed to have convinced himself she was some sort of teenage alcoholic. Also, no doubt, that it was all Nick's fault.

If he was like this over half a bottle of champagne, it took her breath away to imagine what he might do if he ever had an inkling of what else Nick had put into her last night. She could never, ever, hint or breathe or come within a hundred miles of letting out anything about that. She was trapped with her dreadful secret.

Her father came back into the sitting room, breathing fire. "They were out looking for you, at least that lager-lout lodger was. Emma was wringing her hands and preparing to call in the police."

Olivia covered her face with her hands. She had never thought of that. "Oh, God. I'm sorry, Daddy."

He sat down, suddenly looking more tired than angry. "Tell me, Lia, what prompted this spur-of-the-moment change of residence?"

She tried to think. She had to be so careful what she said. She couldn't let on that her mother didn't want her anymore. It was too painful a thing to tell anyone, even Megan, let alone her father. Besides, what would happen if her father didn't want her either? It was better to have each of her parents thinking the other one wanted her, than for them to know the awful truth.

She stared at her damaged feet while she spoke as much of the truth as she dared. "When I came home I heard them talking. Mummy said you'd told her that I wanted to come and live with you, and that you'd said I might be able to stay here for the holidays." She looked up at him. "Is that true?"

"That's what I told her."

"Well, she wasn't very happy about it. She was talking as if it was some sort of insult to her. But Nick said wouldn't it be nice to be alone for a change, and he'd take her on holiday and . . ."

She stopped and swallowed. The bit that would really convince her father was the next part. She had a pretty good idea how he would feel when she told him. She was feeling suicidal all over again, just thinking about it.

"Then I . . ." She scowled at her feet again. "I know I shouldn't have done this, but I was standing there while they were talking about me without knowing I was there, and I didn't want them to know, so I just stood there thinking about how to pretend that I'd only just that moment come in, and I could see them in the mirror. He was feeling her up. I mean *really* feeling her up. He put his hand on her . . ."

She had to stop here. She knew very well what his hand had been doing. She could still feel that same hand doing the same thing to her own clitoris, as she lay in her mother's bed, as she watched herself in the mirror at the studio. But she couldn't say it to her father. She couldn't even think it in front of him.

She went on hastily, "Well, it made me feel sick. He'd just said more or less that he didn't want me around, and I . . . I didn't want to be in the house with him for one minute longer."

She dared to look at her father again. He wasn't showing any emotion at all; he might have turned to stone. He was staring at her as if she were somebody else, not Lia. It was kind of scary, that stare.

"Daddy?"

"All right, Lia." He rubbed his hand across his face to bring himself back to life. "We won't talk about it anymore, we'll go to bed. Let me do something with your feet first."

He went out and came back with a basin of warm water and an armful of newspapers. After spreading the newspapers on the rug and setting the basin on the newspapers, he hunkered down and washed her feet for her and did what he could to take out the glass when she pointed out where it was. Then he dried her feet carefully and carried her upstairs. He hadn't done that since she was very small.

159

Her bed was made up in the spare room, which was actually his study. Althea had put one of her own nightgowns on the bed, and Olivia's father gave her a pair of thick woolen socks to cosset her injured feet.

She sat on the edge of the bed, wondering if she had the strength to get undressed. "Good night, Daddy. I mean good morning. I'm sorry for causing all this trouble."

"Never mind, Lia. Good night."

She decided not to undress, not to put on the nightgown. In the first place, it was Althea's. In the second place, she wanted to go to sleep just the way he had left her, to revel in the knowledge that her father had been mothering her.

20

In the morning Olivia's father persuaded the doctor to come round to the house, on the grounds that Olivia couldn't walk. When the doctor saw the state of her feet he had to agree. He removed a few more bits of glass and told her she was an idiot and to stay off her feet for a few days.

"Can I stop school for the summer, then?" Olivia asked hopefully. "We break up at the end of next week anyway and I haven't got any more exams." When her father vetoed this proposal she said, "But I can stay here, can't I, even if it's not quite holidays yet?"

"How will you get to school?"

"By bicycle. I don't mind doing it that way in summer. And it's only for a little while."

She won that argument. Maybe her father was afraid of finding another policeman at his door in the middle of the night. The argument she lost was about having to phone her mother to apologize.

Nick answered. Olivia briefly considered changing her

voice and asking for Emma, but decided to brazen it out. "May I speak to Mummy, please?"

"I don't know if she wants to speak to you."

"Well, ask her."

"In a minute. She's upstairs right now. What's the big fucking idea of the midnight drama?"

Olivia wasn't even tempted to explain, because Althea was at the window watering potted plants and listening to every word. "It seemed like a good idea at the time."

"Did you think we wouldn't notice you weren't here?"

"I did actually think that. You were both . . . occupied."

He was silent so long that she thought he must have gone to get her mother. Finally he said, "Here comes Em."

Her mother had on her tea-party manners, which made the exchange easier. Olivia made her formal apology. "Mummy, I'm sorry I gave you a scare last night. I didn't mean to."

"I gather you had an unhappy night yourself."

"I did. My feet are too sore to walk on."

"Then we're even, so let's not talk about it anymore. When are you coming home?"

Olivia took a deep breath. "I'm not." When her mother said nothing, she went on, "Daddy says I can stay here for the whole summer. I can ride my bike to school—when I can walk again."

"Is that what you want to do?"

"Yeah." She took a deep breath before continuing. "I'll need my things. Maybe Daddy can go over and get them for me."

"Tell me what you want. I'll pack them and Nick will bring them round."

Olivia tried to think of a polite way to express her misgivings. She said cautiously, "Is that really such a good idea, after all the . . ."

Her mother took the point, but had a few points of her own. "Lia, Ross said some terribly hurtful and unfair things to me yesterday and last night. To be truthful, I feel you've embarrassed me badly by your behavior where he's concerned. I really don't want to have to see him. Do you understand me?"

"I understand," Olivia agreed. What it amounted to was

that her mother was going to leave Nick to take the stick. Well, that was sort of fair, it was all his fault really, more than her mother knew, in fact. And if he didn't want to do it he could just say it was nothing to do with him and refuse.

"What's Nick doing there, anyway? I thought the arrangement was for him to stay in Norfolk on the weekends."

"Well, originally it was, but now he's rented the cottage out till a buyer comes along, so he's going to be living here full-time, at least for the summer. That's why he was so late getting in last night. He'd gone up to clear out the rest of his personal possessions before the tenant moves in on the first of July."

No wonder they were so pleased with the idea of her going to live with her father. "I hope you've put his rent up."

"He's going to be paying for half the mortgage and household expenses. And a good thing too, since I'm not getting anything from Ross anymore."

"I was just about to phone Meg. If it's okay for her to come over here, could Nick give her a lift when he comes?"

"I imagine so. I'll ask him."

"Remind him he promised her a ride in his car."

Her father, when she asked him, said it was all right for Megan to come over. So she phoned Megan.

"I'm at my father's house. Can you come over this afternoon?"

"Sure, but how did you swing that?"

"I'll tell all when I see you. If you phone my mother you can get a ride with Nick. He's supposed to be bringing some things over for me."

"What luck, alone with Nick! I'll ring her right away."

After she hung up she thought about what her mother had told her. How handy, one man's money taking over where another's left off.

That comparison started another one in her head. Her father used to pay her mother money for her. Maybe Nick was paying for her too, without her mother knowing it.

She recalled from *The Naked Ape* a chillingly precise description of what Nick had been buying with his rent money: sexual access. He and her body were in the same house, then in the same bed, then the one was in the other.

It was beneath degradation. She felt like some adolescent ape obliged to service an alpha male gorilla. In such a context, love was the obscenity.

Well, he had outsmarted himself. He had driven her away. And she was safe from him now, in her father's house. Even little apes could get protection from big apes by hiding behind the Old Man.

After lunch the doorbell rang.

All morning Olivia had been trying to think of a polite way to suggest to her father that he should get Althea to answer the door. Althea had no particular grudge against Nick. If anything, she should be grateful to him for taking the specter of the Abandoned Wife off her conscience. But by the time the bell rang Olivia hadn't even worked up the courage to tell her father that it was Nick, not her mother, bringing the suitcase over. She thought of dashing to the door herself, but it would have been more of a crawl than a dash. She had to watch the confrontation helplessly from her propped-up position on the sofa.

When her father opened the door Megan stood on the doorstep. He invited her in.

Megan stayed where she was for a moment. "Nick's coming with Lia's suitcase. We had to park around the corner." She glanced over her shoulder. "Here he comes. It's very sweet of him to lug things around for Lia."

To lug things around for your daughter, Dr. Beckett, when you should be doing it yourself, was her subtext. Having played picador, she didn't wait for a second invitation to come inside.

"Lia, you're an invalid! What have you done?"

"I'll tell you later." Olivia shifted her legs to make room for Megan. "Sit down here and shut up for a moment."

Her father was standing guard in the doorway. Nick appeared on the doorstep and thumped the suitcase down. They did not greet each other. Her father grudgingly uttered a monosyllabic thanks.

"Where's Lia?"

"She can't come to the door. She can't walk." And it was all Nick's fault, her father implied.

Nick glanced past Olivia's father, at Olivia herself on the sofa. "All right, Lia?" His tone of voice suggested that her father might be keeping her in captivity against her will.

"I'm fine, only my feet hurt, so I can't get up."

"Hard luck, having to be waited on."

Her father picked up the suitcase and set it in front of the door to preclude any possibility of Nick inviting himself inside. "Don't let us keep you. You must have better things to do with your time than run errands for my daughter."

Nick said coolly, "That's your job now, innit, mate? We'll see you, Lia."

He had gone before her father could move the suitcase to slam the door in his face.

Olivia hadn't known she had been holding her breath until she let it out. She didn't even know whose side she had been on. Her father must have reckoned that his deliberate rudeness would either make Nick back off or reduce him to inarticulate obscenities. But Nick had beat him on his own ground with a deliberate parody of the working-class wide boy that her father supposed him to be.

"Daddy, can Meg and I sit out in the garden?"

"That's a good idea," her father said in a tone that suggested even good ideas were a bad idea just now. That made it an even better idea, because it meant she would be out of the way of his bad temper.

Althea was not quite so quick to catch on. When he picked Olivia up to take her outside, Althea said, "Should you be doing that, darling? You don't want to pull a muscle."

"I'm not quite dead yet, thank you."

Olivia put her arms around her father's neck and buried her smile in his shoulder.

The garden was not what she would have called a garden at all, more a walled patio. There was a winter cherry in one corner and a grapevine in another and a climbing rose against the south wall and the rest was flagstones, with shrubs in large terra-cotta pots. A stylish Althea sort of garden. But it was warm and sheltered and private. Her father and Althea went out to do some shopping, leaving Megan in charge of her.

"What happened to your feet?"

"I stepped on some broken glass in the dark."

"How did you end up here?"

"A policeman brought me."

"What makes me think you're leaving out a lot of this story?"

Olivia was already fed up with last night's adventures. "Oh, it doesn't matter, Meg. Let's just say I ran away from home."

"Why did you do that?"

"I told you all about it on Tuesday."

"You said you wanted to leave home. You didn't say anything about running away in the middle of the night."

"Well, I came home and heard them talking, and I just couldn't stand it any longer. Anyway, it worked. Here I am."

"For a while."

Olivia shrugged. "Maybe I'll get to spend a week here and a week there. That would be okay. When I can't stand Althea anymore I'll go home, and then when I can't stand Nick anymore I'll come back here. Did I tell you he's moving in, lock, stock, and barrel? Sharing all expenses. None of this lodger crap anymore."

"Is that why you ran away?"

"No, I didn't even know about it then. My mother just told me this morning. We have really excellent interpersonal communications, Mummy and I."

"She was probably nervous about telling you because she knew you wouldn't like it. I don't know why you're so down on poor Nick. He likes you."

"Does he, by God. How do you know?"

"We talked about you on the way over. He was asking questions about you."

"What sort of questions?"

"Oh, you know, if you're any good at school, if you have a boyfriend, and so forth. I told him you're a real dumbo and have a passion for a rugby back."

"I hope he believed you. I thought you were planning to make a pass at him while you had him to yourself."

Megan sighed. "Chance would be a fine thing. Your father sure has it in for him, doesn't he?"

"I really thought Daddy was going to throw the suitcase

at him or something." Olivia giggled. "Maybe he wants Nick to go away so that I can move back home."

"Oh, I don't know, Lia. I think your father loves you all right. He just doesn't know what to do with you. By the way, Nick gave me something to give you."

"He did?"

"Yeah. Just a minute, it's in here." Megan dug around in her bag and produced a tape. "He recorded it this morning, he said, to distract you from your suffering. He said it would be better than a bunch of flowers or a bowl of fruit."

Olivia stared at the tape in her hand as if it might have been a disguised explosive device. There was nothing written anywhere on it to indicate the contents. "Nick said that?"

"Yeah, he did. Well, actually, he said a frigging bowl of fruit."

"That sounds more like it. Meg, can you run upstairs and get my Walkman so we can listen to it? Mummy should have put it in the suitcase."

Megan was back in short order with the stereo. Olivia stuck the headphones in before turning the machine on, just in case Nick had put something on that she didn't want Megan to hear. Perhaps it was the cello music she had heard in his studio. That would be quite romantic, both the music and the gesture.

She started the tape. A piano, not a cello. One of those weather-beaten old black men began to sing. He wanted some seafood, mama. In the next cut he was complaining that your feet's too big.

She might have known that Nick wouldn't do anything romantic. Even the birthday champagne had just served to get her drunk so he could have his wicked way with her.

Megan was watching her. "What is it?"

After her initial disappointment Olivia found herself smiling in amusement at the music. This man was really quite brilliant in his own eccentric way. Much better, after all, than a frigging bowl of fruit. And more cheering than Lloyd Webber's sobbing cello.

"Must be a course in self-hypnosis," grumbled Megan.

Olivia took the headphones off and jammed them in Megan's ears. Then she sat back to watch a broad smile spread across Megan's face.

"This is really excellent."

"Absolutely. Didn't Nick say who it was?"

"Nope. Maybe he wanted to make you guess."

Much later, when her father and Althea had come back from shopping and her father had carried her into the sitting room and then gone off again to drive Megan home and Althea was putting the groceries away in the kitchen, Olivia put the tape into her father's stereo to listen to it properly. The seafood man, it turned out, was only on the A side. The B side was her favorite, Bessie Smith.

In the middle of the tape her father came home. He put his head into the sitting room just as Bessie woke up from her dream of death. She thought he was going to tell her to turn it down. Instead he asked, "Where did you get this remarkable music?"

"It's a tape from one of Nick's CDs."

"Nick?" He looked surprised and skeptical, unwilling to believe that any good thing could come out of Nazareth. He listened to the music again, perhaps hoping to revise his opinion downward. The lyrics of the next song were a series of outrageous double entendres. "This is a bit near the knuckle, isn't it?"

Olivia felt faintly embarrassed. For her father, perhaps, the singer's enthusiasm should have prevented offense, but for herself anything that came from Nick had sex written all over it. "Daddy, if you ever listened to anything but Radio Three you wouldn't even raise an eyebrow at this. It's Bessie Smith. But there's someone else on the other side, I don't know who he is. Maybe you can tell."

She rewound the tape and played the seafood song. Her father was amused, just as she and Megan had been. But he didn't know the answer to her question. "Sorry, I can't help you. Unlike Mozart, the blues don't come with Köchel numbers." He added casually, "Why don't you find out and let me know?"

He meant she should ask Nick. But of course he couldn't say that. That would mean the inarticulate cockney ape knew something the professor didn't know.

21

Relations were not very harmonious on Monday morning. When her father telephoned the school to explain that Olivia had had an accident and wouldn't be attending for a couple of days, he got involved in a very long conversation that Olivia could not quite overhear, since he was in the hallway and she was stuck on the sitting room sofa. The tone of it sounded unpromising.

Sure enough, he was furious when he came back into the sitting room. "Lia, what in the name of God have you been up to?"

"I don't know what you mean, Daddy."

"You don't know you've been hours late for school twice in the last fortnight? You don't know you failed your physics and French exams? Your headmistress said you'd seemed preoccupied, but perhaps comatose would be a more accurate description, if you can't remember any of that."

"I've been having a lot of trouble getting to sleep lately." True, absolutely. "It makes me really dopey the next day. Sometimes I can't get my brain into gear. You know how it is."

"No, I don't." He probably didn't, either. On his honeymoon with Althea he would have been up at eight every morning, scanning the headlines in Italian and keen to get on with the day's menu of antique ruins and quattrocento altarpieces. She had an idea her father's brain never really disengaged. Maybe he even had logical dreams. "I've a good mind to ring up Emma right now. What the hell does she mean letting you sleep in like that?"

"No, Daddy, no! Please don't ring her. It's not her fault, she calls me and then she has to go. Anyway it doesn't really matter now, does it, if I'm living here?"

"Maybe not, for the time being. But I hope you'll let me know if you continue to have trouble concentrating, instead of waiting till you've messed up your GCSEs." He added some remarks about her mother's maternal and intellectual capabilities. They were uncomplimentary and uncalled for but not necessarily untrue, Olivia thought.

She also thought how curious it was that the only things she couldn't blame on Nick were the things that were actually his fault. Maybe he thought that turning up at school an hour late was okay, since he himself had seldom bothered to turn up at all. Maybe he thought that failing an exam didn't matter, because he had never even got as far as sitting an exam.

Or maybe he didn't care.

She didn't want to believe that. He had been insistent, both times, that she go to school instead of playing truant for the rest of the day. Maybe he just didn't understand about school, the way her father didn't understand about hugging and her mother didn't understand about music. If you imagined the different ways in which human beings ought to be able to absorb understanding as being like different colors, then Nick and her father and her mother were all in some way color-blind.

She wondered which colors she herself couldn't see.

After they had got over that initial misunderstanding she was thrilled to have her father at home with her. He was around to look after her on Monday and Tuesday, and for the rest of the week he drove her to school and picked her up afterward—maybe just to make sure she actually got there.

For two blissful days he made bacon-and-avocado sandwiches for lunch and played Scrabble with her. He won every game, but she didn't mind; she was just enjoying being with her father and having him do the things her mother used to do. Whatever Nick's other talents, she was pretty sure he had never played Scrabble in his life.

On Thursday after school her father drove her to Mrs. Stone's house in Golders Green and waited while she had her violin lesson. What with all the upheaval she hadn't had the chance to do much practicing, and Mrs. Stone was not pleased.

She told Olivia's father so. She hadn't seen him for two

years, but she sent the bill to him every month and he paid it. There had been an argument about ten years ago over whether Olivia should take dancing lessons or violin lessons. Her mother wanted her to take dancing lessons because she had had them when she was a child, and her father was pushing for violin lessons because he hadn't had them when he was a child. Olivia didn't remember which side she had been on, if either, but her father had won, and thereafter her mother had considered the music lessons to be his responsibility. Mrs. Stone regarded him as her chief ally.

"Dr. Beckett," she said, making it sound like the German *Doktor* with a *k* and somehow much more illustrious a title, "this young lady says to me, I like this, I don't like that, as if at her age she understood everything about music. I tell her, taste in music is like taste in food and drink. Children like everything sweet, but when you grow up you begin to understand subtlety and dryness. If she would listen and pay attention she would begin to hear this. She has an ear and a brain and her fingers do the right things.

"Romantics all die young, I tell her. Beethoven in his old age, his violins were prickly, not pretty. Well, what do I know, an old woman like me? But you're an educated man, Dr. Beckett, you tell her, maybe she'll listen."

"Lia's living with me now," her father said. "Maybe things will be different."

On the way home he asked if she understood what Mrs. Stone had been talking about.

"Yeah," said Olivia. "Bach."

The problems of three people living in the little house became immediately apparent. Downstairs there was the sitting room and the dining room and a tiny kitchen. Upstairs there was a front bedroom, a back bedroom, and a tiny bathroom. She had to keep her bicycle in the little walled garden, and take it out through the house. Althea nearly had a fit when she discovered this.

The back bedroom was her father's study. It was crammed with books, and he had to move them off the bed before she could go to sleep. If he wanted to do some work, she couldn't hang about in her bedroom as she used to do at home. There wasn't even any room to hang up her skeleton. She wondered how things were going to work out when the baby arrived and needed the back bedroom. Maybe her father had preferred having a study to having a baby.

Fortunately, Althea wasn't around much except in the evenings. She had some incomprehensible job in the City involving swaps, whatever they might be. At the age of twenty-four she made more money than Olivia's father, which he considered a profoundly immoral state of affairs reflecting badly on the values of society, though Olivia noticed that he didn't mind going out to posh restaurants and taking holidays abroad on the strength of Althea's salary, or driving the posh car that her employers provided for her.

Althea said her job was stressful and basically tedious and that she was looking forward to maternity leave. Olivia's father said if she wanted to avoid stress and tedium, having a baby was a funny way to do it. Then he repeated the same story that Olivia's mother had told her, about how she had cried night and day for the first six weeks of her life.

But Althea's baby won't cry, thought Olivia; Althea's baby will be perfect. Or else.

And it would be a boy.

Olivia didn't speak to her mother for nearly a fortnight, until her mother rang up. "I presume everything's all right, since I haven't heard from you."

"Everything's fine, Mummy."

"Don't I get Sunday visiting rights?"

Olivia was a little taken aback. It seemed a very odd idea, visiting her mother. "Do you want me to come and visit you?"

"Turnabout's fair play, isn't it? Come and have Sunday lunch at home."

Her mother said "at home" and Olivia still thought of it as home. But when her father dropped her off outside the house where she had lived for all of the life she could remember, she suddenly felt like a stranger. She had to stop herself from knocking on the door.

Arrangements were less formal than they had been at her

father's under the previous dispensation. Her mother invited her into the kitchen and put her to work peeling potatoes.

Nick was nowhere in sight. Maybe he wasn't at home. Maybe it was going to be just her mother and herself, like old times. She felt both relieved and cheated at the thought. "Where's Nick?"

"He's outside with his head stuck in the innards of my car. It keeps stalling on me. I was going to take it into the garage, but it seems that no real man hands a car over to a mechanic before he's worked out exactly what's wrong with it and can tell the mechanic how to do his job." Her mother shredded lettuce while she talked. "How do you like living with Ross and Althea?"

"So far it's okay. But the house is really small. My bedroom is also Daddy's study, and when I go up to do my music practice sometimes he's in there. He says he doesn't mind listening to me, but I don't know if that's true. I don't know what's going to happen when the baby comes. He can't use it as a study if the baby is trying to sleep in there."

She worried about that a lot. Would she no longer have a bed at her father's house? Would he send her back home when the baby arrived to displace her?

Her mother said briskly, "I expect they'll move."

That was reassuring. Or not, depending on where they moved to. "They can afford a bigger house," Olivia remarked knowledgeably. "Althea makes a bundle. More than Daddy. Did you know that?"

"Althea has money coming out her ears. I believe her grandfather left her a nice little nest egg in his will, which is where the down payment for that house came from. And her parents gave her another one for a wedding present."

Olivia didn't say that Nick had already told her about that. "How nice for Daddy," she said dryly.

"Quite. As I understand it, stockbrokers tend to be wealthier than army officers."

Stockbrokers was Althea's father. Army officers was Olivia's grandfather, Colonel Hardy. He had died when she was still small, and she couldn't remember him very well. But her mother's reference reminded her of Nick's joke about the *Kama Sutra* and the colonel's daughter, meaning her mother.

Her stomach turned over. She couldn't look at her mother. She concentrated on chopping up the potatoes and tried not to think about anything at all.

"That's fine, Lia, don't make mincemeat of them." Her mother took away the potatoes, dumped them into a pot, and turned the heat up high. "Why don't you go and tell Nick it's time to come in for lunch?"

Olivia went out the front door and down the street until she found her mother's car. Nick was revving up the motor by doing something under the bonnet. She called but he didn't even see her, let alone hear her over the noise of the engine. She would have to go up and touch him to get his attention.

He was wearing a white T-shirt. His bare arm was sun-tanned, the blond hairs on it sun-bleached. His hand was splayed out on the wing of the car. She stared at the corded muscles of the arm and the veins that overlay them. For the first time since she had left home, she missed him. She wanted to put her arms around him, to get him to put those strong, sun-browned arms around her.

She ran a fingertip up his forearm and watched the hairs rise in response.

He turned his head without moving his arm. When he saw her he let the engine die.

Her rib cage seemed to have shrunk. She couldn't breathe very well. "Mummy says you're supposed to come in for lunch."

He looked at her a little while longer, squeezing the last cubic centimeter of breath out of her. Then he stepped back and slammed the bonnet down and wiped his hands on a rag. "About time too, I'm starving. How're you doing, kid? How's her royal highness treating you?"

"Althea, you mean? Why do you call her that?"

"I know royalty when I see it. She'd pass the fucking pea test hands down, don't you think?"

Olivia thought of Althea: snobbish, fastidious, autocratic, never knowingly looked down upon. She giggled. "It's true. But you only met her once."

"Once was enough." He put his hand on her shoulder. "Come on, kitten, let's go eat."

Eating lunch reinforced the sense of strangeness. It was as

if her mother and Nick had invited her to lunch at their house, rather than her coming home. It wasn't just because she had taken her clothes away. By the end of the meal she had decided that the main difference was the way her mother and Nick behaved. They were already acting like her father and Althea. Nick wasn't a lodger, he was the man of the house, he was her mother's man. They were living together and this was their home. It wasn't her home anymore.

The thought made a hole in her middle. Althea's baby would have her room in Highgate. If she had to come back here, she would be the lodger, not Nick. She felt like a ghost. Dead people who came back didn't belong anymore.

After lunch she played Scrabble with her mother while Nick did whatever he was doing to the car. It reminded her of the days when she and her mother were first left alone, when they used to play Scrabble to while away the empty Sundays. Long-gone times, thought Olivia wistfully. Then they had been painful days; now they seemed a safe haven lost.

But in those days her mother used to win. Today Olivia came first. "I've been playing against Daddy," she admitted.

"When is he coming to collect you?"

"He's not. He and Althea have gone out to Marlow. I'll have to take the Tube back. It's a bore because I've got some more stuff to take with me."

"I'll take you back, if Nick's finished with my car. Let me go and have a word with him."

Her mother came back almost immediately. "He says he'll take you himself. He wants to try out the car to see if it's behaving properly."

It's not a question of the car behaving properly, thought Olivia. On the other hand, with Nick and her mother so matey, and after what she had overheard him say that Friday night, it seemed likely he really didn't want her anymore.

She told herself it was safer that way.

"Next time we'll go to the seaside," her mother suggested.

Olivia was offended. The seaside was a childish amusement. "I won't be here for next time. I'm going up to Huddersfield for a fortnight to visit Granddad and Gran."

"I'd forgotten. We'll be away ourselves the fortnight after that, so it'll be almost the end of August before next time."

Now her own mother was almost too busy to see her. She would have to fix dates in advance. Her father had always been like that, but her mother . . . It was the end of civilization as she knew it.

She didn't say a word to Nick till they were halfway to Highgate in her mother's car. That was how different things were now, Nick driving her mother's car. She wondered if her mother had got to drive the XJS yet.

"Who was the man on that tape you gave to Meg?"

"I didn't give it to Meg, I gave it to you. Did you like it?"

"We both thought it was super. Who is it?"

"Fats Waller."

"I never heard of him."

"He was a hit before your mother was born. Maybe even before your grandmother was born."

"Daddy liked it too. He especially liked Bessie Smith, but he complained about the lyrics being a bit off-color."

"Too blue for your old man's taste, is she? Maybe he thought you'd be corrupted." He gave her a sardonic half-smile.

She didn't return the smile and changed the subject. "Where are you and Mummy going for your holiday?"

"Crete. Em's idea."

"Don't you want to go to Crete?"

"Sure, why not? Anywhere with sun and a beach and drinkable wine is all right with me."

Anywhere with a bed, she thought, remembering what he had said to her mother that night. She looked at his sun-brown hands on the steering wheel and thought of them stroking her mother's small breasts. A wave of jealousy and black despair passed over her. She hugged herself and closed her eyes.

"Lia? Are you feeling sick?"

He always noticed. He noticed more than either of her parents. Only she didn't want him to notice. She opened her eyes. "No, I'm not."

She wished she had the courage to say what was in her heart. She wished she could say right out, I want you to take me to Crete, I want you to do all the things to me that you're going to do to my mother. But there was no point anyway because he couldn't.

When he stopped the car around the corner from her father's house she got out at once. "Thanks for the ride." She was surprised to see him getting out too. "What are you doing?"

He opened the boot and collected her bags. "I'm bringing these in for you."

"It's okay, I can manage."

He didn't argue with her; he just ignored her. He walked up to the house with her and waited while she dug out her key and unlocked the door. When she opened it he followed her in and shut the door. He went right into the sitting room, dropped the bags on the Chinese rug, and looked around.

"Nice place."

"I'm sure they'd be pleased to know you approve."

"Just the opposite, I reckon. They'd probably want to redecorate at once." He looked back where she hovered in the doorway. His blue eyes were cold. "What was the point of that stunt you pulled the other night?"

Olivia said stiffly, "It wasn't a stunt."

"It was pretty fucking dramatic, whatever it was. And fucking childish. Em was absolutely frantic."

She stepped back into the tiny front hall, away from him. "I'm sorry about that. Really I am. I told her already. I didn't think about that."

"Your old man should have tanned your hide," he growled, unappeased. "I'd have done it for him if I'd caught you."

What if Nick had come looking for her? She shivered at the thought. She couldn't have endured seeing him or her mother that night, not after what she had heard. . . . "It was your fault, anyway. You told Mummy it would be better if I left."

If he was disconcerted to discover what she had overheard, he didn't show it. "You must have thought so too," he said evenly, "since you'd already asked your old man if you could move in."

She put her hand to her mouth and turned her face toward

the wall. It wasn't an answer but she had to say it. "I saw you put your hand on Mummy's . . ."

He could supply the four-letter word for himself.

Nick was not at all abashed. "Serves you right for watching. Anyway, you know bloody well what the arrangements are between Em and me. She wants a steady lay."

Olivia didn't think her mother would have put it like that, or be pleased to hear him put it like that. She imagined her mother introducing Nick to her friends, not as her boyfriend or lover or partner or cohabitee or whatever trendy/genteel phrase might seem to her most suitable, but as her steady lay. That was undoubtedly more honest, but it would never do.

It wouldn't do even for Olivia. She whispered to the wall, "I can't stand that."

"Then you're better off here. What I said was true. Why would it make you light out?"

"I thought you didn't . . ."

She couldn't finish that sentence: I thought you didn't want me anymore. But he seemed to know how it ended. He came close, put his hand on her arm.

"All right, kitten. It's all right."

She turned back to face him. He put his arms around her. She slid her arms around his neck. He kissed her. She wanted to cry because everything was better again and dreadful again.

He unbuttoned her blouse and unhooked her bra and started to stroke and kiss her bare breasts. She wanted that so much it frightened her. But she tried to push his hands away. "Nick, Daddy might come home. You'd better go."

He reached behind her to slide the bolt home across the front door. "Daddy can wait."

"No, no, really, Nick . . ."

He wasn't taking any notice of her, he was sliding the blouse and bra straps down her arms. By the time he had started to unzip her skirt she was in a blind panic.

"Don't, don't, he'll kill you if he comes home, I'll die if he comes home, please go away, Nick—"

He kissed her hard to stop her mouth. "Shut up," he said between kisses. "Your old man's still in Marlow. I'll go in a minute. Jesus, you're beautiful, baby. How in Christ's name could you think I didn't want you anymore?"

He had her naked by now. He was stroking her all over, but mostly her breasts and clitoris. It made her legs go weak when he touched her there. She didn't argue anymore.

She let him force her thighs apart with his own muscular thighs and push himself up into her there. She teetered on her toes because he was taller. In the end he picked her up with his hands under her bottom, and she wrapped her legs around his hips. He thrust himself into her hard, hard, right up to the hilt, to the groin, to the juncture of the thighs, before he came.

Only the door held them up. He leaned against her, pressing her back against the door while she clung to his hips and shoulders. He looked at her with the veiled, remote, unfathomable intensity of an alien race: the race of men and not of women.

He said thickly, "Your daddy should see you now."

That wasn't why he had done it, she knew that much, but it was why he had done it here in her father's house. The thought made her feel sick and shamed. She really would have died if her father had come and found her . . .

She unlocked her legs and wriggled out of his embrace. She started to pull on her clothing with hasty shaking hands. "Nick, you've got to go. Please go."

He had only to pull up and do up his jeans. She was still trying to button up her blouse and her fingers wouldn't work. He did up the buttons for her.

"Don't panic, it's all right."

"It's not all right. You were crazy to do that."

She was on the verge of tears. She couldn't stop shaking. It was disgusting, what she had just done, what she had just let him do. She rubbed her face with her hands and pushed her fingers into her hair, not knowing what else to do with herself.

Nick put his arms around her and pulled her against him tightly, so that her hands were confined against his chest, splayed over the white T-shirt. "Stop doing that. Listen to me, baby." He kissed her anywhere he could. "You know I want you, but you're better off here, at least for a while. You know you are."

She was still shaking, but at least her hands had been

stilled. She laid her head on his shoulder and whispered against his throat. "You're crazy. I hate you."

"Sure you do." He didn't sound offended. "Calm down, sweetheart, nothing's going to happen to you. It's all right now. I'll go away as soon as you stop shaking."

Olivia tried to calm herself. If she had been anywhere else but in her father's house she would have enjoyed being held like this, held by Nick. Any other time it would have made her feel secure rather than frightened. She breathed in the smell of him—cigarettes, perspiration, the earthy tang of engine oil. If her father were a dog he would have been able to tell that Nick had been here. Maybe he would have been able to tell what Nick had done while he was here. If dogs could tell all that, it was just as well they couldn't talk. No one would have any secrets left.

The idea amused her. The shaking went away. After a few minutes Nick went away too.

Olivia went upstairs and stripped and showered. She washed her hair and scrubbed herself all over as if to rid herself of any hint of a scent of Nick, and she put on clean clothes. The skirt and blouse and underwear she had worn to her mother's house went into the washing machine.

The train journey to Huddersfield took about three hours, including a change of trains at Wakefield. Olivia's father had seen her off at King's Cross with one suitcase, her violin, and a bag. In the bag was the personal CD player her father had eventually produced as a belated birthday present, along with three CDs, also part of his present. The *Scottish Fantasia* by Bruch and Vaughan Williams's fantasias were mouth-wateringly romantic stuff, if not quite Jimi Hendrix. The third

CD was Bach. She hadn't looked to see what it was, all Bach was the same dry stuff. She also had a fat fantasy trilogy and her grandfather's birthday present, the Brontë novels. She read *Jane Eyre* on the train because she knew her grandfather would ask.

Every summer she spent a fortnight with her Beckett grandparents. They lived in a little terraced house, even smaller than her father's house in Highgate, and not nearly so chic. The whole town was filled with rows and rows of these tiny grimy houses, going up- and downhill. There was a sitting room crammed with books and a kitchen far too small to eat in, a small front bedroom and an even smaller back bedroom, also full of books, and what must have been the tiniest bathroom in the world. It didn't even have a bathtub, only a shower.

Her father said that when he was young there wasn't any bathroom at all, or any hot water. Her uncle John used to sleep where the bathroom was now. If you wanted to pee you had to use the loo at the bottom of the garden, and if you wanted a bath you had to boil the kettle and fill up a portable tub. If anyone but her father had told her this Olivia would have suspected them of making it up, like the Monty Python sketch about the Yorkshiremen's reunion.

Her grandparents never came to London. Her grandmother said it was because they couldn't afford it, but her grandfather said he didn't like London. They didn't like Althea either. Her father had taken Althea up north once, soon after they moved in together, but the visit had not been a success and Althea had never been back. Maybe, thought Olivia, things would be different when Althea had the baby. Maybe her grandparents would be that glad of another grandchild. Maybe they would forget about her, since her mother wasn't married to her father anymore. . . .

She hugged and kissed both her grandparents when she got off the train. Her grandfather returned her embrace rather stiffly, as if he were faintly discomfited to find a young woman in his arms. "Have you grown again, Lia? I don't remember you quite so high."

"I'm no taller, Granddad. Maybe fatter."

"You haven't a spare ounce on you," scoffed her grandmother. "Only a wisp of a thing like your mother would dare to say fat to you." She was a few inches shorter than Olivia and her mother, but more substantially built. A good solid Yorkshirewoman, she would say of herself. A handsome woman, Olivia's mother had described her. Olivia didn't know how to judge the beauty of grandmothers; they were all too individual.

Her father always made sure she arrived on Saturday afternoon, so as not to spoil her grandfather's Sunday. Having worked as a carpenter all his life, he had "retired" to open a secondhand book shop, where he amused himself during the week. But on Sundays he was never at home.

In the absence of floods or blizzards he spent every Sunday after church walking on the moors. Her grandfather on the moors was like her father on a battlefield. He knew their geology and topography, their human history and animal life, their paths and plants and weather.

He knew the stars too. Every summer he took Olivia up on the moor of an evening and showed her all the stars, naming them as they grew out of the dusk, then naming their constellations as the stars became too many to count. He always picked a night when the stars were falling. Each shower of stars had its own collective name. Leonids, the people of the lion; Ursids, the people of the bear; primitive wandering tribes of heaven. They came too near the earth and were drawn to their doom, small ancient rocks that might otherwise have spent eternity roving peacefully round the sun.

The stars were not the same down in London, not even on the Heath or in her own little local park. All the profligate glory of stellar superabundance got swallowed up by street lamps.

The day after Olivia arrived they all got up and went to the early church service, as usual, and afterward her grandfather took her moor-walking.

Her grandmother never came. She had work to do, she said, without the old man underfoot. She always had work to do, Olivia had observed early on. She never sat down except to eat. She ironed while watching her favorite television programs, or did her mending while the news was on. Olivia didn't know anyone else who did any mending at all, except sewing on buttons or tacking up hems.

When they got home, near sunset, her grandmother had the dinner all but ready, knowing when to expect them. She gave them a cup of tea to keep them going till the meal was served, and asked casually, "How is Emma?"

"She's fine." Olivia hesitated, wondering how best to phrase it. "You know, don't you, that I'm living with Daddy now?"

"No, we didn't know that. How long have you been with Ross?"

"Since—well, more or less since they came back from Italy."

Now it was her grandmother's turn to search for diplomatic phrases. Being a Yorkshirewoman, she didn't quite succeed. "I wouldn't have thought Althea ... with her work and the baby on the way ... even cooking for three instead of two makes it more of a chore."

"Althea doesn't do her own cooking. She has two chefs to do it for her."

"Two chefs?"

"Daddy's little joke," Olivia explained. "Mr. Marks and Mr. Spencer."

"Buying from a fancy food shop like that must come very dear," her grandmother commented disapprovingly. "Doesn't Emma get lonely, living by herself in that big house?"

"She's not living by herself." Olivia decided to abandon circumlocution. Her mother was only doing what her father had done. Nick was no more immoral than Althea. Tell the truth and shame the Devil, as her grandmother herself might have said. "Officially he's some sort of lodger. But actually they ... they're going on holiday together next month."

Her grandmother digested this information and responded heroically, with robust optimism, "So you may have two lots of parents."

I'm more likely to end up with no parents, Olivia thought grimly. But she did not say so.

Her grandmother asked about Althea and the forthcoming baby and Nick and her mother, all in a matter-of-fact manner as if they were not discussing the doings in Sodom and Gomorrah. No doubt she had given up hoping to approve of the world by now and simply sought to understand some small part of it. Olivia was not much help there; she didn't understand it either.

When she had brushed her teeth and settled into bed, the same bed that her father used to sleep in when he was a boy, she realized that she had not thought about Nick since arriving, till her grandmother inadvertently brought up the subject.

Her happiness lasted seven days.

On the second Sunday, when she got out of bed, looking forward to another fine day out on the moor, she was suddenly attacked by a wave of nausea. She ran into the tiny bathroom. After a struggle to control her reflexes she threw up something vile-tasting from her empty stomach.

She came out feeling no better. Her grandmother was waiting for her. "Are you not well this morning?"

She shook her head and put her hand over her mouth. "Maybe you'd better go to church without me."

"It's early yet. You lie in for a while and I'll bring you a cup of tea."

Olivia got back into bed. She didn't feel any better but at least she was in no immediate danger of throwing up again. Her grandmother came back with the promised cup of tea and propped her up with pillows so that she could drink it.

"You've put sugar in it."

"I have. Hot, sweet tea is good for settling the stomach."

Olivia sipped at the tea. Her stomach seemed willing to tolerate it. When she had swallowed half the cup she gave it back to her grandmother and slid down under the covers.

"That's it, you rest yourself while we're at church. Andy won't go up the moor without you."

Olivia dozed off. When she heard her grandparents come back she tried again to get up. She still felt queasy, but nothing dramatic happened. She got dressed carefully and went downstairs.

"That's better now," said her grandmother. "I'll make you a bite of toast."

"Where's Granddad?"

"Weeding the garden. I told you he wouldn't go without you. You'll feel better for a bit of fresh air."

She did feel better once they were up among the heather. By the time they stopped for lunch she was ravenous.

Her grandfather was a dry, reserved man but he had his passions, and the moor brought them all out. There was nothing he did not know about the things that interested him, and he spoke of them to Olivia with such lively intensity that they interested her too, even matters like the maintenance of dry-stone walls. He said that was an art that was quickly learned, because if the stones didn't fit you had to re-lay them, and they were very heavy.

"Sally says you've been practicing your violin every day," he observed as they sat eating lunch.

"Daddy made me promise to." Olivia bit carefully into her sandwich. The bread was delicious, home-baked by her grandmother, but the old lady was apt to put dubious things like tongue or black pudding in the sandwiches. Whatever it was today, it tasted okay, so she swallowed it. "I hope you don't mind."

"Sally likes to hear you play. Are you going to be a musician?"

"I shouldn't think so. I get terrified when I have to play in public. I don't mind in the orchestra, where no one can hear me, but otherwise it's awful. And besides, you have to be really dedicated to it." She thought of Mrs. Stone, in love with music, having to earn her living by making heedless children learn things they didn't really want to know.

"What will you do then, when you're finished with school?"

"Go to university, I suppose."

"What will you read?" He carefully brushed the crumbs off his lap, not looking at her. "Your father always liked to come up here with me as a young boy—not like your uncle John, he was more concerned with games—and I hoped he might take it up for his studies when he went up to university. But he liked other things better, as it turned out." He looked around, a petty monarch surveying his small kingdom. "I've always thought it would be heaven to have someone pay you to consider the lilies of the field, how they grow. Does that interest you?"

Olivia felt a prickle at the back of her neck. She had already, barely fifteen, disappointed the hopes of her parents. Her father had wanted her to be a musician. After his last conversation with Mrs. Stone he had probably given up on that. Her mother had wanted her to be a dancer or an actress or even something more mundane like a textile designer, all of which were nonstarters. Now her grandfather was hankering for her to study natural sciences.

He raised his head to look at her with his bright blue eyes. "Maybe you'd rather be a historian like Ross."

"I like lots of things," she said gently. "I don't know yet if I like one thing more than another."

"It's early days for you," he agreed, not offended. "Nowadays a girl like you could turn her hand to anything. Not like in my day, before the war." He spoke slowly, remembering. "It was another world. Those really were the bad old days. We lived over in Barnsley. All the boys went down the pit."

"The pit?" In the Bible it talked about going down into the pit, meaning hell.

"The mine, coal mine. They're shutting them down now and I say good riddance. There was a song about a mining disaster—two miles of earth for a marking stone. You could say that of the living as much as the dead. Living all day in the dark, in the bowels of the earth, that's not living. More like being in the belly of the whale. The dust eats out your lungs, you end up black inside and out. And the scars on your face. Like the mark of Cain."

She looked at her grandfather. He had an odd, rather alarming look on his face, maybe like a man recalling his own death. To soothe him she said, "I don't think it's so much like that now."

"They haven't taken the sun underground, have they? And cutting coal still makes dust." He cleared his throat. "I won a scholarship to the grammar school. My mother didn't want me to go, she said we couldn't afford the uniform and all, but my father said he'd work extra to pay for it. He was working overtime when he died."

Olivia swallowed the last of her mysterious sandwich. "How old were you?"

"Fourteen. Old enough to go out to work in those days."

Old enough to leave home, like Nick. Old enough to commit adultery, as she had discovered. Going to work sounded like a happy alternative, even if it meant going down into the pit. "Did you go to work in the mine?"

"I had to, my mother said I had to. There were five children younger than me, and we had to eat somehow. And that's all the work there was, as far as my mother knew. The world was a colliery to her. Mining villages in those days, they were like a besieged town, no way out. That's the worst thing, the prison in the mind. That's the sin against the Holy Spirit that shall never be forgiven."

"How did you escape?"

"I didn't jump, I'm sorry to say, I had to be pushed. I walked out one midsummer morning, just like in the old songs, and I was struck with a dread of going underground." He smiled unexpectedly. "It must have been a powerful fear, to overcome my terror of my mother or of going hungry. But I couldn't go down the pit that day. I went for a long wander."

"Then what happened?"

"They sacked me for being AWOL. The greatest day of my life. I never looked back."

Olivia was reminded of Nick again, at the same age, freeing himself of inherited unhappiness. Her grandfather was a generation older than Nick, who was himself old enough to be her father. Things didn't seem to have progressed much in all that time. Nowadays your parents didn't die on you or send you down the pit, and at least in polite society they didn't beat you. But nowadays instead of the children leaving home the parents did.

Her grandfather's voice sounded a long way off, much more distant than the curlews crying in the air above them or the wheatears making a monotonous fuss on the stone wall at their back. "You keep on with your studies, Lia. The best freedom in life is to be able to earn your living in a way that suits your fancy."

* * *

Next morning as soon as she sat up in bed the nausea came over her again. This time she lay back down and fought off the urge to vomit. She knew that as soon as she tried to get up again it would come back. Funny sort of illness, coming and going like this. Yesterday it had lasted only a couple of hours. She hoped it would be the same thing this morning, going away eventually. What kind of flu—?

The thought that came into her head nearly made her vomit anyway. It couldn't be, there hadn't been time enough, it couldn't happen to her, dear God, it couldn't be . . .

She tried to calculate when her period was due. She couldn't remember when the last one had been. Come to think of it, it must have been a while. Her mother had told her she should keep track, but she always forgot to mark it down on the calendar in her diary, and anyway she was so irregular—anywhere from three to five weeks—that there didn't seem much point.

She thought back carefully now. The last time she could remember was the Whitsun holiday, because Megan's family had invited her to go to Broadstairs for the day, and she had made the excuse of the sea being cold to just go splashing in her shorts, rather than mess about with tampons, which she hated. The next time should have been just about the time she went to live with her father. She would have remembered that one if it had happened. But it hadn't.

She tried to reckon on her fingers. That made it eight weeks. Two months. She must have fallen the very first time.

Christ, Christ, she was going to be sick. She grabbed a handful of tissues and held them against her mouth, leaning over the side of the bed. There wasn't much to come up, just a mouthful of bile. She wadded up the damp tissues and buried them at the bottom of the wastebasket.

Now she couldn't remember if her mother had said they were going to Crete next week or the week after. Would they be gone when she got back to London? That would make it eleven weeks before she could see Nick. After twelve weeks they had to do something gruesome with saline injections and it hurt a lot more, she remembered reading.

After twelve weeks it was much more like a baby.

She was nearly sick again. It actually came up in the back

of her throat, scalding like hot acid. How could this be happening to her?

She thought of her grandfather, sent down the coal mine at fourteen. The bad old days, he had said. They weren't over yet. Biology is destiny, who said that? When Megan's cat Mog had still been a playful kitten it came into heat, and two months later produced kittens of its own. She felt like that little cat, trapped into serving blind forces of nature, not a woman but a womb, not an individual but a cluster of imperialistic genes.

She heard her grandmother coming upstairs. She pretended to be asleep. Aside from the nausea, she needed time to get herself together. She had to go downstairs and pretend that none of this was happening: she didn't feel sick, she wasn't pregnant.

She couldn't do anything untoward. She couldn't go back to London early. She couldn't even ring her mother to find out when they were leaving. With the best luck, she would have to wait a whole week, playing a pretense of normality to her grandparents, before she could talk to Nick. With the worst luck she would have to keep her awful secret for three agonizing weeks.

After a while she risked getting out of bed. Everything stayed where it was inside her. She took off her nightgown and looked at her body in the mirror on the little dresser. Her stomach was as flat as it usually was in the morning. She wondered when you started to show.

She felt her breasts. Were they bigger? They got big quite early on, she thought. Megan would know, but she couldn't ask Megan. It was impossible to tell by looking, because hers were already so full. It was obscene and absurd. Her breasts were like that for reasons that had nothing whatsoever to do with her personally, with her immortal soul or her emotions or anything individual to do with her. Even having an ugly face was an individual thing, it was your own face however unpleasing. But she had these large, inconvenient mammary glands sprouting from her chest so that men like Nick would want to impregnate her. Just her DNA propositioning his.

Well, from nature's point of view it had certainly worked.

She went downstairs eventually and apologized to her grandmother for sleeping so late.

"It's the fresh air," said her grandmother indulgently. "All that walking with Andy yesterday caught up with you overnight."

It was the sort of thing one might have said to a young child. Of course, her grandmother saw her as a child. She had been a child up till now.

Now the child was the one inside her.

What would her grandparents do if they knew? They had disapproved of her parents' divorce and her father's remarriage. If they knew what she had done, what she was . . .

Maybe it wasn't true that they would love her in spite of everything.

At least she knew her way this time. There was no dodging through trackless council estates; she followed the right route directly to the right door at the warehouse. She rang the third-floor bell and waited.

Nick hadn't gone to Crete yet; she knew that because she had phoned her mother as soon as she got back from Huddersfield. They weren't flying out till Saturday morning. Olivia tried to ring him this morning after she knew her mother would have left the house, but there was no answer.

He might not have been there, or he might have been asleep. She had reason to remember how solidly he slept. It might have been waking him up that had got her where she was now.

He wasn't answering his doorbell either. She leaned on it for at least a minute. She banged on the door and rattled the locked handle. Finally she hunkered down on the doorstep to wait.

Had he just gone out for a minute or was he out for the day? Would he be here at all today? He might have had an out-of-town shoot. Maybe he was away for the whole week; she hadn't dared to ask her mother.

Please, God, let him come, she begged. I can't waste a day; he'll be gone by Saturday. Would even that be enough time? she wondered. She had no idea how these things worked. Two doctors, you needed two doctors. Did you need your parents' consent? If you did, she was sunk. She thought she was going to throw up right there on the doorstep.

It started to rain. The air was very close, and the raindrops were large and warm, but she was getting wet. She huddled back against the door. It didn't help much. A man drove up in a van and got out. He came up to the door. She stood aside while he unlocked it. One of the other bells, she supposed.

He held the door open to let her go in. But there was no point; she couldn't get into the studio if Nick wasn't there, and she didn't want to be alone in the stairwell. Especially not with this man. He looked her up and down and asked her if she wanted to come inside for a cup of tea. She shook her head, perhaps more emphatically than necessary.

"Stood you up, has he, darling? I'd give him the push if I were you."

And so would I, Olivia thought, if I were myself. But I seem to be somebody else these days.

It was pointless, and maybe even dangerous, to sit on the doorstep all day. She decided to go and find somewhere to have a cup of tea, then come back later.

By the time she found a café she was quite wet. Her shirt was sticking to her in an embarrassing manner. She ordered tea and sat with her arms folded across her front. The place reeked of stale coffee and frying fat, sickening smells. She put sugar in the tea, the way her grandmother had done, and made herself sip it slowly. It was terrible tea, coarse and stewed. She had to swallow hard to keep it down.

When the rain stopped she went back to the studio. This time the XJS was there. She could have fallen down on her knees and kissed it. Instead she rang the doorbell.

When no one came she rang again. She kept her finger on the bell till she heard footsteps on the stairs.

Nick flung open the door, obviously irritated by the insistent ringing. "What the fuck," he said, and saw her and stopped.

She must have made a pathetic sight, she realized, damp with rain and sick with fear and sorry with tears unshed. A lost puppy, not a glamorous lover. Pathetic was the true word.

"Nick?" She stammered over the N. "Can I come up?" He looked at her with impassive blue eyes and she felt obliged to apologize for her presence. "I'm sorry to turn up like this. If you're busy . . . I didn't mean . . ."

She trailed off. He straightened his arm, pushing the door wide open. "Get inside, Lia, for Christ's sake. What the hell have you been doing wandering round in the rain?"

She ducked under his arm, into the shelter of the stairwell. "You weren't here when I came. I waited for ages, but it started to rain and one of your neighbors came along and he tried to chat me up, so I got scared and left."

"Why don't I kill him for you?" He gave her something between a pat and a slap on her bottom to send her up the stairs.

When she opened the studio door she got a shock. Someone else was there.

She stared at the tall woman in a caftan coming out from behind the screens. The woman was cool and self-possessed, bored even. Her features were large and perfect, like an ancient goddess. Her skin was the color of clover honey, her eyes like the sky between the stars. She gave Olivia a quick, assessing glance.

Nick had come in behind Olivia. He must have seen that glance too. His self-possession was equal to anyone's. "My stepdaughter," he lied coolly, to Olivia's amazement and embarrassment. "Lia, this is Jamaica. She's just going."

"If you say so," Jamaica agreed.

"I'll call you when I need you back again."

"Yes, boss," she said sardonically. She was looking carefully at Olivia now.

Whatever she was looking for, Olivia thought, she was

going to be disappointed. Or pleased, depending on the motive behind the look. This woman was clearly a professional model. Olivia at the moment was a drowned rat. No, she was too cowed and timid to be so much as a rat. A drowned mouse.

Jamaica finished her scrutiny and went behind the screens to collect her belongings.

Nick said to Olivia, "You want some coffee?"

The thought of coffee sickened her. "Tea, please."

"Tea, sure."

He went back to put the kettle on. Olivia didn't think anything of that until Jamaica reemerged in jeans, carrying a flight bag. Had she changed her clothes while Nick was back there? Maybe that only meant pulling on a pair of jeans under the caftan. Or maybe it didn't.

Jamaica said, " 'Bye, sweetie," as she disappeared down the stairs.

Olivia waited for the door at the bottom of the stairs to slam before she said, "Are you sweetie, or am I?"

"Must be you." Nick came out carrying two mugs of tea. "She's never called me sweetie before."

Olivia took her mug. It was hot. "She's never called me sweetie before either."

"It just means you're a little girl and she's a big girl."

"I'm not a little girl," Olivia said bitterly. If she were, she wouldn't be in her present predicament. Though she might have been in a worse one. She cradled her tea, painfully hot, staring down into the muddy liquid. It was not sufficient distraction or protection. She walked away from him, still nursing the tea. "Nick, I . . ."

All her prepared speeches had vanished. All courage, all wit, all outrage. She had never really felt any of those things. She had never really been anything but scared and despairing and mortally ashamed.

"What's the trouble, kitten?"

"I'm going to have a baby," she blurted out.

He didn't say anything just for a moment. Then he said, "What d' you mean?"

He sounded faintly breathless. Distinctly harsh. She was more terrified than ever. "You know what I mean. I've missed my second period." She stumbled over that. Having to speak of such intimate female things to a man was as embarrassing as anything else that had happened in the past two months. "I did one of those tests and it came out pink. I was throwing up last week at my grandparents' house."

"Jesus fucking Christ." He came up behind her, and she could feel his fury. "You stupid little slag, you mean you never did anything to stop it?"

She held the mug tightly. It was scalding her hands. It felt good; it distracted her from the horrible ache inside her. "Do what? How could I stop you?"

"You know what I mean." He pulled her round to face him. Hot tea slopped over onto her hands and she hardly noticed. "Haven't you heard of the fucking pill?"

She should have said something like, Haven't you heard of condoms? Or maybe, more to the point, I wasn't expecting to make a habit of it. The gorgeous Amazon who had just gone out might have been capable of those replies. Olivia was beyond anything but stammered apologies and tears. She managed to bite them both back, and nearly threw up in consequence.

"Can I sit down? I don't feel very good."

He looked at her, radiating anger and impatience, but all he said was, "All right, come back here and sit down."

She went with him behind the screen, clutching her tea, and sat down on the sofa at the back. He didn't sit down.

"It must have happened the first time we ... I mean, I should have had a period at the end of June. I didn't notice because of all the fuss about—you know—going to live with Daddy."

"You're sure about this?"

"I told you. I did a test. Twice, two different brands, two days running, just in case it was a mistake. I had to do it in a public lavatory so my grandmother wouldn't know." She shuddered. "I felt like a pervert. And I had to lie in every morning till I didn't feel too sick to get up. They were so nice to me. It was dreadful. If they'd known, they wouldn't ..."

Wouldn't have wanted her there, was her unfinished thought. What she had done was infinitely worse than her father's going to live with Althea. It would never occur to her grandparents that she was even capable of anything so wicked. She felt as if she had already cut herself off from them forever.

"Yeah, well, let's just arrange things so there's nothing for them to know," Nick said briskly. "You need a doctor."

"Two doctors." She had checked that point in the public library.

"If you get the right kind they come in a job lot."

He was already flipping through the telephone directory with the air of a man who knew exactly what he was looking for. That surprised Olivia. Maybe he had paid more attention than she ever did to those ads on the Tube that started PREGNANT? Or maybe . . . She had to have a second go at getting this thought out into the open. Maybe he had done this before.

She should have been thankful, not jealous. It meant that he would know what to do. But she felt wounded by the idea. And she wasn't going to ask.

She sipped tea to console herself. She watched Nick scribble an address from the phone book onto the back of an envelope. He dropped the book on the floor and tucked the envelope into his shirt pocket.

"All right, listen. Are you listening?" He sat down beside her on the sofa, turned to face her, his arm along the back. "You have to do exactly what I tell you or you're up shit creek. Do you understand?"

She shut her eyes and nodded carefully.

"The most important thing is, you have to say you were sixteen last birthday. Make your date of birth a year earlier and work out where you'll be in school a year from now. You'll be going into the sixth form, won't you?"

This time she managed a whispered assent.

"All right, get that into your head and keep it there. Now you're going home to change your clothes. Put on—let me see—that navy blue dress with the short sleeves and the white buttons, and do your hair up. Then come back here. Have you got that?"

Olivia was so surprised by his familiarity with her wardrobe that she failed to answer. If her father had been asked to describe any dress, any one at all, that she had ever worn, he would have failed completely, she was sure. But Nick looked at women's clothing all day through the lens of his camera, didn't he? That probably made him more aware of what she was wearing.

"Lia, did you hear me?" He took her face in his hand and turned her head around to make her look at him. "What did I tell you to do?"

"Wear the navy dress. Put my hair up."

"All right, what else?"

"I'm sixteen."

"Good girl."

He moved his hand up the line of her jaw, caressed her cheek with the broad ball of his thumb. She closed her eyes and felt tears squeeze out from under the lids.

"It's all right, kitten, everything will be all right. We'll get it sorted out before I go away."

"I'm so scared," she whispered. "What if they tell Mummy or Daddy?"

"They won't do that if you don't want them to. That's why you have to say you're sixteen. And you have to look sixteen."

"Won't they check on my age?"

"They're not allowed to." He took the mug of tea out of her hand and set it down on the floor. "Here, come 'ere."

He pulled her onto his lap and kissed her, pushing his tongue into her mouth and sliding his hand inside her shirt to stroke her breast. She put her arms around his neck. The act that had seemed unspeakably wicked and shameful five minutes before began to be the most desirable thing in the world.

"Jesus, I can't screw you now." His voice had gone hoarse. The sound made her shiver. "Some sympathetic quack is going to be peering up your cunt in a couple of hours, and it might put him off if you've just been stuffed."

It was absurd that after all the things he had done to her he could still make her blush by the way he talked. Also she hadn't realized—but of course he was right—that the doctor would want to examine her, even if only to make sure she really was pregnant. And the idea of the doctor knowing that

Nick had just been making love to her ... She was ashamed and afraid all over again.

He took her hand and rubbed her palm against the front of his jeans so that she could feel his erection. The action shocked and aroused her. He said in that husky voice, "What about a hand job?"

She understood in theory what he wanted. She and Megan had discussed it once. Megan said that men liked to be masturbated. It was one of the less disgusting things that gay men did to each other. Also, Megan said you could do it with your mouth. That had sounded pretty off-putting at the time. Now, as she fumbled to unfasten Nick's jeans, knowing what she was about to be confronted with, it seemed quite terrifying as well.

She touched his penis with a tentative hand. The skin was surprisingly silky. She ran her fingertips all the way down, from the tip to the root. It was like a live thing under her touch; it seemed to move and swell and preen itself against her hand.

"More of that," Nick said thickly. He pushed her down off his lap so that she was kneeling between his legs.

She stroked him again and felt him respond. She began to forget her shyness in the pleasure of giving him pleasure. She used both hands. He pushed up against her. She stroked him in his own rhythm. But somehow, even though she was making love to him, he was still in charge. She was an acolyte serving the god, very aware of the strength in his body and the strength of his sexual demand.

"Use your mouth," he whispered.

This was no time to say no. Besides, so far it had been exciting, even exhilarating. Maybe the next bit wouldn't be as unpleasant as she had thought.

She bent forward and touched the satin skin with the tip of her tongue, and felt his immediate response. It was magic. She touched him here and he seemed to feel it everywhere. She held his penis in both her hands and licked the broad, smooth tip as if it were an ice cream cone.

He groaned. It was easy enough to tell when she was doing something right.

He tangled his hands in her hair and drew her head down.

She tried to pull back, but he wouldn't let her up. It wasn't deliberate; he was too close to coming to care about anything but reaching that goal. He told her what he wanted and he made her do it. She had to take him into her mouth.

She could only move as he let her move, because he was holding her head. Even that wasn't so bad, only tiring at the hinges of her jaw. But at the end he pushed in so far she thought she would gag or choke, and her mouth was flooded with salty, slimy fluid. Since she couldn't pull away she had to swallow it.

As soon as he let her go she retched. She clapped her hands over her mouth. "I'm going to be sick." She added hastily, telling the truth and speaking a lie, "It's the baby, it makes me feel sick."

"Go and be sick in the fucking sink," he gasped.

She managed to make it to the sink in time, probably out of sheer embarrassment at the prospect of throwing up on the floor. Afterward she couldn't decide which tasted worse, the sick or the semen. She rinsed her mouth out over and over again to get rid of everything.

Nick came over. "Wash your face and you'll feel better," he told her.

She did, and she did. When she had dried herself he pulled her against him. She put her arms around his waist and her head on his shoulder, facing away from him. She was afraid he would be angry or insulted or disgusted, but his main reaction was amusement. He was laughing to himself; she could feel it shaking his body.

"What's so funny?"

"Nothing. Sorry, kitten, I didn't mean to do that to you. You'll never want to go down on me again, will you?"

She wouldn't, but she didn't like to say so.

"It's your fault." He had stopped laughing now. He pushed her hair aside and brushed her neck with his mouth as he spoke. "You're too goddamned sexy. I got carried away."

She almost forgave him.

24

It was the hardest thing she had ever done, going into the building by herself.

She had begged Nick to come in with her, just to come and sit in the waiting room with her.

"I can't. Jesus Christ, can't you get it through your head? It's a fucking crime, they can send me down for screwing you."

"It's not really a crime. I mean, no one really gets sent to prison for it, do they?"

"They fucking well do. Two years' porridge you can get for it. And your old man would do his damnedest to make sure I did the full stretch."

She couldn't argue with that. Her father might do something even worse, if he knew. The thought made her freeze up with terror again.

"Look, just go in and tell your story. Have you got it all straight in your head?"

"I think so."

"All right, stop worrying. They'll want to help you, not make trouble for you. No doctor with any sense is going to tell a sixteen-year-old kid she has to have that baby. If they ask you anything you don't want to answer, turn on the tears and they'll back off. Tell them everything that needs paying for will be paid. I'll wait right here for you. All right?"

"All right."

It was not all right at all, nothing was all right now. She didn't see how it would ever be all right again. Maybe she would just have to get used to that.

She had brought along a book to read, or to pretend to

read, since she kept finding herself at the same paragraph. She began to feel somewhat better when she noticed that some of the other women waiting looked very nervous.

The doctor was a woman, which made her feel better still. She was asked all sorts of matter-of-fact questions. She remembered to change her birthdate and to say that she was going back to school to begin A-level studies. There was a sticky moment when the doctor asked for her GP's name. Luckily, Olivia recalled that since she was now living with her father she must have a new GP, whose name she didn't know because she hadn't registered with him yet. She didn't even know who her former GP was, because the old one had retired, and she hadn't been back since then, about three years ago. She explained all this at length, until the doctor said she should go to the GP for a checkup a week after the abortion and then let them know the name and so forth so they could send their records.

Olivia lied and said yes, she would do that.

The hard part was explaining how she came to be there. She knew that if she told the truth the doctor would immediately agree to an abortion, but the truth was the one thing she couldn't tell, not even here where she was officially over the age of consent, just in case it got written down and by some horrible bungle came to the attention of either her mother or her father.

Instead she produced a story with elements of truth, about having been out with a boy for the first time and getting drunk and what with this and what with that ... She tried to imply some coercion, something less than rape but more than seduction—was that a definition of date rape? It was certainly a fair description of what Nick had done to her— anyway, she now found herself with child. The imaginary father of the very real baby didn't want to know her anymore, and she didn't want to know him, but he had offered to pay for the abortion. She needed it done quickly so that her parents and her school would never find out.

The doctor seemed to find this plausible enough. Olivia was relieved but not surprised to find that Nick had been right. He was usually right.

"So you haven't told your parents about this?"

Olivia shook her head emphatically. "I can't. Really I can't."

"Why not?"

She thought quickly and fastened on one true aspect of the situation. "It's so complicated I can't even explain properly." She did her best to explain nonetheless, how she had been living with her mother when the event occurred (true), how she had subsequently gone to live with her father because he thought her mother was neglecting her on account of having her boyfriend move in (also true), and how if her pregnancy became known it would cause unbearable ructions between her parents (absolutely and terrifyingly true). By the end of the explanation she was in genuine tears.

After getting over that hurdle, even the physical examination didn't bother her. She had never had a doctor do that to her before. Because it was a woman, she didn't feel as embarrassed as she had thought she would. But it felt very strange to be handled in such a clinical way where only Nick had ever touched her before, not clinically at all.

When she had got dressed again the doctor gave her a funny sort of look and asked her if she wanted to be put on the pill. "It might be best, if you're going to be involved in an active sexual relationship. Abortion is a rather messy and expensive alternative to birth control, you know."

Olivia took a moment to catch her meaning. The meaning was that she didn't believe Olivia's story about how she had got pregnant. Was there some way a doctor could tell how many times you had made love, something like the growth rings on a tree? It wasn't fair. Men's bodies didn't give away their sexual secrets like that.

She didn't know how to answer the doctor. She didn't even know if her sexual relationship was still active, if Nick would ever make love to her again after the abortion.

In the end the doctor insisted on writing out a prescription for Olivia to take away with her. "Just in case you need it," the doctor said. "You wouldn't want to find yourself back here again in a few months, would you?"

Olivia was too mortified to answer. She just took the prescription and buried it in her handbag.

*   *   *

When she came back to the place where she had left Nick, he was leaning against the car, smoking a cigarette. He seemed relieved to see her, which surprised and pleased her. He never seemed to have any nerves at all; she was gratified to find that he did.

"Everything go all right?"

"I suppose so. I've got to go to this place on Friday morning." She gave him the address of the clinic and told him how much they were going to want for it.

Either he already knew the going rate for an abortion or he'd been expecting an even bigger bill, because he only nodded and finished his cigarette. "Friday's a fucking bore. I'll have to back out of a job."

She said sarcastically, "Do you want me to go back and cancel it?"

"Don't be daft, I was just telling you how it is. Any day will do, to get it out of the way."

Olivia got into the car. She had begun to feel very odd. There was this baby inside her, not really a baby yet but it would be if she let it grow. It would be more than a baby; it would be a person just like everyone else who walked the earth. It didn't know that its birth would be a disaster for the two people who had made it. It would knock their lives all out of kilter. It might even send its father to prison. But that wasn't the baby's fault; it didn't know any of that. It was only aiming to be born, and then to be loved. Every baby's birthright, surely.

Instead of having its father talk about getting it out of the way.

And besides, it was Nick's baby. She hadn't really thought about that before. What would happen after she had the abortion, when she wasn't pregnant anymore? Was she just going to forget about him? How could she do that when he was living with her mother? The awful fact was that she was in love with him. And he hadn't shown any inclination to leave her alone. On the contrary.

It was true what she had thought before: nothing was going to be all right again, as far ahead as she could see.

Supposing she had been eighteen when she found herself

carrying his child. Why shouldn't he leave her mother and live with her instead?

Because he didn't love her, that was why. A man didn't cause a scandal of that proportion without being mightily motivated, and he wasn't. She was only a bit on the side, not even a steady lay.

What about the baby? Would he care at all about his child, if it was no longer evidence of a criminal act? She didn't know how he would think about that. He was unexpectedly kind and oddly protective when he was thinking of her as a young girl rather than a focus for his sexual desires. Maybe he would be a good father. Maybe he'd be glad, in the end, of the chance to be one.

All this went through her head while he drove her home. When he pulled off the Archway to let her out she plucked her courage up to say something.

"Nick, what if we didn't do this?"

"What d' you mean?"

She took a deep breath. "What if I just had the baby?"

He looked at her for a long time, impassively. "Why would you want to do that?"

Because it's yours, she thought but didn't say. "I don't know, really. I was just thinking—"

"Daydreaming, you mean," he growled. "Grow up, Lia. Who'd ask to be born to a fifteen-year-old mother? Give your kid a chance. Give yourself a chance."

"But it won't be the same baby, will it, when I have another one?"

She meant to sound dry and logical. Instead she found herself on the verge of tears. It wouldn't be the same, it wouldn't be his. Whoever she married, it wouldn't be him.

He looked at her again for a long time. Finally he reached over and brushed his knuckle across her cheekbone. It was a funny thing to do, an odd way to touch her. A man's way of hugging without really touching.

"I know, kitten." He said gently, "This one has to be the one that got away."

25

The sight of all the blood made her feel faint. In biology class she had calculated that her circulatory system must carry about four and a half liters of blood, and most of that seemed to have just come out of her. She sat down and bled into the toilet for a minute while her head and stomach recovered from the shock.

"Lia?" It was Nick on the other side of the door. "Are you all right?"

"No, I'm bleeding to death."

They had told her at the clinic that she would bleed for a few days, but she hadn't expected anything on quite this scale. She couldn't go home like this. She couldn't, now that she thought of it, go anywhere like this. The industrial-size sanitary napkin they had put on her was absolutely drenched and dripping with blood. She was stuck in the tiny loo below Nick's studio, and Nick was the only one who could rescue her. This was going to be suicidally embarrassing.

"Actually, I do have a problem," she confessed to the door. "I need some more—um—you know, the . . ."

She couldn't say the words. It didn't matter, as it happened; apparently he was telepathic. "You stay there and don't fall asleep. I'll be back in two minutes."

She didn't fall asleep; she was too mortified. She rinsed out her knickers with cold water in the little basin. You had to use cold water for bloodstains because blood was a protein, like egg white, for instance, and if you used hot water it would cook the stains right into the fabric. Her science lessons were really coming in handy today, though she didn't suppose it was quite the sort of situation her teacher had in mind when he tried to convince his class how useful a knowledge of science would be in daily life.

The knickers were going to be horribly uncomfortable when she put them back on, but that was better than leaving a puddle of blood wherever she sat down.

Nick returned with the um-you-knows and handed them to her round the door. What an amazing man, Olivia thought gratefully as she prepared to leave her little prison. She couldn't imagine her father having the cool to go into a chemist's shop and buy sanitary napkins. It was easier to imagine herself buying a packet of condoms. Not that that was in the realm of possibility either.

She emerged with some hope that she might survive after all. She was even beginning to feel faintly hungry.

Nick had made coffee, with milk and sugar. She drank that and felt better. He unearthed a packet of crisps and she ate that. She realized that she hadn't felt properly hungry since that terrible morning in Huddersfield.

She couldn't recall anything about the actual abortion. What she did remember was only a dream. She had dreamt that the place was full of women who had ended up there because the men in their lives didn't want the babies they were carrying. Some of the men appeared in the dream, fathers, lovers, husbands even, none of them wanting a woman with a baby. It was a crazy thing to dream about. But it kept coming back to her, the terrible sense of desolation and despair that the women had felt in the dream, no baby, no man, nobody.

In real life her only complaint had been that they wouldn't let her sleep. They had made her get up and get dressed and told her she had to go home now. She phoned Nick and he said he would come right away. She told the nurse someone was coming to collect her and then she fell asleep again.

The nurse woke her again and said her father was here to take her home.

If Olivia had been properly awake this news would have caused her heart to stop beating altogether. Then she saw Nick standing behind the nurse and understood the mistake the nurse had made.

Nick took her out to his car. He was talking to her but she

couldn't seem to make sense of what he was saying. "You're still doped up," he said at last. "You can't go home like that. I'll take you back to the studio and you can sleep it off."

Anything involving a chance to sleep sounded good to her. She slept in the car all the way to Wapping. He coaxed her up the stairs and sat her down on the sofa.

"You'd better have some coffee."

"Tea, please."

"Coffee, and bloody strong."

She fell asleep again while he was fixing it. He woke her up to make her drink it.

"How d' you feel?"

"My head's not working."

"I can tell. You get that coffee into you." After she had finished most of the cup he said, "I have to go out for a couple of hours. You can sleep till I get back."

She didn't like being left alone, but she was too dopey to argue. She gave him her mug and slid sideways down onto the sofa.

The dream came back to her. In her dream she cried.

"Lia, wake up. What's the matter?"

Nick was shaking her. She grabbed his hand with both of hers. "All those poor women. All abandoned."

"What are you raving about?"

His impatience got through to her. "Nothing. I was just dreaming."

"You were crying." He was still staring at her. She was still clutching his hand. "You're all right, kid. I'm back now. Everything's all right. Sit up and I'll make you more coffee."

It was then, when she sat up, that she felt an ominous rush of warmth and wetness between her thighs. Blood, as she had discovered when she staggered downstairs to the loo.

Bleeding or not, Nick was now insisting that she had to go home. "I've got to get going, kitten. We're supposed to be flying out at an ungodly hour tomorrow, and I still have to pack."

"I wish you weren't going." She wished she hadn't said that. She covered it up by adding, "What if something goes wrong? I could get infected or start to hemorrhage or—"

"None of that's going to happen." He sat down and put

his arm around her shoulder. "If it did you'd just have to go back to the doctor you saw on Tuesday. But it won't happen."

Olivia put her hand on his chest and leaned against him. She didn't want to go anywhere, she wanted to stay just like that. "Nick, you've done this before, haven't you?"

"Done what?"

"You know. The abortion thing." When he didn't answer she said, "Was it your wife?"

He glanced at her in a sideways, speculative manner as if there were something he might have said. But he looked away again without speaking.

She wondered what was in his head. In profile he looked impassive, as always. And beautiful, as always. "Why didn't you want the baby? If you were married, I mean?"

"She didn't want it."

"Why not?"

"I can't remember now. Some shit about her career and not being ready for motherhood."

"What kind of career does she have?" Nothing involving swaps, obviously, if a baby was likely to interfere with it.

"She used to be a model. Now she calls herself an actress."

"Is she famous at all?"

That amused him. "If she was, you'd have read all about it in the papers. What a rat I was, how terrific her new bloke is, all that sort of shit. She goes along with the view that there's no such thing as bad publicity, just make sure you spell my name right."

"Has she got a new bloke?"

"At least one. Why else would she want a divorce right away? Aside from wanting it put down on paper that it's all my fucking fault, of course. And she can screw me for free because her old man is a lawyer."

People got married, Olivia recalled, because the woman was going to have a baby. Now it seemed they got divorced because one or the other had found someone else. That was true of her parents anyway. Maybe it was true of everybody. It didn't sound as if adults made any decisions at all; they just got swept along on the tide of events. Maybe she was as grown-up now as she was ever going to be. That was a profoundly depressing idea.

She didn't want to talk about Nick's wife anymore. She didn't want to think about anything, because she couldn't think of anything that wouldn't make her feel awful. She wanted to stay there forever with Nick's arm around her.

"Lia, we've really got to go."

"In a minute. Give me five minutes."

"No minutes. You'll be falling asleep on me again."

She had to yield and let him take her home. This time he drove up Swains Lane and stopped between the high walls, the cemetery on the left and Waterlow Park on the right, where there were no houses or passersby. She had only a short way to walk from there.

She had gone out that morning with a baby inside her, something that belonged to him and joined him to her. Now she came home with nothing, no baby, no him, no hope of anything to come. She felt . . . orphaned. That was crazy, because it meant the exact opposite of what had happened, but it also described exactly how she felt.

"I'll see you in a few weeks," he said.

That should have made her feel better, but in fact it made her stomach churn. Did he mean when she came over to see her mother, or . . . She wasn't going to ask. Right now the idea of going to bed with him disgusted her, but that was probably partly because of the blood. No doubt by the time she saw him again she would have changed her mind again.

Not that it mattered at all, what she wanted.

26

It was a good thing she was living with her father and Al-thea. She could come home and say she had a headache and go off to bed without their taking any real notice. Althea didn't care, and her father paid no attention to things like other people's headaches, no more than he paid attention to other people's clothes. He could have described to the last detail what a Roundhead soldier might have been wearing at the battle of Edgehill, but the latest fashions that people were wearing on the street outside his front door, or even inside his own home, went right over his head.

As for Althea, she hadn't got the idea of mothering yet. She would have a crash course come December, but even then it wouldn't apply to Olivia.

Althea had developed a substantial bulge by now. She claimed she could feel it kicking. Olivia was surprised what a revolting idea that was, babies kicking inside you. For a week whenever she looked at Althea's belly all she could think of was blood.

Mrs. Stone had given her the Bach partita to struggle with over the holidays. "Come back and tell me you're enjoying it," she had said. The partita had the advantage of being unaccompanied, so she didn't have to imagine Mrs. Stone's piano continuo filling in the bits between. What she played was all there was. Bach at his driest.

She practiced her partita faithfully, more than faithfully. It was beautifully neutral and required her strict attention. It didn't remind her of babies or Nick or where she was going to be living come September.

Her father thought he was being helpful when he dug out

a tape of Oskar Shumsky playing this same partita. It was useful in a way; it told her how she ought to sound. It also told her how she didn't sound. But she had nothing else to do, so she went on trying and feeling frustrated. She listened to Shumsky to remind herself what she was aiming for, even to imitate his phrasing. She found herself humming the music. Usually Bach was an unsatisfactory composer to hum along with; you got through the first theme all right, then the second round started in and you couldn't manage both of them at once. The partita didn't have that problem, though you still couldn't call it a nice, simple tune.

Her mother sent her a postcard. It didn't say, Having a wonderful time, wish you were here; it just said, Having a wonderful time. Olivia tore it up and flushed it down the toilet. She couldn't stand to think of her mother with Nick.

She also couldn't stand overhearing her father and Althea. She was lying awake in the darkness when she heard Althea giggle. Their bed was next to hers on the other side of the wall. She heard the bed creak and one of them shushing the other. It must have been her father, because she heard him say You forgot to shut the door. Althea said Leave it, she's asleep, and she giggled again. After a minute the bed squeaked again and went on squeaking in a rhythm that Olivia remembered. The rest of it was familiar too, the panting and the sounds like somebody dying quietly. Other people's sex lives were disgusting.

So was her own, for that matter.

She asked Megan how people made love when the woman was pregnant, so as not to squash the baby. Megan said from the back, probably.

"What, like gay men?" That was even more disgusting, thinking of her father and Althea.

"No, not buggery. Just doing it from the back."

Olivia considered the mechanics of this proposal. "How does that work?"

"I think you have to get down on all fours."

"Like dogs." This idea was hardly less repellent than the other. Then she thought of Nick doing that to her, and the wave of craving that came over her made her feel quite ill.

"How do you know all these things?" she demanded. Here

was Megan a virgin, and she, Olivia, a jaded voluptuary by comparison, yet Megan was still the fount of knowledge. And not just because Olivia couldn't let on she knew what she knew.

"I ask my mother."

"And she tells you?" Even if Olivia had ever worked up the nerve to ask her mother about anything remotely bearing upon sexual activity, her mother would have wiggled out of answering.

"Well, yeah, she does. But I have to ask her, she never volunteers."

Megan's mother was rather short and quite plump. She didn't look at all like a repository of arcane sexual experience. In fact, Olivia found it impossible to imagine her engaging in any sexual activity whatsoever, though she allowed that this might have been just youthful prejudice against the middle-aged. Still, she looked at Megan's mother with more respect after that.

They were not supposed to be discussing sex just then; they were supposed to be deciding what to do with *Medea*. Olivia's father had made two photocopies of three translations of the play. One was an old-fashioned poetic version full of thees and thous. Another was in more modern verse, i.e., unrhymed and unmetered, and the third was in the most prosaic prose imaginable.

"It should be easy to improve on this lot," Megan announced confidently. "I think we should turn it into a musical."

"It's supposed to be a tragedy, Meg. You can't have a tragic musical."

"Yes, you can. They're called operas."

"Ha-ha. Well, we're certainly not going to write an opera."

"What I meant was, all these bits where the Chorus comes in could be turned into songs. Something really corny and country-and-westernish. And everybody but Medea should speak in clichés, to show that she's the only independent soul. They're all really talking in clichés anyway. Look here." Megan pointed to various speeches, translating them into banality: "Still waters run deep; this is going to hurt me more than it hurts you; all she needs is a good screw . . ."

Olivia was profoundly impressed. "Meg, that's an awesome idea, it really is."

"I know."

"Ms. P. will love it."

"Well, she can't love it if we haven't written it. I'll get to work on the dialogue and you can turn the choruses into something suitable for Tammy Wynette, okay?"

Olivia said okay.

But it wasn't as easy as all that, she discovered when she got right down to it. The trouble was not the invention (or theft) of suitably tragic country-and-western lyrics but the fact that the play was about a woman abandoned by her man, driven to kill her children. It made Olivia think of the dream she had had about abandoned women and aborted children.

It made her think about what she had done to Nick's baby.

Ms. Pankhurst would have been ashamed of her, because it made her cry.

Her mother came back from holidaying in Crete. She invited Olivia over for lunch on the following Sunday, the last weekend before school started again. Her father said he would drive her over there, and her mother said Nick would drive her back. That way neither of them had to knock on the other one's door.

Her mother kissed her when she came in. Olivia supposed that was all right, since they had both been off on holiday. Now that she thought about it, she hadn't seen her mother all summer. She had lived with her mother for fifteen years and seen her every day without fail, except when she went to visit her grandparents, and now all of a sudden she hadn't seen her for seven weeks.

And now when her mother saw her, she kissed her on the cheek. More like a grandmother than a mother. Like she didn't have a mother anymore.

"You look terrific," Olivia said sincerely, swallowing down the sudden ache in her throat. Her mother did look terrific: her hair was almost platinum, her skin glowing golden, and she seemed relaxed, without inner tensions, in a way that Olivia couldn't remember ever seeing her before. She was absolutely beautiful, better than a film star, more real. Olivia felt obliged to add, "Did you have a good time?"

"We had a wonderful time. It was the best holiday I've ever had. We did the ruins and toured the mountains and spent a lot of time on the beach, and everything was just perfect."

Olivia found it much easier to imagine Nick "doing ruins" than her father getting brown on a beach. Her mother was plainly happy. Nick had made her happy where her father had not. What luck for her mother.

She knew the sort of thing she ought to be saying, but she couldn't have said it without choking up. Small talk, it should have been: That's great, Nick must be good for you, I'm glad to hear it. But she wasn't; she hated them both.

She did manage to say something. "Where's Nick?"

"He just popped out to get some cigarettes. Come into the kitchen, you can set the table for us while I make the salad. We're having lasagna, you like that, don't you?"

Cigarettes were a small price to pay for happiness, Olivia supposed. She wished someone would put a price tag on happiness for her. She had already paid a baby and seemed to be no nearer.

In the kitchen her mother had more serious concerns. "You must be starting school again soon."

"Next week."

"Ross said he'd have you for the holidays. What's going to happen when school begins?"

Her mother tried to sound neutral, but her concern showed at the edges. She was afraid that Olivia would come home and merely by her presence change the balance of happiness between her mother and Nick.

No fear, Mummy, she thought, no way am I coming back here. This much at least had been sorted out with her father.

The thing that had really persuaded him was not the glass in her feet or even the policeman at his door but the two failed exams. He didn't trust her mother to see that she got through her GCSEs in proper style. Olivia knew that, because she had overheard an argument between her father and Althea. She had overheard it in the usual way, late at night when they were going to bed and thought she was already asleep. As if she was a little kid who dropped off just like that.

Althea said were they going to get lumbered with Lia forever just because Emma couldn't be bothered to look after her anymore.

Olivia's father said the trouble with Emma was that she had no common sense. She probably imagined that Lia was going to be like her and end up doing something arty, something where formal education and qualifications didn't matter.

Althea said if you asked her, Emma was pretty sharp. As soon as he had stopped handing over money for Lia, she moved her boyfriend in and started freezing Lia out. Now she had got exactly what she wanted—the house, the man, and freedom.

Her father said frostily, good luck to Emma if that was what she wanted. What he wanted was a good education for his daughter.

Althea said it had better be good, the amount he was paying for it, and did he ever think it might be a waste of money.

Her father said what did she mean.

Althea said maybe Lia had got Emma's brains instead of his.

Her father got really huffy and said Lia might have inherited Emma's lack of sense but there was nothing wrong with her brains.

Althea said what would they do when the baby arrived.

Her father said they would be moving, wouldn't they, and would she mind letting him get some sleep.

Althea said there was no call to be rude, she just couldn't help worrying about these things.

At that point Olivia had put her pillow over her head and her fingers in her ears.

"I'm going to stay on with Daddy," she told her mother. "They're putting the house up for sale and looking for a bigger place, but still in Highgate. That's what you said they'd do, isn't it?"

"Unless he wants a baby on his lap while he's working at home, it's what they have to do," her mother remarked acidly. "The baby doesn't quite fit, though. Ross isn't very big on babies. He never showed much interest in you before you learned to talk.''

Her mother had never said such things about her father before. Knowing her father, Olivia was sure they were perfectly true. It was just that her mother had never said them before (a) her father's marriage and the announcement of the baby, and (b) Nick. Since these events had happened at the same time, it was impossible to say whether her mother had given up hope of her father's ever coming home when he married Althea, or whether she had given up wanting him back when Nick moved in. There wasn't any way to ask, to settle the question. But it was interesting all the same that she herself had had to talk, to show a soul, before her father believed she was a person. She wondered if all men were the same about that.

The man she was particularly wondering about came home just then. Like her mother, his hair was lighter and his skin darker. She wondered exactly where he was dark. All over, from sunbathing in the nude? Did men get tanned in their private parts? Megan might know. She would have to ask. Or maybe she would find out soon for herself.

Lunch was terrible. The lasagna was probably delicious; it had smelled delicious in the oven, anyway. It was Nick and her mother who were unbearable. They were like newlyweds. At least her mother was; Nick was incapable of drooling over anybody, but he didn't do anything to stop her. He enjoyed being drooled over. He encouraged her. And he didn't really notice Olivia at all.

After lunch Olivia and her mother played Scrabble in the garden while Nick read the *Sunday Sport*, which he had brought home with the cigarettes. The *Martian News*, Olivia thought it should be called. Maybe that was why he read it. She couldn't make any sense of him at all, but if he were a Martian it would all be explained.

"Oh, Lia," said her mother, "I forgot to tell you. Some boy came round asking for you."

"Some boy?" She didn't know any boys.

"He came ages ago, while you were up in Yorkshire. He said his name was Charlie. I told him you'd be away for the rest of the summer. I didn't want to get into long explanations."

Olivia had to think for a minute to remember who Charlie was. Clare's brother's friend at the pub. He had been quite nice. She wouldn't mind if he wanted to take her out some time. "Well, if he comes back again give him Daddy's phone number."

"How do you know him?"

"I met him ages ago at . . ." She was just about to say "at the pub," but she bit her tongue in time. Her mother thought her experience of pubs was limited to Sunday lunch at St. Albans, and might well be dismayed to learn otherwise. "At Clare's," she finished. "He's a friend of her brother's."

"I noticed he was riding a motorbike. I hope you're not going out on motorbikes, they're dreadfully dangerous. People are always getting killed on them."

There were definite advantages to living with her father. "I've never been on a motorbike in my life," she assured her mother. "The only time I met him, he had his brother's car."

"How old is he?"

"I suppose he must be seventeen, if he was driving a car. Listen, Mummy, I hardly know this person, it's no good interrogating me about him. Give me a list of questions and I'll grill him if I see him. Or else you can ring up Clare's brother and interview him."

"I'm sorry," her mother said, getting annoyed. "I worry about you when I don't know what you're doing."

You'd worry even more if you knew, Olivia thought. She didn't look at Nick, not once.

Afterward they had tea and then Nick drove her back to Highgate. It had come over cloudy and close by now, like rain impending, so she was actually quite grateful for the ride. It wasn't as enjoyable as it might have been because the bad weather meant he had to leave the top up.

"Daddy's home today," she warned him in the car.

"Is that good or bad?"

She didn't know what to say. She had never been so terrified in her life as when he had made love to her against her father's front door. On the other hand . . . on the other hand, remembering it made her want him desperately.

It was her mother's fault. Plainly she was besotted with him because he had been fucking her frantically every day for a fortnight. That made Olivia want him to want her too.

She crossed her arms over her belly. There was something about that terrible desire that made her feel she was about to burst. But it was a gnawing, unendurable ache as well. She felt like the Spartan boy with the fox chewing at his vitals, except she didn't know exactly where her vitals were. She had always thought that meant the heart and lungs and liver, serious organs under the rib cage, but this pain and longing were much lower down.

"I don't know," she confessed.

He turned down the North Hill road to go round the one-way system, but instead of making a right turn he drove straight downhill and pulled over out of the traffic. They were in plain view in plain daylight. Nothing could happen here, Olivia thought. She felt some disappointment.

"Is everything all right? None of those disasters happened?"

"No. I'm okay. I guess."

"What's not okay?"

She knew what she wanted to say, but she didn't know how to say it. She couldn't say it. It was outside the realm of things that she was allowed to talk to him about.

She said it in a roundabout way. "Mummy looks wonderful."

"She does," he agreed dryly. "Isn't that okay?"

"Of course. It's good for her. She used to look so . . . brittle, Meg said."

"That's a good word for it. Meg was right."

She wanted to say *But what about me?* Her throat froze up.

"D' you want to come and see me sometime?"

He truly was telepathic. That was what she wanted more than anything on earth. "When?"

"Thursday's a good day. Make it Thursday week."

Nearly two weeks away. She licked her dry lips. "I have my music lesson on Thursday."

"That's only for an hour. Come afterward."

"What will I tell Daddy and Althea?"

"That's up to you. You're a big girl now."

He was making fun of her for being a child. She turned away and stared out the window, where great, fat raindrops had started to spatter on the glass. It was all lies. Her mother was happy and she was telling lies.

He said, "What have you done to make sure it doesn't happen again?"

"What—well, I—nothing." That was because she hadn't known if they were ever going to make love again. "Can't you, you know—what about condoms?"

"I don't go to bed with my boots on, baby. It's not me that was up the duff a month ago. Didn't that quack say anything about the pill?"

"I told her . . ." Olivia passed her hands over her face. "I told her it had only happened once."

"Why'd you say that?"

"So she wouldn't think . . ."

So she wouldn't think something awful. Olivia couldn't even think what the doctor might have thought. Words came into her head, the words that meant a girl who let men make love to her. Vile words that men used of women they had made love to. Only they didn't call it making love; they had another cesspool of vile words for what it was they did to women.

She started to shake. She thought she was going to cry but she didn't do that. All the sobbing stayed inside her and made her shake, the way she had felt Nick shake with laughter the last time. She couldn't stop shaking, but at least she didn't cry.

"Don't do that." He said it softly, leaning toward her. He put his arms around her. "Don't cry, sweetheart, you're all right."

"I'm not crying."

The huge summer raindrops were falling faster now, streaming down the windscreen as if the car had decided to take a shower. They made an alarming racket on the soft roof.

He kissed her mouth. He couldn't get perfectly close to her because the gearshift panel was in the way, but it didn't seem to matter. He put his hand up under her skirt and down inside her knickers. On Highgate Hill.

"Don't," she said, but it came out as a sigh, a kind of endearment. "Don't do that."

As she said it she was lifting up her bottom to let him take her knickers down. He stroked her genitals. In between kisses he told her what he would have liked to do to her if they had been somewhere else.

She heard him perfectly in spite of the rainstorm. Some of it was things he hadn't done to her yet, and the thought of them made her belly clench like a fist. She thought of what Megan had told her. Like dogs, she had said. Maybe he would do that next time.

His fingers were sliding in and out of her, and she was as wet as if he had already made love to her. They took her up the back way too, the gay way she had thought unbelievably disgusting and now found unbelievably exciting, that he should do that to her by the side of the road. Maybe she said things to him, she didn't know. She loved him. But she didn't say that.

Afterward he pulled her knickers back up for her. Somehow they had worked their way down to her ankles. It was unbearably shameful, but he didn't seem to know the meaning of shame, any more than he understood how revolting it ought to be to stick your finger up somebody's rectum. He didn't get revolted or embarrassed, not by anything.

"You shouldn't have done that."

"You don't mean that."

"Well, not here, anyway."

"Here or nowhere. Are you coming next Thursday?"

She turned her face toward him and kissed his mouth. It was the first time she had dared to kiss him properly, on her own initiative.

"You'd better go back and see that doctor, then."

She didn't tell him that she didn't need to. She already had the prescription in her handbag.

27

She told her father she was going shopping for Megan's birthday present after her music lesson. It was true that the next day was Megan's sixteenth birthday, but she already had the birthday present. She had found it in her grandfather's book shop in Huddersfield, a big book with lots of illustrations about all the appalling things that doctors had done throughout history to their unfortunate patients. The very first chapter talked about cavemen cutting holes in people's heads to cure madness, and the last chapter described neurosurgeons cutting holes in people's brains for the same purpose. If that didn't put Megan off medicine, nothing would.

She went to Mrs. Stone's house in Golders Green after school. For a while she almost forgot about Nick, she was so pleased to be able to play the Bach partita for her teacher. And Mrs. Stone was pleased in return.

"You haven't squandered your summer, I see. It's good to have something to show for your time. And have you enjoyed learning this composition? Do you enjoy playing it?"

Olivia considered. "I wouldn't say enjoy. It's more like cross-country running, mostly pain but sometimes—"

"Sometimes something wonderful," Mrs. Stone finished for her with a smile. "Some people would say that's a description of life, child. Either you struggle and learn, or you lose ground. You never get to stand still."

Olivia went away still pleased, in spite of Mrs. Stone's grim prognostications about life. To get home she had to take the Tube down to Camden Town and then back up to Highgate. She had to go home to get rid of her violin—she wouldn't plausibly have gone shopping with it—and while she was there she changed out of her uniform and put on a short skirt. She wanted to look sexy for Nick, and she was sure he had a fairly conventional view of what was sexy. Doc Martens, for instance, were right out. But she couldn't dress up too much or Althea might notice.

Then she went out again, back down to Highgate station, and went on to Wapping, getting more nervous with each stop and change of train.

She had never done this before. This was different. Every other time they had made love, it was at least on her part unintentional. She hadn't set out to do it. He had done it to her. But this time she had agreed to meet him for no other purpose than to make love. She had started on the pill, it was all premeditated. She had no innocence left with which to excuse herself.

She rang the bell. She could hardly hear it ringing because of the racket her blood was making, buzzing in her ears.

Nick came down. His tan hadn't quite faded yet. His hair was very pale on top, where the Cretan sun had got at it, and a darker shade of blond underneath where it had grown in since he got home. He was wearing jeans and a shirt of coarse white cotton, open at the neck. He looked breathtakingly beautiful.

He smiled when he saw her. "Hi, Lia. Come on in."

She went inside and he shut the door. He knew it was different this time too; he kissed her in the stairwell, before they had even gone upstairs. It was a pretty profound sort of kiss, stating his intentions unmistakably. After that she didn't think her legs would even carry her up the stairs.

She half expected him to take the clothes off her as soon as she had entered the studio. Instead he said, "You'll have to amuse yourself for a few minutes. I was in the middle of something when you arrived, and I can't stop halfway."

"Don't mind about me. I'll be okay."

That gave her some extra time to be extra nervous. He disappeared into the darkroom at the back. She mooched around, looking at things. She was curious about him. She was looking for things that would tell her something she didn't know about him. She didn't know a lot.

220

There was a small bookshelf against the back wall. The books were jammed in any old way, mostly on their backs, some open, some open upside down, which her father had taught her was a shameful abuse of books. That didn't surprise her; she already knew that Nick was untidy, to say the least. What did surprise her was the presence of books at all. They didn't go with the *Sun*.

When she examined them more closely the mystery was solved. Except for a few technical photographic manuals, they were books of pictures. Some of photographs, but also real art—paintings and drawings.

The art books interested her most. The names were unfamiliar to her—not in her father's bookshelf, that meant—and mostly German: Bellmer, Schiele, Beckmann, Grosz. The only name she recognized was Aubrey Beardsley.

There was another name that rang a bell, another German named Klimt, but she couldn't quite work out where she had come across it. The book was lying on the top shelf, buried under a heap of papers. She picked up the papers to move them and realized it was Nick's mail.

Some of it was months old, including apparently unpaid bills. One letter was some sort of legal document, something to do with divorce. Miranda Elizabeth Collinson Winter was the petitioner, Nicholas John Winter the respondent. Nicholas John Winter was being accused of unreasonable behavior. Olivia could imagine Nick behaving in all sorts of totally unreasonable ways, but she didn't know which of them could be called grounds for divorce. She noticed that Miranda Elizabeth Collinson Winter lived down in Kentish Town, not far from Highgate.

She opened the Klimt book and recognized him immediately by the gilt paint splashed liberally through the pictures. She found the very painting that was so familiar to her, the one called *Danaë*. She took the book off the shelf, meaning to tell Nick about it.

There was another surprise underneath the book, a stack of magazines. The one on top was German, the others in English. The German publication was glossy and fairly upmarket but, like the English ones beneath, with a cover featuring a nearly naked young woman in a provocative pose.

221

Out of curiosity she started leafing through. The text was in German, though apparently not the sort of German she had been learning at school, since she couldn't understand most of it. She wondered if Nick could read it. Most likely he wouldn't need to, as it wasn't a literary magazine. The photographs were in glossy full color, nothing freaky, just the usual breasts and bottoms and ... Nick would have called them cunts.

She was disappointed, but she knew she shouldn't have been. It went with all the rest, didn't it? She should have guessed that a man who read the *Sun* and the *News of the World* would have a collection of girlie magazines. They weren't old ones either; the German magazine was the September issue. She wondered if her mother knew.

She also wondered if he got an erection from looking at these pictures. The idea roused her jealousy. The women were all young and beautiful and very well built—too well built for the catwalk, if they had ever fancied being models of a more respectable sort. She imagined herself in some of the more explicit poses, and Nick looking at her. That was surprisingly exciting.

She got a much bigger and more unpleasant surprise when she flipped over to the next page. There was a very unpornographic photo of a girl sitting on a stool, fully dressed in a navy blazer and a prim navy skirt, looking into a mirror. The girl's back was to the camera, but her face appeared in the mirror. It was Olivia.

She sank down onto her knees on the floor. She turned the next page and it was no mistake, everything was there, the whole sequence of photographs he had taken here in his studio, right down to her lying naked on the floor with her legs artistically arranged and her hand between them.

The pictures were quite cleverly done. He had done something tricky with the mirrors. You only ever saw the back of the real girl, at least until she was on the floor at the very end, but the frontal view was meticulously reflected in the mirror. The side mirrors showed an image of the next picture in the sequence. The impression was of a dream sequence: a young girl in front of a mirror, looking at her dowdy school uniform and concocting a fantasy for herself. The last frame of the fantasy clearly implied masturbation.

In the photographs she progressively acquired that blind-eyed bedroom look because that was exactly what had happened in reality. She had been stripping for her lover.

She had been betrayed.

It was possible, she discovered, to survive for quite a long time without your heart actually beating. Hers had stopped the moment she saw the first picture and was only now resuming its duties, as the fist of shock that had squeezed her chest gradually relaxed its hold. But she didn't realize that Nick was behind her until she smelled his cigarette.

She twisted her head to look up at him, the magazine open across her lap. Her voice wasn't working either. She had to have several tries at expressing her outrage, and finally settled for a croaked, "How could you—?"

Compunction was another word like shame, not in his vocabulary. "I thought it was bloody good, actually," he said coolly. "So did they."

She supposed it was bloody good, if you liked that kind of thing. But it was her. Worse, it was her with him. She had done it for him, had that look on her face for him. And he had sold it for the world to see.

"But you knew I'd never have let you take them if I thought—"

"What did you think?" He inhaled and exhaled smoke. "Did you think I was going to frame them or stick them up on the wall over there?"

Over there with the respectable women. His casual contempt for her naïveté scalded her under her skin. She looked at the pictures again. She put both her hands over her mouth, to keep her insides from tumbling out. "You're mad," she whispered. "What if Mummy saw this?"

"She wouldn't be caught dead reading that rubbish. And she's much too well-bred to muck about with somebody else's junk." Unlike you, he didn't add.

Olivia looked at the stack of magazines. Suddenly she understood why they were there. She understood a lot of things all at once. She knew what was in the back of Nick's mind when he looked at women in the street. She knew why the woman Jamaica had been wearing a caftan when Olivia came up the stairs. She even knew, ironically, where the money for her abortion had come from.

She tossed the magazine aside and stood up. He was leaning back against the table, smoking, totally unmoved. He really is a Martian, she thought. Martians are monsters.

"Does Mummy know you take obscene photographs of other women?"

He looked at her coolly, his gaze penetrating the cloud of smoke he exhaled. "I don't reckon she'd be interested, do you? But she might be interested to know how you found out about it."

Olivia understood that too. He meant, first of all, that the bearer of bad news is seldom rewarded. And in the second place he meant that if she told on him he would return the favor.

She could guess, in practical terms, what that would mean for her. Her mother, even if she broke up with Nick as a result, might never forgive her. Her father would throw her out of the house. And probably murder Nick. Disclosure wasn't on. He had sewn her up again.

She didn't know what she was going to say until she said it. "Do you screw all the others too?"

He seemed to find this a quaintly amusing idea. "They're looking for a leg up, not a leg over."

She felt degraded, contaminated, irretrievably humiliated and debased. He had looked at her and seen only the makings of a dirty picture. No wonder he had admired her grotesque breasts. No wonder he'd been so set on getting rid of the baby. Pornographic pictures didn't get pregnant.

She wrapped her arms around herself to keep from falling to pieces. She heard herself saying something from a long way away. "You make me sick," she was saying. "I don't want to know you anymore."

She turned away from him and went toward the stairs. Her legs were working, at any rate. She heard him call her, telling her to come back, but she didn't stop moving.

She ran down the stairs. The lock was on the street door. She had to fumble with that in the dim light. She heard him coming down the stairs after her. Her heart or something was going to burst inside her. She got the door open and ran out into the dark street.

He was still coming after her. She heard his feet, his hard breathing. Her legs weren't working right after all; she hardly seemed to be moving.

He caught her arm. She tried to wrench it free of him. She shouted at him to let her go, to go away. She was actually shouting at him in the street. He had turned her into some sort of vulgar fishwife, the kind of person who has loud quarrels out of doors. She hated him for that as well as everything else.

He was telling her to shut up. Not shouting like her, just speaking in a low, poisonous voice seething with fury and suppressed violence. The sound of it terrified her. He was an utter stranger. She had just had it proven to her that she didn't know anything about him at all. He might do anything to her.

"Stop it, you silly bitch. Come back inside."

"I'm going home. Don't touch me. You make me sick."

"You can't go home without your fucking handbag. You haven't got any money."

"I'll walk, I don't care. Let me go!"

Olivia had worked herself up to a real shriek. He put his hand over her mouth from behind. When she tried to bite his fingers he covered her nose as well, so she couldn't breathe. She thought she was going to die. She collapsed back against him.

He took his finger and thumb away from her nose to let her breathe but kept the hand clamped across her mouth. "That's better," he said, quite cool now that he had the upper hand. "Come back inside, you stupid little cow."

She refused to cooperate. He dragged her back across the pavement and inside, slamming the door behind him. Then he took his hand off her mouth, but he kept his arms around her, holding her hard against him from behind. At least he made no attempt to take her upstairs.

She was still terrified, though she had temporarily stopped struggling. "Nick, let me go. I want to go home."

"You're not going anywhere till you calm down."

"I am calm." She was shaking now with the effort not to be afraid, not to let him see it. "Please, please let me go."

He didn't answer this time. He was still breathing hard. So was she, from the panic and the struggle. His hand, which had been across her midriff, moved down to pull up the hem of her miniskirt.

She tried to grab the hand, to pull it away. "Don't do that. I don't want you to do that to me."

Still he didn't answer, or stop what he was doing. There was nothing she could do to prevent him. It was no use saying no, no, he seemed to consider that a specially enticing sort of come-on. There wasn't any way of saying no to him.

He had her skirt up round her waist and her knickers down round her knees. He was stroking her roughly, intimately, forcing his hand between her legs, pushing his fingers up into her birth canal and bowel. Theoretically disgusting, anatomically invasive, emotionally a graphic two-fingered salute. But sensually, sexually, a total conquest. She could feel her body responding in spite of her terror. It was her head that didn't want him, but her head didn't seem to be working right now.

He made love to her there on the stairs, a brief and rather brutal act. The brutality was not in any particular bit of violence but a subliminal response to her behavior outside. By resisting and rejecting him so vehemently she had raised the stakes, changed the pitch of their sexual interplay. *Don't you like it rough?* he had asked her that time in the park when she had run from him and he caught her. She hadn't understood him then. But she understood now.

She had said to herself just a few minutes ago that she knew nothing of him, but on this primitive level just the opposite was true; he seemed to be transparent to her. As she must be to him, she guessed, and supposed that must be why he never took any notice when she said no. Because after all that, after everything she had felt and thought and said that was perfectly true, she was still in love with him.

He looked down at her in the dusky stairwell, still winded after coming. "I didn't mean to do that. I was going to take you upstairs and do it properly."

"With a camera, you mean?"

"Shut up and come here." He sat on the stair and cradled her. She had been desperate for him to do that. "All right, I shouldn't have done it, not without telling you. It was just so perfect, you were so fucking perfect."

"Perfectly pornographic." But she didn't pull away from him. She wanted him to bring her back to life.

"Anything deliberately sexy is pornographic," he said matter-of-factly. "That's what pornography means. But funnily enough, it's not very often true the other way round."

"You mean pornography isn't very sexy?"

"What do you think?"

"I'm not a man. I can't tell."

He laughed at that. "Well, it tries, kitten, it tries. The dictionary just says that pornography is intended to appeal to the erotic instincts; it doesn't say it actually has to succeed."

She looked up into his face. She wanted to see how he looked when he answered her next question. "Does that mean you don't find the women sexy in those magazines? Or the other ones you photograph?"

He shrugged. "They're just paper hookers. Professional pussy doesn't do anything for me."

He spoke with such casual indifference that she believed him. She supposed she must fall into the category of amateur pussy. Or perhaps unprofessional pussy, though that implied some sort of unsporting conduct—objecting to getting screwed, for instance.

Speaking of amateurs, she remembered the photograph of Althea, taken by her father. She knew she wasn't supposed to mention Nick's relationship with her mother, but she thought she had earned some indulgence. Quite a lot, actually.

"Have you ever taken pornographic pictures of my mother?"

"Just for fun," he allowed. "But she's not the right shape."

"I thought you liked her shape. She seems to think you do."

"I do. She's just the shape she should be. But you're much more—"

"Obvious," she finished for him.

"Generously endowed, I was going to say. Voluptuous."
He cradled her breasts with his hands as he described them.
"I hate it. I wish I were flat-chested."

"That's like saying you're too rich. There's no such thing."
He pushed her upright and stood up himself. "Let's go upstairs and try this again."

28

Things were getting worse rather than better. It was like
discovering you were a gangster's moll. Worse than that:
like finding out the gangster expected you to oblige his
friends—while he was obliging your mother.

Nick had actually apologized and tried to make it sound
like a compliment, but it didn't change the fact that she felt
like a dirty joke. He didn't seem to understand that. He dismissed the magazines as being of no consequence, saying
they were for kids and wankers. That didn't help at all. The
idea of sexual misfits and loners drooling over her naked and
willing body was a nightmare thought.

But the worst thing was that he didn't mind. He wasn't
remotely jealous of all the strangers who would be looking
at her looking out at them with real desire, looking at her
and wanting to do disgusting things to her. If he loved her
he would mind, whatever he said. But he didn't, either one.

She came home feeling as if she had been raped. She had,
actually, she supposed. In literal terms, being dragged kicking
and screaming into a doorway and having your clothes torn
off and getting fucked constituted rape as near as dammit.
But she didn't really mind about that. She forgave him for
that, it had been quite exciting. Very exciting, upon reflection.

But for the rest, desolation.

Althea was watching television in the sitting room. Olivia didn't want to sit around watching the news with Althea, so she went upstairs to her room. Except it wasn't her room at the moment; it was her father's study and he was in it.

At first she didn't want to be in the same room with her father either. Then she thought that he was exactly who she wanted to be near. She went over to her bed, moved her violin to the top of the dresser, and lay down on the bed.

Her father was reading and making notes. The only light was from the desk lamp. She looked at his profile, at the lamplight striking gold out of the shadows in his dark hair. Some of the gold—just a few stray hairs as yet—would be silver in daylight. The wrinkles at the corners of his eyes and mouth and a faintly haggard hollow to his cheeks only made him more masculine and no less good-looking.

She wished she were still enough of a baby to climb onto her father's lap and put her arms around him. She desperately needed somebody to hold her just then and tell her that he loved her and that she was a good girl, a wonderful girl.

It would all have been lies, of course. She was no good.

Her father finally took on board the fact that she was in the room. "How was your music lesson, Lia? You did have one today, didn't you?"

"Yeah, the first one since the holidays. It was good. I think Mrs. Stone was really pleased with the Bach."

"She should be pleased. It sounded good to me too." He would know; he had had to listen to her practice the whole summer.

If he was in a chatty mood she might as well take advantage of it. "Daddy."

"Yes, Lia."

He was only half paying attention; the other half of his mind was on the book, but maybe that was just as well. "Have you ever read any girlie magazines?"

"I don't think reading is required," he said dryly.

"You know what I mean. Have you ever looked at them?"

"I suppose I must have, however briefly. Why do you ask?"

"Meg found some in her brother's room. We were looking at them."

"Was it an interesting experience?"

"Um. Why do men read them?"

"Most of us don't."

"Well, then, what sort of men do read them?"

"Very immature ones, I should think. Probably in search of anatomy lessons. How old is Meg's brother?"

"Eighteen."

"There you are then."

"What about the women in the pictures? Why would they do that?"

"They get paid to do it, don't they? Anyway, perfectly respectable actresses take off their clothes and writhe around in perfectly respectable plays and films, so why shouldn't Sharon and Tracy take off their clothes and writhe around in a magazine?"

"Ms. Pankhurst says it's exploitation."

"I agree. That sort of trash is always ridiculously overpriced."

"Daddy, you know perfectly well what I mean. It's the women who are being exploited."

"Does your Ms. Pankhurst think it should be illegal to photograph young women in a state of undress? Or does she just feel they're not being paid enough to take their clothes off?"

Olivia considered the question. "If it was forbidden to photograph people with their clothes off we'd be going backward into Victorian times."

"An unthinkable situation," her father said dryly. "Maybe she means that the laborer is worthy of her hire."

"No, actually I think she'd think it was worse if they got paid more. She's told us about how Victorian working women were driven into prostitution because of the dreadful wages they got paid, so if posing for girlie magazines pays a whole lot better than waitressing, that would be the same situation all over again, wouldn't it?"

"So she doesn't really want to raise the wages of sin."

That was a joke, Olivia knew, but she didn't get it. "I think what she wants is for women to value themselves too highly to rent out their bodies to be ogled at."

"Maybe they enjoy being ogled. People do like to be admired, you know. If your body is the most admirable thing about you, why not show it off?"

"Daddy, is that what you really think?"

He looked at her then, for the first time. "Is there something wrong with thinking that?"

"It just seems, you know, such a tacky sort of thing to do."

"Tackiness is a question of taste, not morality."

His attention had wandered back to the book. She said, "But how would you feel if I did something like that?"

"I'd be very surprised. Especially since you think it's tacky."

"But wouldn't you mind?"

"Of course I'd mind. I'd expect you to have better taste." He looked up again. "Is this a ploy for getting your pocket money increased?"

Olivia ignored that. "Some of the magazines gave the girl's name and where she lived. What would their families and boyfriends think?"

"Most likely they'd think that young Sharon was famous. The boyfriend's mates would be impressed. A good thing all round."

"Is that what you'd think if Althea turned up in *Playboy?*"

"If Althea were an actress I suppose I'd have to get used to seeing her appear naked in public. But dealing in swaps doesn't involve the same sort of exposure."

That didn't really answer the question, but she didn't think she would get a better answer out of him. He didn't mind discussing the attitudes of Essex Man but he wasn't going to be drawn into anything involving his own emotions. Anyway, she knew perfectly well that if her father found out Nick had taken pornographic pictures of her and sold them to a magazine, he would be absolutely incandescent with rage. So it didn't matter what he said.

And she found the thought of his anger comforting. If Nick didn't mind, her father would.

But his last remark set her thoughts along a different track. If Althea were an actress, her father had said. Nick's wife was an actress, and she used to be a model, he had said. Maybe he had taken dirty pictures of his own wife. Maybe that was how they had met. It wasn't a totally comforting thought, but it did suggest that he might have been telling the truth, that his attitudes were like the hypothetical boy-friend of hypothetical Sharon. Only, what Nick had been most pleased with was not the size of Olivia's breasts but his own photographer's skill, not only in taking and then rearranging the pictures but in getting her to look the way he wanted her to.

All that, and then he got to fuck her afterward.

29

While Olivia and her mother were in the middle of the second round of their now traditional Sunday Scrabble match, the maternal equivalent of a walk round Hampstead Heath, the doorbell rang. "I'll get it," Olivia said automatically, forgetting that she didn't live here anymore.

But it was for her after all. It was Charlie Cahill.

Olivia had forgotten all about him since her mother mentioned him two weeks before. Now she stared at him in surprise and sudden shyness. He seemed to have grown. He had certainly got broader across the shoulders, or developed more muscles or something. Also he was very brown. He looked wonderful.

"Hi, Lia. Remember me?"

"Yes. Sure I do," she added more firmly. "Mummy said you'd been round while I was up in Yorkshire."

"That's right, yeah. Did you have a good holiday?"

"It was okay, thanks. How's your job going?"

"It's the pits, as predicted. They won't even give me time off for a holiday, the brutal sods." He grinned. "But I have managed to get the mother of all suntans. Remind me to show it to you sometime."

Olivia smiled rather feebly. She knew she should invite him to come in, but she was feeling horribly shy at the idea of having to entertain him in the presence of her mother and Nick. Then Charlie fixed his gaze on her bosom and said, "I've got my brother's car. I thought you might like to go for a ride."

Olivia had a sudden brilliant idea: Charlie could take her home. It was a perfectly polite and inoffensive way of avoiding what she had been dreading, namely, being alone with Nick. "I'd love to. I'm just finishing off a Scrabble game with Mummy and then we're going to have tea. If you want to come in and have tea with us, we can go out afterward." She added anxiously, "Is that okay?"

"That sounds great." He seemed to be genuinely pleased at the dire prospect of tea with her mother and Nick. Of course, he didn't know what he was letting himself in for, poor boy.

The first problem was a basic one—how to introduce everyone. Her own surname was Beckett, the same as her father's. Her mother had taken back her maiden name, Hardy. Nick was, of course, Winter. It was just as she had said to Charlie when he first brought her home: she lived in a zoo.

She dodged the problem by doing only half the introduction. "Mummy, this is Charlie Cahill. You met him while I was away, remember? I've invited him in for tea, if that's okay."

"Of course, darling. Delighted to have him. Do sit down, Charlie."

When Nick finally appeared, after Olivia and her mother had got the tea things ready, he got a different soft of half-introduction. Olivia just said, "This is Charlie, this is Nick."

Half an hour later Charlie still seemed to be enjoying himself. Olivia was amazed. She needn't have felt shy about inviting him in; in fact, she didn't even need to be there. He got through three cups of tea and half the plate of Bakewell tarts. Her mother plied him with polite but pointed questions, which he answered with good humor. Her mother's usual social manner was of a lady at a perennial tea party, so if Charlie could cope with her under these circumstances he would have no further problems with her.

After her mother's interrogation, Nick and Charlie talked about motorbikes. That conversation was so successful that Olivia had to interrupt them in order to get Charlie to leave. "Charlie, I've got to go to Highgate. Were you going to give me a ride?"

Before Charlie could answer, her mother spoke up. "Lia, you're not going anywhere on a motorbike."

"I haven't got the bike today," Charlie assured her. "Is Lia allowed to ride in a Ford Escort? It's guaranteed roadworthy, despite appearances."

Olivia's mother agreed that a Ford, even an elderly one, was on her list of approved vehicles. Four wheels good, two wheels bad.

Even four wheels was not as good as it might have been, Olivia discovered when they went outside and she saw the car in daylight for the first time. Either Charlie's brother or the car's previous owner must have been a terrible driver. "Clare said your father was rich. Why doesn't he buy your brother a better car?"

"Why do you think he's rich? Because he gets his sons to work for him at slave wages instead of buying them flashy cars." They got into the car. "Tell me, Lia, why are we going to Highgate?"

"I'm living with my father now. That's where he lives."

He digested that information. "So that's why Nick is Nick. He's not your old man."

"No." Olivia was obliged to say the dreadful embarrassing phrase. "He's my mother's boyfriend."

"Does he live there?"

"Yeah."

"Since when?"

"Last May."

"And would that be why you're living with your father now?"

She looked at him with admiration and relief. "How clever you are, Charlie."

He grinned. He looked lovely when he smiled, all boyish and beautiful, and he smiled a lot. "Will you come home with me and tell my mother, then? And what's Nick done to put you off him? He seemed a good sort to me."

"Maybe he is," she said grudgingly. "It was a case of two's company."

"Was your father living on his own?"

"No. But that's going to be a crowd anyway. My ..." She considered the alternatives and chose the least awful one. "My father's new wife is very pregnant."

"You don't get on with her."

"No. How did you know?"

"I'm clever, didn't you say?"

She laughed. She was beginning to feel at ease with him. Then she noticed that they were coming to the one-way system and the place where Nick had driven down the hill and stopped, when he was taking her home the last time. Where he had ...

She put her hands up to her face, afraid that she must have gone red. This boy would despise her if he knew what Nick had done to her. She went very still and gazed out the window until they reached her father's house.

She was afraid that she had offended him by going quiet on him there at the end. "I'm sorry, I was feeling a bit off just now."

"That's the second time I've made you sick."

She had forgotten the first time. It had been a big thing for her then, the first time a boy had kissed her, but the novelty was quickly overtaken by events. By Nick.

"It's not you," she said earnestly. "Really it isn't."

He said dryly, "Does that mean I can come back again?"

"Yes. Do. I'll be at my mother's again in a fortnight. Maybe we can skip the tea and go for a ride, if you can get your brother's car."

"I thought you might like to go out one night, to a club or somewhere we could dance."

"Well, I would, only ..."

"Only?"

"Daddy wouldn't ... If it was going to be late, I think he'd want to come and pick me up."

He looked at her for quite a long time, plainly trying to decide if this was an insultingly obvious way of putting him off, or if her father belonged to some fringe religious sect. "How old are you?"

"Fifteen."

"Since when?"

"June."

"You mean you were fourteen when I met you?"

It sounded like an accusation, as if she had been deceiving him. She nodded, looking at her hands in her lap. He wouldn't want to see her now that he knew she was still a kid.

"Why didn't you say so?"

"I didn't know you cared."

That made him laugh. "I thought you were the same age as Clare, she's sixteen already. But it doesn't matter. I'll come round to your mother's house in two weeks and we'll go out, okay?"

"Okay, yeah."

"Your daddy won't object to that?"

"Well, he won't know, will he?" She looked at him and smiled.

He stopped smiling. He leaned over and kissed her, not hard, not deep. It didn't excite her. It didn't make her feel sick.

30

They had strangers coming to the house all the time now, potential buyers. Olivia's father and Althea spent every evening poring over, and arguing about, the details of other people's houses that had come in the post. When they went out to look at other houses Olivia came along. It was fun to see inside people's houses and to try to picture which bedroom would be hers, which room her father's study, which one the baby's nursery.

She found it hard to imagine the baby, and harder still to

imagine liking it. It was going to be Althea's baby. If it had been her mother and father having another baby after all this time . . . But it wasn't going to be like that. It would be Althea's and her father's, and nothing to do with her at all.

This year she would be finishing GCSEs, ten of them. Right from September onward her teachers were pushing them all to get on with their projects. Not like the old O levels, they kept saying, where a clever girl could do nothing all year and put on a spurt at the last minute. Olivia and Megan agreed that that sounded like a much more satisfactory arrangement, and that somebody should start a campaign to bring back O levels.

In addition, Olivia had to deal with Mrs. Stone's number-one favorite on the all-time charts, J. S. Bach. She had got quite accustomed now to Oskar Shumsky's partita performances. It was like eating green olives or plain yogurt; you started off by wincing and swallowing fast, like taking medicine, but then you got used to the taste and began to eat it with a kind of private bravado and satisfaction.

She had also listened several times now to the Bach CD her father had given her for her birthday, and that was more like black olives or yogurt with applesauce. Sonatas for viola da gamba and harpsichord, it said on the cover, and then in the small print went on to explain that the two people doing the playing were actually using a cello and a piano. Cheating. But some of the music was really quite beautiful and moving, for Bach, anyway.

The trouble was that anything that made her feel emotional also made her think about Nick. She didn't want to think about him, there wasn't any point, it was sheer self-torture. But in spite of her schoolwork and musical exertions, by the time she had to go back to her mother's house she was having idiotic fantasies that maybe he might love her in the end if she let him take dirty pictures of her. It was just as well she had arranged for Charlie to come and rescue her.

Olivia had thought the last time that her mother had put on some weight, and this time she was sure of it. Even her bosom looked bigger. Nick would like that. Maybe he was fattening her up, as he had joked about doing.

The weight gain definitely suited her. She looked positively blooming. The planes of her face were softer; even the lines in her face seemed to be disappearing. Maybe that was part of the weight she had put on, or maybe it was an aspect of her newfound tranquillity. Olivia had the thought that if her mother had been like this three years ago when her father left he might not have left.

Her mother sang tunelessly as she fussed about the kitchen, preparing lunch. She had no musical ear at all, and had once confessed to Olivia that one benefit of her father's departure was that she didn't have to listen to opera anymore. Olivia didn't imagine that Nick would be urging her to get back into the habit. The song she thought she was singing was one of Bessie Smith's: "I can't do without my kitchen man." Unlike the man in the song, the only thing Nick did in the kitchen was read the *Sun* and drink whiskey or beer, supposedly keeping her mother company while she did boring kitchen chores.

"How are you, darling? How's school?"

"Boring, basically. But Meg and I have just about finished rewriting our play and we've persuaded lots of people to be in it."

"That's not the play you told me about, is it? The one with the gruesome ending?"

"Where she murders her kids? Yeah, that's the one."

"But surely—I mean, that's not really very suitable for a school play, is it?"

"Wait till you see it," Olivia assured her. "We've done it brilliantly. In the original play Medea is a foreigner—she says she's Asian—and when Jason divorces her, she and her children are going to be thrown out of the city, but she can't go back where she came from because she helped Jason steal the Golden Fleece when she left home."

"She doesn't sound like what you'd call an upright citizen."

"Ms. P. says that lots of women are induced into crime by their husbands or boyfriends."

"Lady Macbeth, for instance."

"Mummy, I'm trying to tell you about the play, don't keep distracting me. What Meg and I did, we put it that because her husband has divorced her and she's no longer married to a citizen, she and her children are going to be deported back to her home country, where the despotic government will immediately arrest and torture them as enemies of the state. So when she kills them she does it to save them from a fate worse than death." Olivia clasped her hands to her chest melodramatically, then let them fall. "Sorry, we wrote it all in clichés and it's catching."

"It sounds very interesting," her mother said cautiously. "Would you like to set the table for me?"

This was the third, no, fourth time Olivia had come for Sunday lunch and Nick was never around when she arrived. Maybe he made up some excuse, or maybe her mother wanted him out of the way just at first, to make Olivia feel more at home. Whatever, it couldn't have been an accident. "Where's Nick?"

"He had some shooting that had to be done on Sunday morning in the City. Because there's no traffic then, you see. He should be back any minute."

Olivia tried to imagine. Some tart in a bowler hat and brolly and nothing else, posing between the pillars of the Bank of England, possibly doing suggestive or even obscene things with the umbrella ... The Young Lady of Threadneedle Street.

Her mother was talking to her in an earnest fashion. She had missed the first bit, obviously, because her mother was saying, "I wanted to tell you first. These things get about and it's right that you should know before anyone else."

"Know what?" asked Olivia.

"Do try to take it the right way, darling. You're living with Ross now, so it doesn't really make any difference to you."

This was the way her mother worked round any topic of real importance. Notwithstanding that it wasn't going to make any difference to Olivia, on her mother's own testimony. "What is it you're trying to tell me, Mummy?"

Her mother took a deep breath. "I'm going to marry Nick."

Olivia looked at her mother for quite a long time. "I thought he was married to someone else."

"He is, sort of. But his divorce looks like it's going through now. After that it's just a matter of waiting for six weeks."

Olivia knew about that divorce. Evidently the judge had agreed about Nick's unreasonable behavior. She wondered what it could have been. And she wondered if her mother knew anything about that. "I thought you had to wait two years. Daddy did, didn't he?"

"Well, you can get it faster under certain circumstances."

"What circumstances?"

"I'm not sure. Nick—ah—Nick's father-in-law is a solicitor and knows all the ropes."

Seeing that her mother was so determined to play the innocent, Olivia couldn't be bothered to force admissions out of her. It wouldn't make any difference anyway. Uncleman was going to become New Daddy. Everything was going to be made respectable. Except that her new daddy had been the daddy of her own lost child. But of course her mother didn't know that, and never would. "When are you getting married?"

"Sometime before Christmas." Her mother was suddenly so nervous she put her hands on Olivia's shoulder. "I know you don't like him, darling, but if you'd met him under different circumstances . . ."

Not in the park, for instance, thought Olivia with a strange dispassion. Not in his studio or his car. Not in your bedroom, not in Daddy's house. Where else in the world was there left?

Her mother was still rabbiting on. "It's not as if the old days were ever coming back, Lia. Ross has already remarried and started a new family."

Old days, old family. The words echoed in her head. At fifteen she was already obsolete and discarded. Suddenly what her mother had just said added up in her head: two plus two makes three. Or even six.

"Mummy, are you going to have a baby?"

Her mother went white, then red. "Well, I—well, actually—"

"You are," Olivia said flatly. She could say it only because she had gone dead everywhere else.

"What's wrong with that?" Her mother was defensive, which meant she felt guilty. As well she might.

No, no, it was Nick who should feel guilty. Where were his boots when he went to bed with her mother? But that was one of the forbidden words: guilt, shame, remorse, he never felt or suffered them.

How did he do it? There were five rivers in hell, her father had told her long ago. Maybe Nick's mother had dipped him into Lethe, the river of forgetfulness, just as the infant Achilles had been bathed in the Styx to make him immortal.

But Achilles had had a vulnerable undipped heel. Where had Nick been left unarmored?

"Nothing's wrong," Olivia said. "Everybody has babies now without being married. Why shouldn't you be pregnant by someone else's husband?"

She hadn't thought of it in those terms when she herself had been carrying Nick's baby. She hadn't thought of his wife at all, only his girlfriend, her mother. But what she had said just now had been true then. She had been impregnated by a man who was married to one woman and living with another, and she was not either of them.

There was an old word, by-blow, they used it in historical novels. It meant an illegitimate child. She thought perhaps it would more aptly describe the mother of such a child.

Her mother sank down onto a kitchen chair. "Don't talk like that, Lia. He hasn't lived with her for nearly a year. He's lived here with me since last May. In any meaningful sense he's my husband, not hers."

Olivia sat down in the chair opposite her mother. For all she knew, for all either of them knew, Nick had had another unknown mistress the whole time he had been living with his wife. Knowing what she did of him, Olivia thought that was not at all unlikely. In addition, maybe, in spite of his denial, he had been screwing at least some of the models who took their clothes off and spread their legs for his camera. And what he had indisputably been doing, almost from the day he moved into her mother's house, was shoving his prick up her own cunt.

The word *husband* had no meaning in such a context. Her mother's protestation that four months of fucking was the equivalent of I do before a vicar sounded either naive or cynical to the point of corruption.

Yet she had no right to destroy her mother's happiness. She had no right to say, Your fiancé has been fucking me like a stoat every chance he gets, and I shouldn't be surprised if he's been having it off with other women, whom he photographs in obscene poses for publication in pornographic magazines. It was true, but it wasn't right.

Why wasn't it right to tell the truth?

Megan would know, thought Olivia. If I could have told Meg about this in the first place I wouldn't have been in such a fix. It was like a dream when you tried to communicate something vital to someone and it came out all wrong or not at all.

She had to say something to her mother, something to make her feel okay. Right now it didn't matter about herself and her lost baby, or Nick's wife and her lost baby. All that mattered was her mother and her coming baby, the baby that would be born next spring.

She took a deep breath. "Okay, Mummy. It's okay, you go ahead and marry him, I don't mind if it's what you want. I can see you're happy. He's making you happy, I can see that, and I'm happy for you."

Her mother looked at her in astonishment. "Lia, that's very generous of you."

"It's true, isn't it?"

"Yes." Her mother sounded as if she were confessing to an incorrigible vice. "I am happy with him. He's nothing like Ross. He doesn't get stressed about anything, he just enjoys whatever comes along. And he deals with all the money. It seems like I just don't have to worry anymore about anything. It's like a dream come true. I'd never have thought someone like him . . ." She recollected herself and her audience. "Well, it's just as you said, he makes me happy. I hope I make him happy."

Olivia had to twist the knife in her own wound. "What about the baby? Is he happy about the baby?"

Her mother's fair skin reddened. "Well, yes, he—when he got used to it, he quite liked the idea of having a family."

"Does that mean it was an accident?"

There was a limit to her mother's *glasnost*. She got up and went over to open the oven door. "Yes and no," she said with her back to Olivia. "I got into a bit of a muddle with my pills, so we knew something might happen."

Olivia had to get up herself and go over to the window for fear of how she must look. Her mother had talked of having a family, as if she had none now. She, Olivia, was no one's family, it seemed. Her father had a baby coming, her mother had a baby coming, she had lost her baby and was no one's baby anymore. Not even Nick's.

She hugged herself. She said to her mother, "That's nice. I'm glad for you."

When Nick came home her mother called him into the kitchen. "I've told Lia our news."

He stood in the doorway. He was looking at Olivia, not at her mother. "What did Lia say?"

"She said she was glad for us."

For you, thought Olivia fiercely, not for him. She looked at Nick in the doorway.

The first thing she thought was that her mother might as well be marrying a great cat, for all the influence and leverage she would have over him. The second thing she thought, as she met his impassive blue eyes, was that if he were inside her she would know what he was thinking. She was surprised she could even think that, much less think it in front of her mother. He must have corrupted her in more ways than she had known.

Nick only said, "Good," and turned away from her.

Olivia was so angry, so outraged on her own and her mother's behalf and even on behalf of the unborn baby, that she wished she had asked Charlie for his phone number so she could put him off and go home with Nick instead, to tell him what she thought.

It didn't happen like that, of course. Nick disappeared while she and her mother played Scrabble. She lost the game. Then Charlie came to take her away.

"It's Charlie," she explained to her mother. "He wants to take me out for a while before we go back to Highgate."

"Charlie again? This must be a big romance."

Olivia said flatly, "He's the only boy I know."

Charlie asked her how she was. "Not feeling sick, are you?" he asked, only half joking.

"Well, I am, but not like that. My mother's getting married."

"And that makes you sick?"

"I wish she wasn't marrying him."

"What's wrong with him?"

"I don't like him. Actually I hate him."

"Well, it's not you he's marrying."

No, that's the trouble, she thought. Or half of it. She couldn't decide whether to tell him the other half. It was horribly embarrassing to have to confess that her mother was pregnant by a man who was married to somebody else. That her mother was getting married because she had to, as her grandmother would have said, and doubtless would say now when she heard of the arrangements.

"Actually, she's going to have a baby."

That shut him up for a while. Eventually he said, "That must make you feel kind of funny."

"Sick," she said. "Sick is the word."

Again he was quiet for quite a long time. They were in Highgate already. "It's a nice day, what about a walk? It might make you feel better. We can go out on the Heath."

Olivia thought that sounded like a good idea.

It was a beautiful afternoon, filled with the sort of melancholy autumn sunlight that makes you feel you should have done something more serious with your life, or at least with your summer. Olivia at fifteen felt that she had misspent both. Charlie held hands with her and distracted her with a very funny account of his adventures as a brickie.

"We should go back," she said at last. "My father will be expecting me by now."

"Sure, okay." He added, hesitantly, "Will I be meeting your father?"

"Glutton for punishment, are you?"

He grinned. "I was just thinking, if he got to know me he might be willing to let me bring you home myself, even late at night."

There were not too many people nearby just now. He drew her toward him and put his arms around her. He didn't try to kiss her; he just held her like that. She put her arms around him, too, and closed her eyes. It felt good and comforting. But she wasn't comforted, because he wasn't Nick. And Nick could never comfort her again. Nick was going to marry her mother.

She drew a deep breath and felt it stick in her throat. She started to tremble. "Hey, now, don't cry," Charlie said into her hair.

"I'm not." She tried the deep breath again and this time it

went down to her lungs. She pulled away from him. "I've got to get back."

Charlie came into her father's house for about five minutes, long enough to let her father look him over and decide he wasn't the Devil in disguise. Or that he was, as the case might be. Afterward, out on the doorstep, Charlie muttered to her, "You've got a lot of books in there."

"They're my father's. He has lots more upstairs and in his office."

"What does he do for his living, then?"

"He's a historian. A university lecturer."

He seemed to find this an alarming idea, as if she had said her father was an officer in the SAS. He asked her for her telephone number and went away without kissing her good-bye.

I've put him off, she thought sadly. Or rather, her parents had put him off. Her pregnant mother and her egghead father.

At dinner her father said, "Who is this Charlie?"

"He's just a boy. I met him at ..." Her father wouldn't approve any more than her mother of her going to the pub. "At Clare's ages ago. He's a friend of Clare's brother. He turned up at Mummy's house a couple of weeks back and brought me home."

"He's old enough to drive?"

"Obviously. He borrows his brother's car."

"Where does he go to school?"

"He doesn't." She took a deep breath and came out with all the bad news at once. "He works for his father."

"What does his father do?"

"He runs Cahill Construction."

Her mother might have been pleased with the son of a captain (or at least second mate) of industry, but her father had more exacting standards. "You means he's a builder."

"Well, I don't think he's carried a hammer about with him for a long time now, Daddy. Clare says he's loaded."

Her father looked unimpressed. "Better a successful builder than an unsuccessful one, I suppose."

Maybe she should have lied and said Charlie planned to be a nuclear physicist. Her father didn't know any more than she did—or, more importantly, than Charlie did—about such things. But she had an idea that something in Charlie's conversation would have given that game away before too long.

To take her father's mind off Charlie's lack of intellectual ambition, she said, "Did you know that Mummy's going to marry Nick?"

"I thought he was already married."

"He is, but he's getting divorced. They're getting married in December, Mummy said."

"Out of the frying pan into the fire," her father commented. Olivia saw Althea give him a funny look. "Why the rush?"

"She's going to have a baby."

Nobody said anything for a minute. Then her father said, "That's very original of her. How did this come about?"

In the usual way, thought Olivia. But she wasn't going to give her mother's admission of guile away to her father. "I think it must have been an accident. She said something about him having got used to the idea."

"Useful things, accidents."

"Excuse me." Althea got up abruptly and left the dining room.

Olivia asked, deliberately innocent, "What's the matter with Althea?"

"She's not feeling well," her father said brusquely. "More salad, Lia?"

31

Megan responded more straightforwardly when Olivia gave her the news.

"That doesn't sound like your mother, forgetting something really important like her pill."

"So you think the same as Daddy, she just did it to get Nick to marry her."

"No, not necessarily. Maybe she just wanted to have another baby. You know all this stuff about biological clocks. The older you get the less fertile you are, and the more likely the baby is to have some sort of damage to its chromosomes. So if she wanted a baby, the sooner she got on with it the better."

"Meg, you're so horribly reasonable," Olivia said gloomily. "If she wanted another baby, why didn't she have one ages ago?"

"Maybe your father didn't want another one. Or maybe it's Nick's baby she wants."

Neither of those possibilities did anything to make Olivia feel better. It was quite likely her father hadn't wanted another baby, if he hadn't wanted a baby in the first place. On the other hand, the idea of her prim and proper mother being driven by obscene biological urges, wanting babies, wanting Nick to impregnate her, made Olivia feel like squirming. Not to mention the horrible, haunting image of her mother carrying Nick's baby. The baby she herself had lost.

She told herself that she wouldn't have minded the proposed marriage so much if she thought her mother really knew what she was getting into. It was one thing to marry an up-and-coming fashion photographer whose child you were carrying. It was quite another thing unwittingly to marry a philandering pornographer whose previous children had all been aborted. And it was immaterial that she herself was in love with the philandering pornographer who, et cetera.

Well, not quite immaterial. She could just about stand the idea of her mother's having the baby, provided she didn't have Nick as well. If it was to be just her and her mother and the baby, two abandoned women together again as it had been before, but this time with Nick's baby to raise between them, that might not be too bad. That prospect seemed the least awful outcome of this whole awful muddle.

If there was one thing more than another she resented Nick for, it was that he had made it impossible for her to talk properly to Megan. On the one hand, she couldn't say certain things when certain subjects came up, and on the other hand, she couldn't do what she had done as long as she could remember, namely discuss her problems with Megan and get her advice. She could still attempt to discuss some of her problems, but it wasn't very helpful because she had to leave out the most important bits.

She decided to have a go with this particular problem. "Meg, if you were me and you didn't want your mother to marry Nick, what would you do?"

Megan thought about that. She was so fair, Megan; blindfold Justice had nothing on her. "That would depend on why I didn't want her to marry him. If it's just because you don't like him, you haven't a hope."

"Supposing I think he's the wrong man for her."

"You'll have to be more specific."

"Maybe I think he's not in love with her."

"But you can't really know that, can you? And even if he isn't, maybe she already knows that and doesn't care."

Olivia was scandalized. "How could she not care?"

"Well, if you were in love with somebody who wasn't in love with you, you'd probably be so happy to have him around that you wouldn't worry about whether he really loved you or not. Anyway, there would have to be some reason why he wanted to marry you, and maybe that would be almost as good as having him in love with you."

Olivia looked at her friend, at her wide blue eyes and yellow hair. Rather angelic, really. People like Megan, she thought suddenly, were how religions got started.

Whereas she herself was an example of how they ran aground.

"Suppose I know something really awful about him, that she doesn't know?"

"How do you know she doesn't know it?" Megan said automatically. Then curiosity got the better of her. "Do you really know some dark secret about him?"

"Yes."

"What?"

"He photographs women for girlie magazines."

"Oh, wow." Megan's face lit up in quite the wrong way. "Tell him he can photograph me anytime."

"Oh, Meg, be serious. It's disgusting. Just like that stuff you found under Teddy's bed."

"Maybe it is disgusting, but it can't be any worse for Nick

to take the pictures than for Teddy to look at them. If Teddy was engaged, would you tell his fiancée not to marry him because he looked at dirty pictures?"

Megan had a point. Olivia had one too, but she couldn't say what it really was. It was a terrible handicap in an argument.

"I did have one idea," she said cautiously. "You know he's still getting divorced. I saw one of the papers they sent him and it said his wife had petitioned for divorce on grounds of unreasonable behavior. I thought maybe I'd go round to talk with her and see what unreasonable behavior means. Maybe he did something really rotten to her."

"She'll have a whole list of rotten things he did to her," Megan pointed out. "You need that to get a divorce, if you want one in a hurry. But they're not necessarily true, and your mother wouldn't necessarily believe them even if they were."

"Well, I thought I'd have a go anyway," Olivia persisted. "I don't know what else I can do. Have you got any good ideas?"

"It's tricky," Megan admitted. "Your mother will discount anything you say because you're prejudiced. She'll discount anything his wife says on the same grounds. You'd probably have to prove he's a drug dealer or a child molester before she'd take any notice."

He is, as a matter of fact, thought Olivia gloomily. Only it doesn't help.

She had to talk to Nick. She had to know what he was thinking. He couldn't pretend anymore that what happened between him and her mother was none of her business.

At least now he had given her his phone number, so she wouldn't have to go down and hang around like that first awful time. But when she rang him after school, all she got was the answering machine. There wasn't any point leaving a message; she just wanted to make sure he was there and he wasn't, so she hung up.

She tried again the next day. This time Nick answered.

When she heard his voice her anxiety increased a hundred-fold. What if he didn't want to see her? Maybe he wouldn't, now that he was going to marry her mother.

"It's Lia. Can I come and see you?"

Silence for a moment. "Now, you mean?"

"Is that okay?"

Another pause. "I have to leave at six-thirty."

She looked at her watch. It was four-thirty. She would have to skip her last class. "I'll come right away."

"All right."

He didn't want her, she could tell. Before she had heard him answer she had been ready to go down and tell him she never wanted to set eyes on him again. Now she was terrified that he never wanted to set eyes on her again. She was going mad. He was driving her mad.

When he came down to let her in he just said hi and went back upstairs again, leaving her to come up after him. Not like the last time, when he had kissed her at the door. And when she got up to the top he shut the door and said, "What can I do for you?" as if he were a stranger behind the counter in a shop.

Coming down on the Tube Olivia had thought of all sorts of ways to say the things that she wanted to say, but now it had come to the point so abruptly she knew she wasn't going to say any of them. She was just too scared.

She went over to the windows and stared out at the river, trying to speak without stammering. "I thought you might have something you wanted to say to me."

"Like what?"

That made her angry enough to face him again. "Like about this baby Mummy's going to have."

He looked at her coldly, remotely. "Are you going to get hysterical again?"

She felt like getting hysterical, she certainly had cause enough. But she could see that getting emotional was just going to make him withdraw from her altogether. She swallowed her anger. "I won't. I promise."

"What d' you want to know?"

"Did you know about it beforehand, or was it her idea, or what?"

"Why don't you ask her?"

She had, but she wasn't going to let him know that. "Why

should she tell me? I expect she'd like me to believe she found it under a cabbage leaf."

He ran a hand through his thick fair hair. "I suppose you could call it a planned accident."

"What's that, exactly?"

"Well, it works like this. You go off on holiday, and when you get there you find you've left your pills behind. You can't just pop down to the Greek chemist and pick up another lot, can you? So you say, silly old me, look what I've done, do you want to fuck rubber for a fortnight or would you rather play Russian roulette?"

That was really rather clever of her mother. But she wasn't admiring her mother's cleverness just then. She was too over-whelmed with relief at hearing that all this had happened after her own nightmare. He hadn't made her get rid of his baby while promising to marry her mother who was also carrying his baby. Things were bad enough but not as bad as they might have been.

Resentment at her own fate rose in her again. "So when you got me pregnant I had to get rid of it, but when you get Mummy pregnant you marry her."

He looked at her as if she were half-witted. "Well, I couldn't marry you, could I?"

He was only telling the truth. The literal truth: it was illegal to get married at fifteen, just as it was illegal for him to get her pregnant at fifteen. But in her heart she felt he was telling her something quite different: that she wasn't the sort of girl a man would want to marry. That she could never be his wife because she was his whore.

She really did want to get hysterical now. But if she did he would despise her even more. She made herself speak dispassionately. "How can you marry Mummy when you're not in love with her?"

"You're an expert on these things, are you?"

His dry tone made her wince, as if he had scraped at some raw internal sore. She wasn't any sort of expert on love. Most of her loving seemed to have been one-sided—for her mother, her father, Nick himself. Not to mention André Agassi. But she persisted; it was important. "You can't be in love with her if you've been making love to me all summer."

He came up close to her. She thought he was going to touch her, but he just came and stood close to her, maybe to intimidate her. It certainly had that effect. "Listen, kitten, love is just the word a man uses when he wants to get into your pants. I love you means I want to fuck you. Making love is fucking, plain and simple. That's all there is to it."

Olivia translated what she had just said into the language he had described: you can't be fucking her if you've been fucking me. Patent nonsense, given his premises, his definitions.

He was a Martian after all; he didn't have any human feelings. And yet he could read her mind. She wrapped her arms around herself and leaned against the cold windowpane, staring out into the dusk. "Why do you want to marry her, then? Why do you want the baby?"

Nick was right behind her. He set one hand on the upright between the windows and laid his other arm across her shoulder. She shivered when he touched her.

"That's life, isn't it? People get married and have children. You can screw around forever if you like, but it's only more of the same. I don't want to be living like a kid when I'm fifty."

To her surprise she understood him perfectly. She understood what her mother was to him, and what he was to her mother. Biology was a terrible thing.

His arm around her, his hand on her shoulder, gave her the courage of the damned. She turned toward him and said timidly, "What about me?"

He didn't say anything. He didn't even look down at her. He took her in his arms and held her, leaning back against the window frame, looking out over her head at the twilit Thames and Bermondsey beyond, the place where he was born.

She put her hands up to his chest, her head down on his shoulder, her face against his throat. He should have said it now, he should have said he loved her. Even if all he meant was that he wanted to fuck her.

But he didn't say anything; he just held her. Gradually he began to stroke her: her hair, her arms, her back and bottom.

He turned her face up to his and kissed her several times with growing hunger.

Afterward he spoke to her, when he had taken off her clothes and his own, and laid her down to make love to her. Then, when he was actually inside her, he told her she was beautiful and sexy and had glorious tits and a delicious little cunt and, less obviously complimentary, that he wanted to fuck her mindless.

Mindless was how she wanted to be just then. She didn't want to think about him at all. She just wanted to be close to him, as close as any body could be.

She got her wish, maybe, at the end. He was good at that.

"I love you," she whispered, hoping he would, hoping he wouldn't, hear. She had nothing now to lose either way.

He put his hand over her mouth.

32

"Mrs. Winter?"

Mrs. Winter—Miranda Elizabeth Collinson Winter, that was—didn't deny it, but she wasn't pleased. "Am I supposed to know you?"

"I don't think so." Olivia didn't have to pretend to be nervous; she could hardly keep from stammering. "I'm Olivia Beckett. Your husband's going to marry my mother." She paused to gather her courage. "Could I—could I talk to you?"

She was glad she had come round rather than phoning up first. She had dressed herself in baggy, scruffy clothes and old sneakers, no makeup, to look like somebody's kid rather than somebody's mistress. The woman was obviously more curious than suspicious of this disheveled girl at her door. "All right, come on up."

Olivia followed her up the stairs. The flat was on the first floor of a big old house in Kentish Town. This was the place that her mother said Nick had been cheated out of. Something to do with Miranda's father having taken out the mortgage for her because Nick's income in those days was too irregular—before he had discovered pornography, Olivia supposed—and Nick had made all the payments, but Miranda ended up with the flat on account of her name on the papers. Olivia looked around with interest. And envy: this woman had lived here with Nick.

There wasn't much evidence of Nick left. Maybe it was like her father taking away his books when he left, taking the most important part of his persona out of the house. Or else Nick's persona had been invested in the studio. At any rate the furnishings were sparse and blandly tasteful. Even the pictures on the walls were simply reproductions of familiar paintings, which convinced her that Nick hadn't put them there.

Miranda herself was the most interesting thing in the flat. Olivia didn't know what she had been expecting Nick's wife to look like. If he hadn't mentioned that his father-in-law was a solicitor she would have had her father's image of Sharon-and-Tracy in her head. But this woman wasn't like that at all. At least, she didn't look or sound like that. She was maybe five years younger than Olivia's mother, which made her about thirty. She was taller than Olivia's mother but built the same way, slim hips, small bones, a classically beautiful face, and *Vogue*-sized breasts. Like her mother, this Miranda had fair skin and dark blue eyes, but her hair was black like Althea's and long like Olivia's own.

She was an actress, Nick had said, but not a successful one. She must have been a very bad actress if she couldn't make a living just by standing onstage or on camera and looking the way she did naturally.

Miranda said abruptly, "What did you say your name was?"

"Olivia Beckett."

"I thought Nick was living with a woman named Hardy."

"That's my mother's name. Beckett is my father's name. I live with my father."

"Oh." Miranda sorted this out mentally. "Well, I'm Miranda Collinson, not Mrs. Winter. I never was Winter. You can't keep changing your name if you want to be famous."

"I suppose not."

"I mean, look at Elizabeth Taylor. She's been married eight times, but she's always kept the name she was born with."

Olivia smiled in vague agreement and said nothing. There was nothing to say. She began to have an inkling of where the difficulty with Miranda's acting career might lie.

"Do sit down," Miranda invited. "I think there's still some coffee in the pot, it shouldn't be cold yet. Do you want some?"

Olivia had no interest in lukewarm coffee, but she thought it might make Miranda happier if she said yes, so she did.

"I'll just go and pour it for you. Take your jacket off, it's hot in here. I've had to turn the central heating on, it's been so cold these last few nights. I always like to hold off on it as long as I can in the autumn because the heating bills are so frightful."

Half of this monologue was delivered from the room next door, which Olivia presumed was the kitchen. She obediently removed her jacket. Miranda stuck her head around the door to ask if she wanted milk or sugar in her coffee.

"Just milk, please."

In a couple of minutes Miranda appeared with a mug of black coffee. "Sorry, I couldn't remember if you wanted milk and sugar or not. I know I asked you and you told me, but then I had to heat the coffee up because it was too cold and by the time I'd got it ready I'd forgotten what you said. I'll go and get it if you want it."

The coffee smelled burnt. Was it possible to burn coffee? If so, Miranda was the person to do it. "That's okay," murmured Olivia, "I'll just drink it the way it is."

Miranda sat down opposite her and lit a cigarette. Even her least consequential movements had a kind of self-absorbed gracefulness like a cat, which made Olivia feel horribly clumsy when she was just sitting still. "What did you want to talk to me about?"

"Well, I—it's kind of embarrassing and nothing to do with you really. I just thought you might be able to help." Olivia took a deep breath. "You see, I don't want my mother to

marry Nick. But it's no use my telling her that. I thought—
well, you must be divorcing him for some reason, and maybe
Mummy might change her mind when she hears what it is."

"He broke my nose," said Miranda.

Olivia stared at her, open-mouthed. "You mean he hit
you?"

"Well, he did, yeah. He used to hit me quite a lot. Not
really hard, just a smack when I got him mad or didn't shut
up when he told me to, but it still jolly well hurt. I didn't
say anything to anyone because it's not very nice, is it, having
your husband knock you about like that? I mean, it's frightfully common. Even though he used to make it up to me
afterward."

Olivia listened in a state of shock. It was terribly easy to
imagine Nick doing just what Miranda was describing. As
for making it up to her afterward, Olivia knew exactly what
that involved. He had done it to her, hadn't he, a physical
quarrel and a physical reconciliation? He hadn't hit her, but
he had overpowered her and subdued her with his greater
strength.

Miranda was still going on. "Then one time we had a really
hellish row—I don't remember what it was about, probably
nothing, really, but we'd just come home from a party and
we were both pretty drunk. No, wait a moment, I do remember. We got stopped by the police on the way home and he
refused to blow into their silly balloon, so they booked him.
It put him into a really foul mood and he took it out on me.
He made me so mad I threw something at him. And he hit
me really hard. I mean really hard, with his fist. He broke
my nose. I don't think he meant to do that, but he did it and
he didn't say he was sorry. He just went to bed.

"I rang up my parents and my father came over and took
me to the hospital and then he took me back home—home
to his home, I mean. He was furious with Nick. He hadn't
wanted me to marry Nick in the first place, you see, so we
went and did it on our own in a registry office. Daddy said
plastic surgery was expensive, he couldn't afford to have my
nose fixed on a regular basis, and if I wanted him to he'd
have Nick thrown out of the flat and get an injunction to keep
him away. So I said okay, yeah, and that's what happened."

Olivia felt quite breathless at the end of this. "Didn't he ever say he was sorry?"

"What, him? You must be joking. But I really couldn't forgive him for breaking my nose because you can't be an actress if you've got a nose like a boxer. At least you can be, but you don't get to play romantic parts. And after Daddy threw him out of the flat and got the injunction he was so furious he wouldn't have come back no matter what. I don't mind telling you all this," Miranda explained, "because I had to tell it all to one of Daddy's partners anyway so that he could get the injunction, and then later on for the divorce. So it's all written down officially already, and I'm not giving any secrets away. You can tell your mother that if you like."

Olivia thought she had already heard a great deal more than she had bargained for. She pushed aside the cup of undrinkable coffee and stood up. "Thank you, Miss Collinson," she said politely. "You've been very kind and very frank. I won't take up any more of your time."

Miranda followed her to the door. "Where does your father live?"

"Highgate village."

"That's nice. I like Highgate, all those sweet old houses, only it's too far to walk to the Tube, and uphill as well. How old are you?"

"Fifteen."

"It's too bad for you, having to put up with all this. How come you're down on Nick? He hasn't hit you, has he?"

"No," said Olivia numbly.

"That's good. Well, maybe it's not. If he did hit you it would probably put your mother off him and then your problem would be solved, wouldn't it?"

"I suppose it would." Olivia took a deep breath. "Did you know he does pornographic photography? For sex magazines?"

"Well, of course. How else does a photographer make any money? Sex and violence, that's all that sells nowadays. But it was only make-believe, so why should I care?"

A robust point of view, and one that Olivia wished she could share. There was one more question she wanted to ask, the most important one from her own perspective. If Miranda had been a different sort of person—almost any other sort of person, in fact—she wouldn't have dared to ask it. But this woman was like Nick in a very odd way. They both had something missing, a sense of shame or discretion, which allowed them to admit without disquiet and discuss without a blush things that anybody else would rather have buried in the deepest dungeons of their soul. And also, as a consequence, they neither of them told lies.

At the door Olivia worked up the nerve to ask her question. She had to employ a euphemism to get it out. She thought of apologizing for asking, but there didn't seem much point. "Was he—was he faithful to you?"

Miranda showed no sign of taking offense. "Yes, I should think he was, he had no reason to go anywhere else. We got on amazingly well in bed. That's why I married him."

33

Now that Olivia had the information she had hoped for, she couldn't use it in the way she wanted to. There was no way she could say to her mother on Sunday afternoon, By the way, I was talking to Nick's wife the other night and she told me he used to beat her and she left him when he broke her nose.

Actually, that particular knowledge now seemed to Olivia to be of more concern to her than to her mother. She had no reason to suppose that Nick had ever raised a hand against her mother, or that if he did her mother would put up with it. She couldn't imagine her mother in a violent altercation of the sort described by Miranda. Her mother didn't get drunk or throw things; she never made scenes of any sort. When she was angry or upset she simply withdrew into her emotional shell. No man was going to start hitting somebody who had frozen over.

It was she, Olivia, who had the scenes, whom Nick had threatened to beat. And she was the one who knew what he had done and who had to come to terms with what it meant about the sort of person he was. The sort of person she was in love with.

She wasn't even going to tell Megan. It seemed too utterly shameful, anyone knowing that she had a soon-to-be stepfather who had punched his previous wife in the nose. But Megan asked if she had done anything further about the idea of going round to talk to Nick's wife.

Olivia said well, yes, actually she had gone to see her.

"What was she like?"

Olivia considered how best to describe Miranda. "Beautiful. But pretty dippy."

"Did she mind you coming round?"

"Apparently not. She was quite chatty."

"And did she have any really scandalous and off-putting revelations about Nick?"

Olivia said flatly, "He used to beat her up."

"What, really?"

"Yeah, really."

"How do you know it's true?"

"Oh, she wasn't making anything up. What really got her going was that it was such low-class behavior. Finally he broke her nose for her and she left him because she thought it might mess up her chances of stardom."

"Wow. Are you going to tell all this to your mother?"

"Well, no," Olivia admitted morosely. "There doesn't seem much point. This Miranda person is definitely flaky. For all I know, even my father might have been driven to smack her if he'd been married to her. And if Nick starts to behave like that with my mother, she'll be the first to know, won't she? Besides," she added as a new thought struck her, "she might think it was sort of disloyal of me to go chatting to his wife."

"She might," Megan agreed. "I don't think I'd say anything if I were you."

Which still left Olivia with the problem of how to stop her mother from marrying Nick.

She hadn't heard from Charlie since that last Sunday. I really have put him off, she thought, with a pregnant mother living in adulterous sin and an academic ogre for a father, and she herself threatening to throw up every time he tried to touch her. Why would any sensible boy want to get mixed up with that when the world was full of nice, normal girls with normal families?

Without Charlie to rescue her, she had to go along with her mother's assumption that Nick would drive her home on Sunday. She couldn't really make any excuse, as it was a blustery autumn day and no one without questionable motives would choose to be outside rather than inside a car.

Maybe that was just as well. It would give her a safe—well, relatively safe—opportunity to confront Nick with his misdeeds.

She had read about men who beat their wives. Apparently they all said the same things: either they didn't know what had come over them, really, or it was the woman's fault, she made him do it. Megan would find it of scientific interest, no doubt, to learn which category Nick fell into.

Nick had concerns of his own. As soon as they got into the car he said, "Where's your boyfriend today?"

"Charlie, you mean?"

"How many boyfriends have you got?"

Well, you, for instance, she thought. But he wasn't her boyfriend, he was her lover. He was her mother's boyfriend. There was a dreadful, dangerous difference.

She shrugged. "I don't know where he is."

"Have you gone off him already?"

"I haven't got on to him yet. He's the only boy I know, and I hardly know him." She decided it was time to counterattack. "I went to see your wife the other day."

She expected him to be surprised or dismayed or even angry, but he was only amused. "Did you? What did you think of her?"

"I thought she was beautiful and, er, very sweet."

He laughed at that. "Very scatty, you mean."

"Not too scatty to tell me what you did to her."

"What was that, exactly?"

"Don't you even remember?"

"You mean she only accused me of one heinous crime?"

"She only talked about one, though I wouldn't be surprised if there were others." Olivia clenched her hands together. "She said you used to beat her up."

He still didn't show any sign of concern or alarm or shame or anger, anything like that. He didn't show anything at all; he was impassive as usual. He kept his eyes on the road. "So what did you think about that?"

She had to think carefully about her answer, since it wasn't a question she had been expecting. She said at last, "It scared me."

"You didn't think maybe she was making it up?"

"She didn't strike me as the sort of person to make things up."

He was amused again. "You're right, she's not. It's one of the reasons she's such a bloody awful actress."

"You mean you really did hit her?"

He looked at her then. "Do you really want to talk about this?"

"Yes." She ran her tongue across her lips. His glance made her nervous. "It's important. Really important." When he didn't react she asked, "Don't you think it's important?"

He did respond then. Instead of crossing Finchley Road he turned left and headed north.

"Nick, what are you doing? Where are we going?"

"You want to talk, we'll go someplace and talk. I'm not sitting outside your old man's house for an hour."

She leaned her head back and closed her eyes. She felt dizzy, and it wasn't only because he was driving faster than he should have been.

Ever since she had met him she had been discovering that she didn't really know what sort of person he was at all. Each new discovery made him seem a worse rather than a better person. But after all, she thought bitterly, what sort of redeeming features, what hidden heart of gold, was she expecting to find in a man who would seduce and even rape his lover's fifteen-year-old daughter?

By the time he stopped they were halfway to St. Albans, on a country lane going from Y to Z. It was an unpleasant day, with no sign of life anywhere around. They might as well have been halfway to Mars.

"Isn't Mummy going to wonder what's taking you so long?" Olivia asked with malice.

"I don't have to answer to Em for every fucking minute of my time. You wanted to talk about something really important, remember? I think maybe you wanted to tell me what a shit I am for having broken Miranda's posh little nose."

He had taken the words right out of her mouth, though she wouldn't have phrased it in quite the way he had. "Well, yes, you are."

"All right, get out."

"What?"

"Get out of the car."

"What do you mean?"

"Thick, are you? I mean open the door, get out of the car, and shut the fucking door again so the rain doesn't get in."

Olivia stared at him. He hadn't spoken with particular venom, just with the flat, dispassionate menace that had frightened her more than once before. Was he really going to leave her here in the middle of the countryside?

She got out and slammed the door behind her. She started walking down the road, heading from unknown Y to unheard-of Z. She had no money and no coat. The air was thick with rain posing as mist.

She heard his footsteps on the road behind her. He wasn't running, just walking fast. Faster than her. Her heart was beating fastest of all. Maybe he had made her get out so he could beat her up. She broke into a run.

Not for long. He caught her arm and dragged her round to face him.

"Lia, why don't I thump you right now?"

She whispered, "Why would you want to do that?"

"Suppose you tell me, since you seem so convinced I'm going to do it."

"I—I don't know," she stammered. "Why did you do it to her?"

"She must have told you already. I'd been stopped by the cops for drunk driving and she was being a real cow about it. But I shouldn't have done it. Anyway, I didn't mean to hit her so hard. I just wanted to shut her up."

"Why didn't you say you were sorry?"

"Right then I wasn't sorry. And next morning when her old man came round, I really wasn't sorry for anything after that. In fact, I wished I'd knocked her fucking teeth out. I'd've given him a going-over too, if I hadn't known the bugger would've stitched me up for it."

Olivia put her hands up to cover her ears. She could understand the impulse to violence but not the doing of it. "I still think you're unspeakable. She said you hit her all the time."

"Not like that. I suppose it was really just a stupid sort of game. She'd get on to something and wouldn't leave it alone, she'd work herself up into some kind of hysteria over nothing at all. I'd tell her to cut it out and she wouldn't, so I'd slap her. After that everything was my fault and I'd have to calm her down."

That was more or less what Miranda had said, only it sounded quite different coming from him. Calming her down was what Miranda had called making it up to her. She licked her misted lips. "How did you do that?"

He smiled. "You want me to show you?"

She shook her head. But she did, really. Or really didn't, she couldn't tell which. Her stomach hurt. So did her chest and throat. She hurt all over, as if he had beaten her. He still had her arms in a painful grip. "Let me go," she whispered.

"You want to walk home?"

"No, I—you make me sick." It came out of her throat as a croak. And it wasn't true. It wasn't him that made her sick, it was the want of him.

"Come here and say that." He dragged her hard against him and kissed her mouth with bruising force.

She knew her way from here. Very quickly he had her half undone, her body intertwined with his like ivy on the oak. She thought he meant to have her right there in the road. The thought made her melt.

He said raggedly, "Let's get back in the car."

After he had made love to her he held her for a while. He called her kitten and said he wouldn't hurt her. He told her not to be scared, of him or anything.

But she was scared. He was the most truly wicked, terrifying person she had ever known and she loved him utterly.

34

I'll bet you thought I'd died or gone to Australia."

It took Olivia an instant to place the voice. "Oh, Charlie. No, I didn't think that."

"What did you think?"

"I didn't know what to think," she lied. "I just wondered."

"Well, it wasn't anything personal. My father told the torturers who take his shilling that I had to do whatever the other slaveys have to do. And what the slaveys had to do was work like Trojans seven days a week to get this contract finished before the penalty clause took effect. I complained directly to the management. I said you'd give up on me. But he has a leather boot for a heart, my old man. That's why he's rich."

She laughed at that. "Okay, I forgive you. It's all your father's fault." But she wondered if he had really told his father about her, and if so, what he had said. A daft young girl who gets sick every time I try to kiss her. And his father maybe saying, Stick with her, Charlie, at any rate she'll keep you out of trouble.

"Can you go to a film this weekend? Saturday night? We can go down and back by Tube to keep your father happy."

"That should be okay. I'd like that."

He hadn't said what film they were going to see. Not that it mattered, as long as she hadn't seen it before, only if it was rated 18-only, she would have to do herself up a bit.

She didn't know whether to lurk in her room as long as possible, or to hang about the front door so she could answer it. She had told her father she was going to a film, but she hadn't said anything about Charlie, on the spurious grounds

264

that since all she was doing was going to a film, it shouldn't make any difference whether she was going with Charlie or Megan. There wasn't a lot of trouble you could get into on the Tube.

As it turned out, she was still putting mascara on when he arrived. Her father came upstairs and asked her if she was expecting a young man.

"It's just Charlie, Daddy, you met him before. I told you I was going to a film."

"It looks more like you're going to be in a film, with all that makeup on."

She couldn't explain about the 18-only film because he wouldn't want her seeing one of those. She just said, "Don't you think I look nice?"

"You always look nice. It's not necessary to gild a fifteen-year-old lily."

"Oh, Daddy." She brushed past him, heading for the stairs. "It's just for fun."

Althea was entertaining Charlie. She was actually being quite nice to him. But Olivia wasted no time in getting Charlie out of the house.

"You look fantastic, Lia," Charlie told her.

"My father accused me of gilding the lily."

"Maybe he's right." He looked at her with a grin. "I'd say you probably look best with nothing on at all."

Olivia said breathlessly, "Don't say things like that."

"You're not feeling sick, are you?"

He was only teasing—she hoped—but it still made her feel distinctly uncomfortable. "No, but I will be if you talk like that."

"Okay, we'll talk about something else. What film do you want to see?"

In the end the film they went to was 15-only. All that meant was that there was no buggery or people being chopped into pieces on-screen. But there were some fairly steamy love scenes that made Olivia think of Nick. It should have made her feel sexy, but instead she felt desolate. He had desolated her whole life. Charlie wouldn't want her if he knew about Nick. Maybe that didn't matter, because she didn't really want Charlie anyway. She wanted Nick.

She put all that out of her mind when they left the cinema. Charlie bought her an ice cream cone and they walked around Leicester Square eating ice cream and holding hands. It wasn't a very nice evening but at least it wasn't raining. When the ice cream was all gone they went down the Tube station and got on a train going to High Barnet.

There was nobody else in their half of the carriage. Charlie put his arm around her. "You've got chocolate ice cream on your face."

Olivia looked at her reflection in the window. "I do not."

"Yes you do, right around your mouth. I'll fix it for you."

He kissed her. She didn't pull away, so he kissed her again, this time with his tongue. He had both arms around her. She liked his holding her and didn't mind his kissing her. She put her arms around his neck and kissed him back, but she didn't put her tongue into his mouth the way she did with Nick. Everything she did with Nick was inexpressibly exciting, and it wasn't like that with Charlie. Besides, she didn't want him to know that she knew all about kissing.

They carried on kissing till she suddenly noticed they were at Highgate station. "Hey, this is my stop."

She jumped up and dashed for the doors. They nearly didn't make it. Charlie had to wrestle with the closing door to let her and then himself out. The driver saw him and made the doors open again so he could get off.

He was laughing when he jumped down beside her. "Traveling by Tube is too exciting for me. Next time we'll take a taxi."

Olivia was still breathless from the sudden panic. She let Charlie hold her, and her pulse rate gradually slowed. "That was lucky. This time of night I could have waited ages for the next train coming down."

"Or we might have had to walk back. Terrible hard."

She remembered the last time she had taken a long walk in the middle of the night. She remembered every horrible aspect of it, what had happened, how she had felt. And her father, at the end, carrying her up to bed.

She pulled away from Charlie. "I've got to get home."

When they came to her father's house she invited him in. That was to avoid kissing on the doorstep, which would have been embarrassing with her father sitting on the other side of the door.

Her father and Althea were watching a film on TV. Her father turned the sound right down when they came in. Charlie sat down in an armchair. Althea asked them if they wanted some tea. She said she was just about to make some anyway, which was just the sort of lie that Olivia's mother would have told.

Olivia hung up her coat and Charlie's, and ran upstairs to the loo. Her makeup had got rather smudged, what with all the kissing on the train, and she didn't want her father to notice. She wiped most of it off and put on fresh lipstick before going downstairs again.

Her father was asking Charlie about the film they had just seen. Her father hardly ever went to films, but he knew all about them because he read the reviews in the papers.

Olivia knew that Charlie's idea of a film review was what his friends had thought of it. That was how they had decided which picture to see tonight. His own assessment, which he offered to her father, was that it had been okay but the plot was shaky in a few places. While they drank the tea Althea had made he gave a detailed description of the plot, explaining which particular bits didn't quite hang together and why.

When he left, Olivia deliberately kept the front door ajar while she said good night to him, so that he wouldn't kiss her.

"Are you going to your mother's tomorrow?"

"Not till next Sunday."

"Can I come and get you?"

"Yes, please."

"Okay, I'll see you then."

She closed the door. Her father said, "Is this supposed to be a regular arrangement?"

"It isn't any sort of arrangement. Just because I go to a film with him doesn't mean I'm going to marry him. Anyway, what's wrong with Charlie?"

"Nothing, as far as I know. He may well be admirably suited to take his father's place as a pillar of the construction industry."

"Does he need a degree in mathematics to take me to a film?"

"A degree in English literature might help him to discuss it afterward."

"He explained it perfectly well."

"His grasp of narrative was admirable, I admit."

She thought he was being sarcastic, but she couldn't be sure. "Daddy, don't be such a snob. People can understand things without having to read them in a book."

"I know that, Lia. I'm not being snobbish, I'm being serious."

He was being so serious he was making Olivia nervous. She sat down in the chair where Charlie had been sitting, while her father lectured her.

"Half the pleasure of reading books and getting new ideas from them is being able to talk to other people about what you've read and learned. But that means the person you're talking to has to be interested in learning. I'm not talking about university degrees. My father's formal education ended when he was younger than you, but all his life he's loved to read and learn and to talk about what he's discovered. It's not academic knowledge. He recognizes every living thing he encounters on the moor; he knows the detailed history of the town he lives in. He's a well-educated man, even though by no fault of his own he has no formal educational qualifications whatsoever. Do you understand me, Lia?"

"Yes, Daddy, I understand you perfectly," Olivia said impatiently. "I know how much Granddad knows. He takes me up on the moor and shows me everything."

"Do you enjoy that?"

"Yes, of course. He makes it all really interesting." She added after a moment, recollecting what she had forgotten in the tumult of her life since then, "He asked me if I thought I might like to study natural science at university."

Her father looked at her sharply. "What did you say?"

"I said I didn't know. And I don't. I don't know yet what I want to do or be."

"Well, whatever you decide to do or be or study at university, you want to remember something. You love to read and you enjoy learning things; you're not afraid of having to deal with new ideas. Somebody who thinks he knows it all at seventeen and has no interest in learning more, he's not going to want to talk to you about something new."

This was not the time to tell her father that Charlie was not seventeen but nearly nineteen. "Charlie's not like that," she protested, before remembering to add, "Anyway, Daddy, it's not as if I'm going to marry him, for heaven's sake."

"I expect that's what your mother said to herself when she took up with that yob she's about to marry."

It was funny how understanding came to you, not in dribs and drabs but in great slabs of world knowledge. Olivia suddenly understood a whole new landscape: why her father resented and felt personally insulted by her mother's decision to marry Nick; why after his first reluctance he was now willing that she should live with him rather than her mother.

It touched his pride that his ex-wife should marry a man who read the *Sun* and spelled her name with a haitch. It threatened him with the shadow of a life that his education had allowed him to escape from.

Olivia had never thought about her grandparents in those terms before. She associated working-class culture with tabloid newspapers, television soap operas, dropping one's aitches (or haitches, as Nick called them, though in fact he hardly ever dropped them), and package holidays. Her father's parents had nothing to do with any of these things, so she had never regarded them in that light.

But now she understood, for instance, that her grandmother Hardy would have spoken the same way whether she had grown up in Devon or Derbyshire, or London for that matter, but that wasn't true of her grandparents in Huddersfield. She understood that Althea and Althea's parents were like her mother and Grandma Hardy in that respect. She understood that Nick had to some extent covered his linguistic tracks since he had shaken the dust of Bermondsey from his feet at fourteen, but that he hadn't tried to hide his south London accent entirely. Her father's speech even now was less clipped than her mother's or Althea's, and some of his vowels had a pleasing drawl to them, like a faint echo of her grandfather's voice.

She understood that all these things were important to her father for some reason.

She couldn't answer to any of that. She was fighting her own fight, not her father's, and hers had nothing to do with how people talked or what newspapers they read, if any. It was what they did that was ruining her life, and her father was as guilty as anyone.

"Daddy, Charlie's not a yob. He went to school with Clare's brother, and his father is a lot richer than you. Richer than Althea's father, even. Just because he doesn't go about discussing Einstein's theories doesn't mean he isn't a proper human being. He's funny and sweet and why shouldn't I like him?" She took a breath and added honestly, "Besides, he's the only boy I know."

35

Every time Olivia went to her mother's house she was counting to herself. It was nearly the end of October now. Her mother was nearly three months pregnant. Nick's decree *nisi* had just come through, which meant the final decree was less than six weeks away, about the same time as Althea's baby.

Her father and Althea had found another house to buy, and someone was buying their house. Her father said they had taken a beating on the sale price, but Althea said they had got a bargain on the new house, so maybe it canceled out. The new house was also in Highgate village, larger and younger and considerably more expensive than the present one. It stood at the end of a small Victorian terrace. Every front door was recessed to make an elegant little entrance porch, and each window was set out in a bay, which made the rooms very bright. The rear windows looked out over the old part of Highgate Cemetery. But it was going to be touch and go whether they would be moved before the baby arrived.

Everything would be changed by Christmas. She had an awful idea that the rearrangements were something like a game of musical chairs, and that however it worked, she was going to be out.

She thought of her mother's forthcoming marriage as a particular watershed. Until that happened Nick was only her mother's lover, nothing official. And he was her lover too. She could pretend that things were equal between them, that whatever she did with him was no worse than what her mother did, that she had as much right to him as her mother did. It wasn't true, because she had no right to any man, being not yet sixteen. But she could almost persuade herself that it was so.

Except for two things: her mother was carrying Nick's baby, and Nick was going to marry her mother.

When Nick was her mother's husband, she would have lost him forever. First because screwing your stepfather was a really evil, perverted, incestuous thing to do. Second because she couldn't then pretend in her heart of hearts and secret dreams that he would eventually marry her. It was like the end of her life approaching, and she couldn't do anything about it.

But the more she thought of it, the more it seemed to her that what really made the difference was the baby. Nick was marrying her mother because of the baby; it was the baby, who was part of each of them, that truly joined them together. Her parents had separated and divorced and within a few months would be both remarried and both with a new family, but they couldn't ever really be totally disjoined because of her.

Whereas Nick was only her lover as long as he made love to her. After that she was ex, she was history to him. But if he hadn't made her lose her baby, he would still be joined to her, irretrievably.

It was too late to regret that lost baby. And if she got pregnant again he would only make her get rid of it again. She could say she wouldn't do it this time but she knew she would, because he had all the arguments and logic on his side, not to mention that she always ended up doing what he wanted. He was just like that, she decided. Miranda hadn't managed any better with him, by her own report.

The idea of having a baby was absolutely crackers anyway, she knew that in her head. It didn't fit at all with her other ideas of the future—A levels, university, some sort of career. There was no room in there for an adolescent pregnancy. She knew all that perfectly well.

And yet she carried round, side by side with that conventional image of her life to come, a different pattern of developments, a hopelessly unreal expectation, in which she found herself pregnant again and Nick, against all odds and character and previous experience, not to mention her status as a minor, came to cleave unto her like it said in the Bible.

That was only wishful thinking, she knew that. In her head she knew it. In her heart she yearned for Nick and his baby, and A levels had no significance for her. She despised herself for this lunacy, but there was nothing she could do about it. She wanted what she wanted, she loved whom she loved, whether she wished it or not.

But nobody would have guessed any of this from the way she behaved in her mother's house. In her mother's presence she didn't want to know that Nick even existed, so she paid as little attention as possible to him. She had come, after all, to visit her mother.

When Charlie turned up he came in and socialized for a while. He was good at that. He told amusing stories and discussed inconsequential matters with clichéd fluency. First he chatted up her mother, who obviously enjoyed his attention. After a while he fell into an earnest football discussion with Nick.

Afterward he said to her, "Why don't you like Nick? He seems okay to me."

"I just don't," she said irritably. "Do I have to have reasons?"

"He's easier to talk to than your father. What does your father have against me?"

"You don't go about with your nose in a book. But don't mind him, he'll get used to you." She recalled the football conversation. "Talk to him about cricket next time. He's mad on it. He comes from Yorkshire, they're all cricket-crazy up there."

"I'll remember that." He looked over at her. "What shall we do now?"

"It's a nice day, let's go for a walk in the cemetery."

He looked at her again, a different sort of look. "That sounds nice and depressing."

"It's not. Have you never been to Highgate Cemetery? It's really interesting. The best part is like a jungle, all overgrown, but they only let you in a couple of times a year. The other part is good too. Karl Marx is buried there, and there are lots of strange gravestones. I like going there."

"If you say so."

Charlie went with her down Swains Lane to the cemetery, and they wandered about looking at tombstones. But it was probably no accident that they ended up in a secluded corner of the graveyard. He had brought her there in order to kiss her, and he did.

Olivia didn't mind that. It made her feel good when he held her and kissed her, it eased the aching emptiness that she felt at her core. She had no core. She was empty inside, full of nothingness. Nobody could love nothing.

After several fairly intense kisses, in the middle of kissing her in fact, he put his hand inside her open jacket and touched her breast. The caress was tentative at first—in case I get sick, she supposed—but grew bolder when she did not push his hand away.

She was wearing the bulky sweater her grandmother had given her for her birthday, so he couldn't have felt much more than the round outline. Even that made him breathe more heavily. All it did to her was make her feel nervous.

He slid his hand up under the sweater and T-shirt to get closer to the real thing. Even there he had to contend with her bra, a basic cotton construct designed to do its duty rather than titillate. Her mother, who used to buy all her underwear, maintained that a bosom the size of hers needed all the help it could get in defying gravity, unlike her mother's own small breasts, which hardly required a bra at all, even at thirty-five.

Charlie put his arms around her underneath her clothing,

where he could stroke her bare skin. He kissed her again. While he was kissing her he unfastened her bra and brought his hands around to her front, to push the bra out of the way and hold her bare breasts in both his hands.

She put her hands on his arms. "Charlie, somebody will see us."

"No, they won't. There's no one over here."

They were standing under a holm oak, in a clump of trees near the wall. He was right; there wasn't anyone around. But it alarmed her all the same, his eager hands on her body. He was pushing her back against the tree, pushing up against her and stroking her breasts with shaking hands. She could feel him shaking, hear his rasping breath. Just touching her body was doing that to him.

He lifted her sweater up, exposing her breasts to the open air. She grabbed at it, trying to pull it down. "Stop it, Charlie, don't do that."

"Just let me look at you. You're so beautiful."

Already he had that look on his face that meant he wasn't really hearing her. He was staring at her naked breasts with naked desire. He frightened her.

She managed to push him away and pull her sweater back down. She was trembling now too, but not from sexual excitement. She got her bra refastened, her bosom rearmored. She did up her jacket too, just to be safe.

"I'm sorry, Lia, I didn't mean . . ."

Charlie was stammering. His hand on the sleeve of her jacket was still shaking. She wasn't afraid anymore; in fact, she felt faintly sorry for him. He was so moved and she wasn't.

"It's okay, it doesn't matter now." She put her hands up to his shoulders. "Give me a hug."

He put his arms around her and held her tightly. That was good; she liked that. She felt more in control now. She could get him to do what she wanted, or at least to stop doing what she didn't want. Unlike Nick.

On the way back to her father's house Charlie told her he was going on holiday for a fortnight the next week. "I finally persuaded my father to let me take some time off. This will

274

be the first time I've been abroad in the winter, except for skiing."

"Where are you going?"

"Tenerife. It's supposed to be nice and warm this time of year. Have you ever been there?"

Olivia shook her head. She had never been anywhere but France and Italy, Yorkshire and Devon. Her father didn't hold with lolling about on beaches, and her mother had never had any money for holidays. "Who are you going with?"

"Just a couple of friends." He looked at her with a mischievous grin. "Wouldn't you like to come?"

She smiled back. It was only a joke. "I'd love to, but my half-term break is over tomorrow."

"Rotten luck."

"For who?"

He smiled more broadly. "My friends, I reckon."

He didn't come as far as her father's house; he said goodbye to her on the street corner. Olivia knew that was so that he could kiss her again, which he couldn't very well do, at least in daylight, on the doorstep of her disapproving father. She didn't mind. As long as his hands were outside her clothing he could kiss her all he liked.

36

It wasn't till the last day of her period that Olivia knew what she was going to do. Or maybe she had known earlier but not admitted it. She was going to play Russian roulette.

That was what Nick had called it when he had slept with her mother without using any form of contraception. That's what he was going to do now with her, only she wasn't going to tell him what he was doing. That way God or something would decide her future. If she got pregnant within the next month, she would know in time to tell him, before he married her mother. Then he would have two babies to choose between, two women carrying his children.

In the back of her mind she knew that there were no happy outcomes to such a scenario. Supposing, against all probability and leaving aside the problem of her age, she got what she wanted; supposing Nick chose her instead of her mother and decided to live with her and let her have his baby. That would reveal everything that she had been so desperate to hide. It would leave her mother pregnant and abandoned. And she wouldn't get to live with Nick anyway because her father would probably kill him.

More likely, what would happen this time was what had happened the last time. He would make her get an abortion.

That was too terrible even to contemplate. Not only would Nick have rejected her and chosen her mother, he would be giving her mother everything, marriage and a baby, while taking everything away from Olivia.

She couldn't bear that to happen. She couldn't risk its happening. It would demolish her.

So she had another plan, a safer one that would make both the best and the worst alternatives impossible. If she did get pregnant she wouldn't tell anyone, not even Nick—especially not Nick!—until it was too late. After the fifth month abortion was illegal, and then no one could force her to do what she didn't want to do.

There was another problem here, but she had thought of a solution to it. The problem was that the baby had to have a father, an official father, that is, someone other than Nick. Theoretically she could be mysterious and refuse to say, but in practice she knew very well that her parents wouldn't take silence for an answer. Besides, if she wouldn't say, somebody might think there must be some good reason for her reticence and maybe even guess the truth. Her baby would need a plausible father, and the father had to be someone who couldn't reasonably deny the charge of paternity.

She only knew one boy.

There was no obvious biological reason why Charlie couldn't be the father of any baby Nick had started in her.

They were about the same height and both had blue eyes. Nick was blond and Charlie brown-haired, but since her mother was fair and her father dark the baby could be either without arousing suspicion. There was the tricky question of blood groups, of course, but she had no way of making discreet inquiries about that. Besides, she doubted if either Charlie or Nick would have the faintest idea how those worked in genetic terms, or even what type they themselves were, so it wasn't worth worrying about.

She was amazed that she could cold-bloodedly contemplate seducing Charlie. It would be easy, really. She remembered his hands trembling when he touched her. If he wanted her so much . . .

She could do it in stages. That way he wouldn't know; he would think it was happening the other way round. And he couldn't blame her, in the end, because she wasn't making him do anything he didn't want to do.

That day, the start of a new monthly cycle, she didn't take her pill. After the third pill-less day the die was cast; it was too late to be effective this month even if she started again, so she threw the pills away. She had loaded the bullet into the gun. Now all she had to do was hold it to her head and pull the trigger. Or rather, that was what Nick was going to do.

She went to see her mother on Sunday as usual. Her mother had put on more weight. It suited her, which made Olivia think for the first time that maybe Nick had been right; maybe her mother had been too thin before. Which in turn made her think, also for the first time, that maybe she herself wasn't really too fat. You're the best shape there is, Nick had said. She didn't care so much if that was true; what she cared about was that he should really truly think so.

Since Charlie was still in Tenerife, Nick drove her home. She waited for him to do or say something, but he didn't. He didn't say anything at all, not one word. By the time they got to Highgate she knew she would have to do or say something herself, but she didn't know what. Up to now he had done all the running.

There was nothing cold-blooded about her intentions. On the contrary, just sitting in the car beside him made her painfully aware of the ache in her that wanted him. Maybe he didn't want her now. That thought only made the ache worse.

He stopped the car near her father's house and pulled up the hand brake. While his hand was still on the brake lever between them she laid her own hand over it, timidly. Her heart was thumping like horses on a hunt. When she touched his hand he looked at her.

"Are you . . ." She had to stop and clear her throat. "Are you cross with me?"

"Some reason I should be?"

"I don't know." She ran her thumb across the back of his hand, shyly stroking the veins and tendons outstanding, the coarse blond hairs. She wanted him to touch her so much she thought she would faint if he did. "You haven't said a word to me all the way here."

"What d' you want me to say?"

"I don't know."

She took her hand away and looked away, out the side window. She folded her arms over her stomach, where the emptiness was. Now if he touched her she thought she would burst into tears. He didn't want her, she could tell.

She put her hand on the door handle and opened the door. He said something just as a car went past. Her ears were buzzing and pounding. Without looking at him she said, "What did you say?"

"D' you want to come down and see me?"

She looked at him then. She leaned back against the seat. She managed to say, "When?"

He shrugged, as if it were a matter of no consequence, as if it were not the most important question in the world. "Tomorrow, why not?"

There was a good reason why not tomorrow. The school orchestra had its rehearsals on Monday. They were doing a Christmas concert and she was one of the first violins. Well, that was too bad, she wasn't going to miss Nick for anything. "Okay, tomorrow."

When he came down to let her in from the early evening darkness, she was so glad to see him she put her arms around him as soon as she was inside.

278

"That's nice," he said, amused. He put his arms around her and held her for a minute.

Just for that minute, because he hadn't kissed her or done anything except hug her, Olivia had a very odd feeling. She felt as if he was her father instead of her lover. She felt magically, blissfully safe from any danger or grief. And she felt that he loved her.

It lasted only a minute, like a fleeting dream. None of it was remotely true. He was her lover or nothing. He was the source of grief and danger, not safety. And he didn't love her at all.

She desperately wished that all of it was otherwise. And she wished her real father would hold her like that. She had a vast, uneasable ache inside her, as if her innards had been dragged into a black hole.

She said against his shoulder, "Are you glad to see me?"

She had amused him again. He took her hand and rubbed it across the front of his jeans, so she could feel his erection. "What d' you think?"

She was embarrassed. She hadn't meant that.

Or maybe she had. She moved her hand against him and he pushed against her hand. She wondered what he would think if she undid his zipper and put her hand inside. Maybe that was what he had in mind when he put her hand there. It wasn't something she could ask: Do you want me to . . . No doubt he would have an obscenely succinct way of phrasing it. She just had to do it.

She did it. She had to grope around a bit to get inside his shorts but eventually she succeeded in stroking his erect penis. She could feel it move and swell under her fingers.

Sexual arrangements were an extraordinary thing. It was clear that God was not human, or any earthly creature at all, because He had had no regard for dignity when He organized this most vital function. That men should change size and shape, that women should, as it were, drool over them, that both should become temporarily demented enough to tear off their clothes and rub various parts of their bodies frantically against each other seemed a deliberate demeaning of human pride.

Unless you were feeling that way, in which case it became the most wonderful thing in the world and a stroke of divine genius.

After they had gone upstairs and torn off each other's clothes and rubbed the appropriate parts of their bodies together to their mutual satisfaction, Olivia said to Nick, "I thought you'd gone off me."

"When did you think that?"

"Yesterday. In the car."

"You daft kid, what would make you think that?"

"You didn't say anything. You didn't even look at me."

"That's because I was trying not to think about how much I wanted to screw you."

He was lying on his back and she was lying beside him. She raised her head to look at him, to see if he was making fun of her. But he wasn't even smiling. "Were you really?"

He did smile then. "Would I lie to you, kitten?"

He drove her nearly home and let her out by Highgate station. She was going to be so late she would have to make excuses to her father. Something to do with the orchestra rehearsal, the one she had skipped. If she did it again the teacher would throw her out of the orchestra, and how would she explain that to her father?

She kissed Nick good-bye. She felt like a bedouin taking one last drink from the well before setting out across the desert, even though they had agreed she would come back on Friday. She asked him another question. She dared to ask him only because his strangely shameless honesty meant he would actually answer her.

"Nick, do you want me a lot?"

"You mean how much or how often?"

"Both."

"Yes."

That made her laugh, though it pleased her as well. "Do you want me when I'm not around?"

"Sometimes."

"When?"

"What do you want, dates and times? I've got to go, I'm holding up the fucking traffic. I'll see you on Friday."

It wasn't sometimes for her. She spent all the intervening week thinking about him, the way they say an alcoholic looks forward to the next drink.

37

After school she ran to the Tube station and managed to get to Wapping by five-thirty. It was dark and raining. Nick wasn't there.

She thought perhaps he had been delayed. She didn't want to stand around waiting in the dark, so she walked up to the beautiful Hawksmoor church at the top of the road. Colored light gleamed through the windows. Someone was playing a Bach toccata on the organ. Standing in the outer darkness she felt like one of the foolish virgins shut out of the wedding feast.

No one answered the door when she got back to the studio. She took her walk again and came back and he still wasn't there. She was afraid to wait any longer and she had to get home. Maybe he wasn't coming. Maybe he had forgotten.

Maybe he didn't want her anymore.

By the time she was standing on the platform at the Tube station she was about ready to throw herself under the train instead of getting on it. Coming out of the station at Highgate it was still raining and she realized she had left her umbrella on the train. All in all, a perfect day.

When she got home she took off her wet clothes and had a long bath. She felt like crying but she didn't even have enough inside her to make proper tears. There was a kind of wasp that laid its eggs in a caterpillar and when the wasp larvae hatched they ate the caterpillar from the inside out, saving all the really vital organs till the last so the caterpillar wouldn't die on them before they were ready to go out into the world. Something like that must have happened to her, not in a physical but an emotional sense.

She was roused from her torpor of misery by her father banging on the door. "Lia, have you gone to sleep in there? It's time for dinner and someone's on the phone for you."

"If it's Meg tell her I'll ring her back."

"It's not Meg. I think it's your friend from the construction industry."

That at least gave her a reason for getting out of the bath instead of lying there and drowning. And it was faintly comforting to find that someone still wanted her, even if it was Charlie instead of Nick. She dried herself off hastily and went downstairs to the phone.

"Hi," said Charlie.

"Hi. Did you have a good holiday?"

"Wonderful. You should try it sometime."

"What, Tenerife or a holiday?"

"Either. Both. And I've escaped from the trenches, now I get to make tea for the secretaries at headquarters. Pretty soon they might even trust me with the petty cash."

"What did you do to get a promotion?"

"Well, nothing. It's actually because they don't need any more slaveys. My father says he's having to lay them off in droves. No one's doing any building."

"That sounds rather dire."

"Dire is right. The only thing worse than being a slavey is being an unemployed slavey. But I suppose it's always bad this time of year. Things should start to look up in the spring. Do you want to go to a film tomorrow night?"

"I'm already going to a film with Meg."

"Who's Meg?"

"My friend. You met her, she was at the pub that night. You gave her a lift home."

"I remember. A little blonde, isn't she?"

This seemed such an unlikely way of describing Megan that Olivia had to think for a moment. "Yeah, I suppose she is."

"What if I dig up a friend who wants to see a film and we sort of bump into you outside the cinema?"

"That sounds nice. We'll practice acting surprised."

Megan wasn't totally delighted with the arrangements. She grumbled about it as they walked across Leicester Square.

"What am I supposed to do with myself while you and Charlie are snogging?"

"I think his friend is supposed to amuse you. Anyway, what makes you think we won't just watch the film?"

"Because you're in love, that's why."

Olivia denied it vehemently. "I am not."

"Yes, you are. You're all up and down emotionally. You're going round in a total daze. Classic symptoms."

Charlie turned up at that point with his friend, a slim, fair-haired boy with gold-rimmed glasses.

"Fancy meeting you here," he greeted Olivia. "I told Jon this was a good place to pull birds, and here we've scored in the first two minutes. He'll be very impressed."

She tried not to giggle. "Do I know you?"

"You do now." He pointed to himself and the others in turn. "Charlie, Jon, Lia, Meg, right? Hi, Meg, nice to see you again. Come on, I've got the tickets, let's go inside."

"Jon is big on films," Charlie told Olivia as the feature film started. "After he's explained this picture to me I'll be able to explain it to your old man, symbolism and all."

He was talking into her ear while she watched the screen. In the first three minutes several people had been killed in spectacularly gory fashion. "If you can find any symbolism in this rubbish Daddy really will be impressed."

She had turned her head to address her remarks to his ear. He took the opportunity to kiss her.

"Stop that," she whispered, before she remembered that she was supposed to be in love with him. If Megan thought she was in love, then she had to make Megan believe it was Charlie she was in love with.

She took his hand and held it in both of hers, in her lap where the intertwined fingers would be clearly visible, all for the benefit of Megan. Charlie understandably thought it was for his benefit and took advantage of a night scene to put his hand up her skirt. Since she was wearing tights there wasn't much he could have done anyway, but she grabbed the straying hand and whispered, "Not here."

The way she had phrased her objection meant he would probably have another try on some more propitious occasion, and it was quite possible that her adventures earlier in the week would mean that she would soon be wanting him to do just that and more.

She felt faint at the idea that she might already be pregnant. The odds would be higher if she had seen Nick yesterday. If she were at all regular that would have been just about the right time for ovulation, a fortnight after the start of her last period. That was the sort of useful information she had learned in biology class.

What a hopeless, painful muddle her life was in. There was no good news even to be hoped for, just different sorts of bad news.

After the film they all went to McDonald's for hamburgers; at least the boys had hamburgers while Olivia and Megan shared an order of chips.

"You girls want to have a word with Jonnie," Charlie told them. "He's mad on making videos."

"What are you suggesting?" Megan demanded. "We're not that sort of girl."

Jon went faintly red and blinked behind his fashionable glasses. "This man is a serious artist," Charlie rebuked Megan. "He's doing media studies at college. I was thinking you might want to make a film of that play you and Lia are going to put on."

"That's a brilliant idea." Megan looked over at Jon again. "At the very least you could just come along and video the performance, couldn't you?"

"Well, sure, why not? What's the play?"

"It's a modern version of an old Greek play. Lia and I wrote it and now we're directing it."

"Meg's doing most of the directing," said Olivia. "She's much better at telling people what to do. Also, the whole play was really her idea."

Jon blinked again and pushed his hair out of his eyes. He had fine fair hair like unripened cornsilk, and it tended to flop around. He was looking at Megan with a vaguely dazed expression. "It sounds really good. I'd really like to film it."

"I'll send you my bill for the introduction," Charlie said breezily. "How's the play coming along?"

"We're having casting problems," Olivia explained. "We wanted to give the title role to Devika Patel because it says in the play that she's an Asian woman, but Ms. Pankhurst says we shouldn't do that. She says it's sort of racist to make a point of the fact that Devika's Asian. She says Devika can play any other character but she shouldn't play an Asian woman."

"So you'll have an Asian playing a Greek and an English girl playing an Asian, is that right?"

"That's what she says."

Charlie snorted. "It sounds crazy to me."

"It's not really crazy, it's just sort of deliberately color-blind."

"The big problem," added Megan, "is that Devika's really burned up about it. She really wants to play Medea. She'd be super at it too, she's very tall and dramatic looking."

"Well, I'm sure you'll work something out," Charlie said briskly. "Lia, I'd better take you home before your daddy calls the police. We'll leave Meg to look after Jonnie. They get off at the same Tube station, I believe."

"We'll cope somehow," Megan agreed. "I'll talk to you tomorrow, Lia."

Jon was too distracted to say good-bye. He shook his hair out of his eyes and went on gazing at Megan.

Charlie managed to hail a taxi, no mean feat at that time of night in the West End. He dodged through the traffic on Charing Cross Road, dragging Olivia with him, to catch a cab going down the opposite side of the street. They were nearly run down by a bus. The bus, Olivia noticed when they were safely in the cab, would be going past Highgate station.

"We could have taken that bus," she pointed out.

"What for?"

"It's a lot cheaper, for one thing."

"I'm a working man, remember, not a poverty-stricken schoolboy anymore. Anyway, taxis are much more comfortable. And more fun."

"Fun?"

"Fun. Close your eyes."

She closed her eyes. He kissed her.

She put her arms around his neck and he kissed her again, a long, deep kiss involving tongues. After quite a lot of kissing he put his hand inside her open coat and unbuttoned her blouse. Before she could decide if she really wanted him to do that, he had her bra undone and was stroking her naked breasts.

"Charlie, don't do that, the cabby can see."

"That should make his day. Anyway, he doesn't care, he's seen everything. God, you're beautiful." He bent his head to kiss her breasts, to suck at her nipples.

She leaned back, cradling his head. She liked him to cuddle her, but this was more alarming. She shivered. Not surprising, since being bare-breasted on a cold November night would give anyone gooseflesh. She shivered again. "Charlie, stop," she whispered. "I'm cold."

Charlie raised his head from her breast and looked at her in a way that frightened her, as if he had never seen her before. He's turned into a Martian too, she thought. She couldn't stop shivering. It felt like a fit of fever. She clutched at her clothing.

"I'll do that."

He was shaking almost as much as she was, though he was fully clothed, but he managed to get her bra done up and her blouse refastened. He kept kissing her while he did it, on her mouth, on any bare bit of flesh.

"You're so beautiful, you're the most beautiful girl I've ever seen. I think about you all the time."

"All the time?"

"All day long. I stare at the spreadsheet on the computer and think about your breasts. I get out the tea bags and think about your mouth. While they're explaining costing procedures to me I'm thinking about your legs. All the time."

He put his arms around her and she leaned against him. His overcoat must have been cashmere; it was so surprisingly soft. "You shouldn't do that," she whispered, meaning it, warning him. "You shouldn't do that, it's dangerous."

38

She was so terrified her voice squeaked. "Nick? It's Lia."

"Oh, yeah." An agonizing pause. "Sorry about Friday. I got held up. There wasn't any way I could let you know about it."

She let out her breath. At least he hadn't forgotten. Though his offhand tone did nothing to diminish her other fears. "Can we ..."

She couldn't finish that. And didn't need to. But she didn't get the answer she was hoping for. "This is a bugger of a week. I'm tied up every day. Next week's better."

In her dismay she said aloud, "I can't wait a week." Then she could have bitten her tongue.

"Neither can I," he said more softly. Her heart lurched. "How about Thursday, sevenish?"

"Okay."

It wasn't really okay. She would have to make up some excuse for her father. He didn't like her being out on school nights. But anything would be better than waiting another week. She would have shriveled up and died before next week arrived.

She had another bad lesson with Mrs. Stone, even worse than the last one, because Nick being so much nearer, only a couple of hours away, distracted her so much more.

"You were doing so well this term," Mrs. Stone told her. "I had great hopes, we were making good progress. But the last few weeks we've gone nowhere. Your soul is somewhere else." She looked at Olivia with her piercing dark eyes—Gypsy eyes, Olivia had always thought they were—and said, with surprising gentleness for Mrs. Stone, "Are you in some trouble, child?"

"No, no," Olivia said hastily. "I mean, it will all settle down in a while. It's just that everything is so confused right now at home, what with the baby and moving house and my mother getting married."

Mrs. Stone's nostrils quivered. She had a fine long nose, and a very expressive one. "Baby, marriage? What's all this?"

Olivia explained very briefly. It was all horribly embarrassing, as well as painful. "My father's wife is having a baby next month and they haven't got room for the baby and me and Daddy's books in their house, so they're moving house at the same time, and also at the same time my mother is getting married again and she's going to have a baby in the spring."

Put baldly like that, it did sound like enough to drive anybody to distraction. Only Olivia hadn't been worrying about any of that lately; she was too taken up with Nick and whether or not she herself was pregnant.

"I see, I see," said Mrs. Stone. For some reason the information made her quite angry. "Children," she muttered to herself. "Everybody is children now."

Olivia thought she must have meant everybody has children now, and couldn't think why this idea should upset Mrs. Stone.

"Never mind, child," Mrs. Stone said more briskly. "No doubt, as you say, things will sort themselves out in time. But remember, music is a great consolation, and it never broke anybody's heart."

Once Olivia would have scoffed at this advice. But over the past summer she had consoled herself with Bach's partita and come out of a black time with something good to show for it. The trouble right now was that she couldn't concentrate on anything while she was seeing Nick. Screwing him was destroying her mind.

Walking round Wapping in the dark made her nervous. She had seen a film about Jack the Ripper on TV, which Nick said had been shot down there, on account of the narrow cobbled streets and Victorian industrial buildings and the eerie, misty Thames. She couldn't help thinking about that film as she waited for him to answer the bell.

She heard footsteps coming toward her. Maybe it was the

man she had seen before, who had a place on the same staircase. She didn't dare look round. She wanted to look as if
she was confident of getting inside in just a few seconds. She
fumbled in her pocket, pretending to be getting her keys.

The footsteps came right up behind Olivia. She didn't know
whether to run or what. If it was Nick's neighbor he was
only coming to his own front door.

Whoever it was put his arms around her and pulled her
roughly back against him. She let out a little scream. More of
a squeak, because he had squeezed the breath right out of
her. He said in her ear, "That won't do you any good."

"Nick! You scared the life out of me."

"I know. You shouldn't be coming here by yourself after
dark. I'll meet you at the station next time."

"I've never been attacked here by anyone but you," she
said indignantly. She leaned back against him, so glad to feel
him there, so glad to be with him. When she wasn't with him
it was just Nick she missed and longed for, the whole man
body and soul, but as soon as he touched her she began to
want him in a more physical way. "Are you going to assault
me sexually?"

"Just as soon as I get you inside." He unzipped her jacket
and ran his hands over her sweater, groping her breasts. "Or
maybe even sooner."

She turned to him and put her arms up to his shoulders
and kissed him. She ran her hands down inside his jacket,
across his chest. She kissed the hollow at the base of his
throat, touching his pulse with her tongue. That made his
heart beat faster—she could feel the pulse rate shoot up, and
it encouraged her. She began to unbutton his shirt, one button
at a time, kissing and nibbling her way down his chest as it
was revealed, pinching and rubbing the flat nipples to make
them tighten.

"Hey, wait." He was laughing as he caught her hands, but
she could hear the husky tremor in his voice. She was making
him shake just by touching him, the way he did with her.
"Come upstairs and do that."

He unlocked the door and took her upstairs. As soon as
they were inside the studio he kissed her, his hands jerking
her pelvis up against his. She undid the last buttons on his

shirt, pulling it open and free of his belt. She knelt down and put the tip of her tongue into the hollow of his navel, just above his belt buckle. She began to undo the buckle. She wanted to touch him everywhere, to eat him up. Her craving for him swept aside her shyness and shame.

She had thought after her first awful experience that she could never again bring herself to take his cock into her mouth. But this time it was her doing what she wanted to him rather than him guiding or even forcing her. She had no fear now of not pleasing him. It gave her a sense of great power as she felt his body respond to her caresses. She could do to him what he did to her, she could make him come and cry out . . .

She did, and he did.

He sank to his knees in front of her. She straddled his thighs and put her arms around him, sliding them under his open shirt and leather jacket. He was bare from throat to thigh, and she was fully clothed. He was the sexiest, most beautiful man on earth. She loved him more than she had even yesterday thought possible.

What she said next surprised even herself. "I want to take a picture of you."

The idea amused him. "All right, why not? What d' you want me to do?"

"Just stay right where you are." She went over to pick up one of his cameras. It looked horribly complicated. "How does this work?"

"Move that around to there." He reached over and did it for her. "Now all you have to do is point and press the button."

"If it's that simple, how do you get anybody to pay you to do it?"

"That's only the automatic setting. The photographer's equivalent of the missionary position."

Olivia looked at him through the viewfinder. He was still in the state she had reduced him to, his clothing all undone to reveal his body from neck to crotch. He was smiling at her—not, she knew, because she was about to take his picture but because he found it funny, the sight of her peering down at him through the camera.

She pressed the button.

"Anything else your heart desires?"

Quite a lot, really, she thought, but all of it unobtainable, so she would have to settle for something else. She wouldn't even be able to keep the picture she had just taken, it was far too dangerous. "Can you stand up and make yourself look respectable?"

"Sure I can, but it won't be much fun."

He did it anyway, fastening the jeans and buttoning the shirt but leaving the jacket open. Then he propped one shoulder against the wall and folded his arms across his chest. He wasn't smiling now. He looked faintly challenging, faintly petulant, faintly, well, as if you might be able to interest him if you tried very hard. He looked very sexy.

"You're just like the camera, you do it all automatically. You should have been a model."

"I was."

She nearly dropped the camera. "You—you were? What did you model?"

"Well, it wasn't Moss Bros. clobber. Use your loaf, baby. How would a fifteen-year-old kid keep himself alive in places like Paris and Amsterdam? That's how I ended up in this line of work, when I found out that the man with the fucking camera calls the shots." He straightened up and came over to take the camera out of her frozen grip. "My turn now."

"What do you mean, your turn?"

"I'm going to do some shots of you. Just for fun. I'll burn them all afterward if you want me to."

She wasn't sure if she trusted him. "Promise?"

"Cross my heart." He gathered the front of her sweater into his fist and tugged gently. "Come on, kid, take 'em off."

"What, just like that?"

"This time we'll work backward. You start off starkers and I'll dress you."

When she was all undressed he took off his leather jacket and put it on her, zipping it halfway up. She looked at herself in the mirror. The jacket barely covered her bottom; she might just have been wearing something underneath. To remove all doubt, he told her to put her hands in the pockets and bend forward. As she leaned toward the mirror, the jacket rode up her bottom and gaped open at the front to reveal her breasts. He took a picture of the front and the back view.

Just taking off a jacket could be remarkably sexy, it turned out. He unzipped it and pulled it off one shoulder so that the cuff hid her pubic hair while her breasts were exposed. Then he hauled it further down so that the sleeves dangled empty, with her hands still hidden in the upper part. The jacket covered her hips. He got her to turn slightly sideways so that her left hand inside the sleeve concealed the mount of Venus but her right side was bare all the way up. After that he took the jacket off and draped it over her shoulders. She had to lean forward with her arms folded across the stool, so that her breasts were pushed upward and forward by the frame that her arms made.

He touched her and gave her instructions in that oddly detached manner that she remembered from the other time. "Move your feet apart, keep your knees straight, that's it, more, more, spread your legs, that's right, good girl." She didn't want to think about what the rear view of that particular pose must look like.

Then he took off his shirt and put it on her. She was surprised and pleased, because he couldn't have done this with any of his models; it was too intimate and not at all professional to take off his clothes and put them on her. It was an amazingly sexy thing to do.

All she had on was his shirt and all he had on now was his jeans. They went through the same exercise again, but with quite different poses. The shirt was made of cotton and you could do all sorts of things with it that couldn't be done with an inflexible leather jacket, mostly things Olivia would never have thought of doing.

When he had stripped the shirt off her in photographic stages and she was naked again, he unbuckled his belt and stepped out of his jeans, leaving him in his underpants. He handed her the jeans. "Let's see how you look in these."

"They'll be too big for me."

"That's the idea."

She pulled them on. It was the sexiest thing of all, feeling the rough denim against her soft flesh, the fabric still warm with his body heat, making an unimaginably intimate connection with him.

"Don't do the belt up, leave the zipper halfway. Keep your hands down there. Perfect. Now unzip it all the way, let them slide halfway down your hips, that's beautiful. Hold them up with your left hand and move your right hand down there. Good girl. All right, go down on your knees. No, like this."

He came and stood behind her as she knelt. He pushed the jeans down and her thighs apart. He took her hand and slid it down into her pubic hair, pressing her fingertips over the moist and swollen flesh below. He said in her ear, "Do it for real, baby. Frig yourself for me."

She had never heard that word used in its literal sense before. She had never really touched herself that way before. It would have been embarrassing enough in the privacy of her own room, but to do it in front of him—the thought alone should have made her curl up and die.

She didn't die. It was enormously pleasurable in a sickening, shameful way, both the sensations that her own hand produced in her belly and the knowledge that Nick was watching her do it. He took a picture of her doing it.

Then he laid her down on her back and arranged her to his satisfaction: knees drawn up and apart, jeans crumpled around her ankles, making love to herself.

He must have photographed her like that, but she couldn't be sure because she was so distracted by what else he was doing. He was describing to her in the most graphic and obscenely explicit language exactly what she was doing to herself, how she looked while she was doing it, what effect it was having on him, and what he was going to do about it.

The monosyllables made a lewd litany, a kind of Ur-poetry from the time before true language and true lies came into the world. Cock, dick, rod, prick, stiff, stuff, poke, pork, box, bush, quim, crack, gash, twat, honey pot . . . Another time he might have used those same words to make her blush or laugh, but now it was like he had wired her to the electric mains. She was convulsed with sensation, with shame, with unbearable hunger for him. He was going to talk her to a climax.

She kicked off the jeans. He came into her violently, forcing her, filling her, taking her, making her, wolfing her down and devouring her whole. She came almost as soon as he entered her. It was a long coming, an orgasmic eternity, jolting her over and over as he spilled himself into her. Oh God, he was so good, he was the best man alive... and the least redeemable.

How could he make love to her like that and not love her? Maybe he did and wouldn't say, because he was going to marry her mother; couldn't say, because she was not yet sixteen.

She too was forbidden to say how she loved him, but he had to know, he had to know. When he knew her like that, in the biblical sense, it engendered a deeper knowledge. As if they had become like stars, diffuse and interpenetrative bodies.

She felt like a star all the way home, floating in space and glowing.

39

They were all there, Charlie's whole family assembled at his home to meet her. It was quite terrifying.

It was also quite chaotic, which distracted some attention from her. The little girls, Charlie's nieces, were shy for about thirty seconds before they resumed their entertainment of chasing each other round the house. That provided the background for everything else that went on.

Charlie's father looked surprisingly like her own father. He was about ten years older, shorter and heavier, but with the same dark hair and blue eyes, the same fairly regular features. In his speech and manner he was nothing like her father, but that was scarcely surprising. People like her father didn't exist outside a university.

When she offered her hand to him he held it in both his hands rather than shaking it. She thought he meant it kindly, so as not to seem businesslike. "Hello, Lia. We're happy to meet you at last. Charlie's talked of nothing else for months."

Olivia smiled and nodded and said nothing. There didn't seem to be anything she could say that wouldn't embarrass Charlie. Then she met Charlie's mother, who was about the same age as his father but already mostly gray. His mother didn't like her, she could tell, but she couldn't tell why. A year ago she would have wondered how you could dislike someone you didn't even know, but she had learned a lot in a year.

Then she was introduced to his brothers, Barry and Jackie, his sisters, Katy and Bridget, their husbands (Tweedledee and Tweedledum), and the two shrieking nieces, Maureen and Maeve. She couldn't have identified any one of them if she had met them in the street five minutes later. Her brain had turned to mush.

It didn't matter. Charlie kept a firm grip on her hand or arm and steered her wherever she needed to go. She left them to chatter to each other, which they did incessantly, and answered questions when she was asked.

The house was on the Hampstead side of Finchley Road, of the type that Olivia's father called Stockbroker Tudor (though not in front of Althea's father). It had a very large garden and a four-car garage. There were four cars in the drive but no cars in any of the garages.

All the furniture was obviously new or obviously old. The new things looked more suitable in the context of a modern house, but Charlie's father was very pleased with the old things. He pointed them out to Olivia and described them as if she ought to know what he was talking about. Perhaps it was just that he hoped she would know.

The strangest thing about the house was that no one actually seemed to live there. Everything was immaculate (except where the little girls had taken a hand). There were no books or magazines. The brothers-in-law perched on the edges of their chairs in the huge sitting room. It was only when Maeve (or perhaps it was Maureen) insisted on dragging her into the TV room to show her something that Olivia discovered where they really spent their time.

The furniture here was like an old familiar teddy bear, battered and comfortable. There were women's magazines and Sunday tabloids, a card table and a bag of knitting, a collection of small crystal creatures on the windowsill, and a fat ginger cat curled up in an armchair.

Olivia was sitting on the arm of the chair patting the cat when Charlie came in looking for her.

"My mother would be appalled if she found you in here."

"Why?"

"This is the seamy side of our lives."

"Don't let the cat hear you. Anyway, your niece brought me in here. It's not as if I was snooping around."

Maureen (or Maeve) had wandered off by this time. The cat decided to follow her. Charlie collapsed into the armchair the cat had abandoned and pulled Olivia down onto his lap. "My father's thrilled with you."

"Don't be silly."

"No, really, he is. A professor's daughter, by Jesus, you can't go out and buy one of those like an Old Master or an antique."

It was a good thing Charlie's father was pleased, because her own father certainly hadn't been. When she told him she had been invited to Charlie's house for Sunday lunch he seemed to regard it as next thing to an engagement.

She could answer him quite coolly because it didn't really matter to her. Or to him, if he only knew it. If he knew ... if he knew one-tenth of the truth he would be begging her to go out with Charlie, to fall in love with Charlie. There were worse fates than Charlie.

"Daddy," she said patiently, "if I'd been going out with Charlie like I have and you didn't know him you'd want to meet him, wouldn't you? So why shouldn't his parents want to do the same thing?"

Her father looked at her. She knew what he was thinking: because it's one thing if your son is screwing some unknown girl, and another thing if some yob is screwing your daughter. Nick would have said just that, but her father couldn't say it.

Charlie had turned up to get her this time in a different

car, a larger and newer and fancier one. "My mother's," he explained before she could ask.

"It's nice," Olivia said politely, since some comment seemed to be required. She couldn't tell one car from another, except for flash ones like Nick's XJS. This one said AUDI quite prominently, and by the registration it was three years old. That all seemed perfectly respectable.

But Charlie thought he had something to apologize for. "My father has a Jag, but he won't let me drive it on account of the astronomical cost of the insurance. This one isn't as posh as your father's."

Olivia looked at him, vaguely puzzled. The last car her father had bought was the elderly Volvo he had left with her mother. Then she realized Charlie meant Althea's brand-new BMW, provided free of charge by the bank for which she swapped. For the sake of her father's honor she didn't enlighten Charlie. Instead she gave him a broad smile as she got into the car. "Never mind, I'll slum it for today."

Charlie put the car into gear. "You look great."

"You always say that."

"Because it's always true. Don't be nervous, by the way. I've told them to expect Princess Diana, so they'll be happy with anything upward of Kylie Minogue."

"Am I upward of Kylie Minogue?"

"Well, she's only five feet high and has no tits at all, so I should think you'll be a great improvement."

"Oh thanks, you're lovely," she said, laughing. "Did you know I was considering introducing you to Daddy as a student of nuclear physics?"

"Thank you too. Is he a nuclear physicist?"

"Be serious. He's writing a book about Yorkists and Lancastrians."

Charlie started to laugh. He stopped for a red light while they both laughed helplessly. The light turned green and he sobered up enough to drive on. "Why don't we forget this family affair and go somewhere else? We could go to Brighton for the day. And the night."

"That sounds terrific, but you should have thought of it yesterday. I have to be at school by nine o'clock tomorrow morning."

"Another time, maybe."

"Did you know that Meg went out with your friend Jon last night?"

Charlie was amused. "Did she? I was wondering if he'd work up the nerve. How did that go?"

"Okay, I guess. They went to a film and then discussed it afterwards. Nothing romantic happened."

"Disappointed, was she? I'll have to have a word with that boy."

"I think Meg's quite capable of speaking up for herself."

"I can imagine. She's a fearsome little woman. Jonnie is totally smitten."

"I don't think she cares about that. She just wants him to come and film the play."

"Fearsome, just like I said. What have you done about your leading lady problem?"

"Oh, Daddy solved that. He said if Devika were a blue-eyed blonde would we still want to cast her as Medea? I said yeah, basically we would. You'd just have to make her up, wouldn't you, and that's what Ms. Pankhurst is proposing to do with someone else anyway. So Daddy said, then if you don't give her the part you'll be practicing racial discrimination. So we pointed that out to Ms. P. and she had to give in."

Charlie had kissed her just before they got out of the car. She liked that. He was telling her he was on her side, whatever. Nobody else in her life had ever told her that, much less meant it.

Now in the armchair he kissed her again. She responded, a little uneasily in a strange house. He ran his hand up her leg, under her skirt, which made her even more uneasy. "Charlie, we can't carry on like this in your parents' house."

"Come on, just for a minute, Lia. They won't come in here, they're being all formal in the drawing room."

It wouldn't have done him much good anyway; she was wearing tights and having her period. She had been horribly dismayed, when the period started, to find out she wasn't carrying Nick's baby. Relieved in a way, but mostly disappointed.

Charlie, if he only knew, had reason to be disappointed too. If she had been pregnant he would have got the chance to put more than his hand between her legs. But not now. She told him sternly, "You just keep your hands out from under my skirt."

He took her at her word and started to unbutton the top of her shirtwaist dress. Then his sister Bridget came in to call them for lunch. Olivia was mortally embarrassed, but Charlie and Bridget only looked amused and Bridget went away again.

"Sorry."

"You jolly well ought to be."

"Bridgie doesn't care. Just don't tell them you're only fifteen. They'll think I'm cradle robbing."

"Well, aren't you?"

"Well, am I?"

They began to laugh at the same time. He kissed her again before they went in to lunch.

Afterward when Charlie drove her home he said, "They liked you."

"Your mother didn't."

"Oh, she wouldn't. She's like your father. She'll come round."

Olivia wanted to ask how a builder's wife could possibly take exception to her son keeping company with a don's daughter. But she didn't. The explanation would probably be as complicated as the story she would have had to tell about her father's childhood in order to explain his attitude toward Nick. It was easier just to leave these things a mystery.

40

When Olivia came home from school Althea was already there, though it was supposed to have been her last day at work. She was lying on the sofa, looking pale.

"Althea, aren't you feeling well?"

"I'm not sure. I keep getting pains, but then they go away. I don't want to call Ross and make a fuss if it's only a false alarm."

"Daddy will be home in an hour or so anyway," Olivia pointed out. "You're not going to have the baby that fast, whatever. I'll make some tea."

Olivia went to the kitchen, made the tea, and returned to the sitting room with two full mugs. Althea looked ... distressed was the best word. She was biting her lip and holding her great belly with both hands.

Olivia put the tea down beside her. Althea had always been glossy and polished, in charge of herself and in charge of her world. It frightened Olivia to see her in this state. Althea was part of the adult world, a world of freedom and power. Right now she had neither. She was in the grip of biology. Human rights and dignity, women's rights and empowerment, even the more concrete fact that she was a highly paid and highly valued employee of a large investment bank, had no bearing on her situation now. She was a woman with a baby inside her that had to get out somehow or they both would die.

"Althea," Olivia said timidly, "are you okay?"

"I will be." Althea spoke between gritted teeth. "Wait a minute."

Olivia waited and the pain passed. Althea sat up, took her mug of tea, and sipped gingerly.

"Maybe I should ring the doctor."

"Not yet," Althea said sharply. "It's probably false labor, the damned thing isn't due for another fortnight. I'd feel a fool raising the alarm and then lying around in hospital for hours while nothing happened. Let's wait and see."

At Althea's insistence they waited till Olivia's father came home. For nearly two hours Olivia had to soothe Althea through her pains, which came about every five minutes but didn't seem to get any closer together, as they should have been according to the book, though they did get stronger.

Olivia held Althea's hands, able to follow her contractions by the strength of her grip. "You're supposed to be relaxing," Olivia told her sternly. "Deep breathing or something. What did you learn in your prenatal classes?"

"I'm trying, but it keeps getting worse. I missed half those classes anyway because of working late to deal with New York."

Althea was probably the last person of whom one could demand relaxation, Olivia realized. A woman who traded millions of pounds of other people's money every day—even only notional pounds, whatever they were—was never going to be able to lie back and let nature take its course.

On the contrary, Althea was fighting against it. "I hate this," she confessed to Olivia. "I wish they'd just knock me out and wake me up when it's over. It seems barbaric that women should have to suffer like this."

"You've only been at it two hours," Olivia reminded her. "It says in your book here that the average first baby takes twelve hours."

"It's horrible. I must have been mad."

"Don't you want the baby?"

"It's not fair. Why should I have to go through this for a baby? Having a baby is perfectly natural. It shouldn't hurt at all."

"Dying is perfectly natural too but I expect it hurts," Olivia observed unsympathetically. "Anyway, if you were a termite queen you'd give birth to thousands of babies every day and think nothing of it."

"What have termites got to do with it? You're a weird kid, Lia."

"Here's Daddy."

Her father's first act was to phone Althea's obstetrician. The orders from there were to bring her into hospital sharpish. Althea went into a flap. She hadn't packed, she wasn't ready, the baby's things weren't ready. She was supposed to have two more weeks to do all sorts of things. Olivia had never seen Althea beside herself like this. She seemed to feel that Someone was acting unfairly in starting everything a fortnight before she had expected it. In the end, Olivia had to pack for her.

After her father had taken Althea and her suitcase off to the hospital, Olivia made herself something to eat, did her homework, and played the violin for an hour. By eleven o'clock she was thinking about going to bed. Twelve hours meant that the baby wasn't likely to be born before tomorrow morning.

Then her father phoned to say that the doctor had decided to cut the Gordian knot and do a cesarean. They had just taken Althea away.

Since her father sounded disturbed about this, Olivia pointed out that it was exactly what Althea wanted. "Just before you came home, Daddy, she said she wished they'd knock her out and wake her up when it was over. So she's getting her wish."

Her father did not seem much comforted.

She waited up for another hour without further news. Then she decided to go to bed, but it was hard to fall asleep.

She was dozing off when her father came home. He came upstairs to her room and stood in the doorway, outlined by the faint light from downstairs.

"Lia, are you awake?"

She reached out to turn on her bedside lamp. "What's happened? Is everything okay?"

"Everything's fine. It's a boy."

"How's Althea?"

"She's fine too. She was asleep when I left. They said to come back in the morning."

He had come over to her bedside. She sat up. She felt like the dead king deprived of his funeral, obliged instead to hail his successor. "Did you see it? I mean him?"

"Yes, I held him."

He sat down on the edge of her bed. He had come upstairs straightaway, without even taking off his overcoat. He was flushed with something like triumph; some great thing had been accomplished, a son had come into the world. Olivia wondered if he remembered now what he had said six months ago about learning to like the baby.

This little boy, this infant Macduff, was her brother. Half-brother, anyway. But for her father it was a new family. It replaced her and the old, broken family. She might have had some comfort if she had known she had her own baby, her own family within her, but instead she was alone. Yet she had to be glad for her father's sake.

Her father said, "It doesn't seem right, Althea having missed it all. She ought to have been the star of the show."

"I told you, she wanted it that way. She was really scared." Olivia felt a faint stirring of contempt, however unfair. Althea had evaded the primary obligation of womankind through the miracles of modern medicine. It seemed like cheating.

She looked at her father and forgot about Althea. The lamplight caught a glint of rain in his dark hair. His overcoat was streaked with rain. He had held the newborn baby. She wished he would hold her. The pang of longing was so sharp she reached up to touch his face. His cheek, rough with nearly a full day's growth of whiskers, had raindrops on it too.

"You're wet. It must be raining."

"I didn't notice."

She turned her head away and reached out for him at the same time. His coat carried the cold and damp of the night air. The chill went through her thin cotton nightgown and made her shiver.

"You're cold," he said, maybe feeling her tremble. "You'd better get back under the duvet."

"You're the one who's cold. I'm warm from being in bed. When can I see the baby?"

"Tomorrow, if you like. I'll come home first and take you down with me."

She didn't want to see the baby; she knew she would hate it. More than the baby, she would hate Althea looking smug and triumphant because she had made Olivia redundant.

Redundant meant surplus to requirements. It also meant they didn't want you anymore. And why would any man want a gauche, adolescent daughter who tied him to the wife he had left, when he had a brand-new baby son produced by the new-and-improved-model wife?

"We should celebrate. But you need to get your sleep."

"I wasn't asleep. I'm not the least bit sleepy now."

"There's no champagne in the house, but we could share a glass of wine."

Olivia got out of bed and followed her father downstairs. He took his coat off and poured them each a glass of white wine. When he said share a glass he meant it; they were only half full. Because of the unfortunate encounter after the dinner with Nick, she supposed. He sat in the armchair and she sat on the arm of the chair and they touched glasses and drank to the infant Matthew.

Olivia leaned against the back of the chair, her arm behind her father's head, and sipped her half-glass of wine. "Tell me what happened. Why did they do a cesarean?"

"Something wrong with the heartbeat. These days they wire you up like an astronaut as soon as you go into labor. They know exactly what's happening and take no chances. Quite right too, I suppose."

"Lucky for Althea. She wanted it done like that." She shuddered eloquently. "I'd rather do it the old-fashioned way. Better than being knocked out and cut up."

Her father looked at her with faint surprise. She knew why. Mentally he linked her with the baby being born rather than the woman having the baby. Whereas if she hadn't gone to the clinic with Nick she would have been six months along by now. And her father would have been looking at her in a very different way.

Althea was actually in a maternity clinic, not a real hospital. Her employers paid for private health insurance, so she could have the baby in style. Only, of course, she had missed the whole thing. Tonight she was propped up on pillows in bed, all made up and wearing a fetching nightgown. She looked like a cover girl for a magazine about motherhood.

Olivia asked her how she felt.

"I daren't move for fear of ripping a stitch, but aside from that I'm fine. Have a look at the sprout." She pointed to what looked like a bundle of cloth in a plastic box at the bedside. "He's asleep right now, thank God."

Olivia knelt beside the little cot. There was a face to the bundle after all, not the round, glossy baby face she had expected but a wrinkled, frowning, faintly haggard old man's face, with a surprising amount of coarse black hair on top. It looked more like her father's grandfather than his son.

The baby's hands were curled into fists below his chin, like a boxer preparing to spar. Olivia touched a fingertip to the tiny knuckles.

"Don't poke him," Althea said sharply. "Let sleeping dogs lie."

Olivia drew her hand back from the cot. She was going to get up off her knees when the baby opened his eyes and looked at her. He had cloudy kitten-blue eyes that should have been unfocused. But he frowned intently at her with a mixture of gravity and bewilderment, much the way her father's grandfather might have looked if he had woken up to find himself trapped in a tiny, uncooperative body.

"He's not asleep," she told Althea. "His eyes are open."

"Oh God, I hope he's not hungry again. It's such a nuisance. I'm not supposed to lift anything, including him. I have to call the nurse even to shift him from one side to the other."

Olivia's father had taken a chair on the opposite side of the bed from the baby. "When are they letting you out?"

"On Sunday, God willing. Mama says we're to go and stay with them till we're ready to move into the new house. Next week is your end of term, isn't it? It won't kill you to commute for a few days."

The baby went on staring at Olivia. Perhaps he was trying to work out if he had met her before. Since Althea wasn't watching she touched his hand with her finger again. He opened his fist and closed it around the finger, right hand to right hand—like a handshake, she thought. Maybe she wasn't going to hate him after all.

Her father was saying, "What about Lia? Her school doesn't break up for a fortnight."

"She can go back to Emma, can't she? Emma's taking her

down to Devon over Christmas anyway, she can just have her a few weeks early."

"It might not be so simple. Emma's getting married next week."

Olivia kept her head down and concentrated on the baby. Her father had lowered his voice in some nominal acknowledgment of her presence, but Althea carried on in her usual clear, confident tone. "You mean she's going through with it? She's really going to marry that spiv?"

"At this point I don't suppose she has much choice. She's painted herself into a corner by getting pregnant."

"Not really. What is she, four months gone? She still has time to change her mind about both the baby and its father."

"Well, it doesn't look as if she's going to."

"Silly girl. I can tell her she'll regret it in five months' time. Look at me, I hurt all over."

"Emma knows as much about that as you do," Olivia's father pointed out dryly. "She's already been through it once."

"Once is enough for me. It's lucky for you that you got a son this time, because I wouldn't have tried again for one."

Olivia prized her finger out of the baby's grip. Perhaps feeling abandoned, the baby sent up a wail.

Althea belatedly recalled that Olivia was in the room. "Lia, you didn't wake him, did you?"

Olivia stood up and moved away from the bed and the baby. "I told you, he wasn't asleep. He just decided to cry."

"I suppose he's hungry again, dammit." Althea sighed. "I'll have to ring for the nurse."

"I'll pick him up for you."

"No, no, he's not a doll. Let the nurse do it."

The nurse appeared. Olivia's father sat and watched her pick up the baby and lay him alongside Althea. Then the nurse helped Althea get her nightgown unbuttoned, and helped the baby fasten itself to Althea's right nipple. Everybody looked pleased: the nurse, the baby, Althea, and Olivia's father.

Olivia turned away. There wasn't anywhere to turn away to. She asked the nurse for directions to the loo, and left the room.

When she had locked herself into a cubicle she didn't know whether to vomit or cry. She nearly did both; she wept so violently that it made her retch.

She was nothing but a nuisance to everyone she loved. They all wanted to get on with their chosen lives and there she was, a gawky skeleton at the feast, a parcel passed from hand to hand that no one wanted to get stuck with.

Althea's baby was a Good Thing, pleasing everyone on all counts without even trying. Her own baby had been a dreadful mistake, an embarrassment, a criminal creation. An abortion in all senses.

Last week her hopes of another baby had been washed away in blood. And Nick was getting married next week.

41

Her father rang up her mother to see if she could move back home on Sunday. Olivia listened while he explained about Althea and the cesarean and how she couldn't lift anything and so they would have to go and stay at Marlow where Althea's mother could look after the baby for her, but Olivia couldn't go to Marlow because she still had two weeks of school left in the term.

After he came off the phone he said to Olivia, "Well, that's all right. I'll take you over on Sunday morning before I collect Althea and the baby." He added as an afterthought, "Emma's getting married next Friday but she says it's strictly no frills, so you needn't feel you're interrupting anything."

It was nice to know that her presence in what was supposed to be her own home would not be interrupting her mother's life. The wedding couldn't be very important anyway, she thought with gloomy irony, since neither her mother nor her lover had bothered to tell her about it. No doubt they thought she wouldn't be interested.

She rang her mother to see if she could invite Charlie for lunch on Sunday. Under the circumstances she could do with reinforcements.

"His family invited me over last Sunday."

"Did they? That was nice. Yes, of course Charlie can come for lunch." Her mother paused. "By the way, Nick's divorce has come through. Maybe Ross told you. We're getting married next Friday."

"Daddy did tell me."

"It's not really a wedding," her mother apologized. "Just a formality, really. There won't be any guests or celebrations, so you can go to school as usual and you won't miss a thing."

"You make it sound quite grim." Olivia sounded grim to her own ears. "Don't you want to get married?"

"Yes, of course. It's just that in the circumstances it seems more like tying up loose ends than embarking on something new."

Loose ends. How well her mother phrased it. Olivia herself was a loose end for everyone: for her mother and her father, and for Nick.

He should have been the one to tell her first about the wedding but she had heard nothing from him. To save himself a scene, she supposed. Well, she wasn't going to make a scene. She felt too dead.

Her father drove her down on Sunday morning with her belongings in the back of the car. He said she might as well stay with her mother until he and Althea had moved into the new house. So he was returning her and all her worldly goods to her mother. She wondered if he would really want her back again, or if he would find some excuse to leave her with her mother for good.

To Olivia's relief it was her mother who came to the door. It was only eleven o'clock, so maybe Nick wasn't even up yet. Her parents exchanged a few frosty words, which did not include any mention of babies or weddings. Her father dumped her gear in the front hall.

She followed him back out to the car. "Daddy, will I see you again before Christmas?"

"Of course. I'll ring you."

She had heard that story before. "Have you got the phone number at Marlow?"

"I'll write it down for you."

He tore a page out of his pocket diary and copied the number onto that and gave it to her. A sudden sense of déjà vu swept over her. It was like the first time he had left, only this time she had no hope; she knew he was gone forever and her parents would never, ever be together again with her. They had exchanged each other for Althea and Nick, and exchanged her for a baby apiece.

"Mummy looks lovely, don't you think?"

Her father seemed displeased at the idea, as if her mother's blooming beauty were a personal affront to him. Well, perhaps it was. He said curtly, "They say pregnancy suits some women."

"Did she look like that when she was carrying me?"

He had opened the car door, but he straightened up to look at her. The door was between them. He said more gently, "Yes, she did." He went on looking at her for a minute. "She looked quite a lot like you in those days. I suppose I should say it the other way round: you look like she did."

Olivia pushed her hair away from her face. Normally she would have been delighted, if somewhat skeptical, to be told she looked like her mother. But maybe in this case it was something to be regretted, if she reminded her father of things he didn't want to think about. "Is that good?"

"It can't be bad to be beautiful," he said in his dry way.

She went back into the house. All her things were in the hall, waiting to be carried up two flights of stairs. She picked up the biggest suitcase and hauled it over to the foot of the stairs.

"Just leave it, Lia," her mother said. "Nick will take that up for you. He should be down in a minute."

"I can manage," Olivia insisted. But she left the big suitcase and carried up a smaller one instead.

When she reached the first landing Nick came out of her mother's room.

He looked delicious. He was wearing jeans and a T-shirt

but his hair was tousled and he had a vaguely rumpled air. He had obviously just got up.

It was a painful reminder of the fact that he slept every night in her mother's bed. On Friday night it would officially be his bed too, she supposed. For the last six months she had mostly been able to avoid being confronted with this awful reality. For the next month at least, she would have her nose rubbed in it every day.

"Hi, Lia." He gave her a half-smile and reached for the bag she was carrying. "I'll take that up for you."

She moved herself and her luggage out of his reach. "Never mind, I can manage." She went up the last flight of stairs as quickly as she could.

It was strange to be back in her own room. This had been her fortress, her privacy, her asylum, her own place for as far back as she could remember. It was the only room she had ever really had. In her father's house her bedroom wasn't properly hers.

There was no evidence that anyone had crossed the threshold since she left and took her belongings away with her. Yet now she felt like a lodger.

The lodger. Nick, who had been the lodger, was now, or would be in five days, her mother's husband. In five months they would have a child of their own. She was the interloper, the house guest, the boarder. Even in her own room. Especially in her own room, maybe, since that was where she felt it most.

She was standing at the rear dormer window, staring down at the green oasis of the park, when Nick came into the room with her big suitcase and the flight bag. He set them down and looked around at what had been her domain.

"First time I've been up here."

"What, really?"

"There wasn't any reason to come up. I don't climb stairs for the fucking exercise." He came over to the window and glanced out over her shoulder. "Nice view."

"It's a beautiful view."

She was intensely, painfully aware of him behind her, close to her. She had thought he looked delicious when she met him on the landing, and now she thought she was starving for him. But there were worse fates than starving to death.

When he put his hand on her shoulder she jerked away as if he had burned her, and turned to glare at him. "Don't touch me."

He returned the look, not in his case a glare but a knowing, mildly amused glance. "Whatever you say, kitten."

To call her by that name was a statement in itself. She wondered what he had intended. Nothing much, presumably, with her mother downstairs and likely to come up any minute. Maybe just a quick feel to assert his ownership. Was that how he thought of her, with no respect or regard? She felt sick and shamed, as if she had sold herself into slavery.

She spoke quietly, keeping an ear out for her mother's footsteps. "Why didn't you tell me you're getting married on Friday?"

"What d' you want, an invitation to the wedding?"

"You're disgusting." She could hardly speak, she could hardly breathe. "Go away, get out of my room."

He shrugged, still amused, and went out.

Olivia opened her suitcases and dumped everything onto the bed. She felt like throwing everything out the window. But she had no right to be angry, no right to mind at all. She was the trespasser on her mother's territory. Her mother's house, her mother's man. Her mother's husband, come Friday.

She stayed upstairs, putting her clothes and things away, until her mother came up to tell her that Charlie had arrived.

Her mother came into the room and looked around. "It's amazing, Lia. You've only been back here for an hour and already this room looks like a hurricane hit it."

"If you're so keen on keeping a tidy house, why are you having a baby?"

"I just meant . . . well, it is remarkable. You have a genius for chaos, I think. Why didn't you put your things away directly out of the suitcase?"

"Because I have to sort them. I jumbled everything together and crammed it all into bags in order to get it over here."

"So I see. Well, you'd better leave off sorting and come downstairs. Charlie's here."

She had invited Charlie so she wouldn't have to be alone with her mother and Nick. With Charlie there, everything was friendly and civilized, and nobody would notice if she was very quiet a lot of the time. There weren't any horrible silences.

All she had to do now was avoid being alone with Nick for the next month. Or maybe longer, if her father didn't want her back after all. She tried not to think about that.

After lunch she told her mother, "Charlie and I will do the washing up."

It was hard to say who looked more surprised, Charlie or her mother. At Charlie's house the previous Sunday none of the men had gone anywhere near the kitchen, and it was probable that Charlie had never washed so much as a fork in the nineteen years of his life. But he responded amiably enough to her proposal and helped her clear the table.

She shut the kitchen door and handed him a tea towel. "I'll wash and you dry, okay?"

"I'll think about it." He caught hold of her and kissed her lightly. "Are we allowed to do this?"

She giggled. "Why do you think I shut the door?"

He put his arms around her and kissed her again, more seriously. Then he said, "Okay, you tell me what to do and I'll do it."

When she was up to her elbows in hot water she said, "I'm living back here now. I moved back in this morning."

"Is it going to be six months here and six months there?"

"I hope not. It's because Althea had the baby by cesarean, so they're going to stay with her parents until they can move into their new house. And I still have school for two weeks, so I've got to stay here until they get into the new house."

"When will that be?"

"Who knows? Not till next year anyway." She watched him deal with a dinner plate. "Charlie, you're supposed to be drying them, not just swiping the cloth over them. Give it a good wipe. You can't put it away when it's still wet."

"That's because this cloth is wet."

"I'll get you another one." She opened a drawer and handed him a clean tea cloth.

"I need some encouragement," he said. "Why am I doing this?"

She put her arms around his neck. "You tell me."

"Now I remember." He kissed her several times. "Okay, let's get on with it."

This time he dried everything so meticulously that he fell behind and the dish rack got filled up. She had to leave the pots and pans to help him with the drying. There was a lot of fooling about and more kissing.

In the middle of this her mother came in. They broke apart guiltily. Olivia said, "We haven't finished yet."

"So I see." But her mother didn't seem perturbed, whereas her father would have sounded about fifty degrees below zero. "I just came in to make some more coffee."

"I'll make it," Olivia offered hastily. "We'll bring it in for you."

"That sounds fine. Don't be too long."

Her mother went out again. With any luck she would tell Nick about what she had interrupted.

Olivia said to Charlie, "Mummy must be feeling romantic. They're getting married on Friday."

"That's nice." Charlie looked at her dubiously. "Isn't it?"

"Since she's four months pregnant, I suppose it's the best thing." She added sardonically, "It seems to me that things are getting really bad when somebody marries your mother to make an honest woman of her. Your mother is supposed to be an honest woman by the time you're born. I don't need any moral cliffhangers in the family at my age. Or if there are, it's supposed to be me providing them. I think this is all wrong."

Charlie shrugged. "That's the way it's done. Some of my friends have their fathers bringing home girls hardly older than their own girlfriends. It must be so bloody embarrassing. At least your mother has a man her own age."

"At least," agreed Olivia. It made her shrivel up inside, the thought of what Charlie would feel and say if he knew the truth about her. He would be utterly disgusted for all sorts of reasons, and he would be right on every count. And he wouldn't want her anymore. She changed to a safer subject. "Do you want to come to a concert on Thursday evening?"

"What concert?"

"Nothing exciting, just my school's Christmas concert."

"Are you in it?"

"Why do you think I asked you, idiot? Because I like to see you suffer? I'm playing with the first violins."

"You never told me you play the violin."

"I don't really. It's all a fraud, this is going to be the instrumental version of lip sync. They put on a tape of Beethoven's Fifth and we all pretend to play."

"In that case I'll definitely come. Did I ever tell you that my old man plays the fiddle?"

"He does?"

"The fiddle, not the violin. Different instruments. You can't play Beethoven on a fiddle, only jigs and reels."

"On the other hand," she said to console him, "you can't dance to Beethoven."

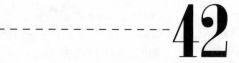

The last rehearsal for the concert went badly, as by tradition it should have, and the teacher conducting it was in a state between rage and despair by the time he told them to go home.

Olivia went home and lay down on her bed. She had had a headache all afternoon, and the racket of rehearsal had made it ten times worse. She heard her mother come in. After a few minutes her mother came upstairs and looked into her room.

"Aren't you feeling well, Lia?"

"I've got a headache."

Olivia was still in her uniform; she had just taken off her shoes and pulled the duvet over her because the house seemed so cold. It was usually warm at the top of the house, even when the ground floor was cool. Her mother came over to the bed and touched the back of her wrist to Olivia's forehead. "It feels like you've got a fever as well. Maybe you're coming down with this flu that's going round."

"I can't be. I can't miss the concert."

"You won't be able to hold a bow, the way you're shivering right now. You'd better get into your nightgown. I'll give you a dose of aspirin and we'll see how you feel in the morning."

She slept through the evening and the night, waking up from time to time in order, it seemed, to be made aware of how dreadful she felt. She wrapped herself up in her dressing gown before crawling back under the duvet because there were inexplicable drafts getting under the duvet and she couldn't stop shivering, even though it made her head hurt more.

In the morning her mother came up and examined her. "You're not going anywhere today, I don't think. And you're certainly not playing at any concert tonight. I'll phone the school and tell them."

Olivia felt too awful to argue. "You'd better let Daddy know too. And Charlie. They were only coming because of me."

"Well, at least now I won't be missing anything by having to go out tonight," her mother observed. "I don't have to be at the gallery till noon. Then if you can cope by yourself for the afternoon, Nick should be home by seven and he can get you anything you need."

"I don't need anything except sleep."

She proved it by sleeping all day, except when her mother came in to give her more aspirin and announce that she was about to leave. "Will you be all right, darling? Do you want to come downstairs and curl up on the sofa?"

"No, I want to stay right here."

She woke again after dark. Her headache had lifted and her fever had broken. The shivers had gone, and she was drenched in sweat. She ached all over, but that was still an improvement.

She crept out of bed and went downstairs to pee. While she was in the bathroom she heard the front door being unlocked. When she came out, Nick was coming up the stairs from the front hall.

"Hi, Lia. I was just coming up to see you. How do you feel?"

"Better. Still rotten but better."

"D' you fancy a cup of tea?"

"That would be wonderful."

He went back down the stairs. She went up to her room. Her nightgown was damp with sweat; she pulled it off and put on another one, the Victorian flannelette gown her mother had given her for her birthday. Then she climbed back into bed, exhausted by all that exertion going up and down stairs.

Nick came up with her tea in a mug. She struggled to sit up so she could drink it.

"Hold still." He raised her by the shoulders and stuffed a couple of pillows behind her. "All right, now you can lie back. Here's your tea."

"Thank you." She took the mug and sipped at it, feeling better with every mouthful.

He drew the curtains on the dormer windows at either end of the room, then came back to the bed. "How's your headache?"

"It seems to be gone. Touch wood." She tapped the side of her head.

He set the inner side, the pulse side, of his wrist against her forehead. "Feels like your fever has gone down too."

"I hope so. I woke up all sweaty, just before you came home."

His hand slid up into her dampened hair, brushing it back from her forehead with his fingertips. "Too bad you've got to miss your concert."

"What do you care? You weren't going to go anyway."

"You didn't invite me."

She leaned back against the pillows. She closed her eyes and opened them again to look at him. She wished he would turn into a toad or something, something ugly and revolting, instead of standing there looking unbelievably desirable. She hadn't been alone with him for ages. She was starving for him still. "Why do you need an invitation?"

He took the empty mug out of her hands and set it on her

bedside table. When he sat down on the side of the bed she put her arms around his chest, like a dryad embracing her tree. She buried her face against his jumper. She ached all over, inside and out, in her bones and her soul.

"I thought you said I was disgusting."

"I lied. No, it's true. We're both disgusting. How can you be doing this when you're going to marry Mummy tomorrow?"

At first she thought he wasn't going to answer. Finally he said, "You're asking the wrong question."

What was the right question? The other way round, maybe: how can you marry my mother tomorrow when you're doing this tonight? But she couldn't ask him that, or anything else, because he kissed her and drove it all out of her head.

"You'll catch the flu," she protested.

"Fuck the flu. Are you feeling too rotten to screw?"

It was a rhetorical question. He was already drawing the duvet back, putting his hand up under her prim nightgown. She wriggled down to a horizontal position, and the nightgown slid up her body at the same time, leaving her nearly naked.

Nick was starving too, it seemed, from the haste with which he reduced himself to the same state as she was in and lay down with her. He was gentle at first, in deference to her debility. But he forgot about that quite quickly, just as she forgot how ill she had been feeling and remembered only how much she had missed him. And why.

She realized afterward what she had done: she had invited him into her bed. Just like her mother. It was her fault now, everything that happened.

She was watching him put his clothes back on, thinking that she would never see him naked again, never again be able to admire his body, so familiar and so alien to her.

"I wish you weren't getting married."

"We've already been through that. And we're not going through it again."

"In six months I'll be sixteen." She said it desperately, shamelessly, before she could think what she was doing and stop herself. "Old enough to marry."

She waited for him to laugh, but he didn't. He just looked at her for a long minute, till she felt like hiding under the duvet. Then he did laugh, but it was more of a grunt. "Not without your daddy's consent. And so what? You're not going to marry anyone at sixteen. You've got a long haul ahead of you—A levels, university, all that lot."

"I don't care about that anymore."

"Don't be daft, of course you do." He sat on the bed again, fully dressed, and took her by the shoulders. "It's not on, kitten, you know it's not. Your life isn't going to work that way. You wouldn't want it to be like that. You've still got a lot of growing up to do."

Olivia put her arms around his neck. There was no point crying. She just wanted him to hold her, and he did.

She said against his shoulder, "I wish you'd never taken me to bed."

"Christ, so do I. Craziest thing I've ever done in my life."

"You said I was asking for it."

"Weren't you?"

"How could I? I didn't even know what—"

"Oh, well, it's all a mistake then." He was laughing, holding her and shaking with laughter. "My misunderstanding. Sorry about that, kitten. We'll take it all back and say it never happened, all right? Now you've got nothing to be pissed off about."

"Nick, that's not funny."

"Isn't it? I thought it was. If you're feeling better, do you want to come down and watch TV? I'll make some more tea, all right?" He reached down to the foot of the bed for her dressing gown and tucked it around her shoulders. "Come on, you'll feel better down there."

He picked her up in his arms, just the way her father had done last summer, and carried her down the stairs to the sitting room. When she was settled and well cushioned on the sofa, he went out to the kitchen, and came back with a mug of tea and an envelope.

Mystified, she opened the envelope. A thrill of horrified pleasure ran through her—or maybe it was only the flu making her shiver—when she saw that it contained the photographs he had taken that last time in the studio. The negatives were there too.

She looked at the pictures of herself as a shameless

stranger. Pictures of herself wearing Nick's clothing. Pictures of herself making love to herself, of her body as she had never seen it. As if she were as alien as he.

Maybe she was. She hardly felt human. She felt hollow and aching within her rib cage where all the vital organs ought to be. Homesick, maybe, for some distant star. For home, wherever that might be.

"I promised I'd burn them, but I think I'll leave that to you."

"Don't you want them?"

"Sure I do."

"Just for yourself, I mean."

"That's what I meant."

"You keep them, then. Souvenirs."

She took out the two photos she had taken of him and gave the rest back to him. She felt worse than homesick; she felt irretrievably exiled.

He glanced at the photos still in her hand. "You can't keep those here."

"I know."

"Best to burn them, like I said."

She knew that, but she couldn't do it just yet. "First I want to stick pins in them. Why don't you take them upstairs and shove them into my school bag? They'll be okay there for now. That's one place she would never look." It was funny calling her mother *she,* acknowledging for the first time, now it was over, that she and Nick had been in a conspiracy against her mother. That she had really and truly betrayed her mother.

When he came back down he sat at the opposite end of the sofa, lifting up her feet to make room for himself and replacing them on his lap. She could feel the warmth in his hands, in his thighs. It was painful to her, as if she had got frostbitten.

"Your feet are cold."

"You warm them up for me."

He pulled the duvet over her feet and stroked them. She supposed that was meant to comfort her for what was going to happen tomorrow, for what had happened last summer, for all the wrong he had done her and the damage he had caused. For having destroyed her life within the short time it took the earth to go halfway round the sun.

They were sitting like that, watching the news on TV, domestic as a pair of old shoes, innocent as the babe unborn, sitting just like that when her mother came home at five past nine on the eve of her wedding.

43

The day of the wedding was less painful than Olivia had dreaded. Her mother invited her to come out to dinner with them but Olivia said she was still recovering from the flu, which was perfectly true. Megan had said she would come over and look after her, and Olivia was looking forward to that. She hadn't been able to hang around with Megan on the old casual basis since moving in with her father in Highgate.

Megan brought over a variety of dishes from the Indian take-away. Olivia discovered that she didn't seem to have eaten for a week, and proceeded to make up for it. "That was really good," she said afterward. "Thanks, Meg."

"If your appetite is that good, you should have gone out with your mother and Nick. I expect they're tucking into something much more upmarket."

"They were only being polite when they invited me along. They really want to hold hands and simper at each other across the table."

"I think that's sweet, at their age. I'm just jealous because I wish it was me holding hands and simpering at Nick."

"Would you like me to tell him that?"

Megan sighed theatrically. "It's too late now, he's a married man."

"He's been married all along, only to someone else."

"Well, he's really married now. You know what I mean. Listen, Lia, we're supposed to be working out stage directions for this wretched play. Is your brain too fevered to concentrate?"

"No, I'd like to do that and get it out of the way. Did you bring your copy of the script?"

"Easier if we write on yours and photocopy it. Have you got it here?"

"It's upstairs in my room. In my school bag."

"I'll get it. You stay here and convalesce."

Megan was already upstairs when Olivia remembered the photographs. She rose as quickly as her aching bones would allow and shuffled into the hall. "Meg, just bring the bag down."

She waited anxiously. Megan's voice floated down. "What?"

"Just bring the whole bag down."

"Okay."

Olivia hobbled back to the sofa. Her heart was still racing in terror when Megan came down with the book bag. And not without cause: as soon as Megan came into the sitting room, Olivia knew what had happened. She could feel herself starting to blush. A dead giveaway.

"You were too late."

"What do you mean, too late?"

"I mean I'd already opened the bag. Why'd you leave them on top?"

Olivia gave up her pretense of innocence. "I was going to burn them, but I didn't want to do it just yet. I was looking at them last night when my mother came up and I just stashed them out of the way."

"You're crazy, Lia." Megan stared at her sternly for a moment before relenting. "Do you want me to keep them for you?"

"What if Teddy goes through your stuff the way you go through his?"

"He wouldn't dare, and anyway, I don't. And besides, he wouldn't know Nick from Adam."

"Well, maybe you'd better. At least until I get back to Daddy's house. If I get back to Daddy's house."

"Okay. I'll put them in a sealed envelope. Even Teddy wouldn't dare open it."

Olivia felt dazed by Megan's matter-of-fact response. "Meg, aren't you surprised?"

"I'm gobsmacked, if you really want to know. You can tell me all about it when I've found an envelope."

While Megan hunted for envelopes, Olivia looked at the photographs. It must have given Megan a real shock, coming across that picture of Nick on his knees with his jeans at half-mast and everything on display. To Olivia's eyes he had an unmistakably postcoital air about him, his smile faintly sleepy and sated, his clothing not merely undone but disheveled. Like a lion after devouring the kill, ready for siesta but still bloody round the muzzle.

Megan came back to the sofa, having found an envelope. She sat down beside Olivia and picked up the fully clothed photo. "He looks appallingly sexy."

"He told me he used to be a model. He ran away from home when he was fourteen and ended up in Amsterdam and did some kind of modeling, but he wouldn't say what it was."

"Fag mags, probably."

"What do you mean?"

"You know. Those grotty shops in Soho put them in their windows. They have pictures of adolescent boys in poses like that." She pointed to the other, incriminating photo.

"But Nick isn't gay."

"Well, you should know," Megan observed dryly. "But all he probably did was take off his clothes for the camera. It doesn't mean he sold his body."

The idea hadn't even occurred to Olivia. She found it horrifying and profoundly unsettling. But there was no way she was going to be able to ask Nick about that.

Megan took the photos and sealed them up in the envelope. And then she said, "Lia, did you take those pictures?"

Olivia briefly considered claiming that she had found them in her mother's room, but she didn't think Megan would believe her. "Yes, Meg, I did."

"Did you go to bed with him?"

Olivia covered her face with her hands, out of cowardice. "Well, yes, I did." She waited for Megan's response. Shock, horror, disgust, incredulity, surely.

Megan nudged her in the ribs with an elbow and said in a Monty Python voice, "Wot's it like?"

Olivia giggled and lowered her hands. "Aren't you going to tell me I'm disgusting and immoral?"

"I will if it makes you feel better, but first answer my question."

Olivia considered. "Well, Ms. P. is wrong."

"About what?"

"Remember she told us the Victorian view was that sex was something that men did to women? Meaning that they had it all wrong? Well, they didn't. Basically it is something that men do to women."

"Maybe he's just not a very good lover, if he made you feel like that."

"You see? You're just proving what I said. You're assuming that if it's not a mutual swooning session it has to be the man's fault, which isn't true. But it is true that the man has to actually, you know, do something, he can't just lie back and think of England. And you can't make him do it if he doesn't want to. Whereas everything the woman does is just sort of helping him along. Or not, as the case might be."

Not wanting Megan to misunderstand her, or possibly anxious to defend Nick's reputation as a lover, she added, "I don't really like that idea, I mean it seems so unfair and unequal, but it's true, it's a biological fact. You know, in physiological terms the sex act basically consists of erection, penetration, and ejaculation, and all that refers to the man. For evolutionary reasons the woman supposedly gets to pick the man who does this to her, and hopefully she enjoys what he's doing to her, but that doesn't change what's actually happening. And it made me feel horribly—well, biological. And vulnerable. Though you do get over that after a while."

It was Megan's turn to consider. "I see what you mean. It's basically the penetration bit that's the problem. I mean, you grow up thinking about your body as if it were your self, thinking you're totally in control. Then all of a sudden, if you're female, you have to come to terms with the experience of somebody actually invading you, even if you've invited him to do it. I guess it has to change our image of ourselves. Men never have to cope with that. In fact, they do the opposite; they get used to the idea of invading other people's body space."

"You make it sound like the War of the Worlds."

"It was your idea, Lia, not mine. I'm just agreeing with you. Now tell me what happened."

Olivia told her the whole story. No, not quite the whole story. She left out the bit about Nick having flogged pornographic pictures of her to a magazine; that was too, too humiliating. She didn't mention having tried to get pregnant, partly because it would sound like total lunacy, partly because it was irrelevant now. And she ended her tale with the time she had taken the photographs. She didn't tell Megan that Nick had made love to her last night, the night before his wedding.

"Oh Lia," said Megan at last, "that's really amazing. No wonder you were so anxious to go and live with your father. No wonder you didn't want your mother to marry Nick. If I were you I think I'd have gone mad."

"I desperately wanted to tell you, Meg, but I just couldn't. It would be unbelievably fatal if anyone else found out." Olivia added anxiously, "Do you think that I'm totally depraved?"

"No, not really. But maybe Nick is. Do you think he's like whatsisname, that film director who has a thing for underage girls?"

"A pervert, you mean?" That was the second time Megan had shocked her by suggesting possibilities about Nick. "No, I don't think so. He likes big tits. That wouldn't suit someone with a taste for Lolitas. And he said he must be out of his mind, the first time, so that doesn't sound like he'd done it before."

"Well, even if he isn't a pervert he's still a rat. It was totally wrong of him to seduce you. He's done you wrong and he's done your mother wrong, even if she doesn't know it."

Olivia felt obliged to defend Nick, though she knew very well that what Megan said was true. "But he wasn't married to my mother then. In fact, he was still married to Miranda, so my mother was committing adultery too. And he's not some kind of Svengali, I mean, it's my fault too, all the times I went to his studio."

"Lia, you can make all the excuses you like, but the fact is, you've been had."

Olivia felt as Victorian as the nightgown she was wearing: seduced and abandoned, deflowered and dishonored, raped and ruined. Worse than Tess of the D'Urbervilles. She felt as empty as outer space. She might have known that Megan wouldn't tell her lies for the sake of comfort.

Quite briskly she wiped away the unavoidable tears. "Well, it's all in the past now. Why don't you make some tea and we'll get to work on these stage directions."

While Megan was in the kitchen, Olivia dug the script out of her school bag. To distract herself she began to scan through it. She blew her nose in a tissue and blinked back tears. The words swam in and out of focus.

> *Can't we just be friends*
> A fool in love
> *The security of marriage*
> I gave up everything for you
> *Respectable women*
> Fatal jealousy
> *Your father's new wife*
> The bridegroom and the bride
> *God is not mocked*
> A baby's sweet soft skin, a baby's breath
> *Child killer*

Megan had come back with the tea. She stood in the middle of room for a minute, looking at Olivia. Then she set down the tea, took away the script, sat down, and put her arms round Olivia.

Olivia wept. Floods of tears. "Oh Meg, I l-love him!"

"I know. I told you. But I thought it was Charlie."

"M-Mummy's having his b-baby and he made me get rid of m-mine."

"Well, he was right. That's the only right thing he's done."

"It's not right, it's wicked. I k-killed it."

"No you didn't, it wasn't properly alive yet. You don't say you've slaughtered a chicken every time you break an egg, do you? Anyway, the soul doesn't come into the body until it's nearly ready to be born."

Megan said this with such casual authority that Olivia didn't dare to ask how she could possibly know such a thing. She sniveled and hiccuped. Megan held up a tissue and blew her nose for her and went on hugging her as if she were a small child in distress.

Olivia rested her head on Megan's shoulder. Megan stroked her hair. She began to feel slightly less desolate.

"He was a magic lover, Meg," she said rather dreamily, between sniffles. "I can't begin to describe how he made me feel."

"I can't imagine him being romantic."

"He's not romantic at all. Antiromantic, even. But mortally sexy. It turns me on just thinking about him. Why are we doomed to be attracted to men when they're such horrible creatures? Why couldn't one of us two be a man, for instance? Then we could get married and live happily ever after."

"That would be just about perfect, wouldn't it?" Megan went on stroking her hair. "You've got beautiful hair, Lia. It's all silky and soft."

"Nick said it was honey-colored." Olivia sighed. "God, I feel dead."

"You know . . ." Megan sounded uncharacteristically tentative. "We don't have to be opposite sexes, you know, Lia."

Olivia lifted her head from Megan's shoulder. "What do you mean?"

"Women can be lovers."

"I know, that's what lesbians do. Oh, you mean . . ." Olivia giggled. "You mean us."

They still had their arms round each other. They looked at each other, half ready to laugh.

"Well, why not?"

"Well, okay, but I don't know what to do."

"What would you do if I were Nick?"

"I'd kiss you."

"Well, do it."

Olivia touched her mouth to Megan's. She closed her eyes and pressed firmly, feeling daring. And odd. After about fifteen seconds she opened her eyes and took her mouth away.

Megan said dryly, "Is that the way you used to kiss Nick? It seems amazingly restrained for someone with a magic lover."

"Well, with a man you're supposed to use your tongue and all. You know."

"Come on, Lia, get into the spirit of this," Megan said sternly. "Sexy is sexy, no matter who you're kissing. Let's try again. Pretend I'm Nick."

Olivia thought about being kissed by Nick. He had kissed her just last night, though it seemed a thousand years ago. The thought made her come over all quivery. She kissed Megan again, opening her mouth and touching her tongue to Megan's. It wasn't much like kissing Nick, maybe more like Charlie. Megan responded with surprising vigor.

Olivia broke off the kiss. "Meg, you're not a real lesbian, are you?"

"Lia, if I were I'd have seduced you long ago, you're the most beautiful girl I know. Don't you want to do this?"

"Yeah, I do, but maybe we should skip the kissing, it doesn't seem to do much for me. Lesbians don't just snog, do they?"

"I guess they do everything except have actual sexual intercourse."

"What else is there?"

Megan looked at her in exasperation. "You're supposed to be the experienced lover, Lia. What else did Nick do? He didn't just lie down on you and stick it in, did he?"

Olivia thought about what Nick had done last night. The recollection of his hands on her breasts made her want to touch them herself. Megan could do that, couldn't she? "Maybe we should take our clothes off."

"Should you be doing that when you've just had the flu?"

"It's okay. I pushed up the thermostat so it's really warm in here."

Olivia stood up and pulled her nightgown off over her head. In a lifetime of friendship she had been naked in front of Megan hundreds of times, but this time she felt slightly shy about it. She sat down on the sofa and tried to casually cover herself with her hands. Megan was briskly removing her own blouse and bra. Olivia felt shy about looking at the breasts she had seen on uncountable occasions.

Maybe Megan was feeling shy too. She reached over hesitantly to stroke Olivia's bosom. "Did he like your breasts?"

"Yeah, I told you, he likes big ones. Also small ones, I guess, since he's married my mother."

"I told you the size doesn't matter."

"Well, I'd still rather have tits like my mother's than these ridiculous knockers."

Megan's stroking became less tentative, more sensual. But her tone of voice was quite clinical. "There's nothing wrong with your breasts, Lia. They're full but they don't slop about. They're firm and really nicely shaped."

"Thank you, Dr. Davies, expert on the esthetics of mammary glands." Olivia was surprised to realize that whatever Megan was doing to her nipples was actually having an effect on her. "That feels good."

"It's supposed to. Close your eyes and imagine I'm Nick."

That wasn't easy. Megan's touch was like a courteous butterfly, whereas Nick's approach to her body felt more like being sniffed and pawed and licked and nibbled by a grizzly with lunch on his mind.

Megan ran her hand down Olivia's stomach, into her pubic hair. That felt good too, or would have if she hadn't been embarrassed by the idea of Megan touching her cunt, and guilty about the fact that she wasn't holding up her end of things. She should have been stroking Megan in return, but she didn't have Megan's nerve.

Or expertise. It became apparent at once that Megan knew her way around the female genitalia as well as Nick did. She was pressing all the right buttons. There was nothing remotely passionate about it, more like being in the hands of a good masseuse. Olivia wasn't sure she liked that. She opened her eyes. "Meg, how'd you learn to do this?"

Megan eased up on the massage. "You're made the same as me, aren't you? If it works for me it should work for you."

"You mean you do it to yourself?"

"Don't you?"

"I'd feel too silly. I feel silly right now, actually. It reminds me of that game we used to play, what was it called? Torture."

They had played that game about five years ago. Not often, because they had to be totally alone in the house for at least an hour in order to play it. They took it in turns to be the torturer and the victim. The torturer took off the victim's clothes and tied her to the bed like an Apache prisoner staked out in the desert sun. Originally the torture consisted mostly of tickling, the victim trying to hold out as long as possible before begging for mercy and confessing to imaginary crimes, the more unlikely the better. But eventually they discovered that a far more enjoyable torture session could be had by pinching the victim's nipples and clitoris to produce deliciously unendurable sensations as well as an awesome aura of wickedness.

Remembering these antics, Olivia began to giggle. It was infectious. Megan broke up too. They ended up rolling about on the sofa in hysterics, groaning and clutching their stomachs, an orgy of laughter instead of the sexual one they had intended.

Gradually they pulled themselves together, emotionally and sartorially. Megan, fully clothed again, went back to the kitchen to make fresh tea because the previous pot had gone cold. Olivia, her nightgown respectably restored, collected the pages of the play script, which had got scattered about on the floor. Then they set to work in earnest on the stage directions, with only an occasional giggle to disrupt the sobriety of their deliberations. Medea's plight had no power to touch Olivia now. And she didn't think even once about Nick, until he came home with her mother.

44

Her father met her at the station in Marlow. He kissed her on the cheek. She was a distant relative again, apparently.

"How is the baby?"

"You'll see."

"Which of you gets up in the middle of the night?"

"Sue and Althea cope with that between them."

"What will you do when you're back in Highgate without Althea's mother?"

"I don't think Althea intends to leave until Matthew is getting a good night's sleep."

She looked at her father, who was looking at the road ahead. "So he doesn't cry all the time, like the last baby you had?"

"He doesn't have a chance. As soon as he lets out a peep, someone picks him up."

Lucky baby, she thought. She had an idea that her father was not among the vigilant baby soothers.

On the other hand, she discovered when they arrived at the house, he didn't need to be. Althea's attention, and her parents', was focused entirely on the infant Matthew.

He was asleep somewhere upstairs when Olivia came in. Because this was officially a Christmas visit, even though Christmas was nearly a week away, Althea and her parents felt obliged to greet her with a kiss on the cheek. That put her father's greeting firmly in context.

Althea's father offered her a glass of sherry, and Althea's mother went off to see about the lunch. A faint complaint drifted down from the floor above.

Althea turned to Olivia's father. "Ross, can you be a darling and bring him down?"

Olivia said, "Daddy, can I come up and see him?"

"He's coming down," her father pointed out.

But Olivia followed her father upstairs anyway and found the baby in his cot. He was in a rage by now, but in that tiny body fury didn't amount to much. He was red-faced with indignation. Olivia, to her surprise, found him comical and sweet and vaguely pathetic. Megan said babies weren't new people but the same ones coming back into the world again. Olivia could imagine how frustrated anyone would be to find themselves back at this helpless stage. It sounded like a cosmic game of snakes and ladders, without any END.

Her father picked up the squalling baby as if the poor thing was liable to do something nasty. Rather, in fact, as if young Matthew were some unpleasant item of wildlife that had got into the house by accident and had to be removed from the premises. Olivia knew less than nothing about babies, but she knew that was not a comforting way to be held. She picked up the blanket from the crib and laid it over her shoulder. "Here, Daddy, give him to me."

Her father handed Matthew over to her. She laid him across her shoulder, folded the sides of the blanket over him, and thumped his little padded bottom quite gently. He stopped crying.

"I'll take him downstairs for you."

Her father followed, obviously feeling that he ought to be playing the parent but acknowledging that by some mysterious biological or psychosexual process she was somehow more at ease with the baby than he was.

When she came down Althea and her mother descended on her like twittering vultures and took the baby away. They took no more notice of her until everyone had gone in to lunch and they were all sitting round the table. The baby by then had had a good bellyful of milk from Althea's breasts and been installed in a sort of infant chaise longue between his mother and his grandmother, with a seat belt to keep him from sliding out.

That was clearly what every newborn baby needed and deserved, a good dose of doting. Olivia's father was equally clearly no good at doting. Althea's father was more interested in and more at ease with the baby than the baby's own father was. Knowing her mother's brittle self-possession and physical reserve, Olivia began to have some idea of why she might have cried so much for the first term of her existence on earth.

After lunch they had coffee in what Althea's mother called the drawing room. It had tall windows looking over the front garden and French windows opening southward to the river and the sort of elegant furniture that Olivia felt she should perch only on the edge of, and even that only because she was dressed up for a Sunday visit. In summer—at her father's wedding, for instance—it was a beautiful, bright, and airy room. In winter airy became drafty, especially when the wind blew along the reaches of the river and up the long lawn. Today was cold and gray, but there was a fire in the hearth. A mingy fire, strictly for cosmetic purposes, since the central heating was supposed to be keeping them warm, but Olivia huddled herself up in front of it, hoping the others would pay no attention to her.

No such luck. Althea's father—now, incredibly, Olivia's stepgrandfather—decided to be matey. "I say, Lia, Ross tells me you've written a play and you're putting it on. That's jolly clever of you."

"I didn't write it, Euripides did."

"Well, you're not putting it on in Greek, are you? Though some of these modern playwrights might as well be performed in Greek for all the sense one can make of them. Which play are you doing?"

"*Medea.*"

"Don't know that one. What's it about?"

Olivia stared at the fire. "It's about a man who leaves his wife for a younger woman with a rich father."

She thought that might shut him up, but he persevered. Maybe you had to have a particularly thick skin to be a good stockbroker. "Sounds quite modern, that. All those old Greek plays were based on myths, weren't they? Full of gruesome doings, but all offstage."

"In our version," Olivia said dreamily, hugging her knees, "she kills her children right onstage."

That put a satisfactory stop to all conversation, until Matthew farted so violently he woke himself up. At first he looked confused and appalled, like a little old man who had inadvertently committed some horrible social faux pas. Then he caught his breath and wailed until Althea's mother picked him up, which was almost as soon as he opened his mouth.

Perhaps embarrassed by her son's behavior, Althea decided to change the subject entirely. She asked, in her clear, carrying voice, "Lia, did Emma's wedding come off all right?"

"I suppose so. At least it happened, but I wasn't there." Olivia added, in case they should guess that she hadn't been invited, "I was in bed with flu that weekend."

"Is Nick going with you to Devon? I suppose Emma can't very well leave him behind, now that she's married him. I wonder what your grandmother will think of him."

Olivia was tempted to reply, Much the same as Gran Beckett thinks of you.

45

Her grandmother Hardy lived in a picture-postcard cottage in a picture-postcard village. The cottage had whitewashed cob walls two feet thick and a thatched roof hanging like a thick fringe out over the upper windows. That made the interior dark and cool in summer, but at Christmas with small daylight and central heating it didn't matter so much. And in the summer her grandmother spent all her time in the garden, which was also of a picture-postcard standard of beauty.

They left home at nine o'clock in the morning on Christmas Eve and arrived at the cottage by noon, thanks to Nick's amazing driving. He was the sort of driver Olivia's father had always condemned by saying they drove like Italians.

Once after they had left the motorway Olivia actually thought they were all going to die, when he pulled out to overtake two cars in a row and another car appeared heading in the opposite direction. Instead of falling back he floored the accelerator and got around both cars with about a second to spare, hardly time for Olivia's heart to start working again.

Olivia also noticed that her mother, who used to get agitated whenever her father went over the speed limit, didn't bat an eyelash when Nick did it. Maybe she thought that if you drove a Jaguar you couldn't help speeding. Whatever, it certainly got you down to Devon in a hurry.

What had been bothering Olivia all the way down, even more than Nick's potentially lethal driving habits, was Althea's question. Olivia too wondered what her grandmother would make of him. She wondered if her mother was nervous about that, and what sort of advance publicity she had given him. She had overheard her mother reading a letter from her grandmother aloud to Nick, about how her grandmother had "told a white lie" to her neighbors by pretending that the marriage had taken place in September. Apparently single motherhood, or any flirtation with it, had not yet become trendy in rural Devonshire.

Her mother had found the story amusing. But Olivia suspected she might have invented some stories of her own about Nick, to make him more acceptable to his new mother-in-law and her neighbors.

When they had arrived and got out of the car Olivia's grandmother told Nick she was delighted to meet him. People always said things like that. Then she told Olivia's mother that she was looking remarkably well. People always said things like that too, but this time it was really true. With her grandmother you couldn't tell.

The first sign of a falling-out happened when her grandmother wanted them all to go to midnight communion. This was one of the things they always did when they spent Christmas in Devon. Not going to church on Christmas Eve was like turning down the turkey at Christmas lunch. But Nick said he was tired; he'd driven across the whole bloody country, and he was going to go to bed.

Olivia was disappointed. She couldn't imagine Nick in

church. Knowing what she did about his background, she thought it quite possible that he had never been inside a church in his life. She had a fantastic idea that something out of medieval mythology might happen, some prodigy such as they used to say betrayed the presence of the Devil.

Her grandmother was even more disappointed, though no doubt for different reasons. "I know you've had a long day, but really you must come, it's such a lovely service and such a mild night. I do think it's really the best part of Christmas."

"Maybe it is, but I'm going to miss it. Good night."

Nick disappeared upstairs. Olivia's grandmother looked at her mother.

"He's tired," her mother said defensively.

"Too tired to practice common courtesy, apparently."

Her grandmother spoke as she did when Olivia had proved wanting in some respect. It wasn't really fair. Her mother hadn't brought Nick up, she had only married him. And at least he hadn't said, Fuck Christmas.

Olivia said, "Never mind, Grandma, we'll go without Nick. It would be worse if he came and then fell asleep in church, wouldn't it?"

The church was at the other end of the village, near enough to walk to. After the service it became clear why her grandmother had been so offended and dismayed. Olivia heard her explaining Nick's absence to her friends and neighbors by saying that he had been "feeling under the weather" and gone to bed early. This was to have been the occasion for displaying her new son-in-law and, more importantly, the father of the visible bulge in Olivia's mother's stomach.

Everyone commiserated with Nick's imaginary ill health and expressed a hope that he would be feeling better in the morning and able to enjoy Christmas. The episode made Olivia wonder how many famous incidents in history hadn't really happened, or at least not like that.

When Nick came downstairs in the morning—the last one down, of course—Olivia's grandmother wished him a happy Christmas with determined cheerfulness. "You must be completely rested now, after such a good night's sleep."

Nick ignored the sarcasm. "Yeah, I feel all right. I'll feel even better after a cup of coffee."

Olivia's mother jumped up to pour it for him. She was like that the whole time they were there, scuttling around like a nervous servant, providing him with anything he thought he might fancy or she thought he might fancy. Olivia thought that was probably to prevent her grandmother feeling obliged to wait on him in any way.

Her grandmother, on the other hand, was conscious of her responsibilities as a hostess, even to an undesirable son-in-law, and also thought that Olivia's mother should be putting her feet up and relaxing on account of being pregnant. This led to a number of arguments along the lines of two people each trying to open the door for the other.

Nick pretended not to notice. And why should he care, Olivia wondered, as long as he gets what he wants?

Everything went smoothly for a few hours. They opened the presents, most of which had been bought by her mother. Presents from Mummy and Nick to Lia, presents from Emma and Nick to Mother, presents from Emma to Nick—with kisses, Olivia noticed as she was handing them out. There had never been any kisses on her mother's presents to her father.

In the end everybody seemed pleased and no one was offended, at least not obviously, though Olivia heard Nick say something under his breath about the tie her grandmother had given him being useful to wear to a funeral. She thought—hoped—that he had liked her presents to him, Jelly Roll Morton (CD) and Ansel Adams (book). Some of the Adams photographs were slightly tritely glorious, like something Pippa might have passed, but others were quite lunar and reminded her of Nick's own work—the Martian pictures, that was, not the professional pussies.

After the Christmas lunch had been eaten and the washing up was out of the way, her grandmother proposed that they should all take a walk to wake them up. The After-dinner Walk was a Christmas tradition almost as sacred as midnight communion, and both Olivia and her mother were on tenterhooks for fear Nick would refuse again. This catastrophe was made more likely by the fact that he had nodded off on the sofa in front of the television while they were doing the washing up, making her grandmother's traditional remark about waking everyone up seem unfortunately pointed.

Her mother said brightly, "That's a good idea, don't you think, Nick? You haven't really seen the village yet, and there's a lovely walk down the lane."

Everybody—that is, all the women—held their breath while Nick roused himself, stretching and yawning. Olivia thought he was like some great carnivorous beast, a saber-toothed tiger maybe, that had found its way into her grandmother's incongruously cozy little cottage and dozed off in front of the fire. When he said, "All right, why not," they began to breathe again and to smile in relief.

During the excursion Olivia kept her grandmother diverted while her mother entertained Nick. Olivia had the harder task. She had to respond to her grandmother's questions and comments in a normal manner while struggling with the emotions raised by the sight of Nick and her mother strolling hand in hand.

Her grandmother was asking about school. Interrogating, actually. "Have you decided what subjects to take for your A levels, Lia?"

"I'm not sure. Physics and biology, I think, but I don't know what else. Math, maybe, but I'm not so good at it."

"You must do mathematics. It's a good solid subject. Emma's headmistress used to say it separates the sheep from the goats."

"Mummy didn't do math, did she?"

"Oh no, she wasn't interested in science at all. Now what about your music? Have you kept up your violin lessons?"

"I'm still going to Mrs. Stone, and I'm doing a GCSE in music."

"I'm glad to hear that. Emma says you've been living with Ross for the last six months. I was afraid that you might have found the music lessons too inconvenient."

"Oh, Daddy would never let me give up the violin. That's what he's most interested in."

"Good for him. How is the baby?"

"He's sweet," Olivia said with warmth and emphasis, so her grandmother would know it was not just the sort of thing people said.

"Most babies are, fortunately. Nature arranges it. How do you get on with your stepmother?"

"So-so. We manage. At least we did before the baby came. I don't know how things will work out now."

"If you can mind the baby for her from time to time, darling, she'll adore you. How do you get on with your stepfather?"

Olivia had to think for a minute to find a politic and noncommittal response. "I don't see a lot of him."

"But wasn't he the reason you went to live with Ross?"

"Did Mummy tell you that?"

"She gave me some story about your resenting him."

"Well, I guess that's true."

Her grandmother walked for a while in silence. Then she said, "Really, you know, if one were matchmaking, one would have matched up Althea with Nick."

Olivia thought about that. It was quite a clever idea. Althea would have been horrified by the suggestion that she was Nick's soul mate, and Nick had no great opinion of Althea, but maybe they deserved each other. They were both totally practical, unsentimental, even ruthless, and they understood how money works—something neither of her parents had ever caught on to.

"Actually, Grandma, I can't really understand it, but Mummy does seem to be happier since she's been living with Nick. Don't you think she looks happy?"

"*Nostalgie de la boue,*" her grandmother muttered mysteriously. "But if he kept his mouth shut he might be a very attractive man. I hope she's happy, darling. There's nothing anyone else can do for her if she's made the wrong choice again."

Olivia was surprised to find herself wishing that adults would stop treating her as if she were one of them. She wasn't ready to know about her mother's relationship with her grandmother, or her grandmother's views on the relative merits of her father and Nick, or what Althea thought about her mother's marriage, or how young Matthew had come to be born. That would all have been quite interesting in a novel, but in her own life it was devastating, because she had no life of her own yet, no distance from which to look back on these family matters. And the most devastatingly adult thing of all, of course, was her own relationship with Nick.

She longed to go back to last Christmas, when she had to cope only with her father's absence and the existence of Althea. Life had seemed fraught and burdensome then, but now she looked back on it as a land of lost content.

There was nearly a row in the evening, when her grandmother wanted to play bridge. This was another tradition. Her grandmother was mad on bridge, and after the death of her grandfather Olivia had been obliged to learn to play it in order to man the fourth hand. This time Nick was to be pressed into service to take her father's place.

Nick had other ideas. "I don't play bridge."

"It's just like whist," her grandmother explained kindly, "but you bid for trumps beforehand."

"I don't play whist either."

"The basic idea is frightfully simple. You'll pick it up in a few minutes."

Nick went on smoking, keeping his attention on the television. "Thanks, but no thanks."

"But we need you at least for the bidding," her grandmother persisted. "After that you can be the dummy and watch television until the next deal."

Olivia bit her lip, torn between her fear of an unpleasant argument and the urge to giggle at her grandmother's perfectly correct but suggestive description of Nick's potential role in the game. "Grandma, if Nick doesn't want to play bridge, why don't we play Scrabble instead?"

"I have an idea," said her grandmother, eyeing Nick, "that Scrabble is another game Nick doesn't play."

"No, he doesn't, but it doesn't matter. We can play Scrabble with just the three of us."

"It would be more polite to choose something that Nick can play. How about Happy Families, Nick?"

He flicked his cigarette ashes at the ashtray without taking his eyes off the television screen. "How about strip poker?"

Her grandmother stared at him. Olivia felt like hiding behind the sofa before the shooting started. But her grandmother said only, "I think not. We're not dressed for it."

Olivia got out the Scrabble box and set the board on the table. That seemed to settle the argument. Her mother and grandmother came over to play while Nick stayed where he was on the sofa in front of the TV.

After a while he got up and went to the sideboard to refill his whiskey glass. Olivia's mother glanced over her shoulder at him as he passed behind her chair. "I'd have done that for you, darling, if you'd asked."

"That's all right, I'm not too pissed to walk yet."

Olivia's mother and grandmother both looked as if they wished he wouldn't say things like that. Nick looked amused; that was obviously why he had said it. He came back and stood behind her mother. He set his right hand with the re-filled glass of whiskey on her shoulder and looked over her head at the board.

Olivia watched his left hand caressing her mother. He stroked the nape of her neck, the long tendons under her ear, the delicate bones and hollows below her throat. The deep V neckline of her black silk dress revealed the curves of her breasts, plump with pregnancy. Olivia was terrified that his hand would stray down too far and touch her mother's breasts.

Maybe that thought had occurred to her mother too, be-cause she put her hand over his. She tipped her head back against his chest and looked up at him. "You're distracting me, darling. Do you want to make me lose?"

Nick brought his hand up under her chin to circle her throat. The tip of his middle finger caressed her carotid artery, his thumb rested on her jugular vein. Olivia knew the strength of that hand. If he pressed down, her mother would pass out. If he squeezed and held, her mother would die. Her mother's baby would die.

He looked down into her mother's face. "You're losing anyway."

"That's because I've had such terrible letters."

"The poor workman blames his tools," Olivia's grand-mother remarked. She laid her word out on the board, setting the Q triumphantly on a triple-letter score.

Olivia's mother pushed Nick's hand away from her throat. "Go away, Nick. It's my turn and I've got to concentrate."

He did go away, but only to fetch and light a cigarette.

Then he came back to stand behind Olivia, whose chair was nearest to the sofa.

"That's right," said her mother, "you distract Lia for a change. She's been winning up till now."

Olivia could smell him. He smelled of whiskey and tobacco, of vice and addiction, of fatal, forbidden pleasures. She prayed that he wouldn't touch her. She prayed for him to go away.

She tried to concentrate on the game. It was her turn next and she had a beautiful seven-letter word, STAUNCH, with no place to squeeze it in. Nick reached over, removed the U, and switched the T and the N around.

The others couldn't see what he had done, of course, and anyway it was a perfectly respectable word he had made, except that she knew he didn't have the respectable meaning in mind. "Stop that," she hissed at him.

He moved the letters again while she watched in horrified amusement: C-U-N . . . Before he could finish the word she knocked his hand away, scattering the tiles onto the table.

Her mother was just spelling out the word RAT on the board. "It's all I can do," she explained. "Do be careful, Lia, you'll jar the board."

Her grandmother didn't even look up from contemplation of her own letters. "Lia, tell Nick the word has to be allowed into the dictionary before it's allowed on the board."

Olivia was so flustered, especially by her grandmother's clairvoyance, that she made the first word she could think of, SCAT, and got a very low score for it. "Now look what you've made me do," she said to Nick. "Go away and watch television."

Her mother pushed back her chair and stood up. "I'm going to make more coffee. Darling," meaning Nick, "will you come and help me carry everything in?"

Darling went into the kitchen with her.

Olivia's grandmother studied the board and rearranged her letters several times. Finally she made the word OKAPI, which put her firmly in the lead.

Olivia called, "Mummy, it's your turn."

"I'll be there in a minute, Lia."

She sounded giggly, which made Olivia suspect that she

341

wouldn't be quite as quick as she had promised. "Do you want us to play your turn for you?"

"Hang on a minute. The kettle's just about to boil."

Olivia and her grandmother waited patiently until her mother returned from the kitchen. Her mother sat down and spelled out MEN in about two seconds and went back into the kitchen.

After quite a long time and a lot of whispering and laughing she came back out with the coffee.

When Olivia's grandmother had won the game, her mother said, "We're going to take a little stroll before bed," and went out into the soft West Country night hand in hand with Nick.

When they had gone her grandmother said, "I think I'll go to bed now, Lia. What about you?"

"I'm tired too. But what about Mummy?"

"I'll leave the door unlocked for Emma. We're unlikely to be burgled before she gets back."

Olivia felt very odd. Her mother was behaving like a teenager. She had gone into the kitchen with Nick to make coffee and they had obviously spent their time in there snogging, just the way Olivia and Charlie did. Even leaving aside the complicating matter of Nick and herself, it still seemed confusing and embarrassing and faintly disgusting. She was even embarrassed on her grandmother's behalf. She felt she ought to apologize for her mother's behavior.

"Meg says"—she waved a hand at the front door—"my friend Meg says this won't go on forever."

"Your friend is right. But it must be nice to feel like seventeen again."

In bed Olivia thought about what her grandmother had said. She knew about that, she realized. It had been some vestigial adolescent version of Nick—maybe the violent, anarchic, fourteen-year-old runaway—who had chased and caught her in the park, made love to her in her father's front hall, spelled out obscenities with her Scrabble letters.

There were other versions of him. There was the Nick who had sold her to a pornographic magazine. The one who threatened her with violence and then told her not to be afraid. One who called her kitten and made her feel like a star. A Nick who ruined his five-hundred-pound suit kneeling at the roadside to comfort a wretched, retching child.

She understood something else; it came to her just then. She knew why he had pushed her away that day and looked at her so coldly. It wasn't her but himself that had disgusted him.

She was sure of that because of what he had said later. He had said she was asking for it. She hadn't been really. She had unwittingly been asking him to love her, when the only thing he knew how to do was to make love. But not even his accommodating conscience could have swallowed the seduction of his lover's young daughter as she wept by the roadside for the loss of her father. Nick was a hard man, but not that hard.

Now, looking back, Olivia didn't know which had been worse: the absence of love or the presence of pity.

Charlie was going to think himself a lucky man tonight. Olivia dressed herself for the New Year's Eve party with the care and forethought of a soldier arming for battle. She put on the red dress she had bought for her father's wedding. Under that she had the black underwear and stockings that Nick had brought her from Paris. It reminded her of what else he had done that day. The thought of it made her feel sexy.

She was more concerned right now with looking sexy. Her own enthusiasm, or lack of it, didn't matter. What mattered was that Charlie had to make love to her. Charlie was about to become a father.

On the twenty-eighth of December—Childermas, her grandmother called it, the feast of the Holy Innocents, who were the babies slaughtered by Herod—it had dawned on Olivia that she might be pregnant again.

She had forgotten about the possibility. When she had failed to fall pregnant in time to (theoretically) stop Nick from marrying her mother, that seemed to be the end of it. The end of the potential pregnancy and of her affair with Nick. But of course he had made love to her one more time after that, almost exactly a fortnight after her last period, the most fertile time, according to the books. And now she was nearly a week overdue.

She went out the next day, after her mother and Nick had gone off to their respective employments, and bought a pregnancy testing kit—two, in fact, as before—different brands, so there would be no possibility of a mistake. She had to know for sure before New Year's Eve. Both tests came out positive, two days running.

Even now, with Nick lost to her, it didn't occur to her to seek another abortion. The knowledge that she was carrying his baby exhilarated her. Her mother hadn't swept the board after all. She would have her own prize, her own bond with him.

The appalling scenes that must sometime take place, when her condition came to light, were too remote to trouble her much. And however shocked and horrified everyone would be, parents and grandparents, teachers and schoolfriends, none of them would ever know the real, awful truth. All they would know about was Charlie.

Nick and her mother were going to a party too. "But we won't be late home," her mother said, "and you shouldn't be late either. Two o'clock at the absolute outside limit."

"My brother's girlfriend is driving," Charlie told Olivia's mother when he came to collect her. "She doesn't drink, so you don't need to worry about Lia getting home."

Her mother did not look particularly reassured. The unstated assumption behind his remark was that he and Barry both expected to be too drunk to drive by the nether end of the evening. "You'd better follow her example, Lia. And remember, home by two at the latest."

The house where the party was being held was north of Hampstead Heath, an enormous, rambling mansion set in a huge garden. Charlie had told her that his friend's father spent most of his time in Bahrain while the boy and his mother lived here in London. Knowing that made the grand house seem rather sad.

When they went in they were sent upstairs to put their coats in one of the bedrooms. The two girls lingered to check their hair and makeup, and on Olivia's part to adjust her neckline downward, since she had been afraid her mother might comment if she left the house looking the way she intended to look.

She studied the result in the mirror. The combination of push-up bra and scooped neckline gave her a cleavage to match any thrusting young starlet. She remembered the first time she had worn this dress, how she had pulled the draw-string to make a high neckline and stop Nick from staring at her breasts. She had come a long way since then, but probably not in the right direction.

Barry's girlfriend was called Lorna. She had an amazing hairdo: determinedly blond, curly, abundant, teased to atten-tion and then artistically knocked about. Olivia was im-pressed. She would never have had the nerve to go about with an aggressive head of hair like that.

Lorna was looking at her in an odd way. "Charlie said you were only fifteen. Was he having me on?"

"No, it's true."

"God, I wish I'd looked like that when I was fifteen. I wish I looked like that at nineteen, come to think of it."

Olivia felt like a brazen hussy. "Do you think I should, um, cover up a bit more?"

"What for? You look fantastic. And you know what they say, if you've got it, flaunt it. Wait till Charlie gets a good look at you."

Despite this reassurance, Olivia kept a modest hand across the visible expanse of her bosom when she came down the stairs.

Charlie hadn't seen her without her coat yet. He was wait-ing at the foot of the stairs. When he caught sight of her he stared in what she hoped was delighted astonishment. Dumbstruck would have been a better word. His jaw had literally dropped open.

She went over to him, both her hands up, fiddling with the chain around her neck. "Well? Say something, why don't you?" She swallowed nervously. "Don't you like the way I look?"

Charlie was speechless for the first time in his life. He took a deep breath and closed his mouth. "My God, Lia, you look like a film star."

"Is that good or bad?"

"Oh, good, good. Christ, you look terrific." He put his arm around her to claim possession. "You'd better stick close to me. I don't want every other guy in the place coming on to you. Can I get you a drink?"

"Okay. A Coke, please."

She stayed with Barry and Lorna while Charlie went off to find a drink. She wondered where Jon and Megan were. So far everyone looked to be much older than her, eighteen or nineteen years old. She felt shy and vulnerable, and very exposed.

Charlie returned with Cokes for her and Lorna and beer for Barry and himself. "It's not so crowded in the other room. Let's go in there."

They made their way to the "other" room, which might have been a banquet-sized dining room or a small ballroom. To Olivia's relief, Clare was there with Alistair, looking quite grown-up in a minimal black dress. The two girls complimented each other perfectly truthfully on their appearance.

After a while Jon and Megan turned up. Megan looked amazingly beautiful in a dress that exactly matched her wide blue eyes. Jon looked just the way he always did, struggling to keep his fine fair hair from falling into his eyes.

"Meg," Olivia whispered as soon as she could, "you look devastating. Charlie says Jon is totally smitten with you."

"He's easily smited, then. You're the one who looks devastating, Lia. You look about eighteen, and positively legendary."

"Legendary, I like that. What does it mean in ordinary language?"

"You don't look ordinary, you look transformed. I can't believe I know you."

"Don't you like the way I look?"

"Who cares if I like it? Charlie likes it, and that's the important thing, isn't it?"

"How do you know he likes it?"

"Oh Lia, you live on the moon." Megan gave her a friendly little shove. "He looks like he's been struck by lightning."

At midnight Barry fetched a couple of bottles of wine from somewhere and poured them each a glass to toast the new year. Since the other girls accepted a glass, Olivia thought there would be no harm in her having one too, in spite of what her mother had said. You couldn't really toast the new year with Coke.

They drank the wine and kissed each other happy new year. Charlie kissed her first and last, though the second time had nothing to do with the new year and went on for quite a long time.

He refilled her wineglass and his own. She leaned against the wall, sipping wine and watching the dancers. Someone had turned off the lights and lit a couple of candles on the table, which had been pushed into a corner and covered with food. Charlie stood between her and the others. He leaned down to say something close to her ear because the music was so loud, and then he used that closeness as an opportunity to kiss her shoulder and throat.

Olivia didn't know what to do next. She was quite sure that he wanted to make love to her, but she didn't know how to go about making it happen. They couldn't use the car, because Barry and Lorna would be with them. It was too cold to go outside, as they had at the pub. And she didn't want Megan to notice anything.

She looked around to see where Megan was, but Megan and Jon had both disappeared. Clare and Alistair were still in the room, wrapped up in each other in a virtually motionless dance, like courting sloths.

Olivia finished her wine and set the glass down. She felt warm and slightly melted inside her skin. She put her arms around Charlie's neck and pulled his head down and kissed him.

He kept on kissing her after that, running his hands over her bottom and pulling her up against him so that she could feel his erection pressing against her stomach. He kissed the upper curve of her breasts. He put his hand down the front of her dress and stroked her nipple till it stiffened. It was too dark for anyone to see what he was doing, and anyway, everybody else was probably doing the same thing.

After a while she said, "I've got to go to the loo. Do you know where it is?"

"I know where there's one upstairs. Come on, I'll show you."

He took her hand and made a way for them through the bodies—upright, supine, dancing, snogging, or drunken in the semidarkness. The staircase was littered with couples deep in embrace or earnest conversation.

One of the conversing couples was Megan and Jon. Actually, Olivia discovered when she stepped between them, they were not conversing but arguing, about organ transplants or some such thing. Megan was so engrossed she barely noticed Olivia going by.

The bathroom was as large as Olivia's bedroom in her mother's house, and twice the size of the room she had slept in at Highgate. It had an enormous round bathtub big enough for a horse, with gold taps. Even the toilet was, as Nick would doubtless have put it, too grand to shit in. Fortunately Olivia only wanted to pee.

When she came out, Charlie had disappeared. Instead there was someone else waiting to use the loo, a boy who had been introduced to her several hours earlier but whose name she couldn't remember. She didn't suppose he remembered her name either, to judge by his drunken grin.

"Happy new year, darling." He leered at her bosom. "Did your boyfriend go home and leave you stranded here?"

"No, he's around somewhere." She tried to squeeze past him without touching him, but the doorway wasn't wide enough. "If you'll just let me get out, you can have the bathroom all to yourself."

"I'd rather share it with you."

To her astonishment and horror, he put his hand down the front of her dress. The only way to get free of him was by stepping backward into the bathroom, but she didn't want to do that in case he followed her in and she found herself trapped. She tried to slip sideways past him, to push his hand away. He forced her up against the open door.

She was too shy and embarrassed to call for help. "Stop that! Let me go, you're drunk."

At that moment Charlie reappeared at the far end of the hallway. Her unwanted suitor must have seen and recognized him too. He released her and slammed the bathroom door, locking himself inside.

Olivia covered her bosom with her arms. She was in tears, shocked and humiliated. The thought of any man, Charlie or anyone, touching her now disgusted her.

Charlie came running up to her. "Christ, I'll kill him! Are you all right, Lia?" He banged on the bathroom door and loudly repeated his threat to kill the person inside.

Olivia caught his arm. "Charlie, please don't make a fuss. I can't stand it. I feel so awful—"

"Jesus, what an idiot I am." Charlie turned and put his arms around her. "Running after that bastard when you're in such a state. Are you all right, my darling?"

She was still holding her arms across her breasts, shaking and crying. She couldn't speak. She wanted to sink into the earth and disappear, or at least to go home right away. She desperately hoped that no one else had noticed the whole awful episode.

"Here, come down here and compose yourself."

"Here" was a bedroom at the end of the hall, where Charlie had appeared from. The house was about five times as large as her father's house and must have had at least half a dozen large bedrooms. There was nobody in this one, but the lamp on the dresser had been turned on. The bed was made but rumpled.

Charlie closed the door and sat her down on the edge of the bed and set about soothing her, holding her and stroking her in a comforting way. He talked to her, calling her my love and my darling. After a while she began to think she liked that.

"Are you all right?" he asked again, offering her another tissue.

"I suppose so." She wiped her eyes and blew her nose.

"But I feel absolutely horrible. And I must look horrible too, with my eyes all red."

"Don't feel like that. It wasn't your fault. It was my fault for not waiting right outside the door. Anyway, you don't look horrible, you look wonderful. Someone said you look like Claudia Schiffer."

She giggled, embarrassed. "They didn't mean my face, they meant my bust."

"What's wrong with having beautiful breasts?" He looked down at her front and cupped his hand around her left breast.

"They're not beautiful, they're just big."

"Let's see." He unzipped the back of the dress and pushed it down off her shoulders, down to her waist, leaving her bust in its cantilevered bra fully revealed.

"Christ," he whispered, which did nothing to settle the argument. "I'll kill him for touching you."

"Never mind him. I don't want to think about that ever again." She put her hands up to cover the bare upper part of her bosom, distressed all over again at the thought of the encounter in the bathroom.

"Here, don't do that. I'm sorry I mentioned it." He kissed and caressed her to calm her down again. After a while he began to kiss the revealed roundness of her breasts. He ran his tongue down her cleavage. That was surprisingly sexy. She felt less like dying now.

Somehow he disengaged her arms from the sleeves of the dress, then unfastened the bra and removed it. That left her naked to the waist, her breasts free and unsupported. Natural woman.

Charlie's response was most gratifying. He all but worshiped her breasts, it seemed. He stroked and kissed and licked and sucked every inch of them, and it felt wonderful, erotic and comforting at the same time. Perhaps it was that sort of enthusiasm that Megan had lacked on her mother's wedding night. She stroked his hair. It was the least she could do.

He maneuvered her into a horizontal position, then lay down beside her and ran his hand up the inside of her leg. His breath quickened when he reached the top of her stocking and touched her bare thigh.

He pushed up her skirt and moved his hand all the way up to her crotch. He was holding her and kissing her when his hand invaded her knickers. She froze for an instant, before she remembered that she had reasons for wanting him to do this. She closed her eyes and lifted her hips to meet the movement of his hand.

"I love you," he said hoarsely, "Christ, I love you, Lia. I've been dying to make love to you since the first time I saw you. Don't say no."

Being accustomed to Nick's more peremptory approach to lovemaking, she was touched that he had even paused to ask. "It's okay," she whispered, all-purpose approval for anything he had in mind.

He took off her dress and knickers but left on the garter belt and stockings, which impeded nothing and added a certain spurious air of sophistication to the proceedings. Then he took off his own clothes.

Naturally he thought she was a virgin and mistook her shyness for anxiety. "Don't be nervous, I won't hurt you."

That amused her and made her feel horrible and fraudulent at the same time. "How do you know you won't? Have you done it before?"

"Well, I have, yes."

"Lately?"

"Not since I met you." He was just about naked by then. He looked good, slim and dark, not as hairy as Nick, but dark so it showed up more. He pushed her legs apart and lay down between them. "Since I met you I haven't been able to remember what any other girl looks like."

"Is that good?"

He entered her at that point. "That's good," he sighed.

Too good to last, apparently. He came almost at once. She was surprised. That had never happened with Nick.

He took her surprise for disappointment. "Oh God, I'm sorry, Lia. Christ, I wait six months and get six seconds."

"Don't fuss." She pulled his head down and kissed him. "It doesn't matter."

"Yes, it does. God, I love you, you're so sweet and beautiful. I don't deserve you."

"Don't say that."

"But it's true. It's all true. Jesus, I love you."

She really wished he wouldn't say such things. It made her feel like the rottenest girl in the world rather than the sweetest and most beautiful. "Charlie, we've got to get dressed. Someone might come in."

It took quite a long time to get dressed because he couldn't keep his hands off her and she had to discourage him from making love to her a second time.

"We can't just disappear for an hour. The others will wonder where we are."

"They'll know very well where we are. If they even notice we're not there."

Olivia blushed at the thought of coming downstairs to knowing smirks. "That's worse. Anyway, I've got to get home, it must be past two o'clock already. Mummy will kill me."

"She's probably gone to bed already."

"Then she'll get Nick to kill me." She pushed him away. "Charlie, please, do, do get your trousers on."

He did up his trousers and put his hand in the pocket. "Christ, I'm an idiot. I brought a condom and didn't use it."

And a good thing too, she thought, there would have been no point otherwise. "Why not? Did you forget?"

"I don't know. Maybe I didn't want you to think I'd plotted this."

"Did you plot it?"

He reached over to stroke her cheek. "I'll tell you, Lia, I've been plotting it since I first set eyes on you. Maybe I fell in love with you then."

She dared to raise the most important question. "What if I get pregnant?"

To her surprise he only shrugged and smiled. "It wouldn't be the end of the world. At least I'm a working man."

That response didn't make any sense to her at the time. It was only later, going home and reflecting, that she realized he had been offering to marry her.

47

By the time Olivia had fixed up her makeup and combed her hair and they had gone downstairs and had another glass of wine to compose themselves and tracked down Barry and Lorna and found out whether Jon and Megan wanted a lift home, it was well past three o'clock.

It was nearer four than three by the time Charlie said good night to her on her mother's doorstep. She had hoped to find the house in darkness, meaning either that her mother was still out or that they had come home and gone to bed. But the sitting room lights were clearly on.

Seeing that she was nervous, Charlie volunteered to take the blame. "I'll just come in and apologize. I'll say it was my fault. It was, wasn't it? You couldn't walk home by yourself." He kissed her for about the hundredth time. "Christ, I wish I could take you home to bed with me."

She disentangled herself from him. "Charlie, I've got to go inside."

"Shall I come in?"

It wouldn't help, not with him plainly tipsy. "Better not. I'll be all right."

"Okay, I'll phone you tomorrow."

He got back into the car and she turned her key in the lock. She didn't know whether to breeze in boldly as if everything was perfectly okay or to sneak inside and upstairs in the hope of pretending she had been home for ages.

The question was settled for her. As soon as she shut the front door, Nick came out of the sitting room. Hastily she shrugged out of her coat. "Happy new year."

"Keep your voice down. Em's asleep."

He didn't look pleased, to say the least. She dropped her voice to a whisper. "I'm sorry I'm so late, I—"

He stopped her in midsentence by grabbing her wrist. "Where the fuck have you been for the last two hours?"

"At the party, what do you think?"

"Do you want to know what I think? Come in here and I'll tell you."

She didn't want to go in with him, she wanted to go upstairs to safety. She could smell whiskey on his breath. He had been out to a party with her mother, and maybe drinking since he got back. She had never seen him observably drunk, not even at Christmas when in one evening he had sunk about half the bottle of single malt her grandmother had given him. But drunk or not, he scared her when he had been drinking.

He dug his fingers into her wrist in some peculiarly painful way that made her feel as if he was about to take her bones apart. "That hurts," she protested, still speaking softly. But she let him take her into the sitting room. He shut the door so that her mother wouldn't hear.

"Em said two o'clock. I heard her say it twice. What the fuck do you mean by swanning in here at twenty to fucking four?"

"It wasn't my fault. Charlie was going to—"

"Sod Charlie. He's just dumped you on the doorstep in the middle of the night, pissed and fucked. I'm surprised he had the sense to put your clothes back on. Not that it makes much fucking difference, the way you're dressed."

She put up her free hand to cover her cleavage. He was only talking like that, he couldn't possibly know what she had done, though it wouldn't be the first time he had guessed what was in her head. Maybe he could smell Charlie on her. Smell Charlie in her. The idea alarmed and excited her.

He pulled her closer, his eyes like sea ice. It scared her to look at him. But it hurt her more, what he was doing to her wrist. "Em told you to get home sober by two o'clock. She didn't tell you not to get fucked because it wouldn't have crossed her mind."

"No," she said as coldly as she could. "That's something you taught me, isn't it?"

He hit her.

It was an open, backhanded blow to the side of her head. It would have knocked her over, except he was still holding her wrist. He slapped her the other way, with the palm of his hand. She was so shocked that she could only stare at him speechless, not even feeling the pain.

He let go of her wrist then. He grabbed the bodice of her hundred-and-fifty-pound dress in both hands and tore it apart, right down the front, just like Mr. Universe with a telephone directory. He jerked the rags of it off her. When he saw what she was wearing underneath, his present to her, he started to call her names in a low, savage tone. He began with common currency like *slag* and *slut* and moved on to language so vile and debased that even coming from his mouth it shocked her. He tore her bra in two. He felled her with another open-handed blow and ripped off the black silk knickers. He was a powerful man, her stepfather.

As he took off his trousers he told her what he was going to do to her, using the obscene idioms of violence and sexual subjugation to describe the act that had moved Charlie two hours earlier to tell her he loved her. He forced her knees up and apart, wrenching her thighs painfully wide. Then he entered her, deliberately brutal, meaning to degrade and humiliate her.

She must have been still wet from Charlie. Nick's cock slid up into her so easily, he would know he had guessed right. Or else he would think that his brutality had aroused her. She didn't know which was worse.

Yet she was aroused. He had struck her in a jealous rage. He was possessing her from jealousy, because Charlie had had her. She had thought he was lost to her. Now she had him again.

She couldn't put her arms around him because he had pinned her wrists to the carpet. But nothing could prevent her body responding sexually to his sexual domination. When he felt her moving to meet him he called her more names, spitting them in her face as he stabbed deep into her. This time the motif was nymphomania rather than promiscuity.

In the end he abandoned words, reverting to the physical language of beasts. That was where his real eloquence lay.

Any human tongue, even the gutter speech of degraded Saxon obscenities that seemed to come most naturally to him, was still a translation from the mystery inside him. Maybe that was true of all men, even her father. Mysteries, Martians, every one of them.

Nick bent his head and caught her throat in his teeth, like a dog or a wolf in mortal combat. It was the skin over her windpipe he had hold of. If he had been a wolf and closed his jaws, she would have died.

But Olivia knew that language too. She tipped back her head, offering him her undefended throat, the way a beaten wolf begs mercy of the victor. But it wasn't mercy she was begging of him, it was love.

"Don't say those things," she whispered. She locked her legs around his hips, the only way she could embrace him while he kept her hands prisoner. She closed her eyes and arched her body up to meet the savage rhythm of his thrusts. "You know it's not like that. You know you're the only man I want."

The wolf's teeth unclenched. He touched his tongue to the place where his teeth had marked her. When she spoke again he must have felt the vibration of her larynx. Maybe her words went through his mouth to his brain, instead of through his ears. Maybe that was how Martians communicated with each other.

"I love you, Nick. You know I love you. Say you love me, Nick."

He stopped moving, his cock still inside her. The blind rage had faded from his eyes. "I told you," he said harshly. "I told you, it's just Latin for I want to fuck you."

"Why don't you say it, then? Don't you want to fuck me?"

He took a deep breath. She felt it shuddering right through him. "Jesus, yes."

He released her wrists and took her in his arms. At last she could, she did, embrace him. He began to make love to her as if he were Adam having just invented it, seizing the pleasure and the woman for which he had been cast out into the wilderness. He responded to her desire with a violent desperation, as if like Adam he had nothing else left to live for.

Again she experienced a sexual clairvoyance, knowing him and knowing that he knew her to the marrow of the bones, to the root of the soul. She loved him, she said it again, she loved him, until coming fulfilled and shattered that perfect understanding.

"All right," he said, "you win, you little witch. I love you. So what?"

"So everything."

She began to cry. Why couldn't he love her as Charlie did, freely and unbegrudgingly? Instead of acting as if loving her was some kind of perversion, as if she were such an essentially and obviously unlovable person that he didn't want to admit even to himself how vulgar and depraved his taste in love objects was.

Though, in justice, having your stepdaughter for a lover was probably about as grossly decadent as you could get. There were stories in the papers every week about that kind of thing, men who had raped and sexually abused their wife's adolescent daughter. Any policeman or journalist or social worker could have made just such a story out of Nick and Olivia. But if it had ever really been like that, it wasn't anymore.

Olivia loved Nick. Maybe Nick loved Olivia. He had said so, for what it was worth.

Not that any of that made it right.

"Don't cry, kitten." He cradled her head and kissed the tears on her face, licking them away with light touches of his tongue like the wolf she had imagined him to be. A wolf with whiskey on his breath. "I'm sorry I hit you. I shouldn't have said all that shit, you know I didn't mean any of it."

With his cheek against hers she could feel the rough growth of his whiskers, five-o'clock-in-the-morning shadow. "Christ," he said in her ear, "I shouldn't be screwing you. You don't want me to love you, baby. I'm a bastard, I'm bad news for you."

"I know all that," said Olivia. "So what?"

48

That was the easy part over and done. Getting pregnant by accident after failing to get pregnant by design, then being seduced by the boy she had meant to seduce. The hard part would be making sure no one found out until it was too late.

Too late was quite a long time, to judge from Althea's remark about Olivia's mother. Four months wasn't safe. Five months, maybe just about. With luck, her mother could be a mother again before she found out she was going to be a grandmother as well.

It might have been much more difficult if Olivia had had to live with her mother the whole time. As it happened, her father was finally completing the purchase of his new house, so she would be able to move back in with him. Assuming he wanted her back. She might have to make a fuss. Hopefully it wouldn't involve getting her feet full of glass again.

Living with her father would have a number of advantages. One, Althea wasn't interested in her and took no notice of her. Two, her father took no notice of anything at all. Three, she wouldn't have to be around Nick. Four, she could find out about babies by keeping an eye on young Matthew. She would be an expert by the time her own baby was born at the end of the summer.

She phoned her father in Marlow on Sunday to ask about the house moving.

"We're completing on Friday, thank God. That works out very nicely, because my term starts the following Monday."

"Do you want some help unpacking? I'm back at school tomorrow so I can't do anything on moving day, but I'll come on Saturday." She added after a pause, when he didn't say anything, "If you want me, that is."

"That's a good idea. You can at least mind the baby so Althea is free to unpack."

"Does that mean I can move in with you again?"

"Of course. You'll have your own room in the new house, and so will Matthew. We won't be living in each other's pockets the whole time anymore."

He wanted her back. For practical reasons she was relieved. For emotional reasons she was delighted. Even if, as her grandmother had suggested, she was going to be a baby-sitter.

The moving man, when it came to shifting her belongings, was by precedent the one in whose house she had most recently been living. That meant that Nick would be depositing her on her father's doorstep. It was Saturday afternoon by the time she had got herself packed. Still, she had no time to feel sentimental about this departure. By the time she moved back again, if she ever did, her mother would have another child. She herself might have a child by then. She couldn't imagine what that would be like. She seemed to have landed on a high-speed conveyor belt to the future, which every now and then threw her off into a new world.

Affairs in the new house were surprisingly chaotic. Althea blamed the baby. She was sitting in an armchair with her feet propped on a packing crate, giving Matthew his afternoon tea, when Olivia arrived.

"Oh, Lia, thank God you're here." That was the first time ever that Althea had shown any interest, let alone pleasure, in Olivia's presence. But Olivia knew why, and Althea was frank about her attractions. "This little monster wants nothing but attention, just when I need him to sit quiet in a corner and let me get on with unpacking."

Matthew carried on sucking at Althea's breast, but he rolled his eyes in Olivia's direction. A pleading look, she thought it was. "He's upset, I'll bet. He doesn't like all the moving around. Cats don't like it either. When Clare's family moved house their cats were in a panic for a whole week."

"Matthew is not a cat," Althea said coldly. "He's a baby, not an animal."

"Of course he's an animal, we're all animals. We're not plants or angels, are we? But I only meant that we can't explain things to him, and he can't explain things to us. And it's the same with cats."

Althea waved these explanations away as too complicated for a woman used to dealing only with simple everyday matters like interest-rate swaps, currency swaps, option swaps, commodity swaps, and the like. "Never mind all that. You'll be calling him a termite next. You really are a loony kid, Lia. But if you can keep him happy when I've finished feeding him, I'll be everlastingly grateful to you."

"I can't do anything for you yet, I've still got to bring my things in. I'll be back in a minute. Where's Daddy?"

"Unpacking his books, where else? His study is the back room on the first floor."

The new house had bigger rooms than the old one, and more of them because it carried on upward for one more story. Instead of being flat across the facade it had bay windows and a recessed front door, and it was made of red brick instead of gray stone.

The front bedroom on the first floor was to be her father's and Althea's bedroom. The back bedroom would be her father's study. The front bedroom on the second floor was to be the nursery (the theory was that Althea could hear Matthew above her if he cried at night) and the back bedroom was going to be Olivia's. There was a second bathroom on the top floor, which she had all to herself. If you didn't count Matthew, that gave her a certain splendid isolation, not unlike the situation of her old attic room in her mother's house.

It also made it likely that she would hear Matthew before Althea did. She wasn't sure whether that was part of the plan or not. The one thing she was already absolutely certain of was that nothing Matthew could possibly do in the middle of the night would waken her father.

Nick was still in the car, waiting to hear if the house was ready for her belongings or not. Olivia went back out to him. "It's okay, we can take all my stuff right up to the top floor."

"Your old man is actually letting me set foot inside his fucking house?"

"He's not taking any notice, he's upstairs unpacking his books. Althea's downstairs feeding Matthew. She said to just take everything up." She added, "Anyway, it's okay now, you're married to my mother. You're my stepfather, just like Althea's my stepmother."

They managed to take everything up in one trip. This meant that Nick had to carry three suitcases and sling the flight bag over his shoulder, but he didn't seem to mind. And after all, she thought to herself, any man who can remove somebody's clothes in about thirty seconds without recourse to a single button, zipper, hook, or lace could surely cope with a pile of luggage.

She waved to Althea on the way up, and her father did not emerge from his study. They landed in her new room, which looked southward over the heath and the cemetery. She thought it was, in point of view, the nicest room in the house.

Nick set down the suitcases and shrugged off the flight bag. He went over to the window to look out, hands in his back pockets. "You get the penthouse suite again, I see."

She stared at the hands in the pockets and at his backside in the worn jeans. She could smell the aura of tobacco smoke that he carried about with him. I'm like one of Pavlov's famous dogs, she thought. When they heard the bell they salivated for dinner. When I smell cigarettes I wet my knickers.

It was dreadful, shameful, worse than addiction. As if he had somehow played Pavlov and trained her to respond sexually to any reminder of his presence. But whether it was his deliberate doing or not, that was exactly what she did.

She came up behind him and slid her hands into his pockets, palm to palm against his hands. It was dangerous lunacy, with her father in the room below.

Nick did not refuse the challenge. He took hold of her hands and brought them around to the front of his jeans, sliding them over the shape of his erection. Had that happened when she touched him, or did he respond to her presence in the same way she reacted to him? Maybe he just knew what she was thinking. He always seemed to know what was in her head.

She leaned against him, stroking him roughly through the denim, pressing herself against his buttocks. He ran his fingertips up her forearm. She felt the little hairs rising up to meet his touch. If there was such a thing as animal magnetism, this was it: a ripple of desire passed upward through her, as if he had run the tips of his fingers up her whole body.

"Daddy's right below us."

"I know that, baby."

"We can't do this. He'd kill you."

"Don't you want it?"

He didn't say, as she would have done, Don't you want me? From the very beginning he had never once, as far as she knew, doubted that she wanted him. Whereas she doubted every day his desire for her. It wasn't fair, men and women.

He wanted her now, at any rate. He turned to face her. He cupped her bottom in his hands and pulled her up against him, riding the ridge of her pubic bone up and down his erect penis, denim on denim, cunt on cock.

"We can't do this," she whispered again. She was clinging to him, longing for him, full of shame and terror. "You're my stepfather now."

"Yeah, that's right, I am." He spoke softly, half smiling, a wolfish sort of smile that alarmed her. "That means you can call me Daddy while I'm screwing you."

"You can't screw me," she said in a panic. "Daddy's downstairs."

"Daddy's right here, and he wants to ram his big stiff prick up into your tight little pussy."

"Don't talk like that." She buried her face in his shoulder. "It's disgusting."

She could feel him laughing. "No, it's not, it's sexy."

He was right, it was sexy. The most disgusting and shameful things were sexy when he did or said them. If it weren't for the danger to him, she would almost have been prepared to lie down for him right there, in spite of her father.

Because of her father.

That made it more exciting. And Nick knew that. He knew everything, every dreadful thing about her, and he didn't seem to mind.

She was depraved, there was no other word for it. How else would anyone describe a girl who was turned on by the possibility of being discovered in flagrante by her father? Especially, unspeakably, in the act of being taken by her stepfather. . . . There were no words in the language to describe such a vile soul.

Well, probably there were. And Nick would know them.

"Lia?"

They leapt apart—at least Olivia jerked away and Nick let her go. She managed to put a decent interval between their bodies in the nanosecond before her father appeared at the bedroom door.

Her father looked from her to Nick with an expression that made her fear her fantasy had come too true. Nick looked from her to her father as if they were both trespassing in some way, because wherever he himself happened to be standing was his own rightful territory. Olivia looked from her father to her stepfather and wanted to be somewhere else.

Her father said, "What's going on?"

Olivia spoke up before Nick could say anything like, What's it to you? "We've just brought up my stuff, Daddy. And I'm going downstairs to get the rest of it right now." Before her father could say something like, I'll take care of that, she added, "It's only a couple of bags, I can carry it up myself."

She made herself walk toward the door, toward her father, not sure even now that he wouldn't seize her and accuse her of unspeakable sins. But he stepped aside to let her go out.

She ran halfway down the stairs before stopping to look back. It was cowardly, she knew, to leave Nick to fend for himself with her father. Yet anything she might do or say on his behalf would only irritate her father more.

Nick was just coming out of the bedroom. He remarked to her father with casual insolence, "Nice place you've got here."

Her father didn't bother to reply, maybe because his preferred response would have involved throwing Nick down the stairs. He came down right on Nick's heels, an outraged tomcat escorting the alley-cat intruder off his property. Nick descended at a leisurely pace, body language to match the coolly provoking tone of his remark. The atmosphere was of a threatened thunderstorm. Olivia began to see how wars get started.

She went out to the car. It was locked, of course, and of

course there was no more baggage inside. Fortunately her father didn't follow Nick out into the street.

Nick came up, near enough to touch her, but he didn't. She could tell that the close encounter with her father had aroused him rather than unnerving him. There was no way he was not going to fuck her now.

Without a word she walked away from the car, toward Swains Lane. He followed her down the lane as far as the narrow upper gate to the old part of the cemetery. Then she turned to face him, her back to the barred gate. "There's no one in here."

He took hold of the bars on either side of her and pressed her right back against the gate, one leg pushing between her thighs. He kissed her mouth. She put her arms around him. She too, now that the danger was past, found herself aroused rather than unnerved. If there had been no alternative she would have let him take her right there, daylight and all, rather than go without him. Lost to all decency, that was the phrase.

"We have to climb over," she said at last. "Give me a boost."

She expected him to give her a leg up, but he put his hands around her waist and hoisted her up. As soon as she was over he came after her.

"What is this?"

"Highgate Cemetery, the really old part. It's like a jungle."

They walked down into the wilderness. "It really is a fucking jungle," he said, impressed. "How come nobody's been round with the lawnmower and Paraquat?"

"It's been like this so long that they've made it into a wildlife refuge. We have to be careful not to disturb the wildlife."

"Fuck the wildlife. The birds and bees are supposed to be the experts on it, aren't they?"

"No, seriously. This is a nature reserve."

"I thought a nature reserve was a nudist camp. In which case, to quote your gran, we're not dressed for it."

He put his arms around her waist, inside her open coat. He ran his hands up under her jumper, pulling her shirttail free of her jeans and unbuttoning the shirt. He unhooked her brassiere and pushed it aside to take possession of her breasts. She had her hands in his hair, kissing and caressing him. She had an idea that he could make her come just by stroking her breasts, but she wasn't likely to get a chance to test that thesis.

He was doing amazing things to her body, pinching and rubbing her nipples, sliding his hand up to surround and stroke her throat—a caress and a threat in one gesture. He knew precisely how to invoke that blend of longing and vulnerability that made her willing to do anything he wanted, however risky or humiliating. As he kissed her she uttered small croaks and whimpers, communicated directly from her tongue to his, no more articulate than an ape's grunts, but he understood her perfectly nonetheless. Because he needed only a simple and primitive answer: Anything you want.

He took her jacket off and slung it over a tombstone as casually as if it were the back of a chair. He pulled her jeans down and stroked her thighs and bottom and between her thighs, until she was almost fainting for him.

By now she was naked from the waist down. It wasn't cold for January, but it was cold enough to make her shiver uncontrollably. The long grass was wet against her bare legs and feet.

"It's too wet to lie down."

"That's what gravestones are for."

She didn't understand him. He showed her: he made her lean over a stone with her legs splayed apart and he came into her from behind.

Like a dog with a bitch. Like a pregnant woman. She was, but he didn't know it.

Pinioned over the tombstone, she couldn't even embrace him. She thought of her father discovering them. Her exposed flesh was cold, but inside she burned with desire and shame. It felt like hot, sticky tar where her guts should have been.

God knew how wicked she was, desecrating some poor soul's grave in this fashion when her grandmother had taught her never even to step on a grave. Her grandmother could never have envisaged her like this, with her stepfather's cock up her cunt and his baby in her belly, and she too young to have a man at all, the law said. It was wildly, perversely exciting, but there was no comfort in it.

She couldn't stop shivering, even when she was fully clothed again. She put her arms around his middle and he held her. She should have said, We can't do this anymore, but she couldn't bear to hear him agree. She was thinking about how he had said that he loved her, and wishing he would say it again.

He was looking about, over the top of her head.

"This place is fantastic. I should have brought a camera. It's like those ruined cities in the jungles of Central America."

"Have you been there? Have you seen them?"

"Yeah, I got flown out there once to shoot some fucking fashion feature. It was bizarre. It cost a fortune to get us there, and here were these stupid tarts getting paid a fortune to wear a fortune in clothes, prancing around on the bones of a dead civilization, in a country where half the people live like dogs. It wasn't that they didn't care, they didn't even notice."

"Did you care?"

He shrugged. "There's a lot of pain in the world. Caring doesn't make it go away."

He moved back about a foot to rest his backside on the tombstone. She came to stand between his legs. She had an arm around his neck. He put his arm around her waist.

He said, "I've always wondered about places like that, big cities, lots of people, how did they get turned into a heap of broken bricks? Imagine all of London in this condition."

"A graveyard, you mean?"

"An overgrown ruin."

She looked around at the cemetery and invisible London beyond. Supposing there was nothing beyond, except more of this desolate wilderness. "How would it get like that?"

"I don't know, but someday it will. What happened to Babylon? How does a civilization die?"

"They get decadent, I suppose."

"Oh, that's simple then." He was laughing; she had amused him. "It's a fucking plague, we all get decadent and die off. A cultural version of AIDS."

"Well, it has to be something like that, doesn't it?"

"What's decadence, then?"

Olivia turned her head to look at him. He was smiling at her. He had stolen from his parents and beaten his wife and betrayed Olivia's mother and debauched Olivia herself in her father's house and her mother's bed. He took pictures of women doing obscene things. Yet he was as clever and perceptive as any man in old Babylon.

But why pick on him? Her father now, there had been scholars and scribes and stargazers upon the perished walls of Babylon, maybe even one who had left his wife and child to commit adultery and impregnate one of his young students. And her mother, yes, there would have been fornicators and adulteresses among the women, and mothers who did their duty by their children without ever loving them.

As for herself, the most famous person in Babylon was the whore of it.

Nick was smiling at her. She took his face in her hands and kissed the corners of his smile. He was the only person in the world she could do that to, and she was forbidden to do it to him.

She said, "Decadence is fucking your fifteen-year-old stepdaughter over a tombstone."

"When you put it like that, it sounds pretty damned appealing."

He started to kiss her more deeply. She knew where that would end up. "Don't, Nick, I have to get back. Althea's waiting for me. And Daddy will get suspicious." She shivered at the thought of what had so nearly happened. It would have been even more disastrous now, now that she was pregnant.

For a moment she thought he wasn't going to let her go, she thought he was going to go on and make love to her again. Could you compound damnation, was twice worse than once? But he only kissed her again, before turning her back toward the gate.

Althea was indignant when Olivia returned. "Lia, you said you'd mind the baby and then you disappeared for an hour."

"It wasn't an hour. Half an hour at the most. Where's Matthew?"

"He's upstairs with Ross. I think he's finally gone to sleep. Where did you get to?"

A vague and evasive reply would only stir Althea's curiosity, so she told the truth. "Nick wanted to have a look at the cemetery. He thought he might use it as a background for something he had in mind."

49

It was easy to be patient, Olivia discovered, when you knew that what you wanted was going to happen anyway, and all you had to do was wait for it. Besides, between now and the birth of her baby there were going to be some excruciating encounters, and she didn't want to wish them on herself sooner than necessary.

If she had been in any doubt about the true state of affairs, it was dispelled a few days after moving back to Highgate. She got out of bed in the morning and was sick.

It was almost exactly six months since her previous bout of morning sickness. This time she felt elation rather than despair. She had had perfect faith in the scientific evidence of pregnancy tests, but in her heart she believed her body. She hoped that Megan was right in claiming that babies were not souls newly created for the purpose but old souls coming back, because she desperately wanted this one to be the same person as the baby she had lost. Who could it be, someone so persistently eager to be born the child of her and Nick?

This time she didn't have to deceive her grandmother, only her father and Althea. That was easy. The hard part was going to school feeling sick. By lunchtime it was over, but the mornings were hell.

She read all of Althea's books on pregnancy. They had titles like *How to Have a Healthy Baby* and described in illustrated detail the events that were going on inside her. She had to sneak the books up to her room to read because the one thing that her father could be relied upon to notice and comment on was her reading material.

Somehow she had to avoid putting on weight. That was

easy at the moment. Although she only really felt sick in the mornings, the smell of food tended to put her off eating much at any time. She bought an array of vitamin pills, which she kept in her dresser drawer and took faithfully every evening, so the baby wouldn't have to suffer from her lack of appetite.

It would be more difficult in the spring. Ideally she didn't want to be found out until the end of May, when she would be six months gone. The baby would be safe after five months, but if Charlie was to be the father she would have to pretend to be one month less pregnant than she actually was. So six months was five months, but five months was only four months—still time, as Althea had observed, for everything to be taken back.

But according to the books, the second trimester of pregnancy was the time when the mother put on most weight, sometimes a pound a week. How was she going to gain so much weight in three months without anyone noticing?

That was something she would have to work out later. Right now she had more immediate problems. What to do about Charlie, for instance.

He had rung up on New Year's Day, when she was still at her mother's. "They didn't kill you after all," he said when she answered the phone.

"No, I'm still alive. Just."

"That bad, was it? Maybe I should apologize to your mother for bringing you home so late."

"Don't bother. She'd already gone to bed. She left Nick to play night watchman."

"Did he give you a hard time?" When she didn't answer, not knowing how to answer, he said, "I'm sorry if I got you into trouble, Lia."

"Don't worry about it, Charlie. It's all right."

"Really?"

"Really."

And truthfully trouble was not the word to describe what had happened: being beaten and raped by her stepfather, then having him say he loved her. It wasn't trouble, it was heaven. But whatever it was, she didn't tell Charlie about it.

"Okay, if you say so." He dropped his voice to a more

intimate level. "Lia, about last night—I mean, you know, what happened ..."

"Yes, I know what happened."

"Yeah, well, what I mean is ..." He cleared his throat, then continued in the same semiwhisper, "I meant everything I said. You're really magic. I can't stop thinking about it."

She supposed that meant he would want to do it again. She didn't know how she felt about that. But she knew she should be saying the same things to him as he was saying to her, and she couldn't do it. Her magic was in another man. And she couldn't even lie; that would be compounding her guilt and deceit. She already felt unbearably guilty and deceitful, toward her mother as much as Charlie.

As she thought that, her mother came into the kitchen. "I've got to go now," she said hastily. "I'll talk to you later, okay?"

"You sound funny. Are you sure everything's all right?"

"I'm okay. Really. It's just—"

"Okay, I get it. I'll see you soon." He blew a kiss down the line, which made her giggle as she hung up.

Her mother said, "Was that Charlie?"

"Yeah."

"What time did you get in last night?"

"Didn't Nick tell you?"

"He's still asleep."

Olivia glanced at the clock. "But it's lunchtime already."

"Which suggests to me that he must have stayed up very late waiting for you."

"Well, I guess he did. Why didn't you both just go to bed? You knew I wasn't likely to get mugged or run over."

Her mother folded her arms and looked frosty. "In the first place, Lia, you're only fifteen. In the second place, after that time you ran away and Ross accused me of neglecting you, I'm not giving him the chance to criticize me again like that."

"So why didn't you wait up yourself, instead of making Nick do it?"

"I didn't 'make' him do it. He sent me to bed and said he'd wait up till you got in. By that time it was already three o'clock and you were an hour late." Her mother's voice grew warmer. "Really, Lia, your attitude to Nick is totally wrong-headed. It wouldn't be any wonder if he resented you as much as you seem to resent him, what with the dreadful way you behave toward him. But he's been good to you, Lia, he really has. He drives you back and forth to Ross's place, he took you out for dinner, he sat with you when you were sick, he ignores it when you're rude to him. And he waited up last night because he cares about you, not because I asked him to. He's a good, kind man, Lia. The way he talks is . . . just the way he talks."

Nowadays a good man sure is hard to find.

Olivia didn't know how to reply to all that. Her mother thought Nick was a good, kind man. Megan thought he was a rat. Olivia, who knew him better than her mother and Megan did, thought his name was no accident. Not Saint but Old.

The weekend after she had moved back in with her father and Althea, Charlie took her to see a film. Afterward they came back to the new house in Highgate and made popcorn in the kitchen.

Althea came into the kitchen to put the kettle on. "Don't mind me," she told them, "I'm just making myself a cup of tea to take to bed. That baby has reduced me to total decrepitude, getting me up at all hours. My dreams are all about sleeping. How are you, Charlie? How's business?"

"Pretty slow. Dead, in fact." Charlie had already told Olivia that he hadn't got the car he had wanted for Christmas. His father had said he couldn't afford it, which Charlie said he would have put down to miserliness if Barry hadn't been given a car the year before.

"Things are tough all over," Althea agreed cheerfully. "But the construction industry's been really hit. Does your father do any property development?"

"He owns some property, yeah. He bought most of it a couple of years ago when interest rates started to drop and he reckoned the market would start to pick up. Now he can't even unload it, let alone develop it."

Olivia looked at Charlie in surprise. She was fairly sure that six months ago he wouldn't even have known what sort of creature an interest rate might be. In another six months, who knew, he might be swapping swap stories with Althea.

"Rotten luck," said Althea. "Maggie Thatcher would never have let things get into this state. She knew better than to alienate her own voters."

"That's what my father says."

"Well, don't let Ross hear him say it. He thinks she's the Devil incarnate for not making up academic salaries to what they are in America. It's sinful, you see, for swap dealers to get paid New York salaries in London, and equally sinful for history professors in London not to get paid New York salaries. The poor innocent hasn't worked out yet that if you depend on the taxpayers for your salary you won't make much money." As she talked she was pouring out two mugs of tea. "There's enough left for you two, if you want it, Lia. I'm going to take a cup up to Ross in his study. And then I'm going to bed."

When she had disappeared upstairs and they were more or less alone, Charlie took the opportunity to kiss Olivia. After a little while she pushed him away. "I have to mind the popcorn. It burns if you don't keep shaking the pot."

"Okay, you get on with it. Do you mind if I watch?"

Watching turned out to mean standing behind her with his arms around her in order to caress her breasts.

"Stop that. You'll distract me and the popcorn will burn."

"It's only fair I should distract you. You're distracting the hell out of me. Why didn't you want to see me last weekend?"

"I told you, I was tired."

"All day Sunday?"

"We were unpacking and getting organized all day Sunday. The house was a complete shambles."

"We could have gone for a walk. Down to that cemetery, for instance."

Her heart lurched. That was why she hadn't wanted to see him, not after Nick ... "I couldn't go out. We had so much work to do, and I was supposed to be minding the baby."

"Then I could have helped you unpack."

"Althea didn't want anyone coming round till the house looked respectable again." The popping had stopped. She took the pot off the heat, removed his hands from her bosom, and added salt to the hot popcorn. "Here, have some. Do you want a drink?"

"In a minute. Come here and stop making daft excuses." He grabbed her and kissed her hard. He was breathing heavily when he raised his head. "Since New Year's Eve I've been dying to make love to you again. I can't think about anything else."

He started to unbutton her blouse. She caught his hands. "Charlie, you can't. Daddy's upstairs."

"I can't not, as long as he's not down here. Just for a minute, Lia, please . . ."

In a good deal less than a minute he had both the blouse and her bra undone and was stroking her bare breasts with a mixture of awe and avidity. "You have the most fantastic tits," he whispered. "Even better than I remembered."

If it was size that impressed him, they really were better than he remembered. Pregnancy made your breasts increase in size, it said so in Althea's book, and Olivia had discovered for herself that it was so. She had had to buy a bra with a D cup because her usual 36C couldn't cope.

Charlie might as well enjoy it while he could. She had decided that she had no objection to going to bed with him, in fact she quite liked the idea. It was better than nothing, when she couldn't have Nick. The trouble was that when she began to show, he would notice if he saw her in the nude.

"Charlie, you have to stop. I'm scared Daddy might come down. Please, Charlie."

He let her go reluctantly. She hooked up and buttoned up her clothes almost as quickly as he had undone them, while he watched with undisguised regret. "When do we get a chance to be alone?"

"Let me think." She couldn't tell him never. She took a handful of popcorn and fed it to him kernel by kernel while she considered how to temporize. "Next Saturday," she said at last. "Daddy and Althea are going out to dinner and I'm minding Matty for them. You can come over then."

When Charlie came over the following Saturday she still hadn't decided what to do. It didn't seem fair to tell him he was out of luck, especially in view of the wicked trick she was going to play on him.

Maybe she should just tell him she was pregnant. She didn't even need to lie to him about its being his child, because it would never occur to him that it could be someone else's. He thought she'd been a virgin until New Year's Eve. A girl who felt sick when someone touched her breasts, a girl whose father insisted on picking her up from a party, a girl like that just had to be a virgin.

But if she told him, he might want her to get an abortion. Or he might want her to tell their parents right away. Or . . . who knew what he might want to do? As long as no one else knew, she was in control of her destiny. That little spark of baby-to-be inside her gave her a surprising sense of power.

She had told him not to come over until she rang him. That was a wise precaution, as it turned out, because Matthew was still asleep when her father and Althea were ready to go out. They hung about for a while but he still didn't wake.

"This is absurd," Althea announced at last. "I'll have to wake him up and feed him. If I don't he'll start screaming as soon as we've gone."

"I'll get him up," Olivia said.

When she went upstairs she found Matthew lying wide-eyed in his cot. She picked him up to bring him downstairs. "Why didn't you speak up, silly boy?" she asked him. "Althea's waiting to give you your dinner."

He wriggled and farted. She giggled and kissed his nose. He giggled too. He was a very advanced baby, able to giggle at seven and a half weeks.

When he had finished his supper Althea handed him back to Olivia. He was pretty soggy by now, so she took him upstairs to get changed. Althea was soggy too, from Matthew spitting up milk as well as from the state of his nappies, so she also had to go upstairs and change.

When Olivia came back down with a dry and happy baby in her arms, her father and Althea were on their way out the door. Althea was complaining to nature or God or fate about the basic incompatibility of babies and a civilized life-style, and Olivia's father was saying I told you so. Althea said she'd had it with breast-feeding, the kid would have to settle for rubber and cow's milk from now on.

When they had gone, Olivia phoned Charlie to tell him he could come over now. Then she put on Jimi Hendrix and danced round the sitting room with Matthew in her arms.

If Charlie had passion on his mind he must have been taken aback when Olivia opened the door to him, still holding her infant dancing partner.

The presence of Matthew in her arms didn't prevent Charlie from kissing her, but it did rather cool the temperature of the kiss. "Shouldn't he be in bed by now?"

"He just got up an hour ago. He's too little to know what's day and what's night."

Charlie followed her into the sitting room. "I thought we were going to make love."

"That's taking a lot for granted, isn't it? How do you know I'm in the mood?"

"I'll put you in the mood, by Jesus. At least, I would if it weren't for the baby."

"He'll go to sleep in a while." She kissed the top of Matthew's head. "Won't you, pudding?"

Charlie watched her. He was really quite sexy, Olivia thought, when he was being dark and moody. "What is it with you, Lia? I thought you liked . . . you seemed to enjoy yourself at that party."

"I did. But that doesn't mean it was a good idea." She was holding Matthew, knowing that it would make it impossible for Charlie to hold her. "Anyway, don't be so impatient. I did warn you I was minding Matty tonight. Daddy won't be back for a few hours yet. I'll put Matty into his baby seat and maybe he'll doze off. He likes to watch the fire."

She settled the baby into his seat and turned on the fake coal fire. Her father said those fires were grotesque but he hadn't had time yet to rip it out and replace it with a genuine Georgian grate burning real Georgian smokeless fuel. She sat down on the rug beside Matthew and put a small, soft blue dog on his lap to keep him amused.

"You mind him for a minute," she told Charlie, "while I make some tea."

Charlie obligingly squatted down on the rug and played

with Matthew and the blue dog for a few minutes while Olivia went into the kitchen to make a pot of tea. When she came back he had turned out all the lights so that the only light was the firelight. She set the tea on the hearth to brew and sat down beside Charlie.

He turned his attention from Matthew to her. She let him kiss her but objected when he put his hands under her T-shirt. "We ought to wait till Matty's gone back to bed."

"Why don't you put him to bed right now?"

"He's not sleepy yet. He'll just cry until I get him up again."

He glanced at the baby, who stared solemnly back at him. "He's okay where he is. He can watch if he likes, who cares?"

"It makes me feel funny. Maybe he knows what we're doing."

"A baby? Don't be silly, he doesn't know anything."

"Meg says they know everything when they're born, because they've done it all before. She says they're old souls. But they forget it after a while and have to start all over again."

"Meg is as crazy as you."

Jimi Hendrix began to sing "Hey Joe." Olivia got up and grabbed Charlie's hand. "Never mind, come and dance."

Charlie put his arms around her waist and she put her arms around his neck and they danced. The slow, strong underlying beat of the music was like a magic web binding their bodies together, making them move as one. By the time old dead Jimi had moved along to "Foxy Lady," Charlie's hands had moved down to her bottom and they were doing more kissing than dancing.

He stopped dancing and started to undress her again. This time she let him continue, until she was kneeling naked on the rug in front of the fire. She unbuttoned his shirt while he kissed and stroked her and told her how beautiful she was. She left him to take off his jeans himself because this was only supposed to be her second time.

He used a condom when he made love to her. Shutting the barn door, she thought. He came quickly, but not as fast as the very first time. Maybe the condom slowed him down.

Far from being distressed or electrified by watching a live

sex show, Matthew had gone to sleep in his chair. He must have been a really old soul.

They didn't get dressed right away. Charlie wanted to admire her body in the firelight. "It makes you look tanned all over. You look like a *Playboy* centerfold."

Olivia had the uncomfortable thought that Charlie might have . . . admired, if that was the word, pictures of women that Nick had photographed. She herself could have been—hadn't been, obviously, but could have been—one of those women. It made her feel like a prostitute, with Nick for her pimp and Charlie the punter.

It made her feel, just for a dizzying moment, like something worse than that: as if she were not a person at all but an object of some small value being bartered between the two men. As if from one perspective, the Martian perspective maybe, the only relationship of any real importance was not between her and Nick or even between her and Charlie, but between the two men who scarcely knew one another, and for this purpose need never have met.

She said to Charlie, "Would you like it if I were in *Playboy?*"

"I would if I didn't know you," he said with a grin. "But since you're my girl I don't want anyone else to see you like that. They'll just have to use their imagination and envy me."

"Do you get turned on when you look at pictures like that?"

"Not anymore. You're better than any of them. I just think about you." He pulled her down onto the rug. "You're like a dream come true. I wanted to make love to you again because I couldn't believe it had really happened."

She wished he wouldn't say things like that. It made her feel like the wickedest woman on earth. She was deliberately deceiving him. He thought she was making him happy but she was going to make him horribly unhappy, and he didn't deserve it.

Just to make absolutely sure it had really happened, he made love to her again. He said he loved her, he said it lots of times. But he forgot about condoms this time.

50

L ia, have you put on weight?"
"Well . . ." Olivia tried her voice and found to her surprise it worked, even sounded normal. It was only Megan
asking, but if she had noticed, other people might. Her
mother, for instance, or Nick. She already had to use a safety
pin to fasten her skirt when she went to school, and jeans
were right out. "I've been feeling sort of fat, but I haven't
dared to weigh myself. It's Matty's fault, I spend all my time
minding him after school for Althea and I never seem to go
out anymore."

Megan took the distracting bait. "How is that working out,
since Althea went back to work?"

"Well, I don't mind, but I don't think Daddy is all that
happy. Althea still had eight weeks left of her maternity
leave, but she said she was bored. She said two months of
full-time motherhood was enough and her brain was turning
to mush. I don't know why she had Matty in the first place
if she's just going to dump him with a baby-sitter after a
couple of months."

"Did your father say that?"

"Oh no, he didn't seem to care about that. What they had
a row about was the nanny."

"What nanny?"

"There isn't any nanny. That's what the row was about.
Althea said she had to have a live-in nanny. Daddy said they
couldn't afford one on account of the astronomical mortgage
they had taken out on that house and anyway there was no
room for a nanny. Althea said there was too; the baby and
the nanny could have the whole top floor if I went back to
live with Mummy."

Megan was scandalized. "She said this in front of you?"

"No, I was upstairs. But I heard them anyway because they were sort of yelling, at least Althea was."

She didn't relate the full argument to Megan. Her father had gone on to say that in the first place he didn't think Emma would be very pleased to have Lia back, what with her own baby coming, and in the second place he was damned if he'd leave his daughter to be brought up by that foul-mouthed oik.

Althea said Lia was pretty much brought up already and wasn't going to be taking elocution lessons from Nick. Anyway, said Althea, she was entitled to her career, wasn't she, and if that meant a nanny then she was entitled to a nanny.

Olivia's father said she should have thought about her career before she got herself pregnant, and if she wanted to live like royalty she should have married one of her tedious illiterate colleagues at the bank. Althea said there was no need to take that tone, he was perfectly happy to have the use of her salary and car and mortgage subsidy, wasn't he? Anyway, Matthew was his child and he had obligations.

Olivia's father said he had obligations toward Lia too. Althea said they would still have room for a nanny if he gave up his study and let Lia have it for her room. Olivia's father said he needed that study and he wasn't going to give it up just so she could have her goddamned nanny which they didn't need and couldn't afford anyway. Althea called him a selfish pig and burst into tears.

After that Olivia went up to her room because she didn't want to hear any more. It was all too adult for her.

The upshot was that Althea employed a lady down the hill, toward Tufnell Park, to mind Matthew during the day. She said it would do for a couple of years, until Matthew started to talk. After that, of course, it would be unthinkable because Matthew would begin to talk like the people in Tufnell Park.

The baby-sitter had a two-year-old daughter in addition to two school-age children, so she had to stay home anyway and said she might as well look after Matthew if it meant getting paid for staying home. She explained all this to Olivia on the first day, when Olivia came to fetch Matthew. Olivia's father dropped Matthew off in the morning because he left the house after Althea, who had to get into the office early to catch Tokyo, she said. Olivia collected Matthew in the afternoon because she was the first one home. It was this afternoon arrangement that disturbed her father.

"Daddy doesn't like me minding Matty after school," she explained to Megan, "because of GCSEs and music practice."

"I suppose Althea really is imposing on you," Megan allowed. "What do you think?"

"I don't mind Matty. I think he's sweet."

"Well, he is sweet, of course." When Megan came up to Highgate she spent all her time playing with Matthew. "But are you sure you're not doing it just so you can go on living there?"

"Maybe I am, I don't know. What's the matter with that anyway? I'd be in the same situation with my mother before long, if I were still living with her. I can't ignore the fact that the baby's there. He's my brother, isn't he? Besides, a hundred years ago everybody had to mind their little sisters or brothers and nobody thought anything of it."

"They had servants," Megan said sweepingly.

"The servants were our age, Meg. My grandfather left school at fourteen because his father was dead and he had to support the rest of the family."

"Maybe that's why your father doesn't want you to do it. Maybe he thinks it makes you like Althea's servant."

Olivia had not thought of that. She had thought in terms of Matthew's needs rather than Althea's. But maybe Megan was right.

Well, that was all very nice, for her father to stick up for her rights and try to prevent Althea the wicked stepmother from turning her into a Cinderella, but where in all that was her father's concern for poor little Matthew? The baby needed to be loved, not just looked after. He didn't know about working hours. All he knew was that sometimes Mrs. Sparrow was there, and sometimes Olivia was there, and for about an hour most days his very own true mother was somewhere around. Quality time, Althea called it.

Megan brought her attention back to the problem they were supposed to be discussing. "What are we going to do about this magic chariot that Medea needs to make her escape at the end of the play?"

Never mind Medea, thought Olivia, I'm going to need a magic chariot myself very soon. But she dutifully put her mind to the problem. "To fit in with the style of the Chorus's songs it should be something like an old-fashioned Cadillac convertible."

"That's a great idea," Megan said sarcastically. "Where are we going to find an old Cadillac, and if we find one how will we get it onstage?"

"We don't want a real one, dumbo. We only need a side view." Olivia considered the problem for a minute. Her usual source for anything arcane was her father, but she doubted that an ancient Cadillac was quite in his line.

She took too long to think. Megan said brightly, "I bet Nick could help."

"Nick?"

"Well, he strikes me as the type to know about old cars. And he could probably find us a picture of an old Cadillac. You don't mind my suggesting Nick, do you? You haven't said anything about him, so I haven't asked. I've been deliberately biting my tongue. Are you really broken up about him?"

"No, not really," Olivia said truthfully. She didn't add that what was preventing her from being broken up was first that Nick had made love to her twice since he had married her mother and even—under duress—said that he loved her; and second that she was carrying his baby and didn't really have time to worry about anything else. She didn't have the nerve to tell Megan any of that.

"Well, you're being very heroic," Megan consoled her. "If I were you I'd be having a nervous breakdown."

"Maybe I would too, if I thought about it. But I don't want to think about it."

"Quite right, too. I'm sorry I mentioned it. But what about the Cadillac? I could ask him if you want, but it might seem funny coming from me rather than you."

"That's okay, I'll ask him."

"Are you sure you don't mind?"

"Positive. For goodness sakes, Meg, I had to live with him

for a whole month at Christmas. We established a modus vivendi."

"Whatever that is," Megan said dryly.

"That's what Daddy told Althea's mother that Althea and I had done. It means you're not trying to murder each other or bursting into tears all the time."

"Does Althea make you want to burst into tears?"

"Not anymore. She can be a real cow when she wants to, but most of the time we sort of get along. And the reason is, I feel like Matty is more mine than hers."

"So you thought Matthew was going to be a problem, and instead he's a solution."

"Well, I—yeah." Olivia laughed. "It's been a lot better since I moved back in. I don't feel quite so much like an intruder."

Charlie had got into the habit of arriving at her mother's house in time for dessert and coffee. It meant he got to eat dessert twice. It was remarkable, thought Olivia, how these routines developed. She knew from fifteen years of living with her parents, together and separately, that neither of them had a real Sunday lunch unless she was officially visiting.

Nick asked Charlie how his job was going.

Charlie shrugged. "Well, at least I've still got one. My father says nothing's going up except crime and unemployment."

"Everything seems to be falling apart," Olivia's mother said. "You daren't go out at night anymore for fear of being mugged or raped or attacked by some psychopath. People have become so selfish and irresponsible, they don't seem to think of anyone but themselves and what they want that very instant. It's like we're going backwards instead of forwards, people are getting worse instead of better."

"It's the millennium," Olivia told her. "Daddy said that everybody gets apocalyptic when we come to the end of a thousand-year period."

"Hey, that's good," Charlie exclaimed. "I'll have to tell my father that. It's not the government, it's the calendar."

Nick pushed his coffee cup over for a refill and lit a cigarette. "Sounds like astrology to me."

"That's another thing. He said everybody starts to get superstitious."

Her mother said, "Ross thinks believing in God is superstitious."

"Then Daddy's wrong, we're getting less superstitious, not more. Gran and Granddad believe in God. So does Grandma, I think. Does anyone here?" Olivia looked round the table.

Nobody answered her question. "Even the bishops don't, these days," Charlie remarked.

"Maybe that's the trouble," said Olivia's mother. "Maybe if more people believed in God they wouldn't be going about raping and murdering and shooting themselves full of drugs."

"But Mummy, you don't believe in God and you're not doing any of those things."

"I haven't the slightest inclination to do them. I'm not even nursing a secret desire to vandalize a bus shelter. But for people who might be tempted, if they don't believe in God maybe there isn't any reason not to."

"Well, you can't force people to believe something. And you've done something that used to be considered much worse than vandalism or drug addiction."

Her mother looked more puzzled than indignant. "What on earth are you talking about, Lia?"

"I'm talking about adultery. If we lived in Iran or Pakistan or Saudi Arabia, you and Daddy and Nick and Althea would all have been stoned to death and I'd be an orphan." She described this hypothetical holocaust with some relish. But of course it wouldn't have happened like that. She would have been put to death too.

Her mother went rather pink. "No one's committing adultery now," she said stiffly. "We're each respectably married to the right person. And that proves what I said about things getting worse. That sort of savagery, it's medieval. Worse than medieval. Even in the Dark Ages people in this country never got put to death for adultery. Why should it matter what consenting adults do in privacy, as long as no one gets hurt?"

What's consent? Olivia wanted to ask. What's adult? What's hurt? She wanted it to matter, what Nick had done.

She didn't want her mother saying, even abstractly and theoretically and in total ignorance, that nobody cared if he had taken her virginity without even asking, if he got her pregnant and made her kill the baby, if he made love to her until she loved him and then married her mother instead. "Didn't it hurt you when you found out Daddy was having an affair with Althea?"

Her mother's first, characteristic response was to glance at Charlie, whose presence was obviously the main source of her embarrassment. Then she looked at Nick, as if hoping he might rescue her. But Charlie showed no sign of vanishing, and Nick went on smoking without speaking. Her mother had to flounder out of this on her own.

"Of course it hurt me," she admitted at last. "But I've realized since that my pride was hurt more than anything. If he'd said beforehand that he was seriously unhappy and maybe we should separate, if we'd broken up for different reasons . . . Anyway, I certainly wouldn't have wanted either of them to die for it."

Olivia wasn't so sure. She remembered her mother's pain and rage in those first dreadful days of abandonment. She knew that her father's adultery had come as a terrible shock to her mother; he wasn't that sort of man, the sort to notice other women. Whatever she might say now, her mother's grief hadn't gone away easily. It hadn't really gone away at all, until Nick came.

And she did know somebody who had died for adultery. The baby Nick had started in her last summer.

She had had enough of adultery. "By the way, you don't have to bother about that fancy gown we were discussing last time, the one for the play. Devika's going to bring a sari."

Her mother looked relieved at the change of subject. "I thought these people were ancient Greeks."

"They are, but Meg says we should be eclectic, and Medea is supposed to be Asian. Anyway, the sari should do just fine. You can get really fancy ones, you know, with gold threads and all. And if the dress is quite exotic it helps to explain why Jason's new wife tries it on right away."

"Why, what happens when she puts it on?"

384

"It's been impregnated with something like napalm, I guess. It starts to eat into her skin and she can't get it off. When her father tries to help her he gets burnt up too."

"Has Ms. Pankhurst approved this?" Charlie demanded. "It sounds dangerously racist to me. Exotic Asian lady poisons blond rival with a sari. You can't trust these wily Orientals, what?"

"Don't try to make trouble, Charlie. I don't want to get into a big argument, I just want to ask Nick if he knows where we can find a picture of a 1950s Cadillac convertible."

She looked at Nick. She hoped there was nothing in her look but the question she had just asked.

Nick shrugged. "That's no problem. But why a Cadillac? That sounds more like Elvis Presley than ancient Greece."

"We thought the play needed to be updated to make people empathize with the characters. So we've done all the dialogue in modern clichés, and the Chorus sings country-and-western songs. We need a chariot, and a Cadillac convertible seems most appropriate."

Nick took one last drag on his cigarette and stubbed it out. "These Greek plays always seem to be about murder."

Olivia's skin began to prickle. "Yeah, I suppose they are. But it's not like Jack the Ripper or the Terminator. All their murders have reasons behind them."

"No more than you'd expect from the blokes who invented philosophy. Where does the Cadillac come in?"

"It's just a joke, really. In the original version Medea's grandfather is the Sun and he sends her a magic chariot to save her from her enemies. It's a deus ex machina, Ms. P. says."

"A what?"

"A sort of deliberately unbelievable miracle. Something hokey that appears at the last minute to rescue the good guys and make sure the bad guys get their comeuppance."

"Like the U.S. Cavalry."

"Yeah, like that. Only in our play it's not obvious if the person being rescued is a good guy or a bad guy."

"That sounds very modern for an old Greek."

"Well, you pointed out that they invented philosophy."

That made him smile. She couldn't stand to see him smiling at her. Not now, not with her mother and Charlie in the room. She jumped up and went behind Charlie's chair and put her arms around him. Deliberately she bent down to kiss the back of his neck. "Come on, Charlie, come and help me with the washing up."

51

Olivia discovered there was something worse than having her stepfather smile at her in her mother's presence. There was having to talk to him on the phone in her father's presence.

If she had known who it was she would have gone downstairs to take the call, instead of letting her father hand her the receiver in his study. "It's for you, Lia. It's always for you. Why don't you answer it yourself once in a while?"

"Maybe I would if I had a phone in my room."

"Your contribution to the phone bill is quite impressive enough as it is."

"Oh, Daddy." Olivia took her hand off the mouthpiece and said hello. She nearly died when she heard Nick's voice.

"I've got a Cadillac for you, Lia. How big do you want it?"

Her brain stopped working. She managed to stammer something. "I—um—what do you mean, how big?"

"Well, it's about four inches by six inches right now. I think your audience would have a little trouble making that out, and your Paki villainess won't fit into it."

"Well, I—I guess we'll have to copy it onto cardboard or something."

"I'll blow it up for you, if you like. Then you can paint it or paste it onto something or do whatever the hell you want with it."

"Oh, that's—that would be very nice."

"Will this weekend be soon enough?"

"Well, I, yeah, that should be okay."

She hung up. Her father wasn't looking at her—which was just as well, because she thought she must have turned bright red—but he had obviously been listening to the conversation. "Was that Conan the Cameraman?"

"Yeah."

"What did he want with you?"

"He said—he'd promised to get something we need for the play."

"Such as?"

"Just a photograph, Daddy. What does it matter?"

"I was just curious."

Her father glanced up at her then while she hovered in the doorway. It was a very odd look, too hot and cold for idle curiosity. For a terrible instant she thought he had guessed something. And then she guessed something herself.

Not curious. Jealous.

She leaned against the door frame, feeling quite faint. Her father didn't know what he had to be jealous of. She remembered Nick against her father's front door, Nick in the room right above this one, where her father had so nearly come upon them in embrace.

What did he want with you?

Call me Daddy while I screw you.

It was because of Nick that she was living here. Not just because he had driven her out of her mother's house, but because he was the reason her father had agreed to take her in. Her father hadn't wanted her until he thought another man was going to take his place with her. And he wouldn't want her anymore when he found out about the baby.

If he ever found out it was Nick—Greek-style tragedies might ensue.

She couldn't just walk away now. She had to say something for her father's benefit. She explained about the Cadillac.

He was amused by the idea. "That's really quite clever. But this production is beginning to sound less like a tragedy and more like a farce."

"Meg says that's the real tragedy. She says people trivialize

human suffering because they can only talk about it in tabloid terms."

"She has a point, but it's not very likely to come across.
Irony is easily misunderstood."

"Funny thing, that's what Ms. Pankhurst said about Euripides."

At Megan's house on Sunday they had a scene-painting
party. For one thing Megan's house was nearest to the school,
and for another thing Althea would have fainted away at the
idea of anyone bringing a lethal weapon like poster paint into
her immaculately decorated house.

Olivia's mother's house was right out for exactly the same reason, though the decorating there was rather more shopworn.
But Charlie took her over there first to collect the Cadillac.

Charlie was her unwitting emotional bodyguard whenever
she went to her mother's house. He transformed her from a
fifth wheel into a couple. He saved her from ever having to
be alone with Nick, even for a minute. Hopefully he reminded Nick that she knew about the other fish in the sea
and was even frying a few of them. Though that could be
dangerous, as she had discovered on New Year's Eve. Maybe
Charlie was her physical bodyguard as well.

On this occasion she discovered she didn't need a bodyguard
because Nick wasn't even there. He had flown to New York for
the week, her mother said. Somebody he had done work for
here in London had got a job in New York and hired him for
a shoot over there. Her mother seemed to think this was promising, careerwise. At any rate he had left the Cadillac for her, and
her mother brought it out and unrolled it.

She hadn't really understood what Nick had meant about
blowing the photograph up. But that was exactly what he
had done: produced an almost life-size image of what he said
was a 1957 Cadillac convertible. Olivia didn't know one car
from another, but it looked just fine to her.

Charlie went down on his knees to study the image un-
furled on the carpet. "That's really excellent. Meg will be
thrilled. What do you think, Lia?"

"She will be thrilled. Ms. P. will be thrilled. I'm thrilled."

And she was, but for an odd reason. Perhaps her father
had been right to be jealous of this favor from Nick. She

didn't know anything about photography, but it must have taken him a little while to do. It was the first, maybe the only, thing he had ever done for her that had nothing in it for him. It was just a favor from the man who, as far as anyone but Megan knew, was just her stepfather.

Maybe he really did love her.

Her mother was looking quite thrilled with it too. Olivia knew what was going on in her mother's head. It was a funny thing, how well she seemed to know her mother now that she didn't live with her anymore. Her mother thought Nick was clever and kind and good, she had told Olivia so. Olivia thought her mother was crazy. But she could see how her mother had come to these absurd conclusions. It was as if she had become her mother's mother.

Her mother held this high opinion of Nick partly because he was so unlike her father. Not that her father was stupid and unkind and evil, even her mother would allow that much. And Nick was no sort of New Man; basically he was unreconstructed Old Adam. But her mother was content, at least in the springtime of their marriage, to fetch and carry the metaphorical pipe and slippers, because he had other virtues to recommend him.

He might well be a better lover than her father, though Olivia wasn't in any position to compare them, but in any case that wouldn't have been his only attraction for her mother. He didn't sulk or freeze up. He didn't purport to find her an intellectual embarrassment. He didn't harass her about money. He didn't expect her to be something she wasn't; he was entirely content for her to be a beautiful woman and the daughter of a colonel. He was happy to be the father of her baby. And he touched her a lot.

That wasn't the same thing as screwing her a lot, though Olivia had a horrible feeling he did that too. And he wasn't one of those people who go about touching everyone as if they were feeling the texture of some interesting fabric. It was just that if you had a touchable relationship with him—which probably meant a sexual relationship—then he touched you like a human being. Casual touches, unconsidered caresses, he did all that entirely naturally. Her father never touched anyone without thinking about it beforehand.

There was another side to that coin, of course. If Nick got mad, he hit you. She didn't think her mother had discovered the downside yet. Maybe she never would. Maybe the baby would. Or maybe not.

Megan and Jon were already at work on the scenery when Olivia and Charlie arrived. They unrolled the magic chariot for Megan and Jon to admire.

"Will it fly?" Jon asked. "It's supposed to fly, isn't it?"

"We can paint wings on it if you want," Olivia told him. "It's the Sun's chariot, we'll paint it red with golden wings. Just so the audience gets the idea."

The hypothetical audience might have got it, but Charlie didn't. "What idea?"

"Medea's supposed to fly away at the end of the play," Megan explained. "Jason says she'll have to be able to fly in order to escape him, and of course she can't fly. Then the chariot comes in, sent down by the Sun to rescue her. Something's happening that can't really happen. Get it?"

Charlie shook his head. "All too deep for me."

Olivia said to Megan, "My father says irony is usually misunderstood."

"This isn't irony," Megan assured her. "It's sarcasm."

52

"Isn't this the week when you're putting on your play?"

"It was, but we've had to put it off. I forgot to tell you, Mummy."

"You were going to let me turn up at school for nothing? That was thoughtful of you, Lia, I must say. Why is it being put off?"

"Devika's in the hospital. She broke her leg." Olivia put

her hand over her mouth to hide a giggle. "When I told Daddy he said she probably didn't know it's not supposed to be taken literally."

"Ross is a very witty man," her mother observed, icily unamused. "When will you be putting it on, then? This is the last week of school before the Easter break and you've got exams next term."

"We'll squeeze it in somewhere. It's only for one night. And Meg says if Devika is still on crutches we can write it into the script."

"That's a brilliant idea," Charlie commented. "If Medea is crippled as well as colored she'll have enough brownie points chalked up already to excuse her infanticide."

It was Olivia's turn to be coldly unamused. "Charlie, this is a serious play, not just an opportunity for you to make racist and disablist jokes."

"I'll bet Ms. Pankhurst taught you that word." Charlie waved to her mother as he dragged Olivia away to the car. "And I'll bet it's not in the dictionary."

"So what?" Olivia let Charlie take her away, still arguing. "Lots of words aren't in the dictionary. It doesn't mean that no one knows what they mean."

"Most of the words they leave out of dictionaries are X rated. Anyone who uses words like *disablist* should wash their mouth out with soap."

He opened the car door and she got in. "You're as bad as Nick."

"What's bad about Nick?"

"Oh, he's a real fascist. He says things like *nigger* and *wog* and *queer* and *dyke* without a second thought. And Mummy pretends not to notice. I wonder what she does when they're out with her *Guardian*-reading friends." She leaned back against the headrest and closed her eyes.

"Are you okay, Lia?"

"Of course I'm okay. Why wouldn't I be okay?"

"You've been looking different lately." She held her breath, but he went on, "Your face looks different. It's thinner, as if you'd been ill."

"I'm on a diet."

"What for?"

"I put on weight over the winter."

"Well, get off it at once. You looked just fine the way you were. This is the first day of spring, isn't it? Why don't we take a ride in the country?"

She didn't want that, but she couldn't say so. "Okay, yeah, it's a nice day."

Eventually he turned into a lane where they had parked before, and pulled over to the verge. She hadn't meant to let him kiss her, but somehow he did.

She definitely had to do something about Charlie today. She was about four months along by now and when she looked at herself she had an unmistakable bump in her belly. She had managed to avoid making love to him for a couple of weeks, but it was nearly the end of term and her excuses would run out by then.

When it came to it, she didn't know what to say. She had to have some reason for not wanting to see him again, but she couldn't think of one that wouldn't hurt him. Well, it was not seeing her anymore that was going to hurt him most, so maybe it would be better to keep everything vague and let him make what he liked of it.

She felt horrible about it because she really liked him. It wasn't fair to him, it was nothing to do with him at all. She was just using him because he was the handiest man. It was unbelievably callous and wicked of her. But she was going to do it anyway. She was prepared to do almost anything in order to have Nick's baby.

"Listen, Charlie," she said. And then she began to cry.

"It's okay, I'm listening, you don't have to cry about it."

"It's not funny." She laid her face against his jacket, turning away from him. "I can't see you anymore."

"What are you talking about?"

"You heard me." She sniffled and hauled out a scrunched-up tissue from her pocket to wipe her nose.

Charlie didn't say anything for quite a long time. Then he said, "Do you fancy telling me why?"

An explanation had just come into her head, one not totally divorced from reality. Also one that didn't involve her rejecting him out of hand. It did, however, mean blaming her father for everything. Which had some justice in it but was basically no less wicked.

She swallowed. "Daddy says I've got too much to do. I've got ten GCSEs coming up next term and he'll kill me if I don't get A's in everything. He says I've got to get all A's to get into Oxford or Cambridge."

"That sounds fine to me. Where do I come into it?"

"It's not you. It's Matthew."

"Your brother? I don't get it."

She started to cry again. Matthew was being blamed now, the poor little mite. At last she composed herself enough to carry on. "It's like this. I haven't got enough time to do everything: school, GCSEs, music lessons, minding Matthew, eating and sleeping, and seeing you. Something has to give. From my father's point of view, it's either you or Matty."

Charlie got the picture with commendable speed. "You mean he wants me to disappear for the next three months."

"Something like that. Or else Matty has to stay at Mrs. Sparrow's house till Althea comes home, and she doesn't get home till after seven most nights."

"You mean you'd rather be with Matty than me?"

"It's not like that. I don't want you to go away. But Matty's just a baby, he wouldn't understand. And you said yourself I look as if I'd been ill."

"You said you'd been on a diet."

"Well, I have. But I have to say I feel as if I'd been ill."

"Are you trying to tell me I still make you sick?"

"Don't say that. You never made me sick. It was . . ."

It was Nick, then and now, but she couldn't say that.

She pulled away from him, opened the door, and jumped out. She ran down the lane. The trees were mostly bare, but the blackthorn was blooming, and the pale yellow primrose and white anemone on the grassy bank. She wished she had been born a rabbit or something, the sort of creature who got fucked by anybody at the earliest age possible and produced dozens of babies, and never had to say no or cope with the moral implications of incest or adultery. And never fell in love.

She came up to a flowering sloe and put her hands around its trunk. She laid her cheek against the purple bark.

Charlie came up behind her. He put his arms around her and the tree. He didn't say anything for a while.

"Lia, do you love me?"

"I don't know." She moved her center of gravity away from the tree toward him, so that she was leaning against him instead of the tree. "I don't know what that means."

Charlie knew what it meant. He itemized it. "Do you miss me when I'm not with you? Do you think about me? Do you get desperate sometimes to make love with me?"

Olivia didn't answer. She didn't know how to. He had just described how she felt about Nick.

He said, "I don't know what goes on in your head."

"Sometimes I don't know either."

He unzipped her jacket and caressed her breasts through the jumper. She knew then that she was going to have to let him make love to her one last time. She owed him that at the very least. Only it had to be done as fully clothed as possible. She would have to do it all for him.

She unhooked her bra so that he could touch her naked breasts under the jumper. She unzipped his trousers and stroked his stiff penis. He liked that so much that she carried on and brought him to orgasm, just with her hands, not her mouth.

He said he loved her. Her conscience smote her. "Don't say that."

"Why not? It's true."

"You don't love me. You just love to do that."

"I do, but that isn't what it means." He had her jumper pushed up and his arms around her, against her bare skin. He kissed her brow and her nose, her chin and her ear, as if deliberately avoiding the explicitly erotic. "I love to touch you and hold you. I love to look at you. I love to think about you."

She knew, she knew; to her despair she knew it all. Only it heartened her perversely to hear a man saying so. It meant that Nick had lied when he defined love.

Much good it would do her.

She began to cry again, more quietly this time. Charlie consoled her. He seemed to take the tears for a confession of love. She couldn't bear to contradict him. There didn't seem much point.

"Don't cry, Lia. If your father wants me to disappear till the summer, okay, I'll do it. Maybe I can meet you after school sometimes."

"On Thursdays. After music lessons."

"Okay, whatever you say. Why after your music lessons?"

"You'll be through your work by the time I'm finished the lesson."

"Okay, that sounds good." He did up his trousers and tucked his shirttail inside and put his arms around her again. "When's your next music lesson?"

"Not till next term," she lied. Nearly a month away.

"Jesus, that's not a week, it's a century. But never mind, it's better than nothing."

She hugged him hard, and felt him hug her in response. She didn't love him like she loved Nick, and she never would. She was cheating him that way. But she did love him in another way and was incomprehensibly grateful to him, because he loved her so thoroughly, in a way, sex aside, that she had never been loved before in her life.

With that in mind she said, no lie, "Oh, Charlie, I love you."

53

That's good," Mrs. Stone said with satisfaction. "The phrasing and tone are excellent. You've been practicing well. And your ear is growing up. I shall give you more Bach to chew on this summer."

Olivia was surprised to find that the prospect didn't appall her. The violin was already providing a release from tension, an occupation when concentration failed elsewhere, an excuse for not going out with her friends when she felt too tired. She was often tired these days. Althea's books said that fatigue was frequently a symptom of pregnancy.

"We'll try it again," Mrs. Stone commanded. "A little more *allegro* this time." She played the introduction on the piano. Olivia raised her bow to play the first notes of Brahms. And had the strangest experience of her life.

Someone kicked her in the stomach. From inside.

She stopped in midphrase. The kick came again. She put her hand down to press on the spot and felt a small, very precise force pushing against her.

Somebody was inside her, wanting out.

Maybe it was the thought of playing host to another being—a Martian, maybe; God knew there were enough of them going to and fro upon the earth. The baby's father was a proven Martian, why shouldn't she be carrying a little alien child within her? Maybe it was that thought that made her faint.

When she came to, Mrs. Stone had laid her out on the ugly green sofa in the music room. Olivia put first things first: "Where's my violin?"

"On the piano. You set it there very tidily just before you fell down."

"Thank heavens. Daddy would kill me if I'd broken it."

"I don't think so. I'll get you something to drink. You stay there."

Mrs. Stone disappeared. She returned with a glass of something. "Sit up, Olivia, and have a sip of this."

"This" was some sort of foreign spirits, schnapps or slivovitz or Mrs. Stone's very own moonshine. Whatever it was, a small sip cleared Olivia's head. She struggled to sit right up. Mrs. Stone urged her to lie back again.

"You stay there. Have another sip. I'll go and make tea."

Mrs. Stone went out again. Olivia sat up and took another sip of Mrs. Stone's firewater. Then she leaned back and tried to relax. She put her hands under her jumper and folded them across her stomach—at twenty weeks a substantial hummock even when she was leaning back—and waited for the prisoner to communicate with her.

She felt it again, a punch or maybe a kick. Or even an elbow nudging what it might have hoped were her ribs. Somebody was definitely inside.

"Wait a bit," she whispered, "you're not ready. You're only halfway there. Lie low for a while."

The baby stopped kicking her after that. Mrs. Stone came back with tea. She had put lots of milk and sugar in it. "It's good for you that way," she explained. She sat down with her own cup of tea and looked at Olivia. She looked at the bulky jumper with the carefully stretched ribbing on the hem, hanging in shapeless folds. She shouldn't have been able to see underneath, to see the zipper that wouldn't do up at all and the two safety pins joined to make a chain and hold the skirt at the waist. She couldn't see any of that.

But like Superman and Olivia's grandmother, she seemed to have X-ray vision. "Are you pregnant, child?"

Olivia opened her mouth. After a while she closed it. Her brain had seized up.

Mrs. Stone looked sad. She might have looked as if Olivia had disappointed her or disgusted her, or as if it was nothing to do with her and she didn't really care about anything Olivia might have done. But she didn't look any of those things, she just looked sad, which Olivia discovered was the worst thing of all.

"Do your parents know? I thought not." Mrs. Stone had acquired Nick's ability to read her mind, apparently. "You must tell them at once."

Olivia crossed her arms over her stomach, defending the baby. "I can't," she whispered.

"But it isn't going to go away, my love."

"It's not big enough yet. They'll want me to get rid of it." Tears were spilling out of her eyes. She couldn't stop them, any more than she could have stopped the baby from kicking.

Mrs. Stone looked at her. Olivia stared at the floor and blinked away the tears. She didn't have the nerve to look at her teacher. Mrs. Stone said gently, "No one can make you do what you don't want to do, child. It's your body and your baby."

"I know that. But they won't." Olivia twisted her hands in her lap. "I don't know what to do."

"Where are you living now?"

"In Highgate. With my father." She added hastily, "I can't tell him, he'll kill me."

"You say he'll kill you for a violin, he'll kill you for a baby. I can't believe either of those things. What kind of man do you think your father is?"

"I don't know what kind of man he is. I just know that I'm not the kind of person he thinks I ought to be. Or even the kind of person he thinks I am."

Mrs. Stone clucked her tongue. "And your mother, didn't you tell me she was getting married and having a baby?"

"She's done all that. I mean, she got married, and she's having the baby next month."

"Why not tell her? She can't blame you so much for doing what she's done herself."

The parallel was much more precise than Mrs. Stone could have known. Olivia had done exactly what her mother had done in going to bed with Nick and getting pregnant by him. Only for her mother it was okay, even a cause for celebration. For Olivia herself it was shameful evidence of a crime.

"I'll ring her up," Mrs. Stone persisted. "I'll say you're ill, she should come and get you. Maybe I don't know you're living with your father now."

Olivia suddenly remembered that Charlie was coming to meet her. "No, don't do that. My ... my boyfriend is supposed to be meeting me when my lesson is over. He can take me home."

"This is the young man who's done all the damage?"

Olivia could tell that Mrs. Stone was not going to be kindly disposed toward Charlie. Poor innocent Charlie.

Well, not so innocent. He was like a burglar who breaks into a house and goes away empty-handed because another thief has already stolen everything of value. Only Charlie didn't know that she had nothing left to give him. He didn't know that Nick had already taken her virginity, her fertility, her love.

Charlie saved her and himself from any unjust direct accusation by ringing the doorbell right then.

Halfway to the door, Mrs. Stone demanded, "What is this boy's name?"

"He's Charlie. But don't say anything to him," Olivia warned hastily. There was no telling what Mrs. Stone might be moved to say; in her frankness and complete inability to suffer embarrassment she was a sort of elderly version of Nick. When Mrs. Stone stopped and looked at her, she had to add, "He doesn't know."

"A very observant young man he must be," Mrs. Stone said dryly. "You have an eventful evening before you, Olivia."

Olivia followed her to the front door, still nervous about what she might do or say. Mrs. Stone opened the door to confront the astonished Charlie. "You are Charlie? Olivia is ill. Please take her home to her mother."

"Ill?" Charlie stared beyond her at Olivia. "What do you mean, ill?"

Mrs. Stone ignored him. He had had his marching orders. "Before you leave, Olivia, I'm going to ring your mother to make sure she's expecting you."

It was pointless to protest. Mrs. Stone was an irresistible force. Olivia waited mutely with Charlie while Mrs. Stone phoned her mother and briskly informed her that Olivia had fainted at her music lesson and was on her way home now, in the company of her young man. Only after that were they allowed to depart.

"Is that true about you fainting?" Charlie demanded, as soon as they were in the street.

"Yeah."

He took her by the shoulders and surveyed her. "I'm not surprised. You look terrible, you've gone all white. Are you really sick?"

"No."

"What's wrong then?"

"Can I sit down somewhere?"

There wasn't anywhere to sit, except on the wall of somebody's front garden. Charlie sat her down there. He was seriously alarmed by now. "Why didn't you tell me you're living with your mother again?"

"I'm not. Mrs. Stone doesn't know I ever left there."

"Why didn't you tell her before she rang your mother? Why did she ring her up anyway?"

Olivia shrugged. "I think she wanted to make sure some-body would be home when I got there."

"But why didn't your mother tell her ... Damn it, Lia, what's going on?" He leaned over her and caught her arms. "Why are you talking like this?"

"Like what?"

"Like that. Not telling me anything."

"Okay, I'll tell you." She patted the top of the wall beside her. "Sit down and I'll tell you."

He sat down warily. "Tell me what?"

Maybe he would stop wanting to see her when he found out she was pregnant. Men did that all the time, not wanting to know about the babies they had made. In evolutionary terms it was counterproductive for them to take that attitude but a lot of them did. Obviously the dictates of biology didn't always have the last word in the human psyche.

One part of her was hopeful, because it would solve a terri-ble dilemma if Charlie didn't want her anymore. The other part of her wanted him to stay and love her.

She took his hand and put it under her jumper, pressing it over the swelling where her waist should have been. "Can you feel that? I fainted because I felt it kick."

She turned her head as she spoke, to look at his face just beyond her shoulder. He might have been about to faint him-self. He had gone white. Even his lips were bloodless. "Christ, you're pregnant."

She said timidly, "Do you mind?"

He put his other arm around her, his other hand under her jumper. With both hands he stroked the baby bulge. "I don't know. I can't think." He drew her back against him. "Jesus Mary and Joseph! Why didn't you tell me?"

She leaned back against his shoulder. "I was scared."

"Scared of what?"

"I don't know. Afraid you'd want to ... do something about it."

"Oh. No. That's up to you. I wouldn't try to tell you one way or the other. It's not for me to say, is it? Ms. Pankhurst wouldn't approve at all of me putting my spoke in."

He went on caressing her. Holding her, hugging her, kiss-ing her hair, her neck, her ear. It should have reassured her, made her feel good. But she felt horribly treacherous and loathsome, because she was deceiving him with silence.

"I did think . . . I tried to imagine what if this happened. After that party, the first time."

"What did you think about it?"

"Well, you asked me then, didn't you? But it all seemed remote and unlikely. I thought—well, you know, if we weren't so young, if you weren't so young . . ." He stopped and hugged her. "It's wonderful, the idea of you carrying my child. I didn't think it would ever happen. You're so cool and remote. I didn't think I'd ever really have you."

She didn't understand what he meant. She wasn't sure she wanted to know. She pulled away from his embrace. "Charlie, we've got to think. I don't know what to do."

"Let's do what your music teacher said. I'll take you back to your mother's house."

Olivia made a last attempt to appease her conscience. "You don't have to come in with me, you know."

"Don't be silly. I won't have anyone saying I'd leave you like this."

"Would you be so brave if it was my father?"

"No, and neither would you."

Olivia was being brave only because she knew that Nick wouldn't be home yet. If she had had to tell her mother with Nick right there she would sooner have run away from home again.

The front door of her mother's house was unlocked. When Charlie and Olivia went in, her mother came out of the kitchen, wiping her hands on a tea towel. Olivia hadn't seen her for almost four weeks, because Nick had taken her to Amsterdam over the long Easter weekend. She was almost at full term by now, at the stage that Althea had described as elephantine. The baby made her slow and clumsy; she moved as if she were afraid of overbalancing. But for all the inconvenience she looked quite content with the world.

Olivia felt a stab of jealousy. It wasn't fair that her mother should be made happy and she herself unhappy by the same condition and the same man. It wasn't fair either, she knew, to blame her mother for her own misery. But envy took away her terror of the coming revelation.

"What's the matter, Lia? I couldn't make out why Mrs. Stone was ringing me. She said something about your having fainted."

"I did."

"But why come here? Why didn't you go home?"

Her mother had said it at last. Here was not home anymore. Her old nightmare had come true, the one where she fled from some terror to reach safety where her parents were, in the heart of her home, only to find that her parents had turned into indifferent strangers and there was no haven anywhere.

She thought she was going to faint again. She stumbled away from Charlie and her mother, into the sitting room, her hand to her mouth. "Mummy, I'm going to have a baby."

She looked back through the doorway at the two of them standing transfixed. Her mother glanced at Charlie and he said, "It's true."

Her mother said, "Oh, God."

Olivia collapsed in an armchair and folded her hands across her stomach. She didn't care what her mother thought anymore. The only thing she cared about now was the baby inside her. Her whole life was in that baby. Nick's baby.

Her mother lowered her bulky body onto the sofa and stared at Olivia with the sort of cold distaste and exasperation she might have shown if Olivia had just been sick on the carpet. I'm a nuisance, an embarrassment, Olivia realized. She doesn't want to have to bother about me now, much less about my baby. She was grateful to Charlie when he came to sit on the arm of her chair and took hold of her hand.

"Oh God, Lia," her mother said, "this is a nightmare. Are you sure? Have you seen a doctor?"

"Yes, I'm sure. No, I haven't seen a doctor."

"You'll have to go at once. I'll take you tomorrow. Oh, God." Her mother passed her hands over her face. Her hands were as fine and thin as ever, but her face had softened during the pregnancy. "Lia, how could you be so irresponsible?"

"I'm not going to have an abortion, if that's what you've got in mind."

"Don't be absurd, you're just a child. You'll ruin your life if you have a baby now."

"No, I won't. Anyway, it's too late. I'm at least four months gone."

"Four months isn't too late, it's just more complicated." That was what Althea had said about Olivia's mother's own baby. "Why didn't you tell me sooner? You're supposed to be an intelligent girl, how could you behave so idiotically? Charlie, why didn't you make her tell me?"

Charlie cleared his throat. "I've only just found out myself today."

"It doesn't matter," Olivia said stubbornly. "I'm going to have the baby."

"You don't know what you're saying, you're just being silly and romantic. I don't suppose Ross knows, does he?"

Olivia shook her head. The real point of telling her mother was so that her mother could tell her father.

Her mother heaved herself up off the sofa. "I'll phone him right now. Oh, Lia, I could really kill you for this."

Her mother went into the kitchen to use the telephone. Olivia realized she had been holding Charlie's hand very tightly. She relaxed her grip. "Sorry."

"Nothing to be sorry for."

She leaned back in the chair, turning her face to his shoulder. "Charlie, you're wonderful. I'm sorry I've got you into this mess."

"I think your father will put it the other way round."

She could hear her mother on the phone. "Ross? Lia's here. You'd better come and get her."

A pause, during which her father must have said something like, What's she doing there and why can't she get home by herself?

"You'd better come and get her," her mother repeated. "She fainted at Mrs. Stone's house and she has some news for you."

Another pause for her father to speak.

Her mother said, "She's pregnant." Then she hung up.

"You'd better go," Olivia whispered to Charlie. "Before my father gets here."

"Are you sure?" He would obviously rather not have been there when her father arrived, but leaving beforehand seemed cowardly. "I'll stay if you want."

"No, you go. I'll be all right."

Her mother came back into the room. "Lia's right, Charlie, you'd better go. We're going to have enough hysteria as it is, without giving Ross the chance to get started on you. Lia, do you want anything to eat? You look as if you've been starving yourself. Your face is too thin. Doesn't Althea feed you properly?"

"I am hungry," Olivia admitted. Ravenous, more like. "I've been feeling too sick to eat for ages."

"I'll get you something to eat."

That was something her mother could get busy with, instead of grappling with the consequences of Olivia's pregnancy. She went into the kitchen while Olivia followed Charlie to the front door.

He kissed her. There was something profound in it, as if he (or more likely she) were a soldier going off to the front. "Tell your father I'm a bastard," he said, only half joking. "Only a real bastard would get a fifteen-year-old pregnant."

After he had gone, Olivia went into the kitchen and sat down at the table. There was an ashtray on the table. It was empty and clean, but it was there.

Her mother set a cheese omelette down in front of her. Her mother was like Megan's cat Mog, she reflected, scrupulously tending to her child's physical and material needs, making sure she was well fed, well-dressed, well rested, well-mannered, but not really noticing or even much caring what went on inside her head.

Her father was the opposite—what was the opposite of a cat?—not taking any notice of what she ate or wore, solely interested in her intellectual development. But they both had the same concern in the end, she thought, which was that she should not disgrace them.

They had failed. Or she had failed them, more likely.

While she ate the omelette and toast and drank tea, her mother talked. The conversation consisted entirely of variations on the theme of How could you do this to me? "This is all I need, with the baby due next month. Ross will go berserk, and he'll find some way to blame me for everything. It really is too bad of you, Lia. Haven't you ever heard of contraceptives? And fifteen is far too young to start a sexual relationship."

Olivia let her rave on without bothering to reply. She fantasized about telling her mother the truth. Tell your husband, Mummy, about contraceptives and screwing at fifteen. If you really want to see Daddy go berserk, tell him it was Nick.

What would her mother do or say with such knowledge? Olivia thought that she knew what her mother's response would be. Last summer it might have been different, but now she had made heavy investments; she was married and about to give birth to a child of that marriage. So now she would blame Olivia herself.

With that thought Olivia began to long for her father's arrival. She wouldn't mind about his rage and sarcasm; she just wanted him to come and take her home.

Somebody hammered on the front door. Her father, no doubt, too angry to use the doorbell, symbolically breaking the door down. Her mother said, "You stay here and eat," before she went to answer the door.

Olivia heard her father say "Where's Lia?" just like that, without any greeting.

Her mother said, "She's in the kitchen, having a meal. She said she's been too nauseated to eat for months. She looks terrible. How could you not have noticed?"

"How could I not notice what you didn't notice, you mean?"

"I haven't seen her for nearly a month," her mother pointed out coldly. "And even then I only see her for a few hours once a fortnight. You see her every day and you didn't notice. You never notice anything, you're so wrapped up in your own petty academic concerns."

"Are you bragging about how little you see of your daughter?" If her mother's tone was cold, her father's was absolutely venomous. "Maybe she's made a connection between your neglect of her and the fact that you're about to present that brainless barbarian with a brat of his own."

"You can call him any name you like, he's still a better man than you ever were, in bed or out of it."

"I don't need any judgments on my sexual competence from an iceberg, thank you very much. Who gave Lia the taste for a bit of rough? She'd never have got mixed up with this gold-plated brickie if you'd brought her up properly."

"Of course you're entitled to say that, having virtually disappeared from her life for two years. But as it happens she hasn't been living here for nearly a year now, so if someone hasn't been looking after her, we know who it is. You couldn't be trusted with a hamster, and that selfish snob you married doesn't even look after her own child. The only reason you agreed to take Lia is so that you could dump the baby on her, since you're too cheap to hire a proper nanny."

Olivia decided she didn't want to hear any more of this. It really made her feel wanted. Also, she was anxious to leave before Nick came home. With her father in this state, it was only a simple safety precaution to make sure he didn't hang around long enough to meet Nick.

She went to the kitchen door and said, "Daddy, will you take me home now, please?"

Both of her parents looked at her. Finally her father said, "Get your things."

When she went into the sitting room to get her coat and violin and school bag her mother said to her father, "She hasn't seen a doctor yet. I'm taking her tomorrow. There's not much time, we'll have to go to Harley Street. Are you going to pay for it?"

"Do you mean if I don't, you won't?"

"I didn't say that. But business is very slow for me right now. I don't see why Nick should pay for your daughter's abortion."

He's already done it once, thought Olivia. But he won't have to do it again. She came back into the hall with her coat on, holding her bag and violin case. "You don't need to have an argument about that. I already told you, Mummy, I'm not going to have it aborted. It's my baby and I want it."

"You're coming to the doctor with me anyway, whatever else you do or don't do." Her mother looked at her father. "All right, Dr. Beckett, I'll leave you to exert your famous powers of logical persuasion."

Her sarcasm was quite justified. Olivia's father had never been inclined to argue a point of practical rather than academic importance. Practical matters were too important to be decided by debate. Whenever he wanted Olivia to do or refrain from doing something, his usual tactics were a mixture of threats and bribes and verbal bullying. Rather like Nick, Olivia thought. She wondered what her father would say if she told him that in spite of his Ph.D. he behaved exactly like the man he had dismissed as a brainless barbarian.

He did it now, with less success than Nick. In the car he told her, "Lia, I don't want a lot of sentimental nonsense about having this baby. You're not having a child at the age of fifteen."

"Sixteen. I'll be sixteen when it's born."

"It's not going to be born. What's the matter with you? All those hormones must be addling your brain. Look, you've got ten GCSEs to get through in the next two months, not to mention A levels and university over the next several years. There's no time for a baby anywhere in there."

"My exams will be over long before the baby arrives."

"How are you going to concentrate if you're worried all the time about having the baby?"

"I'm not worrying about it, I'm happy about it. The only thing I was worried about was telling you and Mummy."

He made a serious and obvious attempt to be patient. "Are you talking like this because you think you're in love with Charlie?"

"I'm not in love with Charlie. I just want the baby."

"But you can't have the baby, you know you can't. Babies aren't dolls, they need someone to look after them all the time. They need a grown-up mother, not a little girl."

"I know what babies are like. You've got one at home." And his grown-up mother hardly ever sees him, she added silently.

When her father got angry his vowels got longer, more like her grandfather's. He must have been very angry now, to judge from the broadness of his speech. "Lia, this is lunacy. You're not having that goddamned baby. I'll pay for an abortion, but I won't pay for you to play house and destroy your future."

"Althea can pay me to look after Matty. That would be better for Matty too."

Her father raised his right hand and brought it down hard and flat on the steering wheel. That was instead of smacking her, she knew. He was driving with both hands close together at the top of the wheel, his knuckles white with fury. Maybe, she thought with surprising dispassion, he wished it were her neck he was gripping so tightly. She had never ever seen him so angry.

"Jesus Christ, you're not going to be Althea's au pair. You're my daughter, God damn it. I want you to get the education your intelligence entitles you to. I want you to be able to do what you want to do when you grow up. I don't want you to end up like my father, his whole life stunted because of something that happened when he was fourteen."

"It doesn't have to be like that. Having a baby isn't the end of the world."

"You don't know anything about it," he snapped. "You're just a child yourself. I'm not going to let you tie yourself up for twenty years at your age."

"Daddy," Olivia said gently, "I don't need your permission to have the baby."

It was true, and the knowledge infuriated him, the limits of his power to control her. "Well, there is one thing you need my permission for, as long as you're living in my house. You're not going to see Charlie again." He added rhetorically, "What kind of depraved halfwit would impregnate a fifteen-year-old child?"

"A real bastard," Olivia said promptly. She felt like laughing, but wisely did not. "He told me to tell you that, Daddy."

54

I didn't see you in school on Friday," Megan remarked when she phoned Olivia on Sunday morning. "Were you off sick?"

"Sort of. Can you come over this afternoon? I'll tell you about it if you come."

"I'd love to. I have something to tell you too. But aren't you supposed to be visiting your mother today?"

"I was, but I've begged off because I'm coming down with a really stinking cold and I feel like death warmed over."

"So you're going to pass it on to me, are you? There's friendship for you. I'll see you about three."

Now that her secret was out, Olivia was anxious to tell Megan. Everyone else at school would be able to see for themselves soon enough. She wanted to be sure that Megan knew first.

The cold was a pain, but she was glad of the excuse to avoid her mother's house. For one thing, she didn't want to deal with Nick. He was bound to be furious. Also, she had seen more than enough of her mother lately, first running the gauntlet on Thursday evening, then the visit to the doctor's on Friday.

That was something else she was glad to have behind her. She had been afraid the doctor would be able to tell exactly how far along she was. Which would have meant, if Charlie came to hear of it, that he would know he couldn't have been the father. But she was deliberately vague about the date of her last period. Sometime before Christmas, she said. After the doctor had examined her he said it could be anywhere from sixteen to twenty weeks, because he could hear the baby's heartbeat but the baby wasn't very big. "Not unusual in cases where the mother is so young," he told Olivia's mother.

Her mother asked about an abortion. Olivia said she didn't want an abortion, she wanted the baby. The doctor said an abortion wasn't a good idea in this case, for one thing because they didn't know how viable the fetus was, but also because the procedure at this stage would be quite a painful and unpleasant experience so it was just as well the young lady was opposed to it.

Her mother didn't press the issue, but Olivia knew that was only because she didn't want to make a scene in front of the doctor. Sure enough, as soon as they came out into the street her mother returned to the subject, applying ice instead of her father's fire the night before.

"Lia, if you were doing this just to embarrass me, you couldn't have made a better job of it. I feel like some sort of slum dweller, having a pregnant fifteen-year-old daughter.

Especially when I'm pregnant myself. It's like a bad farce. What on earth am I going to tell Mother when she comes next month?''

She had a point there. Olivia was more concerned about her grandparents' reaction than her parents' by now. ''Well, she didn't curl up and die when you told her you were pregnant, did she?''

''But I'm a grown woman, and she knew I was going to marry Nick. It's not the same as a silly little schoolgirl. You're too young to be going to bed with boys, never mind having a baby. I'm bitterly disappointed in Charlie. I thought he had more sense.''

''He was drunk.''

Her mother looked at her. ''When did this happen?''

''On New Year's Eve.''

''If it was all a big mistake, why don't you want to have an abortion?''

''It's not a mistake, it's a baby.'' It was Olivia's turn to look at her mother. ''Did you tell Nick?''

''Of course.''

''What did he say?''

''I wouldn't want to repeat it.''

Olivia could understand that. She had never heard her mother utter anything that could be described as bad language. She wondered if her mother found it exciting to hear Nick talk about, for instance, her cunt. But the thought made her feel faint with jealousy, so she put it right out of her head.

When Megan arrived, Olivia invited her to come out for a walk with Matthew in his pram. Like a little dog, the baby was always keen on going for walks. Not that he did any of the walking.

As soon as they were away from the house Olivia asked, ''What's this exciting thing you had to tell me?''

''Well, I don't know about exciting. In fact, I can tell you it wasn't, very.''

''What wasn't?''

''I went to bed with Jon last night.''

Olivia's astonishment was as if she herself had been a virgin. "Meg! Really? I thought you weren't exactly swooning over him."

"Well, he's all right. Basically I like him. It's just he doesn't really turn me on. Or off, I suppose."

"So why did you go to bed with him?"

"I was just fed up with being a virgin. The first time is supposed to be some sort of event, and I wanted to get on with my life without having this big event hanging over me. Apparently in ancient Greece girls used to offer their virginity to the herm before their wedding night."

"What's a herm?"

"It was a sort of phallus carved in stone outside every-body's front door. The bride was supposed to, you know, impale herself upon it."

"Having sex with a stone?" Olivia was appalled. "I thought these people were supposed to be part of Western civi-lization."

"I thought it sounded like quite a good idea. There's sup-posed to be a curse attached to the maidenhead, you know. But we haven't got any herms around nowadays, so I thought Jon would do for a substitute."

"Why would you want to put a curse on Jon?"

"I couldn't really, it's too late. I've already offered up my maidenhead to Tampax."

"Speaking of curses," Olivia added, and they both laughed. "But don't be mean, he couldn't have been as bad as either of those."

"Well, to be fair, he wasn't," allowed Megan. "What I meant was, I was only looking for a handy prick."

Olivia was prepared to be scandalized on poor Jon's behalf until she remembered that for quite different reasons she had done exactly the same thing to Charlie. She swallowed her indignation. "So how was it?"

"Just how you'd expect with two virgins. I can't imagine why anyone would want to get married in that state."

"The earth didn't move for you?"

"No, but the bed certainly did. Teddy was downstairs and I was terrified he would hear and make some evil remark in front of my parents this morning."

Olivia considered the implications of this story as she trundled Matthew implacably up Hampstead Heath. "So are you and Jon lovers now?"

"I don't know. I suppose I could practice my techniques on him."

"What do you mean, techniques?"

"Well, for instance, you're supposed to be able to bring a man to orgasm just by flexing your sphincter muscle. I could try that out on him."

"Are you serious?"

"Why not? Apparently Arab slave girls used to be taught how to do it and they were very highly prized."

"I'll bet they were." Olivia was surprised to find herself outraged. "Are you aiming to be some kind of high-class courtesan?"

"Of course not. I expect they make lots of money, but look what you'd have to go to bed with. They'd all be old or fat or ugly, or else perverted playboys. Nobody you'd remotely want to end up with."

"So why do you want to develop exotic sex techniques?"

"Well, it puts you in charge, doesn't it? You're doing something to him instead of the other way round."

Olivia thought about that. "In charge" was the one thing she hardly ever had been where Nick was concerned, and she didn't see how exercising her sphincter muscle would have changed that. But she understood what Megan meant. "How did all this come about? Did he finally get up the nerve to make a pass at you?"

"I seduced him."

"Oh, Meg." Olivia gazed at her friend in awe. "Did I tell you Charlie said you were a fearsome little woman?"

Megan didn't look pleased at the news. "What made him say that?"

"He meant it as a compliment."

"I should jolly well hope so. Do you want me to push Matty for a while? It's hard going on this path." Megan took over control of the pram and rolled it onward and upward. "You were going to tell me about being sick on Friday. You were very mysterious on the phone."

"Well, it's not a mystery anymore. My mother took me to the doctor. I'm pregnant."

Megan came to a halt. She sounded breathless, as if Olivia had just punched her in the midriff. "You are?"

"You mean you really didn't notice anything? I was so scared that someone would say something before it was too late."

Megan pushed her primrose hair away from her face and stared at Olivia. "Now that you mention it, I don't see how I couldn't have noticed. How far along are you?"

"Five months. But you're the only one who knows that. Everyone else thinks it's four."

"Four months, five months, what does it matter?"

"It makes all the difference in the world. Arithmetic is important, you see, just like they say at school, and so is biology. Four months means Charlie is the father. Five months means it must have been someone else."

"Nick, you mean." Megan spoke slowly and carefully, like someone doing laborious calculations in their head. "Did you do it on purpose?"

"Well . . . sort of."

"What about Charlie? Did you sleep with him on purpose?"

"Sort of."

"What does he think about it?"

"Funnily enough, he seemed quite pleased. He thinks it's his, of course. Only he wasn't pleased when I told him that Daddy said I couldn't see him anymore."

Megan said dryly, "Poor sap."

Without the solace of motion, Matthew had wakened. He sent up a complaint about the lack of progress. Megan jiggled the pram but he only cried harder, knowing a cheat when he met it. Olivia picked him up and tucked him inside her jacket. He stopped yelling almost at once. They all walked on again, Olivia cuddling Matthew and Megan pushing the empty pram.

"You think I'm crazy, don't you?"

"I don't know about crazy. You're in a mess, but it's not totally your fault. Actually, in a way you've been quite heroic. A sort of emotional Charge of the Light Brigade."

"Crazy. I know."

"Well, if you want to mess up your life to prove a point, that's your privilege, I guess. What I really don't approve of,"

Megan said sternly, "is the way you've treated Charlie. It seems to me you've done the same thing to him that Nick did to you. You shouldn't deliberately behave so as to make somebody fall in love with you, if you're not in a position to reciprocate. And now he thinks he's the father of a child, and he's not."

"I could tell him he's not. Afterward, I mean."

"I don't think you should."

Olivia looked at her friend in surprise. Megan had always been absolute for truth, however brutal the consequences. "Why not?"

"Well, for one thing he might be so upset he could do something drastic, like trying to do some serious damage to Nick or telling your father the truth. But really I was thinking about the baby. It's going to want to know who its father is, sooner or later. You're never going to be able to tell it the truth, are you? You can't tell a child that its father is its grandfather. Or would it be the other way round? Anyway, you know what I mean. So maybe Charlie will make as good a father as anyone."

"I hadn't thought of that. From the child's point of view, I mean."

Megan said soberly, "If you're going to have the baby, Lia, that's the only point of view you should be thinking about."

55

Her mother had dealt with the doctor. Now it was her father's turn to suffer public humiliation.

He was going to have to go to school with her on Monday to explain matters to the headmistress. Although he found the prospect desperately embarrassing—as he made sure she knew—he was prepared to do it because as far as he was concerned the most important thing was to make sure that the pregnancy didn't interfere with her education more than could be helped.

"I don't know if they let you stay on," Olivia said doubtfully.

"You're going to stay," her father said tersely. "In the first place it's only one term. In the second place, if they don't cooperate I'll raise the sort of hell they never imagined existed. Do they think being pregnant does something to your mind? Or maybe that your presence will morally contaminate everybody else?"

"I expect they think both those things. But I also expect you'll show them the error of their ways."

"Don't speak to me like that, Lia."

Her father was so angry he looked as if he might actually hit her, for the first time in her whole life. The prospect was more exciting than alarming. She couldn't imagine her father doing any real damage to her, but the threat of it made her think of Nick, who had made similar threats, and what had come of them.

"But Daddy, you said yourself that hormones must have addled my brain."

Her father looked at her as if she had turned into a Martian. No, a Venusian. If her father was a Martian to her, she would be a Venusian, a female mystery, to him. How she could be a mystery to anyone was a mystery to her. It was all perfectly simple. She knew that she was the least complex creature on earth. Nick, who was an unreconstructed Martian, could read her like a book.

"Maybe I should have left you living with Emma," he said coldly. "Perhaps you'd be happier there after all."

"No!"

"Why not?"

Olivia didn't answer right away. She didn't know what to say. She was sitting cross-legged on her bed, in her nightgown. It was Friday night. Althea was downstairs, Matthew asleep across the hall.

This was her home, such as it was.

She knew now that her old home was an emotional nightmare, that there was no home there for her any longer. That her mother didn't love her anymore, if she ever had. That Nick, who might have loved her, who had said he loved her, had chosen her mother instead.

But she couldn't say any of that to her father, not even the bit about her mother. Not only because it would have made her parents' tenuous relationship still worse, but also because she was afraid it would devalue her in her father's eyes. If she wasn't worthy of her own mother's love, who could possibly love her?

She felt dizzy. It was like being drunk. "Daddy, do you despise me?"

"What are you talking about?"

"Do you think I'm a stupid slag?"

"You know perfectly well I don't think any such thing."

"How do I know? People say things like that, don't they, when somebody like me gets pregnant?"

"Don't be silly," he said roughly. "It's not your fault."

"Of course it's my fault. I know how babies are made. They told us in biology class." Erection, penetration, ejaculation, that was how it was done.

Just then she felt a kick inside her. She grabbed her father's hand and brought it over to the seismically active spot on her belly. "It's moving, can you feel it? I couldn't get rid of it, could I, when it's already alive?"

She turned her head to look up at her father. She wanted so badly to be loved, completely, wholeheartedly, body and baby and soul. She thought if she could have been sure that her father would love her like that forever she would even dare to tell him the truth about the baby.

The baby kicked again. She felt it on the inside. Her father must have felt it on the palm of his hand, pressed against her nightgown, pressed flat against her belly.

"Christ!" He pulled his hand away quickly, as if the baby's kick had hurt him. He moved back out of her reach. "Go to bed, Lia."

He watched her slide under the duvet. He didn't hug or kiss her. He didn't call her my love as Mrs. Stone had, or darling like her mother, or baby and kitten the way Nick did. He just said good night and went out.

* * *

Monday's interview with the headmistress was every bit as dreadful as Olivia had imagined it would be. But she discovered, to her surprise and relief, that she didn't really care. School wasn't the center of her life anymore. And the whole conversation was conducted as if she weren't even there.

The headmistress, not knowing what was coming, shook Olivia's father by the hand. She wanted to know what she could do for him.

Olivia's father explained the situation bluntly, saying he had just found out that Olivia was pregnant.

The Head expressed amazement and dismay. She hadn't thought Olivia was that sort of girl.

Olivia's father said there was no such thing as that sort of girl, every girl in the school had been provided by nature with the necessary physical equipment and was capable of sexual reproduction.

The Head deplored this notion. She was running a respectable educational establishment with excellent traditions that largely excluded illegitimate pregnancies. She implied that Olivia had not only let the team down but also lowered the tone of the place. She inquired delicately what steps were being taken to remedy the situation.

Olivia's father said there was nothing he could do; Olivia refused to have an abortion.

The Head said this was unfortunate. She was no radical feminist, but she did think that girls ought to be prepared to fight their corner in what was still a man's world, and that definitely excluded putting oneself hors de combat by getting pregnant before the battle had even been joined. With scrupulous correctness she kept addressing Olivia's father as Dr. Beckett, to rub in the implication that as a scholar himself he should have given his daughter sufficient respect for educational priorities to prevent her doing something so certain to interfere with, if not halt entirely, her academic progress.

Olivia's father said that as far as he knew, having a baby even at fifteen did nothing to retard the mental development of a girl, and if the school was going to teach children how to make babies maybe it should also be showing them how to use condoms.

The Head said schools could teach scientifically objective

subjects like biology but it was really up to the parents to impart moral values and a sense of responsibility to their children. What with the vast increase in broken families and the vogue for cohabitation and everybody thinking that they had some God-given right to personal happiness and that the state had some God-given obligation to pay for the consequences, it was spitting in the wind for teachers to broach the subject of right and wrong or to suggest any merit in delayed gratification.

Olivia's father looked as if he would have liked to respond to this speech with some appropriate physical violence. But that would only have proved the Head's point, so instead he said that right now he was more concerned with damage limitation and ensuring that Olivia did as well as possible in her GCSEs, which was the school's job, after all, and had no bearing on the state of Olivia's morals.

The Head allowed this was so. She muttered about further education classes for teenage mothers.

Olivia's father asked what she had in mind, child care and home economics or something more intellectually ambitious such as word processing.

The Head said it was indeed the case that girls from Olivia's advantaged background seldom ended up, ahem . . .

Olivia's father said that was because they went on the pill or got abortions, not because they were all virgins.

The Head said, in that case, why . . . ?

Olivia's father said he couldn't force Olivia to have an abortion if she didn't want one, could he, for God's sake, and putting a young girl on the pill was equivalent to giving her a license to fornicate, and in any case the doctor had said it was probably too late for an abortion. Apparently the miracles of modern science didn't make it possible to tell exactly how far along the pregnancy had progressed. Nor had Olivia's expensive education enabled her to do the calculations for herself.

The Head said she saw. She asked Olivia if there was anything she wanted to say.

"Yes," said Olivia, "can I wear something instead of my navy skirt, because I have to use safety pins and they keep bursting open and sticking me. It's very distracting in class."

The Head said she could wear something more suitable for her condition, but it would be quite inappropriate for her to flaunt her pregnancy.

Olivia's father looked quite murderous again and said for Christ's sake everyone was going to know all about it anyway and he was surprised the Head hadn't suggested wearing a whalebone corset and pretending there wasn't any pregnancy. He also said he wasn't going to send Olivia back here for A levels under any circumstances. There were schools that knew how to value a child for her brains and ability rather than treating her like a moral and mental cripple just because some yob had taken advantage of her innocence.

Then he said he had to leave, and did.

The Head had a lot more to say to Olivia, but she didn't pay much attention. She was thinking about all the things her father had said.

He had been defending her. He had been on her side.

56

Nobody answered when Olivia rang the bell. Usually her mother came right away. She couldn't just walk in, because the latch was on the door and she didn't have a key. She didn't have a key to what was once her own front door.

It was a sunny day, the first of May. Her mother and Nick might be out in the garden. She pressed the button again. The bell was working; she could hear it ring. She was just thinking about going up to the end of the terrace and along the path to the back gate when Nick opened the door.

It was half past twelve, but he looked as if he had just got out of bed. As if he had got up to answer the door, in fact. He was barefoot and his shirt was untucked and unbuttoned.

He needed a shave. His hair was tousled, his face still puffy with sleep. He looked fantastically desirable.

"Sorry, Lia." He stood aside to let her in, yawning and running a hand through his hair. "I forgot you were coming."

Olivia paused in the doorway, puzzled and wary. "Where's Mummy?"

"I should have phoned you. She had the baby last night. Come in, for Christ's sake." He hauled her out of the way and shut the door. "I was up half the fucking night waiting for the damned thing. I only woke up when you rang the bell."

Olivia was shocked. Her mother's baby had arrived; it was now a real rather than a postulated person. She said numbly, "What is it?"

"A boy. I forget the statistics. The usual number of arms and legs and heads. Sorry I haven't got any cigars. I don't suppose you'd want one anyway."

It had all happened without her knowing. Her mother had given birth to her brother, and she learned of it by accident, as if it had happened to a neighbor. She was devastated, humiliated. She turned toward the door. "I wouldn't have come if I'd known. I'm sorry I disturbed you. I'll let you go back to bed."

He caught her wrist as she reached for the doorknob. "Don't be daft, I wasn't going to sleep all day. Let me get dressed and have a shave and I'll take you out for lunch. Then we'll go round to see Em and the brat."

That sounded almost bearable, having Nick take her to see his baby. Otherwise she would only go home and feel desolate all day. "Okay."

"Good girl. Give me five minutes."

While he was upstairs she wandered around the sitting room, noting changes. There were a couple of strange objects on the mantel among her mother's little figurines. The figurines were her mother's souvenirs from foreign parts. Her mother thought they were valuable enough to forbid Olivia, as a small child, to touch them. Now there were these odd things rubbing shoulders with the sacred objects. One was a greasy thingamajig that looked as if it might have been wrenched from the guts of dead machinery. The other was a crudely cast and badly glazed little gnome with his trousers at half-mast and his bare buttocks presented to the viewer. He was holding a sign that said SOUTHEND-ON-SEA.

Nick's idea of a joke, she supposed. Or else a way of resisting the inevitably embourgeoisificatory effects of living with her mother. No doubt Karl Marx would have been proud of him. On the other hand, that must have been at least partly what he had married her for—her indisputably middle-class status and respectability.

When Nick came down again he was ready to deal with the world, fully dressed, clean-shaven, his hair still damp from the shower, the lines of his face hardened out of their former sleepy softness. He still looked fantastically desirable.

He took a cigarette from the packet lying on the coffee table and lit it, surveying her over the flame. "Christ, you are pregnant, aren't you?" he remarked with brutal bluntness. "I couldn't believe it when Em told me."

For the first time Olivia was embarrassed by her swollen body. Nick looked just the same; she could look at him and want him as much as ever. But when he looked at her he must see someone misshapen, no longer desirable. "You haven't seen me for six weeks."

"Has it been that long?" He stared at her belly, which was covered by a long cardigan. "I thought you were on the pill."

"I went off it when you and Mummy got married. I thought—I mean, there didn't seem much point . . ."

"You misjudged the boyfriend, did you?" He came closer, standing right in front of her. Besides the burning tobacco she could smell the faintly spicy enticing scent of soap and aftershave. "How do you know it's his?"

"I—what do you mean?"

"You know fucking well what I mean. If this is supposed to be the result of New Year's Eve, how the fuck do you know it's his?"

She stepped back and bumped into the mantelpiece. He came after her and leaned against the mantel, one arm on either side of her. She crossed her hands over her stomach. She couldn't let herself even think that she was afraid. If he was angry he might hit her. If he hit her she might lose the baby. Surely, surely he wouldn't do that. . . .

"It's not his," she said in a whisper. "It's yours."

"How do you reckon that?"

She dropped her gaze; she couldn't look at him. "I was already pregnant by Christmas. Before I ever . . . went to bed with him." She blinked back tears. From the cigarette smoke, maybe. "When you were so—so mad on New Year's Eve, I wanted to tell you then. Because I only did it with him so that no one would guess, so they'd never think it was anyone but him. I never even said it was his. Everybody said it for me."

"You crazy little . . ." He didn't voice whatever obscenity he had in mind. "Why did you do it at all?"

"You know why." She took her hands away from her stomach and touched his shirt. Touched his chest, but the shirt was in between. "I didn't mean to get pregnant. I didn't mean . . . You know that time in my room, when I had the flu. That must have been when it happened. And when I knew, I couldn't bear to kill your baby a second time."

She was openly crying now. He flicked his cigarette into the fireplace and put his arms around her. "Jesus, you're crazy. You'll screw up your life, Lia. You shouldn't have done it. You should have told me."

"But I wanted it," she wept. "I want it. It's yours. I couldn't stand to lose it again. Please don't be mad at me."

"I'm not mad. Don't cry, kitten." He was holding her, stroking her, kissing her hair and her face and her throat. "I'm sorry about New Year's Eve. I said I was sorry, didn't I?" He gave her a gently deliberate shake. "But it's not right for you. You're just a kid. You're not supposed to be messing with babies yet."

"I'm not supposed to be messing with you either."

"No, you bloody well aren't. It's nearly a year since I popped your cherry and you're still jailbait. Christ, I feel like the biggest shit in the world."

Olivia didn't contradict him. His feelings on the matter were probably correct. But she still wanted to be kissed and caressed, even by the biggest shit in the world. He obliged her.

After a little while she said into his shoulder, "Nick, are you really not mad about the baby?"

"Not now. Now I'm just glad it's not his."

"I thought you liked Charlie."

"I don't like him dipping his wick in your pussy." He took her by the shoulders and held her away from him, looking down into her face. "Is he still screwing you?"

"Daddy won't let me see him anymore."

His hands gripped her more fiercely, like the talons of a hawk about to lift his prey. "What about before that?"

She knew she was on dangerous ground here. She took the coward's way out. "It was just that once. I told you why."

His eyes were pale and cold, glacial ice, ancient frozen darkness at the core. "You're telling me porkies, aren't you, baby?"

She said defiantly, "If you know it all, why ask?" She tried to shrug his hands away. "I wouldn't need him if I had you."

His fingers dug into her. Maybe the talons were going to rip her to shreds where she stood, not even bothering to carry her away. "One dick is as good as another so long as it's up your crack, is that it?"

It was scary how he could still take her breath away by the crude brutality of his speech. Without lifting a finger he made her feel as if he had slapped her across the face. "I didn't mean that. I meant he loves me."

"Talk is pretty fucking cheap."

"He really does. Not every man in the world has cardiac permafrost like you." She was shaking, stammering, starting to cry again. "Let me go, Nick. You're acting like a d-dog in the manger. It's your baby in me and you d-didn't want it."

Nick let her go, but only to put his arms round her waist—or where her waist had been a few months ago—and pull her against him. She wept into the front of his shirt, lovingly washed and laboriously ironed by her mother.

"I never said that," he growled. "I just said you shouldn't be having it."

That stopped her sobs, at least. But she didn't dare to push him any further.

He started to unbutton her cardigan. She tried to stop him. "I don't want you to see me. I'm ugly, I'm fat."

"No you're not."

"You don't know."

"Sure I do." While she protested, he was distracting her with kisses and continuing to undress her. "Come on, let me look at you, baby."

He had his own way, as he always did. When she was naked he went down on his knees and kissed and stroked her distended belly as if it was the most desirable part of her. She was thrilled and disbelieving. "How can you do that? I look gross."

"Bullshit. You look like a fucking goddess." His fingertip traced a blue vein in her swollen breast. "A fertility idol made out of some rare stone."

Coming from Nick, that was poetry. And he was on his knees before her, as if in the act of worship. Only he was the divinity, not her. She loved him so much she couldn't stand it.

To distract herself from the pain, she made it hurt somewhere else. "Did you say that to Mummy?"

His answer was shamelessly frank and unperturbed. "Em's not built on the right scale. A goddess should look generous—like a feast, not just a square meal." Even while he said this he was stroking, kissing, licking, nibbling her naked body everywhere he could reach, as if she were literally as well as metaphorically a banquet laid out for his pleasure.

When he stood up to strip himself she was afraid he would make love from behind as they had in the cemetery, which was okay for wet cemeteries but not very comforting, and she desperately wanted to be comforted as well as fucked. But he stretched out on the sofa and got her to kneel astride him, so that he could come up into her without putting pressure on the baby. He kissed her mouth and caressed her heavy breasts and told her she was beautiful until she believed him, belly and baby and all. When he came he said her name, *Lia Lia Lia,* the first time he had ever done that, and she loved him even more for it.

"I missed you dreadfully," she confessed. "I didn't know how much until now. Did you miss me?"

"What if I did? There's no point thinking about it."

"Sometimes I can't help it. It's like having a horrible disease and running out of painkillers in the middle of the night."

She had raised her head to look at him. He grunted with

something like laughter and pulled her down to him again. "Yeah, I know. I know what you mean."

"Do you really know?"

"Yeah." He buried his hand in her hair, stroking the nape of her neck with his rough fingertips. "Yes to every fucking thing."

It was only later, when they were going into the hospital where her mother had given birth, that Olivia understood the enormity of what they had just done. If there were degrees of adultery, then screwing your mother's husband on the same day she had labored to bring his son into the world had to count as the highest, or lowest, degree.

She wondered how Nick coped with such thoughts. She knew, though she did not understand it, that he had no sense of shame. Maybe he just didn't have those thoughts—because, as he had said, there was no point thinking about it.

Her mother looked tired but pleased with herself. The baby had just had his very first lunch and was also looking tired but pleased with himself. They had both been through a pretty grueling experience the night before. Though fortunately nothing as difficult as giving birth to Olivia, her mother was happy to tell her.

Unlike Althea, Olivia's mother didn't mind if she picked the baby up. Besides, thanks to Matthew, she had become quite expert at holding babies.

"What's his name?"

"Luke."

When her mother said his name, the baby opened his eyes and looked at Olivia. He wasn't like Matthew at all; he didn't appear the least bit puzzled or frustrated. He looked like a baby who had thoroughly mastered the briefing for his mission on earth and was now ready to relax and enjoy himself until the time came to do whatever he had been sent for. He looked at Olivia with friendly interest.

She asked her mother, "When are you going home?"

"Tuesday, I hope. Mother is coming up from Devon tomorrow to help out for a few weeks."

"That's nice for you. And for Luke, of course."

Less nice for Nick. Maybe the fuss over the baby would

absorb all her grandmother's energies and leave her no time for trying to civilize her son-in-law. She wondered what her grandmother would make of the objets trouvés on the mantel.

She began to feel guilty about hogging the baby. She glanced at Nick, who was standing at the foot of the bed. "Do you want to hold Luke?"

He shook his head. "I'll get enough of that at home."

Olivia had thought she would have to force herself to some pretense of being pleased with the baby, but just as with Matthew she had discovered that her mother's son was a little body in his own right, to be dealt with like anyone else to whom one had just been introduced, rather than an object with EMMA written on one arm and NICK on the other. But though she meant it sincerely, she knew it sounded absurdly formal, like her mother's tea-party manners, when she said to Nick in the car afterward, "Luke is a lovely baby."

"Handsome is as handsome does. Em tells me you cried for six weeks straight."

"I don't think my parents were very helpful. Maybe Luke will be luckier."

"He'll be luckier than I was, at any rate."

She had forgotten about his dreadful childhood. It was hard to think about him as ever having been a young child, when he seemed to her so much the masterful man. Maybe he was hoping to make it up, to do right by his son in the way that his father had done so wrong by him. "Did you ever tell Mummy about your father?"

"That wouldn't be much of a recommendation for me, would it?"

"You mean she doesn't know about any of that?"

Olivia said it spontaneously, without having absorbed the meaning of his answer. When she reflected a moment later, she understood him. However besotted with Nick, her mother might well have hesitated before inflicting on her unborn child a father whose experience of paternal behavior involved abuse.

Before she could apologize for her lack of tact Nick said, "I told you, kitten, it's a big secret between you and me. Not part of the official biography."

When she thought about that, she wanted to tell him to

stop the car. She wanted to say she loved him better than Hero had ever loved Leander or Héloïse Abélard. She didn't really want to say anything at all; she just wanted him to make love to her.

Well, maybe there was something she wanted to say to him after all. "But I know all that, Nick, and I'm having your baby."

He glanced at her with a faint smile. "But you don't count. You're crazy."

She took several deep, slow breaths, to avoid bursting into tears. "My baby counts," she said carefully. "It won't be crazy. It will be just as beautiful and sweet as Matty and Luke. And you're going to be its father. What will you do about that?"

"I don't know."

"What does that mean?"

"It means I haven't had time to think about it. And neither have you. You weren't going to tell me, were you?"

She wanted to take some more deep breaths but suddenly she couldn't breathe. "Can you stop the car? I think I might be going to faint."

Nick stopped very abruptly, turning into a side road and pulling over to the curb. Though the sun was shining, he had left the canvas top up because the wind had a fresh bite to it. She opened her window, leaned back, and breathed in the bright, cool air. Gradually the sense of suffocation receded.

"I couldn't tell you. You would have made me get rid of it, just like you did before." In spite of her efforts she began to cry. "You're happy to have Luke, why don't you want my baby? It's not fair. It's not fair to my baby."

She was weeping quite hysterically by now, enough to prevent her from speaking. Nick pulled her toward him and put his hand across her mouth. "Lia, shut up. Shut up and listen to me."

She didn't do it right away. She put her arms around his neck, subsided into whimpers, and finally buried her face against his throat.

"Now listen. Are you listening? The first thing you've got to understand is that as far as you're concerned I'm a bastard. Have you got that?"

"Yes." She sniffled and giggled.

"What are you laughing at?"

"That's what Charlie said."

"He said I was a bastard?"

"He said he was a bastard. He said to tell Daddy that. He said any man who would get a fifteen-year-old pregnant was a real bastard."

"Well, he was right. About me, not about himself. He's just a stupid kid." He sighed and held her more tightly. "Jesus, Lia. Jesus fucking Christ. You're just a stupid kid too."

"No, I'm not."

"Yes, you are. You don't know fuck all."

"I do know fuck all. You taught me."

He started to laugh. She felt it in his throat, where her face was pressed against him. "Oh Christ, kitten, I wish to hell I knew how to look after you and your baby. But the law won't let me and your daddy won't let me, and I've got Em and Luke to look after. What do you want me to do?"

She raised her head to look at him. "I just want you to love me. And I want you to love my baby, because it's yours. I don't care about anything else—if I hardly ever see you, if we have to pretend, even if I have to let on it's Charlie's baby. I don't care about all that. Well, not very much," she amended honestly. "But I just want to know—"

"You want an understanding, baby. That's what it's called among the nobs." He was silent a moment, looking out at all the conventional suburban houses. "I understand."

She began to cry again, from relief maybe. She kissed him between sobs. "I love you," she said between kisses. "But Nick, what about you?"

"What about me?"

"That's what I want. Is it what you want?"

He put his hand on her breast, cardigan and all. "Right now what I want is to take you home and fuck you again. Have you got time for that?"

She did.

57

"Lia, darling." Olivia recognized her grandmother's voice. "How sweet of you to ring. I know you're very busy with exams right now, but I had hoped you'd be coming up to see us."

"I was supposed to come tomorrow. But I thought maybe it wouldn't be such a good idea."

"Nonsense, I'd love to see you and I'm sure Emma would too. You must be dying to see your little brother."

The warmth of her grandmother's voice suggested to Olivia that her mother had not yet conveyed the bad news. "Well, I'd like to come but I think I'd better talk to Mummy first."

"Just one moment while I fetch her."

Her mother's voice came on the line, rather less enthusiastic than her grandmother's. "Hello, Lia."

"I was ringing up about tomorrow. I know it's my visiting Sunday, but maybe I shouldn't come."

"Why not?"

"Well, you know. You haven't told Grandma yet, have you? About me, I mean."

"No, I haven't." Her mother's tone was definitely cold by now. Not only had Olivia vomited on the carpet, but it was proving impossible to remove the stains and smell. "But it doesn't matter, it's got to be done sometime, doesn't it? It's not going to go away."

"Well, okay, I'll come. Just make sure you've explained before I walk in the door."

"I can tell her the facts, Lia, but you're going to have to explain yourself."

She was not merely the unwanted orphan, she was the

black sheep of the whole family. Like a lunatic or a convict. Worse than that: people could be cured of madness or serve out their term in prison, but a baby lasted a lifetime.

A lifetime and beyond, according to Megan. She would be bound to Nick forever. Hallelujah, she said inside herself, hallelujah and amen.

When she arrived at her mother's house the next day it was immediately apparent that her grandmother had not taken the news well. She kissed Olivia in a markedly formal manner.

"How are you, my dear?" For fear Olivia might try to answer that, she added quickly, "Emma's upstairs dealing with Luke. I'm in charge of lunch today. You'll have to come into the kitchen and help me."

Olivia would rather have gone upstairs to see Luke, but she couldn't refuse to help her grandmother. As it turned out, what her grandmother really wanted was not so much assistance as the opportunity to deliver a lecture. She did this as briskly as she grated the cabbage.

"You have been very foolish, haven't you, my dear? I couldn't believe it when Emma told me. I thought you had more sense than that. Still, I told her it's her fault for setting a bad example. If supposedly grown-up women think it's acceptable to go about openly having affairs and living with other people's husbands and even getting pregnant without any reference to marriage, why should anybody be surprised when a young girl decides to see what the fuss is all about? I know there have always been people on the lower fringes of society who regard the concept of legitimacy with the same indifference as the concept of property, but when respectable people with a proper upbringing and education begin to treat the idea of a normal family as an optional extra which they can dispense with when it gets to be a bore, I really don't know what hope there is for society. Everyone is kicking away the ladders that got them where they are. Everyone thinks they're missing out on life if they don't live like a pop star or a film star—orgies every Saturday night, five wives in succession, every one of them blond, beautiful, and twenty-one. It's all to do with happiness, I understand, but it seems to end in grief most times. I expect you think I'm a boring old dinosaur, don't you?"

Olivia shook her head. She was diligently stirring the gravy, her grandmother being a firm believer in the traditional virtues of meat and two veg. In that belief, if nothing else, Grandma Hardy and Nick had a meeting of minds.

The fact was that she agreed with her grandmother. She wished her parents were still married to each other. She wished that Matthew and Luke were her real brothers, instead of half brothers or even—in terms of shared domesticity—much more tenuous relations than that. She wished she had never set eyes on Nick, never gone to bed with Charlie, had nothing now more consequential than GCSE exams to confront.

But wishes weren't horses, things hadn't happened like that. And as things had happened, she was less concerned with the prospect of giving birth to a child than with the problem of being in love with her stepfather.

There was no way she could have explained all that to her grandmother, so she shook her head and changed the subject. It wasn't really a change, but her grandmother wouldn't know that. "How are you getting on with Nick?"

"He's been keeping out of my way."

"Do you think he'll be a good father for Luke?"

Her grandmother gave her a sharp look. "Do you think he won't be?"

"I don't think anything," Olivia protested. "I just wondered. Because Luke wasn't really his idea, that's all."

"When it comes to human procreation, my dear, the wish is father not only to the deed but to the baby that results. If he's not happy about having a child, he has only himself to blame."

"I don't think he is unhappy about it. I was just asking what you thought, Grandma."

Her grandmother considered the matter. "It's hard to tell. Men don't usually have much to do with small babies. The fact that Nick wouldn't be caught dead changing a nappy doesn't make him a bad father. Emma's father didn't know what a nappy looked like, and I think Ross managed to avoid all that messiness too. Unless Althea's made him into one of these New Men?"

"Not a chance, Grandma. You know Daddy."

"I just thought I'd ask, to be fair to him. I've always thought of Ross as a man dissatisfied with life because it doesn't live up to the billing it gets in books. Whisk this, will you, darling, while I pour in the oil."

"What are we making?"

"Mayonnaise. I don't like the ready-made kind." Olivia whisked while her grandmother poured. "I'll say this for Nick, I misjudged him at first. I thought he was thick."

"What do you think now?"

"He's really rather sharp. Definitely cleverer than Emma. Which is just as well, I suppose. Emma likes to look up to her men. She suffers from the feminine fallacy that they're going to take care of her and protect her from the cruel world. It's the sort of idée fixe that never seems to get knocked on the head by experience." Her grandmother handed her the bowl of mayonnaise. "Mix this into the cole slaw, will you, darling? Then you can go and call Emma and Nick."

After lunch the three women played three-cornered bridge and took turns cuddling Luke. If they all lived here together all the time, thought Olivia, the baby would never have a moment's solitude.

"What's happened to your play, Lia?" her mother asked casually. "Have you and Meg given up on it?"

"No, we're putting it on next week. We hope."

Her grandmother pricked up her ears. "What play is this?"

"*Medea*," Olivia explained. "Euripides."

"Isn't that the one where she murders her children?"

"That's the one," her mother agreed. "Light comedy for schoolchildren nowadays, it seems."

"Well, after all, Emma, what price the death of two children when we watch entire nations being starved or massacred on the nine o'clock news every night? An individual tragedy seems almost an expensive luxury." Her grandmother raised her voice. "What do you think, Nick?"

"About what?"

"About the suitability of Olivia's play."

Nick was engrossed in the sports pages of the *Mail on Sun-*

day. Olivia thought her mother must have nudged his reading material slightly upmarket, at least while her grandmother was here. He turned over a page and refolded the paper. "That's life, isn't it?"

Olivia knew what he meant. Her mother didn't. "What, people murdering their children?"

"They do it all the time."

"They do not."

"I guess they don't put nasty, vulgar news items like that in the red rag you read unless they can work out how to blame the government for it."

Olivia was watching her grandmother. For some reason she desperately didn't want her grandmother to take Nick for a fool, even though Nick himself obviously didn't give a damn what anyone thought. Her grandmother smiled. Not triumphantly or condescendingly, just amused.

"What's the problem with the play?" her mother persisted. "Is it Devika again?"

"No, Devika's fine. Well, actually, she's still hobbling round on crutches, but Meg and I have allowed for that. In fact, it fits in better; it makes her more victimized and helpless. And it makes the bit with the Cadillac better."

"So what's the problem?"

"The Head says it's too close to exams. Ms. P. says it's because of my being pregnant."

"What's that got to do with anything?"

"That's what Daddy wants to know. He's going to make a fuss if the Head really won't let us put it on. He says there's a word for that, but I think he made the word up himself."

"What word?"

"Gravidism. He says it means prejudice against pregnant women."

"That's not quite the right word for it," her grandmother remarked. "The word he really wants is discipulagravidism."

Olivia looked toward her grandmother. "What does that mean?"

"It means a prejudice against pregnant schoolgirls. I expect it's fairly common, especially among headmistresses. And who can blame them?"

Olivia changed the subject again. She was getting quite

good at it by now. She asked her mother what she was going to do with Luke when she went back to work.

"I'm not going back. I'm going to work from home, at least for now. I'll use your old room upstairs as my workshop."

So much for Olivia ever coming back to live here. She was out, finished, grown up and gone away, no longer a member of her mother's immediate family. Her mother had made other arrangements. She swallowed that knowledge and asked only, "Is the gallery going to keep on selling your stuff?"

"They're happy to do that, it sells as well as anything else they're flogging. Besides, I've got the contract with Jack Rae, all his shops carry my creations now. What are you tee-heeing about, Lia?"

"Nothing," said Olivia, who was cradling Luke on her shoulder. "I was just thinking that I'm carrying your creation. And I suppose," she added, "I'm your creation too."

"Once upon a time you were. But you've got rather out of hand since then."

"I'm just bigger, that's all." Olivia appealed to her grandmother. "What do you think, Grandma? Is Mummy still your creation?"

Her mother was oddly embarrassed by the conversation. But her grandmother gave the question due consideration. "Well, Lia, I think giving birth to someone is really just giving them a start in the world. You can help or hinder them but you can't do much about the sort of person they are."

"That's what Meg says. She says they're already real people, they've been here before and they pick the parents to be born to."

Her mother said impatiently, "Then why would so many people choose to be born to impoverished parents in the third world?"

"Maybe that's the best they can do. Maybe there's some sort of ranking system and if you've been a rotten parent last time round you have to take a turn being born to no-hopers."

Her mother seemed to take this personally. "We can't do everything we want to do, Lia. Every child would like to be born into a classic two-parent mother-at-home Western family, but it doesn't work out like that. You can't expect people to sacrifice their whole life to their children. Are they pre-scient, these souls waiting to be born? Can they tell what's going to happen over the next twenty years?"

Olivia considered what Megan had told her. "No, I shouldn't think so. They're just like everyone else, trying to make the best choice they can."

"Well, thank God for that. And remind me what the right answer is, next time you tell me you didn't ask to be born. We're all trying to make the best choices we can. You think you're hard done by because your parents got divorced and remarried. What about Luke? Where would he be if I'd never met Nick?"

"Maybe you and Daddy would have had him."

"And would he have been better off, with parents who couldn't get on together? If it's happily married parents that your new souls are looking for, then he's done well for him-self. Better than you did, my darling."

Olivia put up her hand to cover her mouth. She didn't know, even now, if her father had ever loved her mother, or if he loved Althea and Matthew and Olivia herself. She didn't know if Nick had ever loved Miranda, or if he now loved her mother and Luke. But she did know, quite surely, surpris-ingly, that if Nick didn't love her he didn't love anyone.

But she didn't know where that left her mother. Or herself, for that matter.

"Well, what I think, if anyone's interested," said her grand-mother, "is that we're better off with cottage pie every night of the week than peacocks' tongues on Sunday and bread and water till Sunday next. I also think I'm going to bid two hearts."

When it was time for Olivia to leave, supposedly to buckle down to the tyranny of GCSEs, her mother called Nick in from wherever he had gone to earth, to ask him to take her home.

He did, but not right away. First he took her down to Wapping and made love to her.

58

He knelt on the rug and pulled her down to face him with her bottom resting on his thighs. His thighs were hard and muscular and covered with coarse golden hairs. It was sexy just straddling them, never mind his prick pushing into her.

Her hair fell across his shoulders when she embraced him, like a magical cloak. Maybe if she had been a witch she could have woven a spell with it, to make him love her forever. As it was, all the magic was in what he did to her. His hands on her bottom made her pelvis move in rhythm with his own thrusts. It made her feel thrillingly helpless and overwhelmed, especially toward the climax, when he was so clearly in the grip of some blind erotic god.

Afterward they clung to each other, damp and drained as shipwrecked seafarers after a tropical storm. She pushed the net of hair away from her face and looked down at her bulging abdomen meeting his flat belly.

"How can you want me when I look like this?"

"I'm not that fickle, kitten. And you look great."

"If you think this looks great, you must be a pervert."

"Not me. But there must be plenty of them out there, now that you mention it. A neglected market. Maybe I should take some shots of you."

"Nick, that's not funny." It still made her feel sick and sad when she thought of those pictures. She must have been pregnant then too, though neither of them had known it. She broke free of him. "I have to get home. And so do you."

"They won't miss me."

"Yes they will." She began to get dressed quickly, replacing

436

her underwear and pulling her dress on over her head. "How are you getting on with Grandma?"

"I guess it's harder on her than it is on me. She treats me like a fucking rottweiler—keep it fed and keep your distance."

"I asked her about you. She thinks you're clever."

He grunted in amusement. "She must be pretty sharp herself to work that out." He came up behind her and put his arms around her, linking his hands across her swollen stomach. He had pulled on his trousers but not his shirt. "How about you? What did she have to say to you about making her a great-grandmother?"

"She blames it all on Mummy, I think. Or on society."

"Just as long as she doesn't blame it on me. So she hasn't cut you off with a shilling?"

"Apparently not. I was surprised. I thought she'd be so disgusted and disappointed she wouldn't want to know me."

"Blood is thicker than water, they say. And thicker the older you get, I reckon. All the same, she wouldn't want to take you to church in her village right now."

"You mean she doesn't mind so much as long as her friends don't know about it."

"Don't sound so fucking priggish when you say that. It's the same for you and me, isn't it?"

"You mean you don't mind screwing me as long as nobody knows."

"You want to tell the world, I suppose," he said dryly.

Olivia flushed. "I do, really, except—"

"Yeah, that's right, except. It's nothing so respectable as your granny's embarrassment."

Nick was right. There was nothing respectable about shame and betrayal, adultery and incest. If her grandmother knew the truth she would be more than merely disgusted and disappointed. Olivia pulled his hands apart and away from her, and turned to face him. She wanted to know how he coped with that shame, which should have been stronger for him than for her: he was the married man, the criminal. "What do you think about when you go to bed with Mummy?"

She couldn't tell what he was thinking even now. She couldn't tell if his thoughts bore any generic resemblance to hers, or if they were totally alien. Alien, she guessed, looking up at his impassive face and cool eyes. There was no hope of happiness in loving a Martian.

He shrugged. "What's the point of asking things like that? You don't really want to know."

"Yes I do."

"You think you do. Anyway, it's nothing to do with you."

He was protecting her mother, choosing her mother over her again, shouldering her aside when she threatened to come too close to the relationship between her mother and him. Olivia had a pain inside, like an ulcer in the heart. "What if I said I wouldn't see you again?"

"You're not going to stop seeing Em."

She bit her lip and turned away toward the window. "You know what I mean."

"Tell me."

He was jeering at her. She hated him. She hadn't hated him for quite a while now. "If I said I wouldn't screw you anymore."

"That's up to you."

"You mean you wouldn't care?"

"I didn't say that. I said it's up to you."

It was almost a year to the day since he had come into her life: first as an unknown man in her mother's bed, then an intruder in her home, soon afterward her lover. She thought of the first, the second, and the third time they had made love. Of all the times thereafter, not an incalculable number even over a year. There had never been an occasion when they came together as equals. Which was not surprising, considering what she was and what he was.

"It's never been up to me. I've never had any choice."

"Why not? You know how to say no."

"But it isn't any use."

She looked down at the river, an expanse of stinking mud at low tide, and the endless urban jumble beyond, where he had come from. She was looking out over emptiness. Over Babylon. She felt dizzy and sick.

Nick caught her wrist and dragged her round to face him. He was angry, no longer ironically impassive. She supposed that was some kind of victory. "Are you trying to tell me it's all my fucking fault? You're some kind of fucking puppet without a will of your own, and I'm a dirty old sod who gets his kicks out of stuffing a schoolgirl? Is that the sort of shit you're trying to hand me?"

Olivia shook her head, to deny what he was saying, and to protest his painful grip. "No, no, nothing like that. I'm not blaming you, Nick. That's as pointless as Grandma blaming Mummy. I'm not talking about blame. I only meant that you're a man and I'm a—a stupid kid."

Maybe he had some conscience after all. He let her go.

She turned back to the window. She wasn't sick anymore, just empty. The baby was growing inside a hollow shell. For the first time she wondered if she would be able to love it properly when it was born. Her love for Nick was a craving, a hunger. To love a baby you had to be giving rather than needing.

"If I'd been a woman instead of a stupid kid, would you have married me instead of my mother?"

"I don't know. I never thought about it."

"How could you not think about it?"

He didn't answer right away. Then he said, "If you think about anything long enough you want to go out and cut your fucking throat."

That was an answer of sorts. But she wanted a more direct one. "Think about it now, what I asked you."

"What for? It won't make any difference to anything."

"It makes a difference to me."

She should have been ashamed of herself for begging, but she couldn't even feel shame any longer, only the want of him. Even so, she couldn't look at him.

He set his hands on her shoulders. He slid them up to her neck, under her hair. "Suppose I said yes."

"Why suppose?"

"That's all we can do. It's only hypothetical."

There was nothing hypothetical about the way he was touching her. He caressed the hollow places round the base of her throat. He pushed her hair aside and kissed the nape of her neck. It had to be called a kiss, for want of another word. What he did was he touched his tongue to her skin, then he took a fold of skin between his teeth like some great cat seizing its prey. His left hand covered her throat, his right hand began to unzip her dress.

He lowered the zipper at leisure, trailing his forefinger down her backbone as it was gradually revealed. When he reached her bra strap he unhooked that and continued downward. The fingertip made its way to the base of her spine, to the hollow below her tailbone, at the top of the cleft between her buttocks. Then he began to massage her bare shoulders and her upper arms and back, denuding her as if by accident as his hands pushed her dress aside and down. He knew exactly how to arouse her and how to satisfy what he had aroused—her sexual needs at least. As for any deeper, more than physical aching, maybe he had lived so long with famine that he was no longer aware of such a hunger, in himself or in another. If a person starved long enough their stomach shriveled. Maybe if someone was starved of love their heart shrank.

But by the time he took down her knickers she was ready to melt.

"Do you want it?"

"Yes."

"If you don't want it I'll stop."

"Don't stop."

They sounded like brute beasts, Olivia thought, his voice a growl muffled by her hair, hers a croak from her parched throat. He nipped at the tender flesh that joined her neck and shoulder. Like a tomcat about to mount a female.

That was just what he did. He pushed her down on all fours and took her from behind.

He caught and covered her heavy breasts like a pirate seizing plunder. His thighs forced hers further apart as he rammed further up into her, grunting with each thrust. She felt him as a male force rather than a man—a stallion or stag, a bull or a boar, some powerful, mindless, rutting creature driven by a seasonal sexual storm—and she the female of his species, helpless in her heat, covered and penetrated by his masculinity. They were human only in this, that he had long since successfully started his seed in her and this mating was mere gratuitous lust.

It was the most intensely sexual, intensely exciting experience she had yet had. There would have been no point to the telepathic transparency she had felt on previous occasions; there was no mind, no consciousness, nothing but need and sensation and then at last relief.

They collapsed in no less mindless exhaustion, rolling together on the floor. When the bull and the buck and the ram and the boar had gone out of him and he had recovered his human powers of speech Nick said to her, "Jesus, you're right, you haven't got any fucking choice. I'll never give you up."

59

Olivia didn't need a warning nudge from Megan's elbow to recognize Charlie at the main gate of the school.

It was the last week before half term, before exams began in earnest. They had their dress rehearsal for the play tomorrow after school, and the real performance on Thursday. All quite complicated. But not as complicated as seeing Charlie.

He had his motorbike and was looking darkly moody and romantic, like James Dean. She hadn't really missed him up till now. But now . . .

"I'll see you later," Megan muttered, deliberately heading off in the other direction.

Olivia went up to Charlie. She hadn't seen him for over a month, and had got much more pregnant in the meantime. Maybe just the sight of her, deformed, would put him off.

She couldn't tell. He didn't smile, he didn't speak. He just looked at her.

"You're not supposed to be here."

"I can go bloody well where I please. Your father doesn't own the streets of London."

"But I'm on my honor not to see you."

"Close your eyes, then. Are you hungry?"

It was lunchtime but she hadn't eaten yet. "I am, a bit."

He looked at her, brooding. Scowling, even. Very unlike Charlie. "I'll buy you lunch at the café down the road. Okay?"

To hell with her father. "Okay."

He had to push the motorbike along the pavement because he had only a learner's license and couldn't give her a ride. It looked odd because he was wearing his office outfit, dark suit, white shirt, a tie, and black loafers. He looked very handsome and grown-up in that, she thought. She caught his elbow to keep alongside him in the flow of pedestrians.

"Aren't you working today?"

"At what?"

"Your job, of course."

"I haven't got a job."

She stared up at him. He was looking straight ahead, up the road. "What are you talking about? Your father can't have sacked you."

"He's gone bust. The bank called in his loans this morning. The company's bankrupt. Cahill Construction is kaput. Read all about it in the *Standard.*"

She took her hand away and stopped. "Charlie, you're joking, aren't you?"

He stopped too and looked back at her. "Do I look like I'm joking?"

He looked grim, almost gray. Ashen-faced was the jokey term, but it described him precisely.

She must have been ashen-faced herself, because he put out a hand to take her arm. "Lia, are you okay?"

"I'm okay. I'm just hungry."

He parked the motorbike and they went inside the café. He said he wasn't hungry. Olivia ordered sausages and a large portion of chips. She wasn't all that hungry now but she thought Charlie might be when the food arrived.

"What happens to your father now? Is he out of a job too?"

"Out of a job, out of a home. To keep the company going he put the house up for collateral. So the bank takes the house and we're out on the street."

"What good does that do the bank? They're not going to be able to sell the house. Nick's had a cottage up for sale for a year and nobody's even made an offer."

Charlie shrugged. "Ask the bankers. Who knows how those bastards reckon things?"

Olivia put her hand over his. She felt quite theatrical doing it, but he gripped it tightly, completely, as if it was a vital link to something. When her lunch arrived they ate one-handed. She ate one sausage and he ate the other. They both ate the chips and went on holding hands.

"Is that what you came for, to tell me that?"

He shook his head. "No, that's by the way. Just news." He ran his free hand through his hair. "I came to talk to you about the baby."

"What about it?"

"My father says I have obligations. He says I should be giving you money for maintenance and all that sort of thing." In his words she could hear the echo of his father's voice. Charlie had been born and bred in England, but now when he repeated what his father had said, there was Ireland in his speech.

The idea of maintenance was a totally new one to Olivia. Nick had never mentioned it. But of course Nick couldn't do anything like that. If Nick gave her money, it would invite conclusions to be drawn that had so far never crossed anyone else's mind.

"That's crazy," she said to Charlie. "I could have had an abortion. Why should you pay because I chose not to?"

"That would be like forcing you to have one, wouldn't it? Anyway, my parents are dead against that sort of thing. They were brought up Catholic."

She couldn't take Charlie's money. It would be like defrauding him. But she couldn't say that. "Charlie, you haven't got any money. You haven't got a job now, or even a home, it sounds like. I can't take money from you, not when I don't need it."

She expected him to be relieved, but he scowled more darkly. "You will need it, though. Children are expensive, my father's always telling me, and your father has Matthew to provide for."

"Well, if I need it I can come back to you. I don't need it now."

"What's going to happen after the baby's born? Will you come out with me again? I have a right to see the baby, don't I? Even your father can't stop me from doing that. I could go to court if I have to, they've passed a law about fathers' rights."

Olivia began to feel quite panicky. There were so many things she hadn't thought of, things that couldn't happen the way they ought to, or even the way other people thought they should. It was all much more complicated than she had anticipated. "I don't know, Charlie. Maybe you're right. But I'll have to talk to Daddy about that."

"My father wants to talk to your daddy."

That was even more alarming. "What for?"

Charlie shrugged. "Who knows? Likely when he grew up these things were dealt with man to man, not boy to girl. He's an old-fashioned sort, my old man. Where did you say your father comes from?"

"Yorkshire. Huddersfield."

"I'll bet they did it the same way there, the old men getting together. Everybody used to settle these things like that."

"Maybe they did." Olivia wondered how to put politely her belief that her father wanted nothing whatsoever to do with any member of Charlie's family, still less to be reminded of his own northern working-class origins. There wasn't any way to do it, so she gave up. "I'll have to ask Daddy about that too."

They went out of the café and stood beside the motorbike. "I'll walk you back to school."

"Better not. I've caused enough scandal as it is. The Head probably thinks you're the Prince of Darkness."

"Cheap thrills." Charlie smiled sourly. "Well, if I can't walk you back, I'll have to say good-bye right here." He put his arms around her and pulled her toward him till her swollen abdomen pressed on his flat one. "Give me your best good-bye, okay?"

Olivia giggled. "I can't. We'd be arrested."

He kissed her several times, long, deep, intense physical connections interspersed with pauses for breathless comment.

"Oh God, I've missed you so much. And you look so beautiful."

"Don't be silly. I've gone all fat and shapeless."

"Sod your shape, it's only the baby. You are beautiful, don't argue." After a minute, more raggedly, "And sod your father. I'm not going to give you up without a fight."

Megan caught up with her after school. "What's up with Charlie?"

"His father's company has gone bust. They're going to lose their house and everything."

"You're joking! What's going to happen to them?"

"I don't know. I don't know how these things work out. Charlie will have to go and find another job, I guess. I don't know what his father will do. Everybody seems to be going on the dole, don't they?"

Olivia didn't mean to sound callous; she really was distressed for Charlie and his family, but she had more pressing personal problems to distress her as well. And it was all remote from her, in a way. Her father was a tenured senior lecturer. The only way he would lose his job was if the whole university folded up, than which even the Second Coming was more likely. Megan's father was some kind of lawyer in the Home Office; the entire country would have to close down before he found himself out on the street.

Olivia said more urgently, "Listen, Meg, he actually came round for a different reason. He wants to give me money for the baby."

"How can he do that? He hasn't got any money now."

"That's probably why he's so keen on the idea. And he wants access rights. What am I going to do?"

Megan was less than sympathetic. "You mean he wants to be the baby's father. What did you expect? You told him that's what he is."

"I didn't tell him anything. I didn't tell anyone anything. They just assumed."

"They assumed what you meant them to assume," Megan pointed out dryly. "What does Nick assume?"

This telepathy, there was a lot of it about. She hadn't told Megan that her affair with Nick wasn't quite as finished as she had led her to suppose. Not only not over but never going to end, from what Nick had said last time. But she didn't think she could ever tell anyone, not even Megan, that she had let him make love to her on the day Luke was born. Twice.

"He—ah—he guessed what the situation was."

"You mean he knows it's his baby?"

"That's what makes it so awkward about Charlie."

"What did Nick say?"

"I thought he'd be really mad, but actually . . . basically I think he quite liked the idea. I mean he liked it being his rather than Charlie's. But he also told me I was a stupid kid and I shouldn't have done it."

"I think he's right there. Well, at least he won't have to put his oar in about access rights. He can see the baby as much as he wants to, perfectly legitimately. He can act like its grandfather without anyone thinking anything of it." Megan paused to consider what she had just said. "You really have got everything into a muddle, Lia. What a weird idea, Nick being a grandfather."

"No weirder than Daddy being a grandfather."

"No, I suppose not. Except that they've both just had babies of their own, which makes it even crazier."

"I know. When I first met Charlie I warned him that I lived in a zoo. That's about three times as true now." Olivia returned to the original topic. "But what about Charlie? I need some serious advice, and I don't mean just telling me I've made a mess of everything."

"Well, if you've made him the father, you've got to let him be the father. I don't see that you have much choice. You can't have your cake and eat it too, and you can't shaft Charlie coming and going. At least, if you do I'll never speak to you again."

Olivia looked at her curiously. "Do you like him?"

"Yes, of course, why shouldn't I?" Megan was surprisingly touchy on the subject. "If you really want to know, Lia, I think he's too good for you. You've treated him quite rottenly and he's being very honorable about everything."

"You can have him if you want him."

"Don't be silly, you can't give him away like a slave. That's the sort of thing I mean about treating him badly."

"I know, you're right, I truly am a rat. But I can't really help it. I'm in love with Nick, not Charlie."

"The thing that makes me feel most sorry for Charlie," Megan observed brutally, "is that he's in love with a lunatic."

"His father wants to come and see Daddy. What shall I do about that?"

"Let him come, why not? I expect your father can look after himself."

"It's Charlie's father I was worried about."

"Why, do you think your father will challenge him to a duel on the Heath at dawn? Now that's not a bad idea. If Charlie's father wins, Charlie gets to see the baby. If your father wins, Charlie has to push off. Maybe you should suggest it."

The dress rehearsal went as expected, perfectly dreadfully. Clare, who was playing Jason, forgot her lines in the climactic confrontation scene. One of the murdered children began to giggle in her pool of blood. This touched off an epidemic of giggles, and Megan got quite cross, especially when Olivia caught the plague. "Don't you start, you traitor," she hissed under her breath at Olivia, before denouncing the others for unprofessionalism.

They all dutifully sobered up, but the mood remained faintly frivolous and Megan remained dissatisfied.

"Don't take it so hard," Olivia advised her afterward. "It'll be all right on the night, as they say. Anyway, it isn't some multimillion-pound West End production."

"But I really want it to be good. To show the Head, if nothing else. After all the trouble we went to, to get her to let us put it on this term, and even let you play the Tutor."

"That was only because Daddy lent me his gown, so no one can tell I'm pregnant. Daddy says she's behaving like the waiter in the old joke about the man in the restaurant who finds a fly in his soup: don't tell the others or they'll all want one."

The evening should have been quite light, not yet sunset, only a month from the summer solstice, but the sky had darkened and was threatening rain.

447

Olivia checked her watch as they reached the gate of the schoolyard. "I told my father we'd be finished by eight, and it's nearly eight now. Do you want to wait and get a lift?"

Megan didn't answer. She was staring down the street. "Isn't that Charlie?"

It was Charlie. He came up to Olivia. "I've been waiting for you."

Megan began to move away. "Don't go away, Meg," Olivia begged. "I won't be a minute."

"A minute?" Charlie grabbed her arm. "Is that all I get, a minute? I've been waiting for an hour."

"Waiting in the pub, by the smell of you." She spoke sharply, but her inward response was dismay rather than annoyance. Her father would be here any minute, and Charlie was drunk. "How did you know I'd be here tonight?"

"Jon told me. He said he's going to be filming your play tomorrow night. Can I come and see it?"

"Better not."

"But I want to. I didn't get to hear you play the violin, so I want to see you onstage."

Olivia remembered what she had done that night instead of playing the violin. She had invited Nick into her bed and he had impregnated her. It frightened her, illogically, that Charlie should mention it.

Megan had stopped at a discreet distance. Olivia tried to move Charlie in the opposite direction, into the shadow of the wall. "Charlie, you'd better go. Daddy will be here right away."

"Did you ask him?"

"Ask him what?"

"You were going to ask him. The professor knows all the answers, you said. Can I see my baby when it's born? Can he spare my father a few minutes of his precious time? Yesterday you said you'd ask him."

"I—I forgot. He was out last night. I didn't have time."

"Then I'll hang about and ask him myself when he comes."

"Charlie, you can't. He'll go berserk when he sees you. He'll be furious with me. You don't want to get me into trouble, do you?"

"I've already done that, haven't I?" He put his hand on

her swollen stomach, his arm around her so she couldn't pull away. "It's my sodding baby, not his. Why should he have all the say about it?"

"Because I'm his baby."

"No, you're my baby too." His hand moved up to her breast. He groped it roughly, not like Charlie at all. "Christ, I'm dying for you, Lia. I can't stand it, not seeing you. Your daddy doesn't need to know."

"Charlie, please don't do that." She tried to push his hand away. People were going by, looking at her and Charlie. "He'll know all about it if you don't go away right now."

"Don't you want me? You haven't gone off me, have you?"

"No, no, of course not." She let him kiss her to prove it. "Now will you go away?"

"I want to ask your father—"

"He won't talk to you, he doesn't want to see you. Please, please, Charlie, do go away."

She was nearly in tears from terror. That sobered him a little. "Will you ask him?"

"Yes, yes, I will."

"Promise?"

Megan reappeared. "Lia, your father's coming."

Olivia pulled free of Charlie and walked over to the curb, resolutely keeping her eyes on the traffic and the approach of her father in Althea's BMW. She heard Charlie call her. She heard Megan say soothingly, "Come on, Charlie, Lia has to go home. So do I. Will you walk me home, since Jon's not here?"

60

Between the ending of the school day and the start of the play, Olivia had to dash up to Golders Green for her music lesson. Theoretically she could have skipped it because it was the last one—the last before exams, before the summer holidays, and now the last one ever because of the baby—but in fact that made it impossible for her to miss. There was something faintly tragic about it. Mrs. Stone and the violin were accidental casualties of her chosen course of action. She had grown rather fond of the old lady and her Johann Sebastian.

The affection was mutual, perhaps, because when she left, Mrs. Stone gave her a present, Bach's *Art of Fugue* on a CD. "The string arrangement, not the organ," Mrs. Stone explained. "You can hear the parts more clearly."

Olivia thanked her, feeling surprisingly tearful.

"Good luck in all your exams," said Mrs. Stone. "An A in music at least, eh? And good luck with your baby. What will you do afterward?"

"Go back to school, I suppose. But not to the same school. Daddy had a row with the Head."

Mrs. Stone said mysteriously, "He's quite a good man, your father, but maybe not so good as he ought to be, an educated man like him." Then she astonished Olivia by embracing her with tears in her eyes. "Bring your baby to see me one day, child."

Olivia blinked back her own tears. "Promise."

From Mrs. Stone's house she had to head directly back to school to help Megan get everything ready, herself included.

Everything certainly needed getting ready. When she arrived the place was in chaos. Ms. Pankhurst immediately pressed her into service as a makeup assistant.

Clare as Jason wore a wig that gave her a receding hairline, which was enough to give anyone the giggles if they knew about the curly red mop underneath. Medea's children wore short trousers and round caps like Billy Bunter–ish schoolboys.

Glauke, Creon's daughter, was in pigtails, a child bride marrying Jason at her father's bidding. That had the effect of making her, almost as much as Medea, a victim of Jason's and Creon's conniving. It also made her an innocently excited child, rather than the greedy, gloating woman Olivia had envisaged, when she tried on the fatal gold-threaded sari.

The play was going to be performed in the art room, because that had movable screens and also made a more intimate environment for an informal production, Ms. Pankhurst said. Actually, it was probably because the Head wouldn't let them use the stage in the auditorium. But she had a point about the intimacy, since the audience was going to consist entirely of the families and friends of the cast. The cast was not large, and neither were their families, except for Devika, who had dozens of cousins, all apparently eager to attend her stage debut.

Olivia's family contingent was supposed to be her father (Althea was minding Matthew at home) and her mother and grandmother (leaving Luke with Nick). Matthew would be okay with Althea, but Olivia hoped for Luke's sake that he slept soundly till her mother got back. On the other hand, he was probably in better hands with Nick than Matthew would have been with her father.

Megan had very relaxed views about the mystery of the theater. Anybody who was not actually onstage at any given moment was allowed to sit on the floor at the front to watch the performance, sneaking behind the screens at the last minute before they had to go on themselves.

That arrangement meant that Olivia got to watch most of the play. She was only on twice, and not for all that long either time. But she was in the first scene, so it was just as well she had been too busy beforehand to work up a case of nerves.

The Nanny came on first to explain the situation to the audience, pretending to talk to herself the way actors do. Here's Medea, a king's daughter, divine blood in her veins, could have had her pick of men, but she chose Jason. Gave up everything for him, made him what he is, presented him with two sons, and now he's left her for another woman. A younger, richer woman, heiress to the kingdom when her father dies. A much better bet than the aging, disinherited daughter of a faraway foreign king, dead or deposed by now, no doubt. Just like a man, eh? But Medea won't take this lying down, you wait and see.

The Tutor (Olivia) entered in her father's academic gown and her grandmother's half-moon reading glasses, with Medea's children in tow. Her big news is that Medea is going to be deported as an undesirable alien, now that she's no longer married to Jason, and the children are being sent away with her.

Olivia felt a small thrill when Medea came out. Devika's long black hair had been plaited over her shoulder. She dragged herself onstage between crutches, straightened to her full height, and looked about, her black eyes sweeping first the audience, then the Chorus. Nobody uttered a squeak.

Medea describes herself: a woman, a foreigner, her family dead or estranged, and far away in either case. A woman whose life has been shattered through no fault of her own, cast off by her husband like a suit of old, ill-fitting clothes. A mother with no means of supporting her children. But Jason isn't going to get away with this, oh no. She'll teach him what it means to suffer.

Creon marched onstage, Jason's new father-in-law, a gray-haired person in a suit, carrying a briefcase. He has come to deport Medea and her children. Medea begs him for time to find somewhere to go. If she is sent back to her own country she'll be arrested and tortured and executed and so will her children. Creon says he's a merciful man, he'll give her till tomorrow morning, and he went away.

Jason arrived (Clare in a wig). As a friendly gesture he

offers to lend Medea some money to make a new life for herself in another country.

Medea tells him at some length what he can do with himself and his money.

He tells her not to make a scene. Just like a woman, and a foreigner to boot—they don't know how to behave, they don't appreciate logic and democracy and a stiff upper lip. Furthermore she's too aggressive in bed. Puts men off, that does. Having sealed his own fate with his big mouth, Jason stomped off.

Medea lays her plans. She will send the children with a poisoned gift for Jason's bride Glauke. That will gain her revenge. But what will she do with the children afterward? She can't leave them to suffer or be sent home to torture and death. If it comes to dying, she would rather kill them herself.

Devika said this looking quite steely. But in the next scene, when Medea persuades Jason to take the children to Glauke with the gift of a golden sari, she kept breaking down, bursting into tears.

Then it was time for Olivia's next entrance, to tell Medea that Glauke is delighted with the present and she and Jason have decided to let the children stay and live with them. So the children are going to be all right. Only Medea will be sent away in the morning.

Only Medea knows it's too late. They're all doomed by the fatal sari.

A Messenger arrived to tell the horrible tale. Upstage, while the Messenger is speaking, a freckled, pigtailed Glauke models her fancy sari for the benefit of Jason, her husband, and Creon, her father. She starts to scratch, then to tug at it, then to scream. She rolls over and over across the stage like someone trying to smother a fire. Jason, her husband, stands by looking quietly appalled, maybe at the hysterical scene she is making. Creon, her father, tries to get her to stand up and ends up rolling about and screaming along with her. Finally they stop screaming and lie in a twitching heap. Beautifully gruesome, thought Olivia with satisfaction. And no giggling either. Megan would be pleased.

The Messenger tells Medea she had better leave quick because a mob is on its way to kill her and her children. Cries offstage of Kill the witch! Kill the spy! Kill the foreign scum! Megan and Olivia had wanted to use more topical epithets, the kind in Nick's vocabulary, but Ms. Pankhurst vetoed that.

Devika/Medea throws her crutches away and sits down on the stage. Her children come out and she cuddles them. The Chorus wring their hands at the edge of the stage and beg somebody to do something. They also beg Medea not to do anything she might regret. She looks at them as if they are ghosts, or maybe she is the ghost.

Then she takes out a knife and tenderly, maternally, cuts the children's throats. There is blood everywhere. Tomato juice, actually.

Jason came storming in. This was the scene that Clare fluffed at rehearsal, but she didn't fluff it now. He sees the Chorus first, and says he has come to rescue his children before the revenge mob arrives. He describes in lurid but unoriginal terms what he is going to do to Medea. He asks where she is.

The Chorus all try to speak at once, not answering the question but defending themselves, saying they didn't think she was serious, it wasn't really any of their business, the authorities should have, et cetera. While they are gabbling, the fiery Cadillac with gilded wings drives itself onstage and parks in front of Medea.

Devika arranged herself behind the Cadillac so that she appeared to Olivia and the audience to be in the driver's seat. She looked like a tragic queen. She tells them all to shut up.

Jason sees her then, and the dead children. He calls her an unnatural abomination. Women aren't supposed to commit murder, especially they are not supposed to kill their own children, most especially they are not supposed to commit such horrible crimes in order to avenge a husband's rejection, it is so unfeminine. He makes all this clear. He adds by the way that he also regrets losing his children.

Medea says he should have thought about that when they were going to be sent away.

They have a terrible row, blaming each other for everything. It sounded so much like the argument between her own parents the night they found out she was pregnant,

Olivia could hardly believe all this had been written more than two thousand years ago.

Jason is still calling down curses on Medea as she drives away in the Cadillac with the dead children. When the car has disappeared he sits down in the puddle of tomato juice and covers his face with his hands.

The lights went out, because they had no curtain. In the darkness all the actors in the front row got back on the stage, and bowed when the lights came back on again. The audience applauded with varying degrees of enthusiasm. The youngest members seemed best pleased, the older ones mostly looked politely bewildered.

Olivia, still in her father's gown, sought out her mother and grandmother. "What did you think?"

"It was—ah ..." Her mother searched for the mot juste. "Quite interesting."

"Quite," her grandmother agreed, "if a trifle bloodthirsty. Never mind, you all appeared to be enjoying yourselves."

Her father was hovering in a meaningful manner. All he wanted to do was tell Olivia that he would wait outside for her, but he was obliged to acknowledge her mother's presence and to exchange some chitchat with her grandmother, whom he hadn't seen for over three years. Olivia warned him that she might be a while because of having to clean up. Then her mother said she had to get home because Luke would be wanting his feed, he was still waking up at night. Olivia gave her grandmother back her reading glasses and thanked her for the use of them.

All three went out together. Olivia felt a pang of nostalgia for the days when her parents used to come and go together all the time.

By the time they had finished clearing up and restoring the art room to relative normality, Olivia and Megan were the only ones left. Jon, who had come to film the play, nobly stayed to help them tidy up.

"That's it, then," Megan announced, having satisfied herself that there was nothing the Head could reproach them for tomorrow. She dispatched Jon to collect his video gear. "Lia, are you coming with us to Ms. P.'s party?"

Olivia shook her head. "My father's waiting out front for

me. I'm so tired I just want to go home. Thanks for taking care of Charlie last night, by the way. Daddy didn't even notice him."

Megan said gloomily, "You won't thank me when I tell you what happened."

Olivia looked at her apprehensively. "Why, what happened?"

Megan sat down on a bench. Collapsed, more like. "I went to bed with him."

Olivia collapsed onto the bench beside her. "You what?"

"You heard me." Megan added defensively, "You said I could have him, didn't you?"

Olivia repeated numbly, "What happened?"

"Aren't you even jealous?"

"Of course I am." Olivia knew that Megan was indignant on Charlie's behalf. But Charlie would have been pleased to know what Olivia was feeling right now. She was doing just what she had accused Nick of, being a dog in the manger. "But I haven't really got any right to be jealous."

"Well, you don't need to be," Megan confessed. "He was drunk and I didn't know what to do with him, so when I got home and no one else was there I took him up to my room and laid him out on the bed. I pulled off his shoes and made him drink coffee while he kept telling me how much he loves you. He was literally crying on my shoulder. I was just sort of comforting him, you know, and, well, I think he was just pretending I was you, and what with one thing and another ... well, I told you what happened.

"Then he fell asleep and I couldn't wake him up. So I had to leave him there and go to sleep in the spare room."

Megan told this story with her hands clasped tightly in her lap. Olivia stared at those hands while she listened. She felt as if she herself, rather than Charlie or Megan, was the villain of the tale. "Are you in love with him, Meg?"

"It doesn't matter, does it? He's not in love with me." Megan stood up wearily. "Let's go, Lia. Your father's waiting for you, and Jon's waiting for me."

61

"That was quite a remarkable piece of theater," her father said on the way home. "Your Devika is a real actress."

"Don't sound so surprised."

"A moving performance is always a pleasant surprise. Though in this case perhaps pleasant isn't the right word."

"Didn't you like it?"

"Was I supposed to? I rather thought the whole production was designed to offend. A presentation by Angry Young Women."

Olivia sighed. "Maybe it was."

"You don't sound very sure. It was your play, Lia, you ought to know what it was meant to convey."

"Well, I—actually, I came to a different conclusion about it tonight," Olivia said slowly. "I decided Jason is right."

"What, right to leave Medea?"

"No, right about what he says at the end. Medea really does behave like a man in getting her revenge, instead of letting it go like the Chorus advises. And if every woman behaved like a man, then—well, I don't see how the human race would survive."

Maybe there was no such biological entity as the human race. Maybe it was something like lichen, a symbiotic association of two species, Martians and Venusians. If the Venusians started doing what the Martians do, the symbiosis would fail. There would be no new generation. Or if the Martians began to behave like Venusians . . . An unimaginable state of affairs.

"Not so much angry as alienated, I see," said the Martian beside her. "Do you think that's what Euripides had in mind when he wrote the play?"

457

"Who knows what he had in mind? Maybe he wasn't sure himself. Irony," she observed reflectively, "seems to be a two-edged sword."

Althea came to meet them at the front door. "There's someone waiting to see you, Ross," she told Olivia's father. Under her breath she added rapidly, "It's Charlie's father. He rang and I told him you were out. He asked when you'd be back and I said around nine, so that's when he turned up—and he's been sitting there ever since."

Olivia shrugged when her father looked accusingly at her. "I don't know anything about it, Daddy. I'm starving, I haven't had anything to eat yet." She fled to the kitchen, leaving her father to cope with the uninvited guest.

Althea followed her into the kitchen. "What's all this about?"

"I don't know. Why didn't you ask him yourself?"

"I did sort of hint around, but he just said he wanted to talk to Ross." Althea looked affronted, like Tabitha Twitchett. She had made it clear from the beginning that while she had no moral objection to Olivia's pregnancy, she regarded it as extremely low-class behavior for a schoolgirl, as well as evidence of stupidity and incompetence. Now, thanks to Olivia's indiscretion, she had an Irishman in her sitting room. "How long is he likely to stay?"

Olivia shrugged again, her mouth full of cheese-and-tomato sandwich. To avoid further questions she took her sandwich and a glass of milk upstairs. At least she started up the stairs, but after a few steps she sat down to eavesdrop on the conversation in the sitting room.

The burden of Charlie's father's speech was that his family had always been upright men who paid their debts and honored their obligations. He didn't want Olivia's father to get the wrong impression about that. Charlie had done wrong in getting Olivia pregnant but he was prepared to stand by her and give her financial support. He understood that Olivia's father had discouraged her from continuing to see Charlie and he couldn't but agree with that, seeing what damage Charlie had done. They did things differently nowadays, didn't they, young people; there was no telling them anything and they took things for granted that would never have been tolerated when he himself was a lad. In his day if you got a girl pregnant you married her. Though of course Olivia was too young to marry just yet, and Charlie too for that matter, nineteen was really too young for marriage nowadays, wasn't it?

Olivia's father said he hadn't realized Charlie was nineteen.

Charlie's father said nineteen last November.

Olivia's father said that if he'd known that, he would have stopped the whole relationship before it had even got started. Evidently Charlie didn't understand what underage meant, or that there were laws designed to prevent feckless young men from seducing naive little girls.

Charlie's father said it wasn't like that. He himself hadn't realized how young Olivia was until all this trouble came up. Of course Charlie would have been willing to do the right thing by Olivia if she hadn't been so young. Quite stuck on her, he was.

Olivia's father said sharply that there was absolutely no question of marriage or anything else like that. Olivia was only fifteen and this was an unfortunate but temporary interruption to her education and she would be back at school as soon as possible in the autumn. It had all been a terrible strain on her and there was no point prolonging the unhappiness. Olivia didn't need or want any money from Charlie.

Charlie's father said with some heat that the fact that his business had folded up on account of the recession didn't mean that he was incapable of meeting his personal obligations and making sure that his sons did what was right or paid for their mistakes, by Jesus.

Olivia's father said it wasn't a question of whether Charlie could afford to support a child, though he didn't suppose Charlie had given much consideration to that before setting out to seduce Olivia. The whole thing had been a mistake from beginning to end and it would be best if Charlie got himself stuck on somebody his own age and maybe worked out how to use a condom while he was at it.

Charlie's father said that his wife said the same thing, that it had all been a mistake from the beginning. She said it was what came of letting a young girl go out with boys when she was too young to know what normal, healthy young men were like and what effect a low neckline and a miniskirt could have on them, especially when worn by a girl like Olivia, who was a beautiful girl and very well built if her father didn't mind him saying so.

Her father did mind. He said that Olivia had a first-class brain as well but he didn't imagine Charlie had noticed that, and if Charlie had cared at all for her he wouldn't have stupidly jeopardized her future in this way.

Charlie's father said if Olivia was really all that clever she should have minded her own future and kept her knickers on. Even at fifteen she must have known how babies are made; she surely knew how to get herself up to look older than her years.

Olivia was too embarrassed to listen to any more. She fled upstairs.

She scrubbed her face and brushed her hair to make sure all the makeup and powder had gone. Then she undressed and pulled on her nightgown, put on her personal stereo, and wrapped herself in the duvet.

Her first exam was going to be biology. She looked at her biology notes. It all seemed to be concerned with reproduction. Spores and gametes, stamens and pistils. The pistil, she read, was the female organ of a flower, comprising ovary, style, and stigma. Funny, that was exactly how Charlie's father had just described her. The ovary was where babies started from, the style was a low neck and a miniskirt, and the stigma was letting Charlie screw her, with the result that all the world knew what she had done. She could just imagine the words Charlie's father would have used if he found out it wasn't Charlie at all.

She shut up the books and closed her eyes and concentrated on the stereo to try to ease her agitation. The music was Mrs. Stone's parting present, the *Art of Fugue*. She had already listened to about half of it on the way back to school after her music lesson. It began very simply with a short unadorned theme easy to follow, as Mrs. Stone had observed, because each part was played by a different section of the string orchestra. Then came variations on the simple theme: it was played backward, and upside down, and both ways at once. It was like being drawn into a novel that started like a good mindless read but gradually developed unexpected complexity, till she found herself somewhere she had never thought to be. It was some of the most moving and beautiful music she had ever heard. Mrs. Stone was right after all, she had misjudged JSB.

She was so absorbed that she didn't know her father was in the room until he touched her on the shoulder. She opened her eyes and removed the headphones.

"Shouldn't you be revising?"

"I'm listening to the CD Mrs. Stone gave me."

"What is it?"

"You have to guess."

She handed him the headphones. After a few seconds he handed them back. "It's *Die Kunst der Fuge.*"

"That's right. It's lovely."

"Better than Jimi Hendrix?"

"Much. But this wouldn't go down so well at a party, would it?" Since he didn't show any sign of going away, she switched off the player and looked at him. "Has Charlie's father left?"

"He left quite a while ago. It's taken me some time to cool off. I don't enjoy having my daughter called a trollop, especially by the father of the yob who seduced her."

"He doesn't really think that," Olivia protested. "He was just talking like that because you were saying rude things about Charlie."

Her father looked at her coldly. "You heard, did you?"

"Just that bit. I was going upstairs."

"Maybe it's just as well he came. It reminded me there are some things we have to sort out."

"What things?"

He didn't sit down on the bed the way her mother would have; he stood and looked down at her. "For one thing, you're never going to see Charlie again."

"What, not ever?"

"Not while you're living here."

"But he wants to see the baby. He says he has rights."

"He's not seeing the bloody baby," her father all but barked, his BBC accent falling further by the wayside with each word. "You're not going through this to provide him with some entertainment, or whatever the hell he has in mind. If he wants to get awkward about it I'll have him charged with unlawful intercourse and corrupting the morals of a minor. After he's done his goddamned best to ruin your life without a second thought, the idea of him going on about his paternal rights is a total farce."

Olivia thought about that. It seemed hard luck on Charlie, but not such hard luck as Charlie himself would suppose. He wasn't to be allowed to see a girl who wasn't in love with him, and he wasn't to be allowed to see a baby that wasn't his. Only he didn't know that.

"What if I say I'm going to see him anyway?"

Her father went white with anger. He said in the flattest, iciest voice she had ever heard him use, "Then you can go back and live with Emma, and you can do it right now. She doesn't appear to care what you do or whom you do it with, but I'm not giving you room and board and paying for your education while you screw around like a tramp and waste the brains God gave you."

She had never heard him speak like that to anybody ever, never in her life. She folded her arms across her swollen body as if to defend herself from his rage. She felt herself trembling—not with terror, that was too ordinary an emotion. Something more terrible than that, she didn't know what it was, except that it came from the old nightmare in which her parents turned into strangers.

Her mother had already become an indifferent stranger, as her father had just observed. Now he was showing his own alien soul. He seemed to have turned into her headmistress and Charlie's father rolled into one. He didn't love her for whatever she was, he loved her only for being good and clever and a credit to him. A well-trained dog could have earned as much affection, and got more pats. And if she wasn't going to be the way he wanted, then he didn't want to know her.

She pushed the duvet aside and stood up. She walked past him to the door.

"Lia, did you hear what I said?"

She didn't look back. "About my being a tramp, you mean?"

He said something she didn't catch. She was already half-way down the stairs. He came to the top of the stairs and called her to come back, God damn her. She ran down the lower flight of stairs to the front hall, clutching the hem of her Victorian nightgown with one hand so she wouldn't trip on it. She could hear her father storming down the stairs as the front door closed behind her.

She didn't know where to go. She couldn't go back to her mother. She couldn't turn up on Charlie's doorstep, if he even had a doorstep anymore. She wanted to go to Nick, but she couldn't do that. She couldn't even run away from home, barefoot as she was and wearing only a nightgown. Maybe if she could find somewhere to spend the night she could come back tomorrow, when her father and Althea were out, and pack her things. And then go—where?

She was standing irresolute in the middle of the street when her father opened his front door. He called her name in that terrible, icy voice. He called her Olivia.

Olivia ran.

She ran down the street to Swains Lane. She ran down the lane to the cemetery gate. She couldn't run very fast because of the baby, and when she got there she realized she couldn't climb over because of the baby.

She leaned against the gate, in the corner by the wall, cling-ing to the bars to hold herself upright. She was out of breath and had a terrible stitch in her side. The baby was kicking her, the poor thing didn't like being bounced about as she ran. And she was cold. A nightgown wasn't really outdoor wear, not even a long flannelette one on a mild May night.

She huddled down in the corner of the gate and drew up her knees as close to her body as the baby would allow. She pulled the hem of her nightgown down over her feet and hugged herself to try to stop herself from shaking all over.

It had been much colder the day she climbed over this gate with Nick. She remembered what he had done and what she had done and it made her go hot with shame, but that didn't stop the shaking.

She had been wearing this nightgown when the baby was

begotten. She had thought that was the last time Nick would ever make love to her.

Better if it had been. Her father was right after all, she was a tramp and a trollop. She was worse than that. She was all the awful things that Nick had called her on New Year's Eve. She shook with shame and self-loathing.

She wanted Nick to hold her.

Or even Charlie. It didn't matter, what Charlie had done with Megan. It would have been better if he did love Megan, then at least there would be two people happy. She herself had no right to him at all. She had ruined his life, and maybe Megan's as well. But she wished he was here to hold her, to make the shaking go away.

She saw her father coming down the lane.

He approached cautiously, stopping at a distance to call her, like someone trying to coax back a runaway cat. "Lia?"

She didn't answer, she didn't move. She was shaking too much.

He came closer, still wary. "Lia, are you all right?"

Still she didn't answer. He came right up and looked down at her. Then he went down on one knee in front of her, not touching her, holding one bar of the gate with his right hand to steady himself or something. He was still wearing the suit and tie he had worn to school to see the play. It made him look stern and formal, but he was on his knees.

There was a light from nowhere shining on his face. It was the moon. She could see his face clearly. The expression on it was oddly frightening. He looked as if something was hurting him badly inside.

His left hand touched her knee, about six inches from her face. His touch was hesitant, as if he wasn't sure how she would feel—hot or cold, wet or dry, good or bad. "Lia, what's the matter with you? Why are you doing this?"

She licked her frozen lips to give them the power of speech again. "Doing what?"

"Running away from me like that."

Her teeth were chattering. "You called me a tramp."

"I didn't say that. I said—oh, hell, just forget that." He took his hand away from her knee and combed it through his dark moonlit hair. "Why are you having this baby? You did it deliberately, didn't you? Maybe not getting pregnant, though you must have known perfectly well how to avoid that and you didn't do it. And I don't know why you didn't, since you said you're not in love with Charlie. But then you went to a great deal of trouble to hide your pregnancy. The only reason for you to do that, when you knew it wasn't going to disappear, was to make sure that it couldn't disappear. Do you have some profound moral objection to abortion that I haven't heard about yet?"

"No, Daddy." She knew she didn't because she had already done it once.

"Then why are you so determined to have it? What are you trying to prove? That if Althea and Emma can have a baby, you can too?"

She shook her head. She didn't know what to say. "I don't know. Why are you talking to me like this?"

"Like what?"

"Like it was important."

He looked at her sharply, as if she had said something seriously mad. "What do you mean?"

It was her turn to speak flatly. Not because she was angry, as he had been, but because she didn't dare to let her feelings come out. She didn't know exactly what her feelings were, but she knew her father wouldn't like them. So she took all the feeling out of what she was saying.

"You're supposed to be my father. For two years I only saw you every second Sunday and you let me kiss you hello and good-bye like some old aunt. I wouldn't have seen you at all if I'd left it to you. No, I wouldn't, you know I wouldn't have. You treated me like a nuisance. When I couldn't stand living with Mummy and Nick I asked to come and live with you. I begged my father to let me come and live with him and he said, well, he didn't know. I'm only here because I ran away from home and got picked up by the police. Just now you told me if I don't behave the way you want me to I must be a tramp and you don't want anything more to do with me. You also told me just now that Mummy doesn't care about me. So if you don't care, no one does."

She took a deep breath. It had been a long speech. "Now

you're asking me why I got pregnant. And I'm asking why you want to know now."

"I see," her father said.

He got up off his knees and stared through the cemetery gate, holding the bars with both hands like a prisoner in a cell. Olivia knew what he was looking at; it was a familiar scene to her. Right at hand was the black night of an ancient charnel house, beyond that the lights of London dancing its way to the grave. And overhead the summer stars, Altair, Vega, Deneb, Arcturus, flying endlessly apart from each other, neither knowing nor caring what patterns they made in their flight, patterns visible only to the eyes of earthly creatures.

Her father cleared his throat. "Did you by any chance think that once Matthew was born I wouldn't want you here anymore? That you wouldn't be invited to move into this house?"

"I did think that," she admitted. "I was all ready to hate poor Matty. But when I met him he was a different sort of person than I'd expected, and I quite liked him. Besides, I don't think you and Althea treat him the way you should."

Her father glanced down at her. He was smiling, a dry, crooked smile. "What do we do wrong?"

"You do everything wrong, Daddy. You're hopeless, you're just not interested in him at all. Because he can't talk, I suppose. Althea's a lot better, but he's sort of inconvenient for her."

"So you're trying to make up for our deficiencies."

"Well, somebody has to, poor little mite. I don't want him to grow up wondering if anybody loves him."

"Is that how you grew up?"

"It wasn't bad until you left. And even then I thought Mummy did. But now you're both strangers."

"So nobody loves you now."

"Matty does. Meg does." She took a very deep, very shaky breath. "And Nick."

That got his attention. The dry, faintly amused tone disappeared. "What about Nick?"

"I think he sort of loves me."

Her father said harshly, "What does that mean?"

She tried to articulate Nick, leaving out everything physical. "He notices everything about me. He understands what I'm thinking. And he talks to me straight, like one real person to another, not an adult talking down to a child."

"Christ almighty." Her father gripped the bars of his cage. He was angry again, but not at her. Not even at Nick, maybe. Just at himself, because a man he despised could do something right that he did wrong.

And that was so, she thought, no matter what else Nick had done, things that he ought not to have done. Her father was the other sort of sinner: he left undone the things that he ought to have done.

She felt vaguely sorry for him. He was a blind man in Cyclopean country. She relented, unbundled herself, and stood up beside him, stiff and cramped. Even her fingers were numb when she touched his hand on the bars.

He started at her touch. "Your hand is like ice."

"I am a bit cold."

He took off his jacket and draped it across her shoulders like a cloak. She put her arms around his chest. He put his arms around her, over the jacket, and held her tightly. Just like Nick. She felt the warmth of his body radiating into hers through his cotton shirt and her nightgown.

Gradually the shaking went away.

He was talking to her. She could feel his warm breath on her hair. "I'm sorry, Lia. I didn't mean what I said about— about what Charlie's father said. I don't want you to go anywhere else. I'm glad you love Matthew and I hope you love me, even if I don't deserve it."

"Of course I love you, Daddy. You know that."

"I don't know anything, it seems. Are you warmer now?"

"A bit."

"Then let's go home."

He actually kept his arm around her as they walked back up the lane.

"Tomorrow we'll have to talk about your A levels."

"Not in the autumn," she said.

"What do you mean, not in the autumn?"

"Not this autumn. I want to be with the baby for a while. It's going to need a mother, isn't it? I can look after Matty at

467

the same time. Althea can pay me. I'll go back to school the year after. I'll only just have turned seventeen by then. Meg's already going to be seventeen in September."

She couldn't guess what he was thinking, but it didn't really matter as long as he wasn't angry. As long as he had his arm around her. "All right, Lia," he said at last. "If that's what you want."

When they got back up to the house he had to ring the bell, because he had come out after her without taking the door off the latch. Althea opened the door and stared for a moment as if she had never seen either of them before in her life. "What are you doing out there?"

"Looking at the stars," said Olivia.

When she was back alone in her room she put the headphones on again. The music was gearing up, taking a breath before the final push to the finish line, working up to the most beautiful and moving passage in the whole work.

And then it stopped.

She thought the stereo must have turned itself off. But she could see the disc revolving. Then she thought the headphones had got disconnected. She checked them and they were okay.

She skipped back a track on the CD and there was Bach in all his stereophonic orchestral glory. When she reached the same place again it stopped again.

She took the disc out and went downstairs to find her father. He was in the dining room, pouring himself a glass of whiskey. Rather a stiff one, she noticed.

"Daddy, there must be something wrong with this CD. It stops just before it should be getting to the end."

"That is the end," her father said. "He died before he finished it."

"He died just like that, with his quill in his hand?"

"Not exactly. He had a stroke and died a few days later."

"That's really spooky. And sad."

"Not quite so sad. He'd been blind for years, and with the stroke he suddenly regained his sight. So he had other things to think about just before he died. They seemed more important at the time, I expect."

"I wonder what things seemed important to him after he died."

Her father gave her a funny look. "Well, nothing. That's the end of it when you die. Nothing is important after that."

"Granddad doesn't think so. Neither does Meg. She says we all come back again."

"Meg would know, of course."

Olivia was not intimidated by her father's sarcasm. "Meg knows as much as you do about it," she pointed out irrefutably. "Anyway, if nothing is important after you die, why is anything important before?"

Her father couldn't think of an answer to that, not at least in the five seconds she waited. Then she went back upstairs to listen to the last part of Bach's last work again before falling asleep.

During the night she dreamt of how the music should have ended. But the baby started kicking inside her and woke her up, and by then the music had gone.